Tide of War

AJ Cooper

Tide of War
Copyright © 2015 Andrew James Cooper
Published by Realms of Varda
www.vardabooks.com

Front cover art © Nejron | Dreamstime.com

Back cover art © Rainbowchaser | Dreamstime.com

ISBN 978-1-958724-21-7

100 miles
Western Ocean
Westwood
Zarubad
Ardogne
1. Vale of Roy
2. Duchy Valais
3. Duchy Lessant
4. Duchy Ajernon
5. Duchy Duranche
6. Duchy Voraigne
7. Duchy Ajernon
8. Duchy Arvogne
9. County Garrone
10. County Rannier
11. Silvan March
12. Cavon March
13. County Belidere
14. Montée March

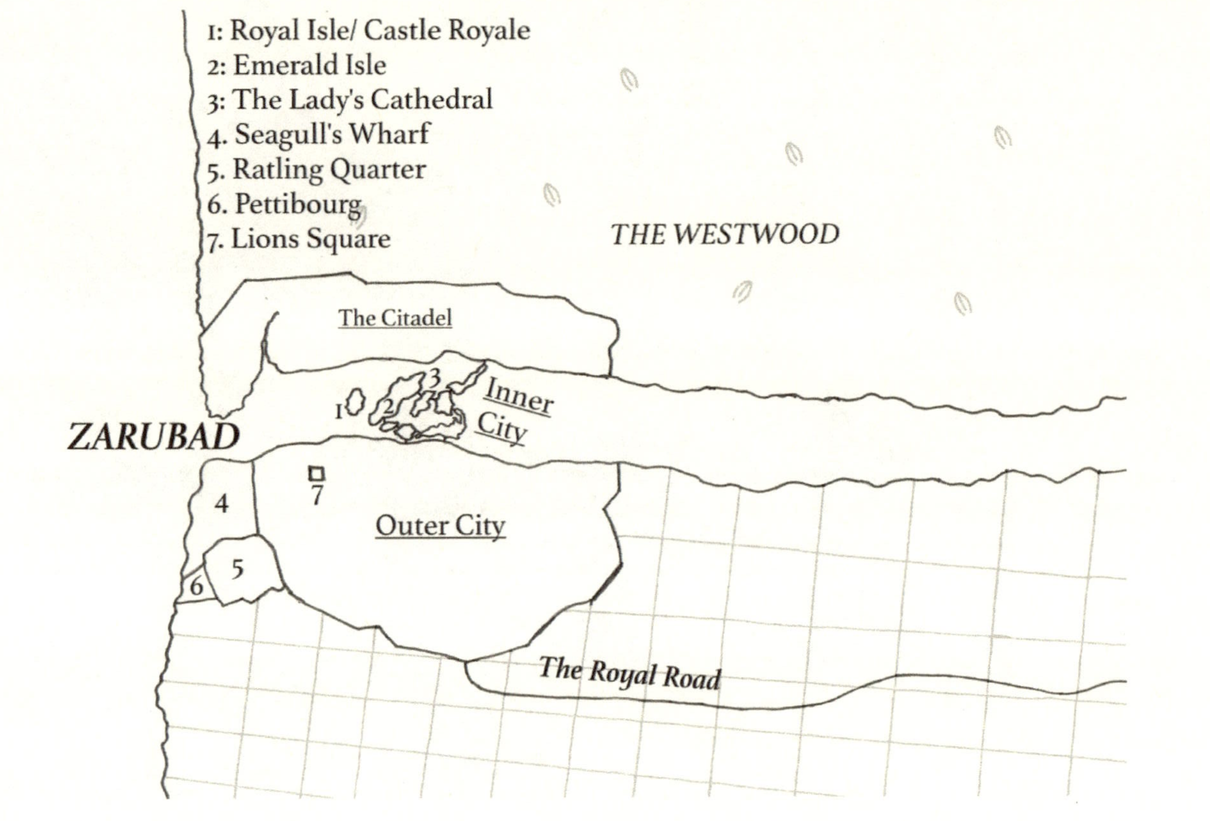

ZARUBAD
1: Royal Isle/ Castle Royale
2: Emerald Isle
3: The Lady's Cathedral
4. Seagull's Wharf
5. Ratling Quarter
6. Pettibourg
7. Lions Square
THE WESTWOOD
The Citadel
Inner City
Outer City
The Royal Road

Prologue:
Storm Clouds Gather

Gray waves crashed against the beach amid the stormy skies. Traders in Port Bratteau cursed at the weather. No sailor or fisherman dared go out. Far away, on the Isle of Storms Observatory, the Royal Observers Society could hardly believe their spyglasses: the cold water, bubbling as if in a cauldron—and amid the waves, fleshy tentacles slapping and wriggling.

The peasants in the port spoke of "The Storm of the Ages." In the seaside chapel, the Reverend Heloise prayed earnestly for the Goddess's aid. Yet within an hour, the storm had dissipated into blue skies; the water had stopped its bubbling; and the tentacles had sunk back into the depths. The matter was forgotten.

The Lion in Autumn

The Pretender loomed high above her with a flail of spiked steel and armor of the blackest black. Yet the Maid of Naines did not tremble. Instead she took up her sword, called upon the Goddess, and drove the length of steel through his heart. He fell that day, and there was much rejoicing.

—from *The Ajernine Chronicle* by Martin vis Abrenard

Chapter One:
Pork Lysene

Danitari

It was a sight that threatened the fragile world order, a sight that could not be ignored, nor forgotten. It was a sight that the traders in their tall townhouses observed in horror, that the beggars, the laborers, and the elven slaves like Dan viewed with no small amount of glee.

King Jourmande vis Bretagne, sovereign of Zarubain, ruler of the kingdom, the hand of god on earth, rode weakly on the saddle of his horse with only a dozen knights in his retinue. The proud lion rampant banners of the House Bretagne were nowhere to be seen; no doubt they had fallen into the southlanders' hands. His haggard, weak face, his wheezing breath, his careening ride on the horse, all spelled without any doubt "defeat."

King Jourmande had taken the Road Saint-Genevieve, a chipped, pothole-covered road stained with the ages-old remains of chamber pots. Dan watched the sick seventy-four-year-old man as he hurried through this backwater part of the capital, looking down, not even daring to meet the gazes of the street folk. *This is a man ashamed,* Dan thought as an unstoppable grin fell over his face.

"Dan!"

Dan whipped around and offered an apologetic look, as he'd learned to do. His master's wife, Mignette, stood in the doorway with a dark scowl on her face.

"What is stealing your attention, Dan? What is *so* interesting that you paused your work?"

Even five years into his servitude, the name "Dan" was

strange to him. *Danitari*, his parents had named him, in Elvish *"the holy."*

She stormed over to the window, saw the king in all his shame. "Goddess bewitch us all!" she cried. "Those damned southlanders… they are so low-born, almost as low as you elves…" She turned and Dan met her gaze. "But that is too grievous an insult. The elves are lower than southlanders, lower than pigs and milk-cows, lower than the bugs I stomp on with my slippers."

It was not long ago that the Elven King had lost a war to Zarubain. He had defended Danarion, the City of Light, and kept the Elven World free, but tens of thousands of elves had perished.

Of his battalion, only Dan was unlucky enough to be alive.

"You are happy to see his defeat," Mignette snapped at him, and Dan drew back. "You are happy to see the sovereign humiliated, are you not?"

Her words were true. Sometimes Dan missed Master Jouliver while he was away on his trade journeys. At least Jouliver allowed Dan a moment's reprieve, a second's rest. Mignette had no such mercy.

"I can see it in your eyes—you are joyful to see the king's humiliation."

"I am heartbroken, just like you. The Zarube people are superior to all others in Varda… there *must* be an explanation. He must have won." In Dan's youth, he had detested all lies and falsehoods, but here, in the human world, they were nothing less than necessary. Now, lies rolled easy off Dan's tongue, and he had grown adept at telling them.

He could not resist her or raise his voice against her—an elven slave, saying one cross word, was worthy of death in the eyes of the law.

Mignette's expression softened just a slight bit, enough to show that she believed Dan. "Tonight I shall want Pork Lysene, with apple savories and a great big bottle of *gerusivel.*"

Gerusivel was what the Zarubes called elven wine. The west of Zarubain was known all across the kingdom for its viniculture, but even the westerners could not produce such a delicious drink as *gerusivel.* She could not afford a single cup, let alone a bottle, nor did she have room in her budget for apple savories.

"I realize you do not know what Pork Lysene is, Dan, but if you do not find out and make it for me, I will punish you severely."

Down in Mignette's cellar were her instruments of torture, where—months ago—she had gone too far with Dan's once-companion Samné. She had been whipped and beaten until she lost consciousness. She had never woken up. In the dark of night, Mignette and Dan had dropped her lifeless body in the River Zarube.

Often, Dan envied Samné, who was now at peace.

"I have left a bit of money on the table downstairs," Mignette said. "It is not enough, but you will have to find a way to make it work." A smile grew on Mignette's freckled face.

~

It was late when Dan returned from the market, carrying a basket filled with all manner of things—yellow onions, carrots, a pink slab of pork, and hot pepper. No one knew what Pork Lysene was, so Dan would only make a pork soup and accept whatever abuse followed. Perhaps, tonight, he would be as lucky as Samné—fall asleep, and never wake up. Perhaps, he too, would have a watery grave, a place of eternal rest beneath the waves of the sea.

He lit a fire in the kitchen and brought a pot of water to boil as he chopped the pork into bite-sized bits. For a half an hour he let the pork cook, along with the carrots and lettuce, hot pepper, and a dash of salt. Steadily, the bubbling water turned brown, and a delectable smell filled the kitchen. This, Dan knew, was a dinner fit for a king. But he would have to eat his masters' stale bread, or some foul left-over meal from days ago.

"Mignette!" Dan shouted.

In an instant she had appeared in the doorway.

"Your Pork Lysant—" The last syllable was swallowed by Dan's gasp.

His master's wife wore her nightclothes. "You silly elven fool," she said. "Pork Lysene has only vegetables… Some in the House of Lys think only meat is acceptable. In the Book of Manners, it says not to serve the Lysenes pork, or beef, or chicken."

"Why are you only wearing nightclothes?"

"I think you shall like your punishment tonight, my little elf."

"Goddess, no."

Mignette's smile dimmed, then grew bigger.

"Elves are the lowest of all creatures, you've said, lower than dirt, lower than worms. Why would you defile yourself so?"

Mignette laughed. "Sometimes, it is the dirt I need."

"I will not do this to Master Jouliver."

"You will."

"I will not."

She stepped closer to him, laid her eyes on him, grabbed the plain woolen tunic that Dan wore. "You will," she said, close enough to kiss him.

I will not, Dan thought. *Never.*

Chapter Two:
A Victory Wasted

Ramir vis Rambée, Duke of Lessant

The court was buzzing with anticipation about the king's battle. "I wonder," Ramir's wife had told him, "what the king will do with all this money. Perhaps he shall build another palace in the Westwood, or add a gilded ballroom to the palace!"

Yet the king was nowhere to be seen, and no messengers had heralded his arrival. So when the double doors of the Castle Royale's Great Hall were thrown open, the last person Duke Ramir expected to see was the king, Jourmande vis Bretagne.

The wrinkled old man was wheezing, perhaps ill. A yellow dribble trailed from his nose to his mouth. His white hair and beard seemed sparser than before, somehow. His purple robe was caked with mud and grime. His eyes had a weak, desperate look, the look of a dying man. In the span of several months, it seemed Jourmande had aged ten years—up to his death bed.

"Father!" Princess Clarysse came running up to her father and met him in an embrace. "Goddess, you look tired. But I am sure the Imperials look worse."

The Imperials, Ramir knew, owed the Zarube Crown seven hundred marks as a price for peace. Could it be possible that the southlanders had stooped to an all-time low, that they had somehow defaulted on their debts, had resisted the army, even—Goddess forbid—defeated Jourmande?

"Our army is scattered," Jourmande snapped. "Away from me, daughter!"

She fell from his embrace.

"We are defeated. I am ashamed. I must rest. Good night."

Clarysse looked most offended out of all the kingdom's notables in the Great Hall, with bulging eyes and an incredulous expression. The High Priestess Alse-Lorie, leader of the kingdom's faithful, had opened her mouth so wide Duke Ramir could fit a cudgel in it.

But Duke Ramir, as always, kept his reactions firmly in check. Months—or was it years?—ago he had defeated the Imperial Army himself, risking his own life to ensure the kingdom's honor. Now King Jourmande had brought it all to ruin—in an instant snatched away all Duke Ramir's progress, brought him low by incompetence.

"Now, a song of harvest time," shouted the court jester, Honey Crumbles. "A song of the famous Harvest Haunt, who tempts the peasants to stay indoors, to eat, drink, and be merry."

Goddess, how Ramir loathed that silly waif. He had often joked how he'd like to knock his head off, to see how far he could send it flying into the distance. It would be a great show, a better contest than knightly jousts. Only rarely did jousts end in death. A bloody battle was only ensured in the arenas, which were forbidden by the high-minded folk of the royal capital.

"What shall we do?" Clarysse cried. "What shall we do, when my father returns in defeat and shame?"

"We shall pray!" Alse shouted. The High Priestess had dressed in bright fairy pinks and greens, arrayed herself splendidly with no idea that tragedy awaited them all.

"I will avenge this," Ramir said. "On my honor, I will extract those seven hundred marks from the Empire, if it is the last thing I do." Yet war no doubt was the last thing Clarysse and Alse-Lorie and all these minor nobles gathered here wanted.

In his guest apartment, Ramir drew his sword from its sheath and laid it lengthwise across the bed. Its pommel was forged into the bear-head of the House Rambée, and its steel was of a quality a blacksmith could never make today. He had plunged its blade through an Imperial soldier's throat. He knew firsthand that the Imperials were human, that they bled and died as every other people. They were not gods; they were not even superior in prowess to the Zarubes. Yet somehow, with a mustered army of ten thousand, the ineffectual and incompetent King Jourmande had thrown away all the country's gains, had made a severe and irreparable blow to the royal treasury. Yet still Duke Ramir clung to his loyalty—but why? Why, indeed, when he could rule better?

Perhaps because the House Rambée had stood steadfastly with the King of Zarubain for centuries. In the seemingly eternal rule of the House Bretagne, their right to rule had never been questioned.

Duke Ramir should not question it now.

"Your Honor." A woman's voice called out to him.

He turned and beheld a slender figure in the doorway.

It was Princess Clarysse Bretagne, a woman of less than seventeen, unmarried, blonde-haired blue-eyed and beautiful but undeniably—Duke Ramir knew—vapid and dumb. "I am scared," she said. "If the nobles rebel against my father—"

"They will not," Duke Ramir answered boldly, and spoke— as far as he knew—the truth. "All the great lords and barons and dukes benefit from the current order of things. Do not worry, Princess Clarysse. I will protect you, as always."

As she left, Duke Ramir remembered Princess Clarysse's innocent blue eyes. He grabbed his ancestral sword and slid it into his sheath. Then he turned and left down the Castle Royale's winding corridors, knowing, in his heart, exactly where he was going.

~

The guards let him by and Ramir entered the royal quarters, seeing—as he had expected—the king Jourmande with his nubile young lady wife, Queen Alysant. The beauty from the minor county of Renseur had her slender pale hand wrapped in Jourmande's wrinkled one. "All is well, my husband, my life-fire. All is well," she purred.

Yet King Jourmande was staring out into space, his eyes devoid of all thought, so absent he did not look up at Ramir. All around him, the splendid wealth of the Zarube Crown lay: gold-framed pictures of butterfly-winged pixies and glowing blue will-o'-wisps painted by the famed artist Ranoul; a wardrobe large enough for a giant, carved intricately enough for the Goddess herself and washed in varnish; glass displays of ruby-inlaid goblets, diamond-encrusted necklaces, and sapphire-studded bracelets; and shelves of rare, illuminated books each worth more than a minor barony. Yet their owner—the sovereign of Zarubain, the King on the Lion Throne, the vicar of god on earth—had lost all hope, had lost all optimism, all joy about the future.

"Your Majesty," Ramir said, and dropped to one knee.

Jourmande turned his eyes to Ramir, but they were the eyes of a dead man.

"You still have the kingdom's allegiance. You still have *my* allegiance."

"I have failed, Ramir," Jourmande answered. "I have failed myself, I have failed you, I have failed everyone. I was told the Empire lay on the brink of ruin, but now I know I had misjudged them. I have brought about a defeat worse than any the kingdom has had to suffer through. Things would have been better if another successor had been chosen—even the Bastard Prince."

Jourmande, an elderly cousin of the childless former king Gylles, had been chosen according to the laws of succession. Gylles had vanished one night in the midst of the Castle Royale, disappearing with the blue wizard, Lemuel, who also was never heard from again. "I doubt anyone could have done better, Your Majesty," Ramir said. "Least of all the Bastard Prince. I have heard terrible things about him, Jourmande. I have heard things that the laws of courtesy forbid me to repeat."

Jourmande's eyes peered deep into Ramir's. "You brought about the Empire's defeat, imposed a crushing indemnity… I brought your plans to ruin. It is *you* that must continue this war. It is *you* that must command the army, and bring the kingdom the resolution it deserves."

"Surely you do not suggest another war," Ramir said.

"We tire of war, but war does not tire of us."

Jourmande knew something Ramir didn't.

"Whatever you require, I will do, my king," Ramir said.

"Very well, Ramir, Duke of Lessant." Something like a smile touched Jourmande's face. "Commander of the Army, savior of Zarubain."

Chapter Three:
Secrets

The Black Count

The trees in the Royal City and in the Westwood had begun turning shades of gold—at least, the few trees that were not pines. The Count of Garrone had arrived by river-boat in the king's city very early for the Feast of Saint Ignáce.

He wanted to come early, he told the suspicious nobles, for he had left everything important in the command of his bailiff and shire reeve, and the common *villeins* had done splendid work this year in the harvest, and the grape harvest of 1227 promised to be the best in the county's history. His wife he had left behind in the Castle Garrone, and no doubt that woman was lying with the hostler or some dirty-fingered peasant in his absence, or worse, the Bastard Prince who lived in the Montée March nearby. His wife was a Lysene woman, having little scruples and littler self-control, but she did not matter in the Black Count's mission here. She did not even know the truth of why the Black Count was here. No one did, nor would they be able to guess. The Black Count had pushed the truth so far down beneath his surface thoughts that sometime even he believed his own ruse, that he had arrived for the Feast of Saint Ignáce early.

In truth he had no reverence for Saint Ignáce, the peasant girl who became a warrior and saved the kingdom. After all, a story of a peasant who donned armor and rode into battle, helm, sword, and all, might give the *villeins* improper ideas. Rather than revere Saint Ignáce, why wouldn't they focus on the story of her death, burned at the stake by the very ones she saved?

"Your Honor," a guard said at a bridge that led into the

cobblestone streets of the Inner City.

The Black Count offered the man a slight nod—all he would afford to a common man-at-arms. He pressed on, finding the overwhelming stench of the Outer City fade slightly. Here, where the notables of the realm resided, a little bit more attention was paid to sanitation and hygiene. No chamber pots were emptied out windows with a shout of "Look out!" The cobblestone had only wear and tear as you might expect from windy, rainy Zarubad.

The bells tolled in the Lady's Cathedral, filling the city with their resonant notes. The noon prayers had begun. The cathedral's giant façade was visible even where the Black Count stood, and in the cool, cloudy light of the morning, the laughing pink-and-red portrait of the Lady—etched in stained glass on the rose window—glowed like fire. The high priestess, Alse-Lorie, had a gift for managing coin and for building strong relationships with the sisters across the realm; the Church of the Lady's wealth had almost doubled during her tenure. But she had a secret; the Black Counts informants told him she had been seen alone with a knight, even though priestesses were forbidden to marry. The Black Count dealt in secrets; he had ears from Zarubad to Carribor, and secret-gathering was why he had come.

He crossed three more bridges before he reached Emerald Isle. Here, every duke, count, and marquis had a temporary residence for when the king needed them. The Black Count had his own, but he was not predisposed to visit the capital. That would make the task ahead more difficult.

In a winery, he purchased two bottles of *gerusivel* for a king's ransom of ten gold crowns, more than all the peasants in County Garrone made in an entire month. Then, receiving the go-ahead by the castle guards, he took the ferry through the gently-flowing River Zaros and landed at the island upon which Castle Royale was built.

Inside, a dour and defeated-looking King Jourmande was slumped in the Lion Throne. *He is demoralized*—the Black Count took a mental note.

"Jorjé," the king said the Black Count's name, a rare thing for him to hear. "It has been at least ten Yules since I saw you last."

The Black Count nodded. "Your Majesty. I have brought you two gifts."

"*Gerusivel*," the king muttered it like a curse. "I do not drink anything crafted by the inferior race."

The Black Count did not show his disappointment. "Pardon me, Your Majesty. I apologize. You *did* deal the elves a crushing defeat."

"Untrue," the king said. "It was my young cousin, Gylles vis Bretagne. Everything good that has happened to this kingdom in the past quarter-century is squarely due to him."

Shall I try to comfort the king and call him a liar, or shall I say nothing? He hurled the *gerusivel* on the ground. The bottles shattered into a hundred pieces and the ruby-red liquid spread like blood across the stone floor. "You are a good king, Jourmande. Everyone I know says so." It was a lie, but a little bit of the sadness faded from King Jourmande's eyes.

"You have wasted a fortune, Jorjé."

"A small price to pay, for our good king to listen to reason."

"I shall enjoy watching the servants clean it up."

"Then it is not a waste. I am glad you liked my gift," said the Black Count.

He spent the rest of the morning in the Castle Royale, wandering its corridors and speaking to King Jourmande when he had the chance, even eating the noon meal in his presence, learning little—learning nothing, in fact, except something dark was bothering the king, like a cloud hanging over his head.

Does he know?

Chapter Four:
Signs of Unrest

The Reverend Alse-Lorie, High Priestess

Alse-Lorie had never seen a sovereign so dejected. Of course, at age twenty-seven, she had only ever served under two monarchs. As she exited the Lady's Cathedral down the pink-carpeted aisle, she uttered a prayer for him: *Goddess, give the master of your beloved nation strength, courage, and honor.* Honor was what was sorely needed in the king's spirit, a realization that if the monarch is afraid, the nation will be afraid.

Two reverend daughters—Varysse and Elouette—met her in the cobblestone promenade outside the cathedral. They had a task ahead of them, a task that Alse-Lorie loathed but one she was required to undertake at least once a year. She would leave the clean, well-kept boulevards and avenues of the Inner City and meet with the lowborn merchants, traders, and street rabble in the filth of the Outer City.

"Oh, how I despise this," said Varysse, a woman of nineteen who had left her pampered life in Duchy Ajernon for the pink-and-green robes, all to avoid an unsavory marriage.

"Me as well," said Elouette, whose story was much the same, but further away, in County Miere.

"You will learn to like it," Alse-Lorie said. An empty promise was a small sin in the eyes of the Goddess.

The riverboat had already been prepared; it would take the two reverend daughters and the reverend lady to their too-close port of call. Ten knights were on board, ready protect them with swords and shields.

Thank the Goddess, Sir Loy was not aboard. He, too, was a sin, a grave sin that made Alse-Lorie wonder if her connection to the Goddess was forever severed.

In too short a time, the riverboat docked on the south bank of the River Zaros. The smell was not terribly pleasant in the Inner City, but here the combined stench of emptied chamber pots, of pigs and cattle running wild, of tanneries and of befouled fish hit Alse-Lorie like a wall. The plague of 1221 had wiped out a third of the city, and Alse-Lorie thought the capital was well overdue for a new one. Perhaps then, everyone living in this squalor would flee, and only the clean cobbled roads and stately flower gardens of the Inner City would remain.

Three lowborn boys in ragged gray clothing caught sight of them through an alley, and immediately began jabbering. Alse-Lorie sighed, prayed to the Goddess for strength, and hiked up her gown as she climbed onto the sturdy wood of the dock. She had a great task ahead of her, a most onerous and unfortunate task. She had to pretend the nobles of the realm were concerned with the lowborns' affairs, to soothe the lowborns' woes with promises of the afterlife, and to make certain the lowborns would not revolt.

Leaving the dock, she noted the dirt roads had been recently cleaned—a small comfort, that the king's men had thought of her so—but as she passed through the cramped streets underneath the shaky timber houses, she could not help but see the garbage piled in alleyways. Flies buzzed everywhere, and the flea-bitten peasants gawked at her, even as they ducked away to let her by.

The dirt road segued into a cobblestone thoroughfare. It, too, had been cleaned, and Alse-Lorie comforted herself with the fact that Lions Square was only a short walk away.

She stumbled, nearly falling face-first on the road. She cursed. The road was chipped and filled with potholes. The king did not care for the Outer City's roads. She looked up to laughing faces—the faces of starved men, and of merchants and merchants' wives only slightly fatter. There were elves, too, with their pointed ears and slight builds, dour-eyed and stormy-complexioned. All by law were slaves, talking tools, commodities to be sold and bartered.

Cursing again, she eyed the road, dodging potholes and broken crevices, seeing—as a result—that the hem of her gown was stained black with mud. A light drizzle began.

The drizzle had turned to a misty rain by the time Alse-Lorie reached Lions Square.

The stone square had as many potholes, scars, and crevices as the road, and the four lion statues guarding the center had been worn by rain and wind, but worst of all, the square itself was crowded with lowborns. Traders had set up stalls along the perimeter, heckling passersby about shoes, tunics, cuts of pork, heads of lettuce, carrots, chicken-bones, candles, and blankets. As Alse neared the high lectern, the smell of ripe fish overwhelmed her, threatening to knock her off her feet.

Like flies to a rotted carcass the lowborn gathered around Alse to hear her speak. She could not believe how many souls lived in this city, how many of these lowly people gathered to listen. The ten knights formed a protective wall around her, Varysse and Elouette. When she had seen as many gather as she could bear, she began to shout:

"My dear subjects of the His Majesty King Jourmande vis Bretagne, 1227 is a good year to be a Zarube." *They are so dirty, so poorly garbed, so ridden with rashes and ailments of all kinds.* "As is customary I shall enliven you, as the faithful children of our lady goddess Feanara, with the good news that springs forth better and brighter each day." *It is good that the Goddess loves them—no one else does.* "The lords and ladies of the realm have enjoyed great harvests of wheat, grapes, apples, and fruits, and they are content and not restive. The king's sovereignty is not questioned by any, and there is no sign of discontent among the nobles." *Already they look bored.* "Zarubain has once again claimed victory over its enemies…"

"*What of the southlanders?*" shouted a peasant in that grating Outer City accent she'd come to despise. "*We don't got a victory against them, do we?*"

She was surprised these lowborns knew anything about that, or about anything outside their insular, seven-square-mile Outer City world. She debated a moment whether to answer him, but found herself shouting back a second later: "We shall not fear a nation where the lowborns choose their king!" They responded to her with dull, dead eyes, utterly uninterested. "Be assured their insolence will not go unpunished! Soon their lands will be divvied up amongst the lords and ladies of Zarubain, and their lowborns will know their proper place!" The customs of the southlanders were barbaric, but look at what Alse-Lorie was doing now: answering a peasant's foolish queries openly, giving him the undeserved honor of a response.

"*What of the Storm of the Ages?*" shouted a peasant girl.

"*Enough!*" Alse howled. She did not know what the fool girl spoke of, but even the shrill rebuke was more than she deserved. "Let me continue: there is no better time to be a Zarube. Our future is bright." *Ours, not theirs.* "Food is plentiful!" *For us.*

The crowd had already begun to disperse.

"The Lady loves us all, lowborn and high. If you cling to our goddess, to her words and to her hope, one day you—like the nobles of the realm—will live in her kingdom."

A few faces brightened. She had done her duty. She left the lectern, desperate to return to the Inner City, eager to leave the smells, the squalor, the lean-to wooden houses and the chipped, uncared-for roads behind.

She departed under the protection of the ten knights. As she left, she caught sight of the statue of the king on the west entryway of Lions Square. The lowborns had tied a noose to it, and spattered it with pigs' blood. Such a thing was a capital crime, a worrying sign of discontent. At such a troubled time, Alse-Lorie, reverend lady, High Priestess of the Goddess Feanara, would not tell King Jourmande and add to his worries.

Chapter Five:
When Duty Calls

Ramden the Bold

Ramden wore the blue bear-rampant symbol of the House Rambée on his surcoat, and was never afraid to have it so boldly displayed on his armor, not even in the presence of his enemies. Even now, riding his horse alone beside the vineyards of Ajernon, he had no fear. His friends in Lessant, which the House Rambée ruled, called him Ramden the Gallant or Ramden the Fearless. His father, the duke Ramir, had spoken to him countless times of the dangers his bold adventurism could get him into, but Ramden had never listened to him, not once in his twenty years of life.

In the wake of a war between Ajernon and Lessant, Ramden had fought alongside the House Rambée's knights, risked death numerous times and had personally fought in the battles that brought the war to a close. His father Duke Ramir had given him an earful every time he'd bragged about the exploits to his friend, even given an empty threat of cutting Ramden out of the line of succession, of giving the duchy to his younger brother Ramone or even his sister Ramonette.

What would Father think now?

Just hours ago, in the manor house, Father's knight Guliver had met Ramden in the yard, said, "I dare you, Ramden the Bold, to go to Abreville and bring me back a bottle of Ajernais gold."

The other knights gathered there in the manor yard had laughed at Guliver, thinking Ramden would never in a hundred years follow through on the dare.

But Ramden *had* followed through, and wearing the Rambée

symbol on his surcoat, no less.

Four miles of hard riding, and the town of Abreville appeared. Its thatch-roofed stone buildings lay in the shadow of the Castle Rose—a fortress built upon a rock hill, its stone exterior overlaid with bricks the color of a summer sunset. The Castle Rose had never fallen, not once in its six-hundred-year history, though many had tried. The town of Abreville, lacking walls, had been destroyed countless times, but not so the Castle Rose, home of the Dukes of Ajernon.

Ramden galloped headlong into the town of Abreville, coaxing his stallion to leap over rocks and high ground. A peasant on the town's outskirts raised the hue-and-cry: "*Hey, there's the Wild Bear o' Lessant!*"

This time of day, the market square of Abreville lay in the direct shadow of the Castle Rose, but the air was still humid and warm from the sun and from the countless bodies packed inside. The air was heavy with the scent of baked bread, mixed with less savory things—ripe fish, laying out in the hot sun, and the contents of chamber pots in the outlying streets.

"I want some famous Ajernais gold wine!" Ramden shouted, and realized the market had gone quiet in the wake of his presence. "I can pay full price for a bottle!"

"Here, sir!" A peasant was shouting in the east corner, lifting up a bottle. "For twenty coppers, or a *denier* if you've got one!"

Ramden grabbed a coin from his pocket, the only coin he'd brought—a gold *libre* with the king's head cast into the metal. This was the peasant's lucky day. Ramden galloped up to him and flipped him the coin.

A nun stood next to the peasant, wearing a dark green coif and pink wimple. "The audacity!" she howled. "It is Ramden,

Ramden the Fool!"

At her words, a knight appeared, riding in on a horse. Ramden only had to glimpse at the Ajernais swordfish symbol on his surcoat to know it was time to flee. He grabbed the bottle of gold wine, yanked the reins to wheel his horse around, and took off at a gallop.

"Your father will pay a pretty ransom!" the knight shouted as their horses leapt down the high ground and rocks toward the road. "When will you learn your lesson, Master Ramden? Only fools are as bold as you!"

As Ramden touched ground on the road, there was a loud horn peal. He looked back, saw the mustachioed knight blowing a horn to summon his friends.

Three knights joined Ramden's pursuer as the vineyards of Ajernon flew by. The clouds had cleared momentarily, baring the bright blue sky. "Lovely day, isn't it?" Ramden shouted at them. "A day beautiful enough to capture in a painting, wouldn't you say?"

"Our lord Ramden is a girl!" one of them shouted. "Perhaps he belongs in Valais with Roland and Lord Mars!"

Ramden's horse at last broke its gallop, but so did his pursuers' steeds. The river appeared—the very border with Lessant—and the bridge that forded its wide waters.

"Do not think we will not follow you!" one of them shouted. "The ends of justice know no borders!"

"Ah, but they do!" Ramden shouted.

As he expected, two knights and ten men-at-arms stood watch at the bridge, and the pursuers slowed to a halt. Ramden was home free, a bottle of Ajernais gold in his hand, the dare answered and completed. He laughed.

"We will catch you one day!" one of the knights shouted as he galloped across the bridge. "This, I swear!"

"Sure, you will!" Ramden laughed.

He paid no heed to the guards at the bridge as he flew by. The day had faded to dusk, the sun reduced to a faint twinkling on the horizon.

In the woods just outside Castle Silvergold, a dark shape emerged on the road. For some reason Ramden stopped, though he normally never would. The reason, he realized quickly, was fear—his body gone cold, his skin crawling with gooseflesh, his breath gone short and rasping. The size of the shape grew, and in the fading sunlight it took form: a woman five feet tall but with the presence of a giant. Her filthy gray hair fell in tangled knots down her gown of tattered wool. Her pruned old face was marred with boils and cysts. A peasant, surely—and yet in her hand was a gold lantern that shrank and then grew in size, and within it a glowing green orb.

A woods witch, Ramden realized, a friend of the fey, a devotee of the Lady Goddess but without all the trappings of the state-sanctioned church. Ramden's father Ramir had made it a point to root out all witches—"woods witches, bog witches, and witches who hide in peasants' clothes"—and burn them at the stake. Yet neither he nor any of his successors had made a lick of progress. The witches remained, and had won the support of the lowborn, entertaining their simple minds with light-shows and cursing the peasants' oppressors with nightmares, poxes, and hag's eye.

"Ramden the Bold!" the woods witch thundered.

Ramden's stallion reared up on its hind legs and let out a shrill whinny.

Shaken autumn leaves whirled about her and landed near her feet. Her gold lantern swelled again, then shrank; the green orb within blazed brighter until it had turned white. "The Lady is concerned with you. She worries for your safety."

"How dare you speak of the Lady, witch," Ramden snapped, but a lump had grown in his throat. "You, who disobey her vicar on earth, the king." He reached for his sword, tried to draw it, but it wouldn't budge—it seemed as if the blade had melded with its sheath.

"*You* speak of the Lady," the woods witch answered, "a far greater offense. You highborn think you can honor the fey goddess with cathedrals and churches of stone... She detests those rose windows, those buttresses, those pointed arches which you used *iron* to carve. You claim to honor her, yet you exude disrespect in every way."

"Have your say, woods witch, before I strike you down."

"You cannot strike me down, Master Ramden, but I will have my say nonetheless." Her prune face wrinkled into a smile. "The Lady is concerned for your welfare. She sees your boldness as a sign of great gallantry. Yet it will lead to disaster... utter disaster before the winter's end. Trouble is coming, Master Ramden, great and terrible trouble, unless you heed my words."

"Be gone, witch," Ramden hissed. He would not listen to a witch's advice, even if it did come from the Lady's mouth.

That night, Ramden ate a sumptuous feast in his father's hall, and every knight drank a cupful of Ajernais gold. But even in the bright warmth of the hearth, the sounds of laughter and music, and the taste of crisp pork, a vision assailed him—of darkness and shadows taking shape, of a demon in human form beckoning him close and bidding him to stay nearby.

Chapter Six:
Watching Eyes

The Knight of Lorh

"Hey-nonny, hey-nonny, hey-nonny, hey!"

The Ardognese dancers spun in circles, twirling green and red streamers and leaping into the air. The Bull Leapers' Dance was not quite as impressive without bulls, but King Jourmande did not allow animals into his hall. It was a pity, for Sir Darius, Knight of Lorh, enjoyed bear-tamers as much as anyone else, and none had ever been seen in Jourmande's hall. At least these dancers were different from that ridiculous jester, Honey Crumbles, who had plagued the Great Hall the past seven nights.

"Hey-nonny, hey-nonny , hey-nonny, hey!"

An Ardognese man and an Ardognese woman jumped in the air and locked hands mid-leap. A flash of red and green streamers soon followed. At the high table on the dais, a wide grin had overtaken King Jourmande's face. His expression had been dour just yesterday, when Honey Crumbles had resorted to beating himself with a stick; this foreign dance from exotic Ardogne had driven the nation's ills far from Jourmande's mind.

Sir Darius, Knight of Lorh, still thought bulls would make the dance better. The thought of wild animals in the palace terrified King Jourmande , it seemed, yet he had no qualms about the steel bastard sword Sir Darius had slung across his back. For all King Jourmande knew, a conspiracy by one of his relatives could be brewing in the Great Hall, yet he had no sign of worry. There were younger and wiser men in the House Bretagne, distant cousins and second-cousins, nephews and great-nephews, that could try to take his place.

"*Hey-nonny, hey-nonny, hey-nonny, hey!*" An Ardognese dancer leapt on a woman's back, then back-flipped high into the air. The same woman leapt on his shoulders and back-flipped twice the height. King Jourmande clapped his hands, positively delighted at the night's entertainment.

Yet when there were not great pig roasts and plates of apple and lemon savories, bottles of sweet, sparkling *gerusivel,* and endless entertainments, Sir Darius knew the mood of the king's court was dark. He had arrived seven days ago, after all, in preparation for the Feast of Saint Ignáce, which all the great dukes and duchesses had been invited to. Sir Darius knew things would change, and soon. There was trouble on the border, signs of impending war—that, after all, was why the Knight Grandmaster of Lorh had sent him here. The southlanders were a fearsome force, vengeful and without honor.

"*Hey-nonny, hey-nonny, hey-nonny, hey!*" A dancer leapt off another's back and pirouetted in the air, sending her black hair twirling.

In Sir Darius' morning prayers, a terrible feeling of apprehension had filled him. Nothing unusual had happened throughout the day, though he had been watching fervently each hour. He scanned the room, looking for anyone who did not belong.

The Young Duke, Roland of Valais, sat at the table, having barely touched his plate of pork. The bailiff whom Roland had ennobled and raised to the rank of baronet—the one called Lord Mars—sat by his side, half again the Young Duke's height. They had just arrived from Duchy Valais this morning in preparation for the Feast of Saint Ignáce. If they had any reason to harm the king, they showed no signs of it. But the Young Duke—from all accounts— had no great ambition, no desire for anything except pleasure.

"*Hey-nonny, hey-nonny, hey-nonny, hey!*"

The duke Ramir had been in the king's court for more than a month and showed no signs of leaving. The tower of a man had an ugly face, scars running across his arms, and a head of black hair quickly going gray. He had left his wife in Lessant but she was coming in time for the feast-day, he said. He was the king's most trusted advisor.

"*Hey-nonny, hey-nonny, hey-nonny, hey!*"

The dancers were spinning and jumping in a frenzy. The Black Count sat near the king. The Black Count was a man of mystery, an oily serpent which you could never pin down. Yet murder was not his way.

"*Hey-nonny, hey-nonny, hey-nonny, HEY!*"

A dancer had leapt halfway to the ceiling, and a knife was in his hands. Sir Darius had only a moment to react. He rushed through the Great Hall, up to the dais, but hadn't made it halfway across the room before the dancer landed. The king was laughing uproariously. The dancer had balanced the knife-point on his head.

"Calm down, Knight of Lorh," Duke Ramir thundered. "My father once said, 'He who is suspicious of evil at every turn is an evil man himself.'"

Sir Darius answered the insult with a glare. Perhaps he had been too trusting of this duke Ramir. Perhaps Ramir did not have the king's best interests at heart.

"Tell your king you have pleased me greatly!" King Jourmande shouted. "I do believe our friendship with Ardogne will continue, if I had to guess based on this lovely Saint Ignáce Day gift. I would dare say the peasant savior of Zarubain is smiling in heaven as we speak. Hail Ardogne, hail Saint Ignáce, and hail King Roderigo—may he live a hundred years!"

In the shadows, Honey Crumbles in his jester's hat was glaring at the Ardognese dancers, his face burning with jealousy. Sir Darius wondered why he had not considered that ridiculous buffoon before. He had been slighted, jeered, and insulted enough to perhaps take up employment for the enemy.

But Sir Darius realized he had been a fool all this night—

why would an assassin commit a brazen assault while everyone was awake and laughing, and a host of knights and red wizards stood guard in the Great Hall? The trouble would not happen until after dark, when the king had gone to bed.

In the entrance to the royal wing of the castle where the king slept, Sir Darius stopped at the stone wall perpendicular to the door. He wetted his finger and dipped it in his pouch of moon dust, then drew a Lorhish rune of vigil. With the invisible mark, no one who entered or exited the inner rooms would escape Sir Darius' eye. He breathed all his magic power into the fine dust and asked Orbuus, god of mysteries, to keep the ward safe.

The night turned cool, but Sir Darius did not return to *The Tabard Inn* on Emerald Isle. Instead, he flipped the hostler two silver *deniers* to keep him quiet, entered the stables and ducked inside an empty stall. There, sitting amid the hay and forgotten horse stool, Sir Darius used his third eye.

The hallway lay empty, save two knights with swords and shields who guarded the entryway. The minutes dragged on, and yet they spoke little. No doubt King Jourmande had already retired to bed.

The minutes turned to hours. The sconces on the walls shone the same flickering light on the red Fharese rug; further down the hall, the gold-bordered painting of Saint Genevieve did not move from its place. The only sound was the wind, slowly building outside, the steady patter of rain, threatening to lull Sir Darius to sleep.

Time went on, slow like a river frozen-over. The knights talked idly amongst themselves.

Sometime in the dark of the night, new knights switched places with the first two, assuming the guard duty. The rug was red as it had ever been before; the portrait of Saint Genevieve in her flowing gown of white samite did not move.

~

Morning light pierced the high windows of the stable, waking Sir Darius from his slumber. He had no idea when his watch ended and at what time the sleep had overtaken him. Either way, he left into the morning light filled with shame, and smelling of hay and horse.

A shout rang out as Sir Darius wound his way through the Castle Royale. "Why! Why, O goddess!"

Sir Darius took off at a run. The man shouting was the Black Count, standing at the entry to the Great Hall.

A storm of indistinguishable shouts and cries had overtaken the once-tranquil castle. "What is wrong?" Sir Darius cried.

The Black Count fixed his eyes on Sir Darius—twin black orbs contrasting starkly with his ashen complexion. "The duke Ramir! The great duke Ramir is dead!"

Sir Darius cursed himself for focusing overzealously on the king. "Goddess help us!" he shouted. He ran into the Great Hall, into a scene of panic.

Tears were running down King Jourmande's eyes, who sat rigid at the high table on the far end of the room, against the wall. He had aged ten years overnight. Beside him, his young Renseurian wife, Queen Alysant, had locked her pale white hand in his. She had an expression as gloomy and dark as her raven hair.

No one had touched the trenchers of fried bacon or the

plates of fairy cakes that graced the long tables. The Young Duke had stood up, appearing unsettled; his friend Lord Mars had stood up also, but had an unconcerned, dullard's expression.

Could it have been him? The Lord Mars had been raised to the nobility from his status as a common bailiff. The hearts and wills of peasants were easily shapeable; for a little money, they could be bought. But why would Lord Mars endanger his privileged life in the royal and ducal courts?

"Two guards dead, too!" cried the Black Count from outside the Great Hall. "And the killers had the key! Somewhere, somehow, we have been betrayed!"

That much was clear, but by whom?

Alivere and Esmette from Duchy Arvogne had just arrived this morning; they, surely, had nothing at all to do with the duke's death.

"Whoever did this—I will cut out his heart!" thundered Sir Loy.

At the knight's words, the high priestess, Alse-Lorie, stood up. A pained look was on her face—a look of discomfort, perhaps guilt.

Could she have done this?

Chapter Seven:
The Wizard Speaks

The Reverend Alse-Lorie, High Priestess

Each time she heard Sir Loy's voice, Alse-Lorie felt vulnerable, ill at-ease, unsafe. He was a reminder that she had broken her sacred vows. Each day she fretted that the Grayman's beard she consumed day after day would fail, that she would find herself with child, that her sins would catch up to her, expose her as the fraud she was.

How despicable, she thought, *that at a time of such crisis, I am so worried about myself.*

That Knight of Lorh, Sir Darius, was staring daggers at her from across the room. Alse had always despised the Order of Lorh—the king had dragged them kicking and screaming into the Elven War, and now they spoke ill of the decision to sell elves into bondage.

"The Lady is with us all!" Alse-Lorie shouted. *But not with me.* "The duke Ramir now runs through the flowered fields of the Otherworld." *But I will not, I will never.* "The Lady will protect us all." *But she will not so much as think of me.*

Sir Loy had drawn his sword. His cheeks had turned some shade of pink. Despite his wrath, he had never looked so gallant, in his gold-enameled breastplate, his gorget of steel, his giant pauldrons that tripled the size of his shoulders. "Who did this?" he howled. "The southlanders must be behind it!" He lifted his two-handed sword above his head, a weapon that would topple a lesser man.

"Enough!" Alse-Lorie howled.

King Jourmande had slumped in his seat at the high table.

The court had quieted its panic at Alse's word.

"We must not lose heart or hope!" she continued. "Most of all, we must not lose our minds. We must launch a formal investigation—a calm, collected, rational investigation."

The three-dozen or so knights in the court had looks of inconsolable rage, a rage that forbade rational thought and demanded violence and bloodshed. Every knight, that is, except the Knight of Lorh, Sir Darius, whose eyes scanned across the room, examining, calculating. In a moment's span, Alse-Lorie had no doubt in her mind that Sir Darius was involved.

"Uriel!" King Jourmande shouted, and at His Majesty's loud voice the court had a silence deeper than it had ever seen before.

The green wizard, Uriel, appeared from the dark shadows, clutching a knobbed staff of wood half again his height. In the right corner of the room where he had hid silently, knights and servants alike cleared away from him, fearful of his great power. "What do you seek of me, Your Majesty?" The dim torchlight illuminated his ancient gray eyes, his long gray beard. He turned his steely gaze to the king.

Uriel never failed to unnerve Alse-Lorie.

"What say you?" Jourmande continued. "Who committed this heinous crime?"

"I am not ashamed, Your Majesty, to say that I do not know," Uriel began. "Not even the wisest can see all. And not even the All-Seeing Orb can look into the past."

"You disappoint me, Uriel," Jourmande growled.

"Then your expectations are too high," said Uriel. "I am not here in your service. I serve only the Council of the Twelve and its All-Seeing Eye. I am not even here to protect you, but only to watch you, and keep an eye on the goings-on of the Lion Throne."

Only a wizard would dare speak so rudely in the Zarube king's court.

"And yet," Uriel said, "I have my suspicions."

"Then say them," Jourmande said.

Sir Darius had fallen back into the crowd, perhaps hoping to disappear.

"I believe your enemy is here in this room, among us," Uriel said. "I believe someone standing here plunged the knife into Ramir and his guards, betrayed you utterly, and is working under the pay of your enemies."

There were a few gasps; lords, ladies, and knights looked around at each other, wishing Uriel spoke a falsehood but secretly believing he had told the truth.

"I believe," Uriel continued, and the room again turned quiet, "that the southern Empire is on the march. They are warmongers, King Jourmande. Having sensed the nation of Zarubain's weakness, there is little doubt that they will arrive at your borders… assault your castles and towns."

King Jourmande's face was little changed; he already had the look of a man defeated. Alse-Lorie wanted nothing more than to soothe his worries, to awaken the lion within him once again. But she had no recourse except to pray to the Lady—the Lady who, by all accounts, had abandoned her.

"Do not listen to the wizard's lies!" Alse-Lorie recognized the voice of Fabient, Minister of War, who kept accounts of all the kingdom's knights, horses, and men of fighting age. He hated to be contradicted. "There is no evidence! There is no need to worry… no need to panic on account of *Uriel*… a man of no noble birth."

Fabient spoke truly; the wizard Uriel, as a child, had been of no noble birth—the son of a common cooper in Altdorf, by a stroke of fate he was born with magical talent. Though trained and educated, and now a powerful wizard, he had the stain of peasantry about him, a stain he could never remove, no matter how diligently he tried.

"Ignoble or well-born," Uriel said, his face calm and unchanged, "if the king's court does not value my counsel, I shall take it elsewhere."

King Jourmande was glaring at Minister Fabient. "Do not listen to him, Uriel," he snapped. "Your presence is valued here; and your counsel may be true. A month ago, the Viceroy of Mekara said something similar."

Alse-Lorie gasped. The king had kept this news hidden, a dark secret held close to his heart.

"What did Lord Seven Sous say?" exclaimed a knight.

Lord Seven Sous, or Lord Falerien as respectful people called him, was far from the concerns of the capital, the viceroy of a backward region little cared-for in the minds of the court.

"Reports of an Imperial army massing," Jourmande continued. "Of soldiers so numerous they could not be hidden; of forests chopped down to build catapults, trebuchets and siege engines; of a resurgent southland Empire, more confident and vengeful than it ever has been before."

Eons ago, Alse-Lorie knew, the emperor Tidus had established trade between the Empire and Zarubain, signed declarations of peace and mutual friendship. In the past decades their centuries-old alliance had evaporated.

But Jourmande, apparently, was not done. "Lord Falerien has said they have not yet made their move. But preparations are underway. That is why I summoned the Dukes of the Seven Gems to the Feast of Saint Ignáce, and every border march from Silvan to Miere. We must prepare for war. We tire of war, but it has not tired of us."

~

Alse-Lorie left the Castle Royale and entered once again the Lady's Cathedral. At the altar she collapsed, laid her hands on the pink cloth that covered the stone, and fell into fervent prayer.

"Save the nation, O Lady; do not turn your back on the

country, or to your vicar, the king."

She felt the presence before she heard the voice. "Alse, my sweet."

Of all the people I do not want to see... She stood up, clutched her dress, and turned around. Sir Loy stood there, a tower of a man with thick chestnut-brown hair. The eyes that gazed upon Alse were blue as the sapphires on Jourmande's crown. Still he wore the breastplate, and the thick gorget covered his neck. He was the fiercest fighter in Jourmande's employ, courageous, lion-hearted, bold to a fault. It was he that made Alse regret joining the priesthood; it was he that made her break her vows. *Just this once,* she said, *and I will never do it again.* Then she had done it again—against the wishes of the Lady, against the vows of the priesthood—sinning week after week, month after month, for three years to the day.

"Trouble has come to Zarubain." Sir Loy was not smiling. "Must I comfort you?"

Alse-Lorie scowled. "You are too brash, Sir Loy." There were no priestesses hiding among the pointed arches or worshipers sitting in the pews. Still, she loathed it when he came here. If caught, her hair would be shorn; her body would be clothed in rawhides or rough wool; her underlings would parade her through the filthy streets of the Outer City before formally excommunicating her, or worse. "Go away, Sir Loy," she said. Tears had formed in her eyes. "Go away and never come back. I cannot bear the sight of you."

A look of hurt crossed Sir Loy's face. Then, his expression hardened in anger. "Very well," he said, and stormed off out the cathedral's double doors.

Alse wept, laid her hands again on the pink cloth of the altar, crying but unwilling to pray, for her connection to the Lady was severed, her relationship with the Goddess forever ruined. She wept for her lot, for her life in ruins.

That night, she summoned Sir Loy.

Chapter Eight:
Lies

Danitari

For refusing Mignette and honoring his master, Dan now slept in a thin iron cage, and for the past two weeks had eaten nothing but befouled river water. He sat in his own filth, just as Mignette demanded. Now, each day, when she descended the stairs to the cellar with her whips and prods, she had to cover her nose with a cloth. Her torture since the starvation began had lessened, but now Dan shook constantly from the lack of food. The growing stench sickened him. He knew he had caught some kind of illness; a constant dribble trailed his nose, his head burned with a virulent headache, he felt cold even in his ample clothing. *This,* Dan thought, *is what hell must feel like; and yet it is for a good deed that the gods are punishing me.* That, of course, was how things seemed to always go. If he had run from war, refused to defend the City of Light and its King, he would never have been sold into slavery.

One morning—or was it night?—Mignette returned to the cellar. So focused on reading her expression—whether those rosy freckled cheeks and bright blue eyes exhibited wrath—that Dan did not immediately notice the man standing next to her.

The head of the household, Jouliver Jourdanis, had apparently returned. He still had on his traveling clothes—thick woolens caked with mud. A stench of many days and weeks without bathing hung heavy about him. Yet no doubts he had returned twice as wealthy as before.

"Master Jouliver," Dan said. "Hello!"

Jouliver had furrowed his brow; his normally fair

complexion had turned red in splotches. His brown moustache and eyebrows were quivering. "I will not give you the honor of a greeting, Trash. I return from Miere, from a journey of many hundreds of miles, and I hear what you have done. I paid six-hundred *deniers* for you, you scalawag, you traitor, you piece of garbage."

"I have done nothing but sit here in this cage," Dan growled. He could no longer play the submissive fool. It was not fitting for elves to serve as slaves—elves, the Light's firstborn.

"The Royal Road is filled with bandits, pickpockets, and unscrupulous robber barons. I traveled well over four-hundred miles just for silken clothing—and in the *best* of circumstances I will barely turn a profit." Still, Dan did not know what lie Jouliver had been fed. "The last thing I deserve," he went on, "is a home under threat."

"You do not have one," Dan sneered. "And still, I don't know what you are so upset about."

"Your attempt to seduce my wife, of course." At the voicing of the lie, the red splotches on Jouliver's face increased.

"She lies!" Dan snapped. "I do not love human women, nor do I even like them! Mignette has ensured that."

"Quiet, Trash!" Mignette hissed.

"Who shall I believe?" Jouliver howled. "My dear wife, or an elf?"

"You know less about your wife than you think," Dan said.

"Kill him!" Mignette howled.

"No," Jouliver answered. He had stopped quivering. "His life is worth six-hundred *deniers* to us. We owe it to ourselves to get back our investment. I shall lie about him, and to the poor sap's disadvantage. Danitari, you are back on the market."

Could it get worse? Danitari asked himself. *Yes,* he determined after a little thought. *Yes, it could.*

Chapter Nine:
Unexpected News

Ramden the Bold

Ramden was wandering the castle yard, sword in hand—plotting his next daring escapade but failing to think of anything that would top his journey into Ajernon—when a rider came galloping through the open portcullis. Ramden brandished his sword, called out, "Hail!"

The rider came to a sudden stop, sending up specks of dirt and mud. "I come bearing bad news. I must speak to Lady Narysse."

"My mother is inside."

"And where is the heir apparent?"

Ramden's gut clenched. Could Father truly have died in the safety of the capital? "I am he."

"Ramone?"

"Ramden."

"The duke's will states that his son Ramone shall inherit his title."

"Impossible!" Ramden cried. "I am the heir!"

The rider seemed to have lost interest in Ramden. He rode his horse further to the stable, then dismounted and hurried inside. Ramden barreled ahead, after him.

His brother Ramone sat in the feasting hall of Castle Silvergold—a fitting place to find him, since it was there he spent most of the day. Against the laws of primogeniture, Father had chosen Ramone—twice as wide as Ramden was tall, inactive, slow in body and mind, unwilling to fight for anything. Mother sat nearby him, flanked by two fairy priestesses. Ramone gripped a haunch of pork in his greasy fingers. Ramden had the love of the knights, the ladies, and the peasants—yet Father had chosen this monstrous hog to inherit Castle Silvergold and all its holdings.

"The great duke Ramir is dead!" the messenger shouted.

Mother gasped. Ramone instantly began to cry. He stood up—perhaps for the first time in his life—and shouted, "Truly?"

"Truly," the messenger continued. "It brings me no pleasure. A knife took him in the heart. It is a dark day for the nation."

"A knife!" Ramone cried. "How is that possible? He was in the Castle Royale, with all the safety of the knights." Tears had formed in the pig's eyes. Ramone loved Father but he was still useless.

I deserve Castle Silvergold, not him.

"It was an act of treachery," the rider continued. "A sign of weakness, to stab someone in the middle of the night. An unmanly act, for certain. And there is more… Master Ramone, I have something for you."

Only then did Ramden notice the leathern sack in the rider's hand. He removed its contents—a sword of cold gray steel, with a silver crossbar and a great sapphire jewel affixed in the center.

"*Kingmaker!*" Ramone cried.

"And the duchy is yours."

Mother eyed Ramden, hoping for a muted reaction, her lack of surprise proving that she had known all along. Against all law, all traditions, all rules of primogeniture, Ramden's fat fool of a brother had taken what was rightfully his.

"But Ramden—"

"Yes, indeed!" Ramden shouted. He swept his own sword out of its sheath. "But Ramden!" He charged wildly ahead, slammed the blade down, slicing straight through a wooden bowl and halfway through the table. "Goddess damn Father, and Goddess damn all of you!"

"Calm down, Ramden!" Mother howled and stood up, daring to wear an angry expression on her face, daring to indicate that somehow *he* was in the wrong.

He jerked the sword out of its place, swung back again, and sliced a melon in two.

"Enough!" Mother howled louder than before. Even through the white powder makeup her face had turned a shade of red. "You are only proving our beliefs!"

"Your beliefs!" Ramden screamed. "*Your* beliefs! So it was you, too, Mother, who betrayed me. It was you that poisoned him against me, wasn't it?"

"It was not me, no less than your Father," Mother snapped, having the gall to be angry.

"Sir Martin! Sir Percival! Sir Guliver!" Ramden shouted. "Come with me! We are going to Zarubad, to answer this illegal travesty! I will have Mother and my pig brother hanging from nooses, and my father buried in a pauper's grave."

"Stop it, brother!" Ramonette had appeared in one of the feasting hall's many doorways. The only daughter of Duke Ramir was sixteen and still unwed, her political use as yet unexpended. No doubt the fat fool Ramone would find a way to further his control over Lessant and Castle Silvergold.

That evening, Ramden departed with a purse-full of gold coins stolen from the treasury. Neither Sir Martin, Sir Percival, Sir Guliver, or any knights followed him on his journey north; and no ladies or maidens cheered him farewell. Alone and friendless, with just his sword and steed to keep him company, he left on the northward-leading road to right this great injustice, to force the world to give him his due.

Chapter Ten:
A Coming Storm

The Reverend Alse-Lorie, High Priestess

At last, the loathsome preparations, the fourteen days and nights of cooking, the awkward hellos and how-was-your-journeys had dissipated. The dukes and duchesses, counts and countesses of the Western Heartlands had arrived, along with all their children, grandchildren, and distant relations, servants, and elven slaves. The Feast of Saint Ignáce had begun in earnest, and here—in the Hall of Mirrors—the more than a thousand party goers had gathered. Alse-Lorie had worked her blonde hair into elegant plaits and wore a sapphire-encrusted gown of gold cloth that some might say did not belong on the body of a High Priestess.

In truth, not *all* the Western Heartlands were in attendance. The Duke of Lessant, Ramir, had passed on, and his family was now in grief. Here, in the Hall of Mirrors, his death seemed a distant memory.

Two trumpets pealed. The double doors opened at the top of the grand staircase, and the partygoers at the ball turned to look up.

"Lord and Lady Roland Valais of Duchy Valais!" shouted a servant at the top of the stair.

The Young Duke had never looked so handsome in his scarlet houppelande and wide-brimmed black hat. His wife Elsie had on a gown of gold and silver tissue with a train that followed behind her as she made her way down the stair. The somewhat homely daughter of the Count of Belidere wore a smile on her face, yet it seemed—as always—strained. She had not borne the Young Duke any children. For a reason Alse did not know, she had expected Lord Mars to be up there, alongside them.

A servant walked by Alse with a silver tray of apple savories. She did not dare take one. Her gown of gold cloth still fit her and she intended for things to stay that way. On a table within arm's reach were puff pastries and baked apples drizzled in honey, cream-filled tarts and plates of fairy cakes, giant silver ewers filled with dessert wine, apple pies, apple cobblers, candied pears and loaves of sweetbread. The people of the Outer City often complained to the priestesses of their lack of food, but here, in the Hall of Mirrors, was a veritable paradise on earth.

"Lord and Lady Eurelien Námois of Duchy Duranche!" the servant shouted.

Another duke and duchess began their slow journey down the grand staircase, and were greeted with applause. The noise echoed off the polished silver mirrors that lined the walls. All around her the sounds of joy and chatter echoed. The men and women gathered here had been lulled into such calm. Just days ago a man had been murdered, and here they stood, gawking at the gowns and jewelry of the duchesses. Disaster was one false step away, and these fools were gathered in the Hall of Mirrors, thinking nothing of the gathering storm.

A servant passed by, his tray lined with silver goblets of wine. Alse grabbed one despite herself. She held the cold metal up to her lips, took a drink, and eyed the revelers.

Many wore masks of feather or glittering silver, though the king had never explicitly called for a masquerade. How many of these could have a knife in their possession—ladies, too.

"Alse."

Alse screamed and turned around. Sir Loy stood there. She had spilled some wine on the ballroom floor. He was not half so gallant and handsome in the dress of a civilian, with his tunic of green-dyed fustian and his loose-fitting brown trousers. Seeing Sir

Loy in plainclothes was almost enough to frighten her away from him for good.

"There is something wrong," he said. "I can feel it."

Alse cursed. Sir Loy was a dullard, for certain, unable or perhaps unwilling to keep their love discreet. "Get away from me," she hissed. Though, she, too, felt a sense of impending danger she had not felt since the day she and Sir Loy made love the first time. *There is something dreadful in this room*, she thought. *Something dreadful and terrible.*

A roll of thunder echoed, loud enough to be heard in this heavily-insulated corner of Castle Royale. A patter of rain was audible too, even above the chatter, the heaviest downpour Alse had ever heard.

"Lord and Lady Gouldair Voraigne of Duchy Voraigne!"

More cheers, more applause, echoed in the Hall of Mirrors. A servant passed by, with pear savories. She grabbed it and ate it to calm her nerves. She had heard from someone that pear savories were less fattening than apple savories. The light, sugary crust melted in her mouth, and the syrupy pear filling exploded with flavor. She took a swig of wine. Another roll of thunder echoed through the Hall of Mirrors.

"Lord and Lady Alivere Alerie of Duchy Arvogne!"

Lord Alivere had robbed the cradle with his wife Esmette, who could be no older than seventeen, but she was as splendidly arrayed as a lily with her parti-colored blue-and-yellow gown of silk and her jewel-encrusted flame chaplet. Lord Alivere, an old gray man of no younger than seventy, looked overly proud as he descended the grand staircase with Esmette in tow.

"Lord and Lady Dunstan Abrenard of Duchy Ajernon!"

Out of the doors came the second-most important duke of the Seven Gems after Ramir, Lord Dunstan. Alse knew he hated show and pomp, and he had dressed accordingly: a thick tunic of jet-black wool cinched in a leather belt with a gold buckle, tan pants, and a red cape. The gray-bearded Lord Dunstan had a wife of a more appropriate age, Lady Jaine, but whatever problems Lord Dunstan had with show, she had none. Alse knew Jaine had outdone all her competitors; she wore a billowing purple gown with floral patterns woven in gold thread, a pair of white samite gloves, and a diadem of gold cloth encrusted with white diamonds. Behind her, two maidservants in flame-colored flannel held up the train of her dress.

Some partygoers gasped in awe; others even clapped. Alse-Lorie only took another drink of wine. Sir Loy had vanished into the crowd. She could not shake the nervous feeling. Another roll of thunder echoed through the room.

"Absent today is Lord and Lady Ramir of Duchy Lessant!" the announcer shouted. "May the Goddess comfort his family in their grief." His dour expression brightened. "And now, without further ado, the centerpiece of the evening, the moment we have all been breathlessly waiting for: the sovereign of the Goddess's beloved nation, the ruler of the people, the holder of the Zarube Crown, His Inimitable Majesty, King Jourmande vis Bretagne!"

The trumpets blared and instantly the orchestra in the far corner of the Hall of Mirrors began to play *The Lion on the Ramparts*—lyres, lutes, trumpets, shawms and horns all—as applause and cheers rose.

King Jourmande began his journey down the grand staircase, his procession twice as slow as any of the dukes before him. Queen Alysant had on a dress of white samite interwoven with gold thread, simple though twice as expensive as any clothing before her. Her small crown of gold was inlaid with purple jewels and lined with silver. King Jourmande's crown, twice as large, gleamed in the lamplight with radiant gems of red, blue, green and white. His royal robe of purple was lined with white fur, and in his hands he held a gold scepter.

Even now, as the receiver of all this adoration, his expression remained dour, his eyes had the look of a man five-hundred years old and not seventy-four, and his shoulders slouched as if the weight of Varda had been thrust upon them.

Thunder rolled again, louder than before. Alse-Lorie took another swig of wine until her cup was empty. The crowd of partygoers cleared a path for King Jourmande as he made his way, waving ceremoniously, toward the royal podium that rose above the door. He climbed the red-carpeted stair with Alysant in tow, and took his place in front of the wooden lectern, just as *The Lion on the Ramparts* ended. The crowd quieted, expecting a rehearsed speech of glad tidings, maybe a mention of Ignáce, the peasant girl, the victorious Maid of Naines. But Alse knew this speech would be nothing of the sort.

"Great dukes and duchesses, counts and countesses, marquises from Silvan March to far-flung Miere and even beyond," King Jourmande began, "words cannot express my gratefulness for your longsuffering loyalty, your love for the Goddess and her beloved kingdom, and for your first and foremost duty—to fight for the realm. For as men and women of the most privileged class, that is our most ancient call—to fight, to risk our lives, to defend the nation and the sovereignty of the Zarube Crown."

The mood in the room had visibly darkened; quite clearly the lords and ladies of Zarubain wished for nothing more than peace, for life to consist of an endless rotation of grand balls and midnight parties.

"A terrible foe has arisen, a shadow in the south," King Jourmande said. "Not content with our defeat, the southlanders have left north from their ancient border, the great wall. The Viceroy of Mekara has braced himself for battle in Castle New. Our beloved Lord Seven-Sous may lose his life. The storm clouds of war are gathering, my friends and beloved compatriots. Every bridge must be fortified and garrisoned, every castle must be stocked with arrows and munitions. Every town and city must be filled to its full capacity with fighting men. All of fighting age must prepare for battle; all knights must be summoned. A levy must be taken. A long and difficult road is ahead of us." Jourmande frowned. "I love all of you dearly but that is not why I was so insistent that you all visit for Saint Ignáce Day. I wished to appoint Ramir War Lord but he has passed on too soon from a coward's knife; thus I shall appoint Lord Dunstan Abrenard, if he will accept."

All eyes focused on the elderly duke, who looked utterly baffled. "I… I… of course, Your Majesty. Who better?"

"Indeed. Who better?" A sad smile crossed King Jourmande's lips. "Now is not the time for cowardice, O lords and ladies of the realm. Such revelry as this, we will not know for months, maybe a year or more."

Alse-Lorie felt her heart sink. Indeed, she had expected something terrible all this time. She wished her goblet were not empty.

"The southlander general is a tactical genius, it is said," the king continued, "a prodigy in military strategy from his earliest days. Do not underestimate Marcus Sylla, even if he is the son of a farmer."

"Why shall we fear a lowborn peasant?" shouted Fabient, Minister of War, somewhere in the crowd.

"I have said my piece," the king finished. "Try as best as you can to enjoy Saint Ignáce. Use the model of our nation's great savior in the coming months. Tomorrow, depart; and prepare for war."

A maelstrom of death awaits us, Alse-Lorie thought. The king had not spoken the complete truth. *A storm of destruction, a nationwide massacre, until the River Zaros runs red.*

Thunder exploded overhead, rattling the mirrors. At the noise, Elsie, Duchess of Valais, screamed; a servant tripped and crystal cups shattered; and all the color left Alse-Lorie's face.

Chapter Eleven:
Dismissal

The Black Count

All the puppet strings had been pulled and played to perfection.

Morning peeked through the high windows of the Great Hall. Some peace had returned to King Jourmande's face as he feasted on duck-liver pastries and sipped his breakfast tea. The burdensome news had been released, the ill tidings delivered. Most of the party guests had departed to make preparations; only Roland vis Valais, Lord Mars, and servants remained. Even Roland's wife Elsie had departed; perhaps only she had a mind for the trouble to come.

"I don't understand, uncle," Roland cried. He stood before the dais, in the shadow of the high table. "Why can we not simply make peace with the southlanders? Why must we fight, risk death and destruction?"

King Jourmande regarded the Young Duke sourly. "What they say about you is true, Roland vis Valais. You are faint of heart. You care only for peace and safety."

Roland's hand went to the hilt of his sword; an action of incredible rudeness in the presence of the king.

A voice answered, not the one the Black Count expected. Deep and commanding, the wizard Uriel said, "Your nephew has the right solution, if not the right motives."

The Black Count turned; the green wizard had appeared unexpectedly as always, this time in the Great Hall doorway.

"The southland empire is strong, Jourmande, stronger than any here might believe. It would be best for you to meet the general

Sylla in person, ask for terms, and do whatever he requires—indemnities, reparations, and payments, even up to the whole of Mekara."

Jourmande slammed his fist onto the table. "I have endured much, wizard, and given you the benefit of the doubt always, but such counsel I will not tolerate. If you wish for the Lion Throne's defeat, be gone, old man, and never return."

"That is not my wish," Uriel answered.

The Black Count feigned anger.

"I have never had the kingdom's fall as my desire," Uriel said. "The Council of the Twelve takes no sides in any wars except its own—"

The king bared his teeth and his face turned a shade of pink; Uriel was only angering Jourmande further, driving himself away from Jourmande without the Black Count's help.

"Do not be wroth with me, Jourmande," Uriel said.

The king looked ready to pounce.

"I am not your enemy. There is an enemy still here in the castle, an enemy who drove a blade of steel into Ramir's heart."

The Black Count's hands turned clammy. He feigned agreement—or should he have feigned anger?

"I have told you what I think is best—" Uriel's words were swallowed up by Jourmande's screams.

"Get out, old man! Get out, and never return!"

Wordlessly, unfazed and emotionless, Uriel nodded, turned around, and left.

"You have alienated a great ally," the Young Duke said.

"An ally," the Black Count shouted, and walked toward the dais, "who openly advocated for surrender."

"An ally whose wisdom and power is greater than any in this room," the Young Duke said. He turned to the Black Count and sneered. "Giving our king advice he does not wish to hear is not a crime."

"What you do with Lord Mars is a crime, Roland," the Black Count snapped.

The Young Duke laughed coldly. "There is no crime for a nobleman."

"The king can make it so."

"Enough!" King Jourmande snapped. "Jorjé, I fear you have overstayed your welcome."

The Black Count was unaccustomed to people using his name.

"Your insults and accusations of my dear nephew are unwelcome," Jourmande said. "They have been fervently denied and contain no kernel of truth. You should go back to County Garrone, and do not feel you need to return for Yule-tide. I will make it clear when your presence is welcome again."

Roland vis Valais was smirking at the Black Count. If the love and concern for the king the Black Count professed were genuine, he might have been insulted, even crushed, by the king's denouncement. But instead, it was only a minor setback, a small disappointment in the longer run.

The seeds of the coming catastrophe had been sown; in weeks, they would bear fruit.

Chapter Twelve:
A Vow

Ramden the Bold

The streets of the Outer City of Zarubad had turned to thick mud, and the bridge to the Inner City only narrowly rose above the flooded River Zaros. A great storm had ravaged the capital the prior night, Ramden had heard, a terrible affair of crackling lightning, voluminous rain, and howling winds.

Now, the rain and clouds had all disappeared, making way for a bright blue sky. The sun beat warmly on the Inner City. The lords and ladies, nuns and priestesses, wandering the cobbled streets were taking full advantage of the weather, but a shadow seemed to have fallen over the capital. He had heard scarce bits of rumor in the villages and marketplaces he'd passed by on his day-long journey from Lessant to Zarubad. There was trouble, people said, a rumor of a levy being called up. That could only mean war.

At Emerald Isle, in view of the spacious townhomes and lion statues, the ferryman recognized Ramden and allowed him to cross the water to Castle Royale.

~

In front of the Lion Throne, Ramden knelt before the King of Zarubain, sovereign ruler, god's vicar on earth.

"Ramden the Bold," Jourmande said. "To what do I owe this great pleasure?"

"My father is dead," Ramden said. "Against all our laws, against every one of our customs, my slothful younger brother has inherited Castle Silvergold. By rights the duchy is mine. I demand you force my mother to appoint me duke. It is no less than I deserve."

"Indeed, it is," King Jourmande said. The light of the torches on sconces glinted in his eyes, and a smile crossed his face, the jolly, knowing smile of a grandfather. "Yet I am not in power over your father's will, and your father made it clear."

Ramden snarled some curse.

"You do not seem to grieve for him," King Jourmande added.

"How can I, when he has done so great an injustice?" In truth he had not been shaken by the death, even before he learned of this great betrayal.

"The southlander Empire is marching north, young Ramden the Bold." A bit of that grandfatherly smile faded. "It has assembled siege weaponry—trebuchets and catapults, and arrow-launchers that can impale an armored host ten knights deep. The general Marcus Sylla is by all accounts a tactical genius, and bent on destruction. Surely your grievance can wait."

"It cannot," Ramden quipped. "There is nothing more important to me."

"I will make you a vow, Ramden," Jourmande said. "You are by all accounts an excellent warrior, a man of unmatched bravery and courage, strong of arm and quick of reflex, a master of sword and shield."

Ramden smiled at the compliment; such words were worth as much as gold, when coming from the king.

"Long ago," Jourmande continued, "King Cyrien, the father of my predecessor Gylles, had a bastard child by a Vale of Roy peasant; against all the warnings and cautions of the lords he raised the bastard as his own. He was King Gylles' half-brother; a closer relative to Gylles than me, eligible to the throne if he were not a bastard. Even now the Bastard Prince lives. He was spoiled in Castle Royale against all warnings of the nobles and the High Priestesses.

He came to believe that nobility and power were what he deserved. In the end King Cyrien had a problem on his hands; he needed to quiet the situation, to put him away as best he could. He married the marquess of Montée March and swore to defend Castle Holmgray and the bridge."

"Why are you telling me this?" Ramden knew much of it already; the Bastard Prince, an enigma, rumored to be a madman, perhaps even a murderer, was a subject most decent folk avoided in conversation.

"I am sending you to Montée March, to Castle Holmgray. A great number of men-at-arms and archers are gathering there as we speak. My Ramden, I make this vow to you." Jourmande stood up from the throne. "Defend Castle Holmgray and its bridge, prevent—at all costs—its fall to the Imperial Army, and I will make you Duke of Lessant.

"Bring me the head of Marcus Sylla—and I will make you my heir."

Interlude:
The Demon

Lord Falerien vis Alerie, Viceroy of Mekara

The head of the battering ram at last burst through inner keep's door. The people of Castle New were screaming. Marcus Sylla, the Dark One incarnate, had promised no quarter to anyone, but only a long, painful death.

Lord Falerien—or Lord Seven-Sous, as most called him—had always thought the gods were good, that the denizens of heaven looked after her children. He had instructed the townsmen in that regard and considered that instruction paramount in preventing their rebellion. Now, he had no such certainty. He had donned a suit of armor, a greathelm through which he could hardly see, a giant cleaver of a sword and a thick wooden shield, but even through it all he was shaking. Whimpers he never intended to utter were sounding from his lips. In the heat of the torches, in the heat of the armor, Lord Falerien vis Alerie was colder than he'd ever been in any winter. His gut churned at the thought of what would come next. Marcus Sylla, the Dark One incarnate, had promised to burn Lord Falerien alive.

"Surrender!" Marcus Sylla had shouted at the gate of Castle New. "Otherwise we will crucify your citizens and burn your leader alive!"

Lord Falerien had ordered the gates to open and prepared to establish terms. Yet Marcus Sylla, the Dark One incarnate, had betrayed his word, had charged into the city and immediately begun a great slaughter.

Now, holed up behind the city's last defense—the keep— Lord Falerien and all his knights watched as all their hope faded, as the southlanders breached all their defenses, as the gate broke to pieces with a sundering *CRACK!*

Lord Falerien ran.

In the armory, the Imperial soldiers found him. Falerien dropped to his knees, knit his gauntlets together, begged for his life to be spared.

Instead they had him remove his armor, and dragged him—wearing only smallclothes—outside into the burning town of Castle New.

~

Where once the blue-gold lion flag of Zarubain flew was the red-gold eagle flag of the Empire. The thatch-roofed houses of Castle New burned bright with flame. True to Marcus' word, some of Falerien's subjects were screaming on their crosses. Sparks and flames drifted up into the sky and choking smoke was ever-present. The peasants' cries for mercy were short-lived and answered with violence.

A soldier threw a collar around Lord Falerien's neck and yanked him down the steps by a chain, like a dog. He stumbled and fell. "The king will pay a fortune for my release!" Lord Falerien screamed, but his voice was drowned out by the roaring flame, the anguished cries, the triumphant shouts of the Imperial soldiers. The soldier yanked on the chain again and Falerien fell again, bruising his kneecaps, tearing his skin on the crude stone steps.

Lord Falerien had envisioned a new life here in the kingdom's most newly-acquired province, a life of quiet as he developed these undeveloped plains into great pastures and wheat fields, as he grew the small town of Castle New into a bustling, thriving city. The Mekari natives had posed no true threat to him; how, then, could it all end like this? How could the sum of everything he feared be thrust, now, upon him?

At the town square, surrounded by the blazing inferno, a pyre of wooden logs had been erected. *They mean it—they will burn me at the stake. Me, a nobleman.*

Sylla stood there. When Falerien first laid eyes on him, he had expected a red-skinned demon with horns and glowing yellow eyes, sulfurous breath and long black claws. Instead it was a man in a shirt of light chain, beardless like his soldiers, with close-cropped brown hair and the most piercing blue eyes Falerien had ever seen. His nose was strong and aquiline, his face noble, handsome, save for a scar that ran across his eye. In his right hand was a shortsword, the same plain steel weapon he always bore. In his left—oh, his left!—there were no fingers at all. Over the demon Sylla's face a smile had formed, a dark smile like a child dissecting an innocent animal.

"Please!" Lord Falerien cried. He fell to his knees; the collar and tight chain strained against his neck. He knit his fingers together. Tears formed in his eyes. "The king will pay a great ransom for my safe return. Ten marks, twenty… a hundred, even! And do not burn me—it is not fitting for a noble to be burned alive. Such is a fate only for the lowborn, and for heretics!"

Sylla laughed. Even above the deafening noise of the flames and the screams of the crucified, his voice arose, powerful, commanding: "Lowborn, high, or born in heaven, all my enemies receive the same fate. My father was an olive farmer, Falerien. Your words only dig you deeper into the grave… yet you will not receive a grave."

"*Please!*" Lord Falerien screamed. "*Mercy!*"

"No mercy," Sylla answered. "By the authority of Numa, emperor and god, I affix you to this stake… and I will gladly hear your screams."

~

And screams he did hear, until the roaring pyre at last

swallowed them up, charring Falerien to blackened ash.

59

The Eagle in Winter

THE KINGDOM OF ZARUBAIN IS THE MOST
CIVILIZED NATION-STATE IN THE BARBAROUS
NORTH. ITS KING HAS ABSOLUTE POWER OVER
HIS SUBJECTS, AND THE NATION HAS NOTHING
RESEMBLING AN ELECTED COUNCIL OR ANY
FORM OF DEMOCRACY AT ALL. THE KING AND
HIS NOBLES ARE PRIVY TO FABULOUS WEALTH
BUT THEIR SUBJECTS ARE DESTITUTE AND POOR.
THEIR MILITARY IS THE GREATEST IN THE
NORTHERN WORLD BUT FALLS FAR SHORT OF
THE IMPERIAL LEGION.

—from an intelligence report to the Imperial Council

Chapter Thirteen:
The Man in the Mask

Ramden the Bold

Under a gloomy steel sky, Ramden traversed the winding dirt roads of Montée March. Much of the region was covered in bogs and marshes, overrun with wilted brown reeds and bursting with purple swamp flowers. As he drew near the River Zarube, a few vineyards appeared, but the black pine trees and hemlocks never disappeared. A rain began. It was late in the day when Castle Holmgray appeared, a giant edifice of stone with sky-high turrets, walls with iron spikes, and skeleton reliefs that ran under the parapets. With a castle such as this, it was little wonder that rumors abounded of the Bastard Prince's cruelty, of torture devices in his dungeon where he ripped the tongues out of prisoners of war. The castle itself was connected to the bridge which spanned the entire River Zarube, forbidding entry from the outside world, barring any unwelcome visitors to the Goddess's favored kingdom.

In the shadow of the castle lay a peasant village of wattle-and-daub huts, sunken dirt roads, and a makeshift village green. Ramden could not imagine a gloomier place to live. The creatures of this village were equally gloomy: a hunchbacked woman walked across the way, carrying a bucket of water from the well; and following behind her were two little children with gaunt, hungry faces. The only hopeful thing in the village was a small stone chapel with pink-and-green stained glass windows, and above the doorway, the words: "The Goddess Loves Us All." No doubt the hundred souls who lived in this village could not write their own names, much less read the false hope etched above the chapel doors.

Ten men-at-arms stood guard at the gate of Castle Holmgray, clad in thick hauberks of chainmail and bearing halberds half again their height.

"Ramden the Bold," one said. "I can tell it is you by that blue bear on your surcoat, though the thing is filthy and covered in mud."

Ramden eyed the shirt he wore over his mail. Indeed, the long travel through the dirt roads and the rain had stained it almost to black.

"His Excellency the Marquis has been expecting you."

~

Through winding stone passageways and corridors Ramden made his way through Castle Holmgray. All the dark rumors of the Bastard Prince took on a new meaning as he passed by macabre pictures of the unquiet dead and by real skeletons on display, dressed in bronze suits of armor. Once, a knight told him he suspected the Bastard Prince was a necromancer; another said his wife, the former Leyna Grandvail, dabbled in the dark arts. In the coming war, there were few Ramden would less rather have by his side than the Bastard Prince.

The corridor opened into a throne room no less gloomy. The throne was of chiseled stone, a dark gray color but lined along the armrests with bright friezes—skeleton-men and crossbones. And on that throne was one who could only be the Bastard Prince.

A coat of scarlet-colored flannel fell to the throne's pedestal, lined with black-spotted white fur. Two black gloves covered the Bastard Prince's hands, and a wolf mask covered his face. The Bastard Prince's dark eyes peered at Ramden through narrow holes. So detailed and accurate was the mask that Ramden might have believed a snarling, gray-furred, black-whiskered creature of the night sat before him, had it not been for the human body below.

Ramden dropped to one knee—more an honor than this strange man deserved—and rested his hand on the hilt of his sword. "Your Excellency."

"'Why is he wearing the mask of a wolf?'" the Bastard Prince said. 'Why does he have skeletons in suits of armor?' 'Why does he have such an obsession with death?'"

"Why does he ask himself questions?" Ramden quipped.

There was a pause, then a deep belly laugh which Ramden considered more odd than comforting. "The Bastard Prince is a strange fellow, is he not? I will answer your questions, Ramden, right now. As a young man I wished to see the world. I wished to visit the southlands—the Empire I had heard about in passing from our dignitaries. I had heard of streets that crisscrossed the whole Southern World for thousands of miles along its extent, resistant to rain and damage and crowned with white stones. I had heard of cities where the emperor's subjects lived in houses a hundred feet tall, of a capital so large it makes Zarubad seem a backwater village. I had heard of a nation with stringent laws, where torture is forbidden, where captives are well-treated, where prisoners of war live in rented villas by the sea.

"Yet I did not go, Ramden. My father said it was too dangerous. In the end, only my half-brother King Gylles traveled there. My father Cyrien only allowed me to visit places within his realm—so I did. I traveled hundreds of miles down the Royal Road with only a hundred knights to protect me, until I found myself far away, in the Eastern Region, where the Zarube king has only nominal control. There, in the town of Parballon, I partook in the Wolf Dance. I donned this very mask and locked hands with the peasants as we revered the wolves, hoping to avert their hatred. I realized the best way to face wolves and all dark things—death, plague, famine— is to surround yourself with it, to celebrate it."

What a strange man, Ramden thought, but kept his words under control. "I am only here to defend Castle Holmgray," he said.

"So you tire of my story?" The Bastard Prince rose from his throne. "Very well. You should prepare yourself for battle. Ours is a strategic place, a bulwark against the enemy. The general Marcus Sylla will have a fight on his hands."

Some five-hundred peasant-archers were hidden within the stone walls of Castle Holmgray, and another two-thousand men-at-arms; they ate in their own private quarters, where no doubt pottage and—in the best of times—leftover scraps of pork were served. In the knights' quarters, a meager but well-cooked meal of chicken had been laid on trenchers. Only the most watered-down wine was served; Goddess knew the southlander general could seize upon them at any second, and they had to be of right mind at all times.

A knight sat down opposite him from the great wooden table—a man with piercing blue eyes. Long locks of hair fell down his back, so blond they were almost white. His face was pallid, almost unhealthily so. All these factors—and the unnerving, mystic air he projected—made it clear this was a Knight of Lorh.

Ramden stood up and left the table, taking his trencher with him. He would rather drown in the River Zaros than fight alongside a weak, Goddess-hating, elf-loving coward—in other words, a Knight of Lorh.

But what did Ramden indeed have to fear from the Empire—a nation which held itself to extreme ideals of compassion even in wartime, which took prisoners gladly and kept them in a villa by the sea? Ramden the Bold had never felt bolder. With such little risk, he would do everything in his power to find Marcus Sylla, bring back his head to King Jourmande, and be made heir-apparent to the throne.

Chapter Fourteen:
A Necessary Mission

The Knight of Lorh

Sitting alone at a large table, Sir Darius consoled himself with the fact that he'd been treated this way before. The Knights of Lorh, the most hated of all the knightly orders, had a surfeit of false gossip and malicious rumor. The weight of accusations was heavy, but thoroughly untrue. They betrayed the country in the Elven Wars—false, for the Knights of Lorh had fought alongside the king's army, even if they disagreed with the elves' mass sale into slavery. They hated the Goddess—no, they respected the Goddess, even made offerings to her holy church, they only revered the Orbuus lord of mysteries and knowledge above all. Other unspeakable rumors developed because of their practice of celibacy. Yet how many Knights of Lorh slipped up on their vows? How many had slipped into the Outer City of Zarubain and visited its brothels? How many, on missions to Ardogne, had not frequented its legendary bordellos?

Now, Sir Darius had only himself for company, and a plate of overcooked chicken for dinner. Even the wine was foul, watered down until only a trace of its rich flavor remained. Nonetheless he had a mission here, even one beyond the defense of Castle Holmgray. He had begun to suspect the Black Count was a traitor. The Bastard Prince had always been at his side. Some would call him crazy, but he had expected something bad to happen the night the Duke of Lessant was murdered.

He finished the meager chicken and vegetables and had half a thought of eating the trencher, which had soaked up all the broth and chicken juices. He ignored it, swallowed a great gulp of watered down wine, and retched at the horrid taste.

He stood up and left the mess hall, disappearing into the dim corridor.

For his next endeavor, he would use up every last bit of moon dust in his possession. The expensive ground-up crystal would have to be refilled sometime after this battle—if he even survived it—when he returned to the main commandery in Tournay. He had every intention of surviving this battle, but still… there were questions Sir Darius had, questions that had to be answered before he offered his life in service to the marquis.

He lifted the moon dust pouch high above his head and let the shimmering white powder fall all over him. Then he reached out with an invisible hand into the Wellspring of magic which lay all about him. He let every particle of crystal soak deep with magic, allowed every infinitesimal shard to cloak him in a wall of ignorance, so that no one in Castle Holmgray would see him.

In the light of dusk, Sir Darius walked openly into the castle yard, drawing the suspicious looks of no guards.

For an hour he waited, until the moon arose, until the stars spread out in their radiant patterns, until a high-ranking servant passed into the keep's doors. Sir Darius entered with him.

The winding passageways of the keep were ill lit, so that Sir Darius often stumbled. At each corner was a skeleton in full arms and armor, bearing a sword or halberd or great-axe. This, Darius knew, was proof and confirmation for all the rumors swirling about the Bastard Prince. Sir Alvyn, Knight Grandmaster of Lorh, had reason to believe the marquis had initiated a program of butchering the Mekari natives south of the river, then burning the flesh off their bones through alchemy. Sir Alvyn also claimed Lady Leyna, the marquess, had amassed a great collection of books on necromancy, and intended to become a death wizard, but had found her innate magical talent lacking.

From the feasting hall, low murmurs had arisen. Sir Darius entered quietly, and found, as expected, the Black Count with the Bastard Prince. Leyna Grandvail-Bretagne was there too—an old woman with long gray hair and the darkest, most piercing eyes Sir Darius had ever seen. The rations of the inner court did not look much better than those of mess hall; indeed, the only thing different were the silver bowls and cups, and the wine that looked a bit stronger than the foul, watered-down concoction Sir Darius had drunk.

Sir Darius drew near the dais where the marquis sat enthroned. Even here, in the private company of his wife Leyna, the Bastard Prince wore that ghoulish wolf mask lined with gray fur, which allowed his soulless black eyes to send chills across Sir Darius's skin. "It is a matter of great importance," the Black Count was saying. "Everything rides on this… if not, we are done for…"

"Our plans are solid… do not question them now," the marquis murmured.

"Wait!" Leyna Grandville-Bretagne snapped. "Hush! Listen!"

Sir Darius gulped. Beads of sweat were dripping down his invisible-to-them skin. He had gone cold as an Eastern winter; his heart beat audibly, at least to him.

"Another one of her hunches," the marquis noted sourly. "I swear, dear wife, you will take ill after all your suspicions and paranoid visions."

Paranoid. So they are *hiding something.*

"I hear it, too," the Black Count said. "Soft, so soft… the beating of a human heart. The slight intake of breath."

Sir Darius cursed himself for this foolish mission.

"Is there a wizard in our midst?" the Black Count murmured. "No, worse… that blasted Knight of Lorh… *Richilieu, shut the door!*"

At the word the double doors to the feasting hall slammed

shut. Sir Darius' throat was tightening; he could envision it now, his tortured end, the skin slowly flayed by the hand of the Bastard Prince, the Mad Marquis. He could already feel the stinging pain as they rubbed the raw flesh with salt, and then set him, screaming, on fire. He could hear his fellow knights' shouts of gladness, saying that the elf-loving coward had gotten exactly what he deserved.

Lady Leyna had risen from her seat. She was flinging out her hand, grasping at nothing, feeling around the air like a blind woman. Sir Darius backed up, cursing himself, cursing his foolish action. Was it not according to the Law of Lorh to serve your liege without faltering, to obey him without questioning? And yet Darius had been brought to this by his own worries, by his noble concern for the kingdom and the safety of Zarubain, never once considering his own safety.

"The heartbeat grows louder. The breathing more desperate," she said.

"Now, even I can hear it." The Wolf Man stood up with a silver goblet in hand. He tossed its contents forward, missing Sir Darius' body by only a fraction of an inch. "The traitor will regret his mistakes."

Sir Darius kept backing away, not knowing what else to do. Could he try to fend them off, even kill the Mad Marquis and Leyna Grandvail-Bretagne? Could he bring himself to break the Law of Lorh so severely, all to save his skin from flaying?

Chapter Fifteen:
New Masters

Danitari

The air in the capital had turned gloomy as signs of war proliferated and few had any hope of long-lasting peace. Yet still Mignette and Master Jouliver had stripped Danitari to his smallclothes and set him on a pedestal in Lions Square. Already a great crowd had gathered.

Mignette stood to his left and Jouliver, to his right. "A great warrior!" Mignette said. "An elf willing to die for his master and for grand ideals of honor… an elf used to the harsh rigor of the battlefield!"

Dan realized that—in all his years of service—he had told Mignette and Jouliver precious little of his life in the Elven World. He had, indeed, fought in the service of the King. He had fought with sword and spear against the marauding human hosts. But Mignette and Jouliver had not been worth enlightening.

"One-hundred *deniers*!" cried an old hag of a woman, bound up in a flea-bitten gray hood.

"He is also great at farm work, and will gladly serve in the country, toiling endlessly with a smile on his face!" Master Jouliver hollered.

That, he could not bear—a too-short life working himself to the bone, a hard existence before he finally died of exhaustion.

"One-hundred and one *deniers*!" a tall man shouted. He was dressed in a leather jerkin and had a longsword hanging from his belt.

The old hag snarled. "One-hundred and fifty *deniers*!" she howled. Dan wondered what this woman wanted from him—surely not battle. Perhaps she needed a gardener, or some youthful company. Either way, she could not be worse than Mignette.

"One-hundred and fifty-one *deniers*!" the tall man shouted.

The old hag growled curses and turned away, forfeiting the auction.

"A strong elf, strong with sword and axe!" Mignette advertised. "A keen elf, keen with sling and bow!"

The crowd was mumbling; it appeared only the tall man was intrigued.

"An elf of great health, good with plows and shears! He shall turn your farm into a green Otherworld, bursting with vines and life!" Jouliver lied.

"Two-hundred *deniers*!" shouted a portly man with graying hair.

"Two-hundred and one *deniers*!" shouted the tall man.

"Two-hundred and fifty *deniers*!" the portly man answered. He had turned a bright shade of pink.

"Two-hundred and fifty-one *deniers*!" the tall man shouted.

"Goddess damn you!" the portly man howled. "Six hundred-and-one *deniers* and three *astonnes*."

"Six-hundred-and-one *deniers*, and four *astonnes*." At the tall man's words, the portly man let off a string of curses and profanities, then ducked away in defeat.

"A good elf!" Mignette shouted. "Good by day or by night, strong, hard-working, diligent and wise!"

But the crowd had begun to filter away, leaving only the tall man.

"Very well, my good man!" Mignette shouted. "Danitari is yours now. Put him on the front lines of battle… he is an expert in war."

From the tall man's bulging coinpurse, he handed Mignette the sum in a collection of *sous*, *deniers*, and *astonnes*. Then he beckoned Danitari, and left with him through Lions Square.

The man was not only tall, but muscular, with great thews of arms that bulged from his leather jerkin. In a quiet alley off the Road Saint-Jermaine, he at last turned to face his new slave.

"You are a warrior, no?" A bushy black beard, crudely shorn, contrasted starkly with his fair skin and piercing blue eyes. "Danitari? *'Holy'*—do you live up to your name?"

"You know Elvish. *Illunaddori vadan,* my friend," Danitari answered. "Ever since I was sold here, people have called me Dan."

"It rolls off the tongue better, here in the Kingdom of Zarubain." A slight smirk crossed the man's face. He had the look and the presence of a commander of warriors. "I shall do you one better. I will call you Danny."

That is even worse, Dan thought, but managed not to voice the thought.

"I am Brandon… Bran, for short. Some call me the Black Fox."

In passing, Dan had heard Jouliver speak of the Vale of Roy, immediately south of the city. A group of vagrants and bandits had harassed the region for years, Jouliver said, waylaying caravans and picking off the king's men as they took the southward-leading road. The once-tranquil and safe region had become unsafe and dangerous—all because of the bandits and their leader, the Black Fox.

"I believe I can trust your discretion," Bran said.

"Of course," Dan said. What elf would betray that trust? What elf, living a life of servitude and misery, would be believed in a court of law? The judges did not even consider killing an elf murder—only a destruction of property.

"The Black Fox supports the elves all across the kingdom… he draws them into a kingdom of his own in the Vale of Roy, gives them sword and spear and bow. He gives them a purpose, a stake in this land… and an eternal friendship. *Illunaddori vadan,* indeed, my friend."

"Friendship" is what this Black Fox called it. Dan was no closer to freedom, no closer to returning home. This Black Fox was no true friend. A true friend would set Dan free. He had forgotten what freedom felt like; his servitude had only been years, and yet it felt a lifetime. He had exchanged one master for another… but still, he was a mere puppet, a chess-piece in the Black Fox's hand.

Chapter Sixteen:
A Dangerous Gambit

Ramden the Bold

In the middle of the night, Ramden awoke in his bunk to cries of pain such as he had never heard before. They were faint, distant, but so desperate he could make out the screams for mercy. Someone was being executed—a traitor, perhaps, who had pledged allegiance to the Imperials? Or could it be something else?

More and more, Ramden had grown to hate Castle Holmgray. It frightened him more than any of his youthful dares, more than any battlefield he had ever fought upon. At least, in the front lines of battle, you had a sword in your hand, a breastplate on your chest, a helm on your head, and a clear and discernible enemy. But who could face Castle Holmgray and its seemingly harmless horrors—the skeletons dressed in ancient armor, the stone-carved graveyard reliefs that ran along the walls? How could he fight the soulless black eyes of the Bastard Prince, hidden behind the ghoulish wolf mask? How could he fight the cold, calculating gaze of the Black Count, whom he was supposed to battle alongside?

The screams of pain reached their fever pitch. There was a loud metal *clack!*—a device of torture reaching its final setting perhaps, and the cries drowned to a loud moan, and then nothing. He thought he might recognize that voice—a fellow knight, perhaps, but he could not think of who.

It was a long hour after that unsettled scream before he fell asleep again.

Ramden woke before dawn. When he entered the castle yard

the sky was still black; when he reached the top of the castle wall, a faint glow had begun to show on the clouds. Archers had been posted on the wall and had their bows at the ready, their arrows within arm's reach. When the sky had lightened, revealing shifting clouds, a pair of sentries came galloping northwards across the bridge. "They are coming! They are coming!" one cried. "The Empire is only two miles away!"

An archer blew a horn, and more horns sounded. Ramden rushed down the wall, still in his sleeping-clothes, and ran into the armory.

Four servants helped Ramden don his full armor. He squeezed his feet into the sabatons and felt the heat of the padding as the servants helped him into his greaves. More armor followed; the skirt of mail, the steel-plate tasset. He fit his fingers into the gauntlets, his arms into vambraces. Over them fell the heavy pauldrons and the steel gorget, then the greathelm which limited his vision but protected his vulnerable head. Over all this the servants laid the surcoat of the House of Rambée, a thick shirt of white wool with a blue bear-rampant. Once he had worn it proudly; now, it only reminded him of Father. His sword and shield came next. The fine steel blade had brought him out of many dire situations, had allowed him many victories. It was, in many ways, Ramden's most loyal friend.

Over the helmet they attached the bright blue and white feathers of the House Rambée.

"Thank you," Ramden breathed. He had no battle nerves. He had no doubt he would survive this battle, even thrive in it. He had no doubt he would send the Imperials into a quick rout, perhaps single-handedly. The Imperial Army was notoriously lightly armored, its cavalry and knights a laughing stock compared to those of Zarubain.

In the castle yard the men-at-arms were piling onto the battlements. Castle Holmgray was a place of horror, but its fortifications were strong, its walls sturdy, its upkeep impeccable. More knights were walking out of the armory: Knights of Marabelle in dark-blue surcoats, Knights of the Sun in whites and yellows, and Knights of the Pillar in whites and golds. Some were mounting fully-barded horses with the help of servants.

"Sir Ramden, where is your horse?" cried a voice Ramden recognized as Sir Gaitan. "The Lord Grandvail-Bretagne is opening the gate… he expects to deliver a devastating charge straightaway!"

It seemed folly to Sir Ramden, not to allow the siege to take its course, to slowly wear away the Imperial Army and *then* rout them. But Sir Ramden had survived and thrived on such reckless adventures before. And once in the open, fighting his way through the Imperial Army, would he not have a chance to take the head of Marcus Sylla? Would he not have a chance to become the next King of Zarubain, and show his brother Ramone who was the better of them?

When his horse was fully barded, arrayed in all the blue and white colors of the House Rambée, two servants helped him on the saddle, and Ramden kicked his sabatons into the stirrup. He prepared his lance as horns blew—this time, from far away yet deafening in their volume and piercing in timbre.

All one-hundred and fifty knights had readied themselves in formation, spreading out in ten rows in the castle yard. The gate of Castle Holmgray was not narrow, but nonetheless the charge would have to take place in waves. Ramden, much to his disappointment, was in the farthest of the rows.

The sound of stamping feet grew louder. The archers on the battlements had fearful looks about them.

The Imperial Army is larger than they thought, Ramden guessed, but still he had no battle nerves. They would win this fight; they would emerge victorious and Ramden would have Marcus Sylla's head. There was nothing he was surer about. The gate was cranked open. A horn pealed. The first row of knights flew ahead, and the bridge rattled under their pounding hooves. The next row of knights followed. There was a loud *whoosh!* and a sound of splitting flesh. The archers on the walls cried out and ducked under the merlons. The next row of knights refused to charge. Ramden's fellow brothers-in-arms had begun to back away.

"Cowards!" Ramden screamed. He yanked the reins of the horse, urged her to a gallop, and barreled ahead, circumventing the stalling knights. The bodies of thirty knights lay splayed on the bridge, each row of knights pierced by steel-headed javelins, twitching in their death-throes. The Imperial Army had erected fifteen wooden contraptions—scorpions, they called them—at the entry of the bridge.

Ramden almost backed down, but swallowed his nerves and charged across the bridge. The scorpions were almost fully-loaded again. The Imperial soldiers laughed at him as his horse's hooves pounded on the wood. As the iron-headed spears clicked into place on the scorpions, Ramden's horse barreled off the bridge in a long leap and landed on the damp soil.

A wing of Imperial soldiers folded in to protect the scorpions. Their steel helmets, cuirasses, shields, and shortswords were quality, but nothing compared to Ramden's lance. "For king and country!" Ramden cried and charged full-tilt into the Imperial host. Only now did he think he might die—only as his lance shivered and cracked apart on the Imperial's iron shield and the rest of the soldiers circled in like hungry wolves around a lone stag.

Ramden swept out his sword. Twice the Imperial soldiers struck; one glanced off his shield, the other scraped uselessly against his steel greaves. Then there was a biting pain, to his left, as a sword punctured the armor in his shoulder, and the blade bit deep.

Ramden's horse whinnied wildly; no doubt she was struck, too. She reared up on her hind legs, throwing Ramden back with her. Ramden could see death all around him. The scorpions had been swallowed up by the army; endless rows of Imperial soldiers were marching unmolested into the castle. Volleys of arrows fell from the castle's battlements but they bounced uselessly off the Imperial soldiers, now ducking under their shields.

Another piercing stab throttled Ramden with pain; the masterfully-forged Imperial sword had pierced his tasset and mail skirt and punctured his side. Ramden urged his horse to gallop ahead. With a rush they broke free of the ambush.

Outside the gang of soldiers they found themselves in a veritable sea of Imperials. Ramden could feel the blood leaking through his armor, dripping through his padding. He charged ahead through the ranks, sending Imperials leaping out of the way, breaking up their formations, bashing with his shield when he could.

At last the soldiers became an immovable wall of steel. His horse fell to her knees, succumbing to the Imperials' cruel wounds. Ramden stood up, dizzy from the loss of blood, feeling he was living in a dream world. He was not yet ready to go to hell. He was not yet ready for the tormenting demons and the incubi and succubi. He blocked a blow from an Imperial shortsword, but then the row of soldiers in front of him charged in unison, locking shields, and knocked Ramden forcefully to the ground.

This is it, Ramden thought. He could scarcely see anything through his visor. The sounds and sensations of battle bled into one nightmarish cacophony. Ramden was overheating in his armor. The sun was burning hot.

Vultures were circling.

"Wait!" some cried. "Do not kill him!"

Ramden succumbed to his lack of blood, the heat of the armor and the helmet, the deafening cacophony. He shut his eyes, and did not open them.

He awoke in Castle Holmgray. He was in the servants' quarters, in a rough bed. Could the disastrous defeat have been a bad dream, a mere nightmare? It seemed entirely possible. Why, after all, would the marquis open the gates and send the knights on a foolish charge?

He was lying on his stomach and biting a strip of leather. Something sharp pricked him on his side, and he screamed through the leather. He scanned his environs and saw he was not alone. A dozen men in leather jerkins stood there. Their vests were embroidered with an eagle in yellow thread. They were brown or black of hair, with not a single blond among them, dark eyed, and tan of complexion.

"Signore," they were saying, and "signor"—the only words he recognized. These were Imperials, and a medic was stitching up Ramden's wounds.

The thread tightened, burning like fire as his wound was closed. Ramden let out another scream.

"Quiet, little girl!" someone said in Zarube.

Ramden turned around, meeting the medic face to face. He had a thick head of brown hair, cut with extreme care, and a scar running across his right eye. His blue eyes were the most piercing Ramden had ever seen. His gaze was cold, unnerving, almost reptilian. The tunic he wore was simple but dyed in rich red and gold, and made of silk. His trousers were a dull reddish-brown and made of fine wool.

"What is your name, captive?" the man said.

"Ramden," he answered. "Ramden the Bold."

"Indeed you are bold," he continued. "My name is Marcus Sylla."

Ramden's heart was seized with cold. His breathing stopped an instant as he righted himself on the bed. "You are the general of the Imperial Army? And you are… a physician?"

Physicians were the most hated members of any king or

duke's court. Often they were lowborns who had studied medicine, of no noble birth or ancient blood.

"I am an amateur," Marcus Sylla said. "In battle, I have sewed up many wounds. The human body is a most fascinating thing."

The words sent shivers through Ramden or a reason he did not know. Perhaps it was the blue-eyed, reptilian gaze.

"Did you know the human heart is an oddly-shaped thing, connected to the body with all sorts of veins and ventricles and tubes? It is not a perfect shape as we often think, nor is its color uniform."

Ramden didn't know what to say. This Marcus Sylla was clearly a lowborn fool who had no business as a general. He did not know how to have a polite conversation, which things to mention and not to mention. He would lose this war for the Empire, and quickly. "My father… err—brother… will pay handsomely for my return."

"Your father is your brother? So your brother married your mother? Interesting."

Marcus Sylla's social ineptitude was already wearing on Ramden. "The House Rambée is wealthy. My family will pay ten marks, or more, to see me safely returned."

"But what if I want to keep you?" Sylla said. "What if I do not want you to leave my sight?"

"Please," Ramden said. Still, this Sylla did not scare him. He was lowborn, a commoner, who spoke terrible Zarube, though he had a glint of reason in him that few lowborns did. "My family is very wealthy."

"Come with me," Sylla said.

Ramden stood up and a rush of dizziness fell over him. He steadied himself on Sylla's shoulder. The stiches on his side burned like fire. He wondered if Sylla had fed him a harsh liquor to stem the pain. He did not feel himself; he could not quite think clearly.

Ramden followed Sylla through the winding corridors of Castle Holmgray. The halls showed signs of struggle: tables overturned or split apart, skeletal guardians knocked down or robbed of their armor. The blood of knights and men-at-arms was spattered on the walls, but the bodies were gone.

In a spacious room, most likely the late marquis's bedchamber, Sylla had made his own. Imperial flags—gold eagles on fields of red—were draped everywhere. And there were other things.

The door shut behind them, and a lock clicked into place.

A panic was rising up in Ramden, a shaking cold, a freezing, blood-curdling fear burning through his veins. On the window-sills and on the bed's end-tables were jars filled with yellow fluid. Within were human hearts, human hands, a human foot. "Goddess preserve me! What have you done to the marquis?"

"No," Sylla cooed. "His Excellency the Marquis has received Imperial citizenship, and has fled south with his wife Leyna. These are not Zarube parts… no, these are Imperials, and a decade old, long before I attained the rank of general. It is you, Ramden, that may be added to my collection if you do not submit utterly to my command. *Put these on!*" From the folds of his shirt he had produced rusted metal handcuffs.

Ramden, shaking all over, slapped on the rough metal binds. He could scarcely breathe. A trickle of urine was running down his leg, soiling his trousers. "Please, Goddess, preserve me."

"There is only one god here, Ramden the Bold," Sylla said. "There is only one god in Castle Holmgray, and if you defy him you will find yourself in a hell of your own making."

Chapter Seventeen:
Betrayal

The Reverend Alse-Lorie, High Priestess

In the Great Hall, Alse-Lorie eyed the supper before her and grimaced. Jourmande had not often, in the past, served the so-called high cuisine of Zarube chefs, but it seemed he wanted a challenge tonight. A silver bowl lay before Alse-Lorie, piled high with butter-fried lamb eyes in a thick duck blood sauce. Eating one without gagging would be an accomplishment indeed. Her only comfort was the silver goblet of hot spiced wine. The Feast of Saint Ignáce had come and gone, and Yuletide approached quickly. Soon the Castle Royale would be lined with evergreen wreaths, holly berries and mistletoe.

A man appeared in the open door. He was dirty, covered in mud and sweat, and his thick woolen tunic was matted with dried blood. Most rudely of all, a sword dangled openly from his belt. This was a knight, and his news could only be bad. "Castle Holmgray has fallen. The Imperials have crossed the River Zarube. They have entered the kingdom. His Excellency the Marquis has disappeared; he has fled, or fallen. The Black Count is gone as well—he is fleeing to Garrone. It is a dark day. Let us all pray to the Goddess, for her mercy."

Alse-Lorie, shepherd of the people, would pray to the Goddess on their behalf, but the Goddess had long turned her favor from her. She was far-removed from Alse-Lorie, as far as heaven was from hell.

An exhaustion sank into King Jourmande; in a moment's span he aged five years. The knights and castle servants began to shout in anger. An illness seized Alse-Lorie. She wanted nothing more than to return to her quarters in the Lady's Cathedral, to forget the nation's ills. The Imperials were savages, bloodthirsty and merciless. They would have no compunction in slaying the highborn along with the low. In their backward society there was little distinction between the noble and the common. "Goddess preserve us," she muttered, but her pleas were empty, her requests futile.

The knight who had relayed the news left their sight. Only then did Alse-Lorie notice he was limping, suffering from a grievous wound.

"Enough!" Alse-Lorie howled, and the uproar quieted. "We must not panic, or curse the Goddess! We must keep our wits, our courage, our heart! Above all, we must not abandon hope!" But what hope was there? "We must not lose our courage!" But why not? "We must fight—for we are the lions on the rampart!" An empty assurance to a doomed people.

King Jourmande rose. His wife Alysant rose with him. "If only Ramir was with us," he said. "If only we had not been betrayed, perhaps things would have turned out for the better."

Hours later, hungry and weak, Alse-Lorie returned to the Lady's Cathedral. Sir Loy was there, waiting for her. Against all protocol he wore his sword openly on his belt. Sir Loy knew how much she loved to see him armed, gallant and brave. He knew that all the minor priestesses and attendants had gone to bed. He knew they were alone.

"I noticed they were serving high cuisine," said Sir Loy. "I went to the Outer City. I brought bread loaves and seared fish… and a bottle of sweet wine."

"Goddess bless you," Alse-Lorie said. The blasphemy of what she said struck her quite clearly. "I do believe the nation is done for."

Sir Loy shook his head. "The nation is not done for, Alse-

Lorie. The Empire is already vast and overstretched; to add Zarubain to its holdings would be madness."

"Madder things have happened," Alse-Lorie said. "Like risking excommunication and shame… for your kiss."

Sir Loy leaned in to kiss her and she did not resist. Her face flushed hot. She thought she heard a footstep, turned around and scanned the cathedral. No junior priestess was hiding in the choir. No servant hid behind the lectern. She—and they—were utterly alone.

Sir Loy left in the dark of night. Alse-Lorie drifted off to sleep. When she awoke to the morning's light, a slip of paper had been pressed underneath the door. Nervously she rose, utterly naked, and slipped on her shoes. She picked up the message, turned it over, and read:

I know what you did.

It was signed, Varysse.

Alse-Lorie fell, bruising her knees on the ice-cold stone floor. A shaking overwhelmed her. A sickness settled into her stomach. Varysse, the junior priestess she Alse groomed to take her place one day, knew the lies her life was founded on. Varysse could use this to her advantage, weasel her way into the High Chair, publicly shame Alse-Lorie and remove her from power.

Varysse wouldn't get the chance.

Chapter Eighteen:
A Dark Calling

Danitari

A heavy rain was pouring in the Vale of Roy. The hemlocks and firs dripped with rain, and the roads had turned slick and muddy. Lightning flashed and thunder rolled across the vale. The winds howled, and clouds blotted out the sun. At some point Bran, the Black Fox, led Danitari off-road into the woods. Amid the dark pines, a sense of isolation began to grow. The woods were empty, silent, and vast, but Bran navigated them like an expert, pressing on in a straight line, arrow-like in his determination.

"Quiet here, ain't it, Danny?" said the Black Fox.

"Yes," Dan answered. The nickname was even more insulting than Dan, but what else could he expect in this cruel nation? What else could he expect, as a slave?

"I hear, Danny, that some elves take up in the country, in tiny self-sustaining villages. They call them *ayris*. Ain't that interesting, Danny?"

"Truly?" Dan asked. For a moment excitement overwhelmed him, but the abject gloom of his situation quickly cut it down. What chance did he have, trying to find an *ayri*? What chance did he have, trying to escape from Bran?

"Don't get any ideas, Danny," the Black Fox said. A grin crossed his black-bearded face.

Shortly before dusk, the trees opened up into a vast clearing where a collection of low wooden houses were built. On each door, a fox head was painted in black. Fires were burning in the open, and around each of them were the bandits, wearing leather jerkins and wielding spears or swords—and all, every single one of them, elves. The Black Fox had created his own slave army.

He caught sight of an elf with a lute, plucking a familiar Lamen melody. Relief washed through Danny, knowing he'd be with his own kind.

Someone was approaching—a tall elf with thick brown hair and smooth grayish skin. *Nurnen.*

"General Estilas," Bran said, and Danny could hear his smile. "We have a new arrival. Now there are five-hundred elves, fighting strong."

Estilas nodded. "What is your name, friend?"

"Danitari," he answered.

"*Illunitari vadan*, Danitari," he said.

"The same to you," Danny answered.

Estilas bristled at the reply. Perhaps he was unused to such informality among his men. "You are our five-hundred and thirty-first warrior. You are Lamen, no? A soldier in the King's armies?"

"We were all soldiers in the King's army," Danny answered him. "But yes, I come from Lamdar." Danny had thought less and less of Lamdar, the center of the elven world. Even now its lush green grass, its blooming apple trees, its hilltop villages and quiet temples seemed a remote, unreachable dream. The land of Light and Life had been stolen from him. The times of plenty, the love of his family, the comfort of his home, were all gone, stolen away, burned to ash and carried away by a fell wind.

"Indeed we were," Estilas answered, looking suddenly pensive. He snapped back to attention. "You have a new king now… King Bran."

Danny eyed the wily Black Fox and in his dark warrior's eyes he saw just what this man wished to accomplish. He was not a mere bandit… no, he was worse: a rebel, a pretender to the throne, using his ill-gotten money to purchase ever more and more warrior slaves.

This Black Fox wanted to sit on the Lion Throne, with a crown on his head. Worst of all, Danny knew this man's plans would come to ruin, and Danny, and all his hundreds of fellow elves, would pay the price. "King Bran," Danny repeated softly.

"Not king yet," the Black Fox answered. "But one day."

"Indeed." Danny could not bear to meet his gaze.

"Get my good friend Danny outfitted, General Estilas."

~

For a band of rogues and ne'er-do-wells, the Black Fox's men outfitted Danny well. He received for himself a jerkin of studded leather, no doubt stolen from one of their victims, a wooden shield and a fine spear. The jerkin fit poorly—it was crafted for a human larger than Danny—but it would block the blows of the enemy. Against the Black Fox's usual victims—innocent traders, merchants and caravans—it would do well to enable the bloodshed.

In the last throes of twilight, the Black Fox met him near a campfire and sized him up. "I think you will make a great addition. Your king is pleased."

For Bran to call himself a king was punishable by death. Yet the gravity of his goals seemed lost on him; the great danger he had thrust himself into, the torturous death he might one day receive, did not seem to faze him. He was smiling, jovial, confident.

This was now Danitari's dark calling—to fight in the name of a rebel, to serve selfish ends, to fight for a cause he did not believe in, to sacrifice his very soul in order to preserve his life.

Chapter Nineteen:
A Change of Heart

The Black Count

The Black Count was a consummate actor, the equal of any professional performing in Lions Square and twice as good as any amateur performing a mystery play in the Lady's Cathedral. But for a reason he could not explain, he dreaded returning to the king in defeat. So afraid was the Black Count that he was days late, and had stopped in the seaside town of Avermere in Lessant and taken up lodging in that most ignoble of places—a common inn.

The Black Count had betrayed his country. A shaking had overtaken him, and the only thing that stopped his overwhelming nerves, his icy sweat, his knotted guts, was cup after cup of wine. A cold terror seized him whenever he thought of what he had done. He knew well the ancient punishment for treason; he had falsely set up many innocent men. Each arm, each leg, would be bound tight with a length of rope. Each rope would be tied to a horse. The horses would be sent off galloping in every direction, until the sinews and strands of flesh at last snapped off. There was no more painful death.

The peasants would watch him in glee. The Black Count emptied his glass of wine. It was poor stuff, watered down, harsh and bitter. His noon meal of poached eggs was little better, unseasoned except with salt. He did not fit in here, in this filthy establishment, and people did take notice. The fat peasant serving wench was eyeing the Black Count every few seconds with a dumb, dull stare. The innkeeper often looked in his direction too, but his focus was on the dark woolen cloak that the Black Count wore, and the gold clasp, fashioned into a stag, that bound it together.

Another peasant watched him too, a tall man with thick brown hair and a lazy eye who was eyeing his sword. None dared talk to him and that was just as well. The Black Count was a troubled man, assailed with visions of what might be, but he still had his dignity. No lowborn would ever approach him to talk, or treat him like an equal.

Two peasants were talking in the corner. "Did you hear about the storm?" one said, a male. "Off in Rannier?"

"No," someone answered, a female.

How was the Black Count to get up the gumption to show his face? Would he buckle down before King Jourmande? Knowing the stakes were so high, the punishment so severe, would his lies be convincing? Could he look at Jourmande's face, and not betray his crime?

"It washed away an entire village," the male said. "And people who tried to escape were grabbed by tentacles—like the ones you see on a sea-monster, but much bigger!"

"Goddess preserve us!" cried the female. "Where did you hear of this?"

"A merchant, passing through town," the male answered.

The innkeeper was looming before him. The Black Count gasped and looked up. He saw in the innkeeper's blue eyes something like those of Jourmande. "Do you want another cup, my lord?"

"Yes," the Black Count lied, but his words seemed unconvincing to him as they poured from his lips. Proof for his suspicion, the innkeeper paused, examining the Black Count's eyes.

"Truly?"

"Would I lie to you, lowborn?" the Black Count hissed.

"No, my lord." The innkeeper grabbed the pewter cup and left the Black Count's side, walking down the stairs of the wine cellar on the far end of the main hall. As soon as the innkeeper was out of sight, the Black Count left, and cursed the Dancing Bear Inn and the whole town of Avermere as he exited through the door.

Outside the sky had turned dark and gloomy, and five-foot waves were crashing on the sandy beach. Frightened fishermen were returning on their boats. The once-tranquil fishing village had taken on an air of worry. The Black Count could see it in the lowborns hurrying into their hovels, of the quickened pace of their walks. In the marketplace on the shore, the fishmongers had no buyers and the nets were full of fish that, this late in the day, had begun to turn rank.

The Black Count fetched his horse from the stable. His gut twisted into a knot as he rode north, forcing his worries away, ignoring the terrible feeling that a cruel death awaited him. *I am the consummate actor, a master of deceit.* An hour later he crossed the bridge into the Vale of Roy.

It was near dusk when the smell of Zarubad finally reached his ears. Most noblemen entered Zarubad via boat, in order to avoid the disgusting squalor of the Outer City. More than two-hundred thousand merchants, craftsmen, street urchins and slaves lived in that cesspool of humanity, and the numbers only increased each year as poor peasant-farmers lost their livelihoods to the much cheaper slaves. The Black Count remembered, in his youth, a time when Zarubad had far fewer people, when he could only smell its horrid stench from a mile away and not ten.

ZARUBAD – FOUR MILES

At the sight of the northward-pointing signpost, the terror returned to him anew. He had pushed the thought of a tortured death far inside him. Now the phantom returned, hovering over him, spreading its long dark wings around him. He had scarcely ridden three strides before he yanked the reins and yanked his horse around.

He would return to Castle Holmgray. He would ask Marcus Sylla for Imperial citizenship, because he was too afraid.

Chapter Twenty:
Hell

Ramden

Clothed only in a loin rag, Ramden—bound by four chains and bleeding in countless places—hung suspended in Marcus Sylla's room. He could no longer call himself Ramden the Bold, for now he had offered a thousand different pleas, promising his castle, his horse, his sword, even his family's lives, for freedom. Marcus Sylla had denied each request. Now Ramden's legs were raw and burning after a hundred defecations, the stink so severe he would have vomited, had he not already emptied all the contents of his stomach. Marcus Sylla had not today given him his rations of dry moldy bread and foul marsh water.

The door opened and Ramden screamed. He saw Marcus Sylla's face, but only seconds later did his eyes register that this was not Sylla, nor a man at all, but a woman in a gray russet gown. Her lush red lips widened into an "O" and her bright blue eyes bulged in horror. She let out a scream.

"Help me!" Ramden screamed. "Help me!"

"I cannot help you!" the woman cried. "I am just a whore from Monteville!"

The door slammed behind her. Ramden had blocked out the shape behind her, so terrible was it. The grim omen, the harvester of souls, the dark reaper stood before him, staring at him with demon eyes.

"She cannot help you, Ramden," Sylla said in his staccato Imperial accent. "She is just a whore from Monteville." He slammed the door shut behind him. A lock clicked into place. "Poor Crystelle serviced five legionaries last night. She got ten silver coins for her troubles."

"Please, Sylla! Let me go! Have her instead."

"*What?*" Sylla called out. "What did you call me?"

"I am sorry! I am so sorry, Master!" How could he have forgotten? "Master! Master! Master!"

But Sylla picked up the whip and cracked the thong against Ramden's bare chest, opening up a new wound. The blood trickled down a hundred older wounds, a hundred different terrifying memories.

"What is *that?*" Crystelle cried, pointing to the jars of Sylla's previous victims.

"Do not worry about what things are," Sylla said. "You are just a whore from Monteville."

Sylla walked closer to Ramden and Ramden screamed.

"You scream like a woman," Sylla said. He touched Ramden's bare right hand and undid the shackle. The chain struck the filthy floor. His arm fell uselessly down, as unresponsive as jelly. Three more chains he undid, and Ramden hit the waste-stained ground. His legs and arms would not respond. He could not move. "Get up!" Sylla ordered.

"Yes, Master!" Ramden said, but his legs would not respond. They struggled against the filth of the floor and would not do as he commanded, so raw and gelatinous were they. His arms, sore yet lifeless with disuse, would not respond either. He screamed, "Sorry! Sorry, Master! Sorry!"

He flopped across the floor like a fish, until nausea overtook him. His head grew heavy and a deep sleep seized him. Sylla was howling with laughter.

When Ramden came to, a bit of the life had returned to his arms and legs. He flopped across the filthy floor and finally stood up, before slipping on something and hitting the floor hard. He could feel Marcus Sylla behind him, a dreadful wraith with long dark wings.

"Crystelle!" Ramden cried. "Crystelle, help!" He crawled forward but only moved an inch.

A hard-soled boot struck Ramden on the leg. He looked up, saw Marcus Sylla wearing chainmail and a steel helmet with a red horsehair crest and in his hand a shortsword of steel. "Your Master has a battle to win, a province to take for his own. All of Montée March must be secured, every village, every town, every hold and keep and fastness."

He was speaking to Ramden like a human being.

"Try to escape, and I will disembowel you myself," said Sylla. "I will stretch your innards out like ribbons across Castle Holmgray. I will keep your head in a jar. I will eat your heart."

Ramden whimpered. The door opened. Sylla left. He tried to crawl his way toward it, but the door shut, the lock clicked. "Crystelle! Crystelle!"

"Isdar help me!" he heard her say.

Ramden turned around. The Monteville girl was on Sylla's bed, her hands and legs bound with rope. She was dead, her eyes shut, her throat slashed. She was at peace.

"Isdar help me!" she said again. Ramden was hallucinating.

How Ramden envied her, dead and at peace. She was in heaven with the Goddess, and Ramden remained here, in hell.

Why has he left me alive? Ramden wondered. *There must be a reason… he must have a purpose!*

Hours later the feeling fully returned to his legs. He stood up. The air was thick with stench and every kind of foul odor. The iron barred window let in cool air, but the wind wasn't enough to drive it away. Ramden staggered toward the window and looked down. The Imperial Legion had left long ago, but still the endless columns were visible, marching down the dirt road. The kingdom the Goddess loved had no chance. The kingdom that had endured hundreds of years of discord, war, and plague would endure not a month more. The gods had vested all earthly power in the hands of a deranged murderer and madman. Everyone would soon be butchered. Only Ramden would be left alive.

"Only I will be left alive!" Ramden cried. "Only I will be left alive!" A strange joy filled him. "Only I will be left alive!"

Marcus Sylla must have a purpose for him. There was a reason. There had to be.

Chapter Twenty-One:
How It Begins

The Reverend Alse-Lorie, High Priestess

"Six-thousand men at arms, eight-thousand peasant archers and two-hundred knights were sent to Montée March!" King Jourmande howled, his voice echoing through the Great Hall. "And we were defeated?"

"Moreover, the honorable Lord Dunstan vis Abrenard, Duke of Ajernon, has taken an arrow in the chest, and the black wilt has set in," the messenger continued. "He will no doubt die within days. Montée March is fully under the control of the Empire."

"Goddess preserve us!" King Jourmande cried, and eyed Alse-Lorie, whom he still viewed as a saint.

She could not help but glare. Varysse now knew Alse-Lorie was a fraud, a walking lie, a vow breaker. No doubt in the small circle of high-ranking junior priestesses, word would quickly spread. *Goddess help me!* She still asked the Lady for her help, reactively, instinctually, though she was as far from Alse-Lorie as Zarubad was from Alzdorf. Varysse had promised not to tell, but Alse knew Varysse's character well; like so many of the junior priestesses, she was spiteful, petty, and cruel. *What will they do to me?* In recent times, an excommunication from the Fairy Faith was punishment for vow breakers. In the most severe of times, the offending priestess was shorn of her hair, branded as an adulteress, stripped naked, and set on a cucking stool in Lions Square for all the lowborn *villeins* to see. She would live the rest of her life in shame and disrepute. She could not let that happen. She would wring the life from Varysse's neck before she allowed that to happen.

"A dark day!" King Jourmande wailed. "A black storm-cloud hovers over our nation, bringing darkness and doom."

"All men-at-arms and knights in the Western Heartlands must be called up!" cried Queen Alysant.

For once the vapid wife of King Jourmande had ideas of her own. She had spent all her years in the court perfecting her hair and presentation—a good art in good times, but poor in times such as these. Alse-Lorie cursed them all, wondering if somehow they knew, if somehow Varysse had told them.

The guests in the Great Hall had dwindled to only a dozen, not counting the ten guards standing motionless in their heavy armor and faceless in their greathelms. The blue and gold of the House of Bretagne, and Zarubain itself, was painted boldly on their shields. The great lords and ladies of the Western Heartlands were preparing for battle, or more commonly, hiding in their castles and keeps. In Duchy Valais, Roland and Lord Mars were cowering in Castle Sunbow.

"I think the elves had something to do with it!" Princess Clarysse shot up, spilling her fruit bowl. "Those wicked, shifty, crafty elves!"

"Perhaps," King Jourmande murmured.

Alse-Lorie could not bear the conversation any longer. "I shall say a prayer for us all!" she lied, and promptly left.

In the Lady's Cathedral, before the great stained-glass portrait of the Goddess, a few dozen worshipers had gathered, scattered among the pews. Their heads were bowed, their arms lifted in prayer. They were muttering, begging the Goddess for mercy. They were begging the Goddess for a victory—a Goddess with deaf ears and blind eyes. If the Goddess was real, she was cruel indeed, to force chastity on her priestesses at risk of shame and degradation.

She passed the dais, the High Lectern and the gold and silver High Chair, and turned toward the narrow door that led into the inner cathedral.

She almost ran into Varysse. "Where are you going?" the junior priestess snapped.

"Am I beholden to you? I am High Priestess—"

Varysse caught Alse's mouth in her hand like a slippery fish. "Is Sir Loy with you?"

Alse shook free of her grasp and spat at her. "Silence! You will not speak of it... ever again."

Varysse smiled at Alse coldly. "I have kept my promise. Cross me, Alse-Lorie, and I will tell the world of your sins."

"Will you?" Alse huffed. She could feel the eyes of her parishioners, but even in this silent place they were too far away to make out her words. "I can still make your life hell on earth."

"And I can see you publicly shamed, stripped of the priesthood, and excommunicated from the Fairy Faith," Varysse said. "By the way, I've tossed your Grayman's beard into the river."

Alse sputtered some curse. She could buy more in the marketplace easily. She would not have to fear pregnancy for long.

"You had best watch your tone around me, Alse-Lorie, or I will let your secrets out into the open."

Alse looked down, for once submissive, but Varysse blocked her way. The catty junior priestess had a new confidence and fire in her blue eyes. "I want to be ennobled, Your Fey Radiance," she said. "I am only a reverend daughter. I want to be raised to the rank of full priestess. I will be the Reverend Varysse." The torchlight in the cathedral glittered on her pink-and-gold robes.

"I cannot give titles so easily," Alse-Lorie said. She worried she might sob. She was eyeing the stone floor, utterly undone.

Varysse grabbed her by the shoulder, dug her nails deep into Alse's flesh. "You will find a way, Your Fey Radiance, or I will see you naked and shamed, displayed for all to see in the Outer City on a cucking stool."

Alse-Lorie cried out at her words, spun around and ran to

the cathedral doors.

The spires, statues and gargoyles of the Lady's Cathedral had never looked so ominous or baleful. She could not bear to look at the rose window and see the Lady's laughing, carefree face glowing red and pink in the sunlight. What Varysse asked was uncalled for, and she knew it. Her service had been less than exemplary, and few attained full priesthood before age thirty. Alse had been an exception. Varysse's career as junior priestess had been undistinguished, at best forgettable. If Alse succumbed to the snake and promoted her to full priesthood, Elouette and Cherie-Byssant and all the junior priestesses would be filled with jealousy, and worst of all, suspicion. Alse cursed the situation.

She ran from the Lady's Cathedral, the grim gray prison of stone that forbade all love, and fled toward the bridge. Nuns in pink wimples glared at her as she ran. Never before had they seen the High Priestess in such clear distress. Beyond the bridge, on Plumtree Isle, amid its brick-face townhomes and great inns, a shirtless man stood crying out nonsense. He was whipping himself. He wore the coarse woolen trousers of a peasant. *Ah! He is a flagellant.*

"We have displeased the gods!" he was crying out. Blood trickled down his suntanned back like streams. "The gods in High Heaven look down upon us! They hate us for our drunkenness, for our endless song and merriment, for the adulteries of the heart! That is why the Empire is winning! That is why our country is failing—for our darkness within, for our secret sins!"

"Away with you!" Alse-Lorie howled. "Away!"

The flagellant backed away, timid, but he did not stop whipping himself. He kept shouting nonsense: "We have displeased the gods in High Heaven! We have drunk too much wine! We have danced too often and sung too much!"

"You speak of all gods, when Zarubain serves the Goddess!" Alse-Lorie howled. "You speak of all gods, when the Lady is our patron; and she is jealous! *Away with you!*"

The flagellant backed away further, but whipped himself again, drawing more blood, adding to the crimson flow trickling down his back and legs. "Forgive us, gods! Turn away your wrath from us! Accept this punishment, my bleeding and my pain, as atonement! Turn away your wrath, and let the godless Empire fall!"

"Godless!" Alse was approaching him like a forest cat. A crowd of Plumtree Isle residents were watching them. "You are the godless one, *priest!* Your male gods are foreign! Your vows of celibacy and poverty are foreign too!" At least fairy priestesses were allowed to marry at a certain age. "I see, to our great detriment, that you have not taken a vow of silence!"

"Forgive us, Alabaster! Forgive us, Heron! Forgive us, all gods, all Heaven!" He whipped himself again.

"Get out!" Alse howled. *"Get out!"*

"Forgive us all—even her!"

"Get out!" Alse howled, and made a dash at him.

He dropped the whip and bolted away.

The crowd of wealthy nobles was staring at her. "Alse-Lorie!" said a man in a thick green cloak trimmed with ermine, whom she knew only as Lord Sylvien. "I have never seen such fire from you." His tone sounded forced; neither his eyes, nor his face seemed approving.

Alse flushed with shame.

"Goddess be with us all!" cried an old cow of a woman Alse knew as Lady Colette-Aimie, the wife of some minor baron. "Never has our High Priestess been so angry! She does not like those flagellants, does she?"

"Nor male priestesses!" said a man Alse did not know.

The embarrassment turned her blood hot. All that outburst had been unfair, a funneling of her shame and fear upon an innocent priest. She turned and ran back toward the Lady's Cathedral, toward the grim gray prison she had fled from moments ago. All this shame, all this fear, could no longer continue.

She would name Varysse full priestess, and surely an earthly hell would follow in its wake.

Chapter Twenty-Two:
The Devil He Knew

The Black Count

On the north-west edge of Montée March, in a dreary brown landscape, the Black Count arrived at his destination. In the shadow of Castle Moongold, the signs of battle lay all around... or more accurately, a great slaughter. The bodies of peasant archers and men-at-arms lay rotting in the sun, and the stench was worse than any swamp the Black Count had been to. Carrion birds pecked the eyes out of corpses. And there were worse things: lining the road, bodies nailed to wooden crosses. The Black Count had heard of this Imperial punishment, a slow and agonizing death for cowards and traitors. It was difficult to tell whether Imperials or Zarubes had been crucified, for they were naked and long dead. But they served as strong messages amidst the massive carnage in which thousands upon thousands had lost their lives. The Black Count had heard the Duke of Ajernon had taken an arrow in the chest and perished days later.

The Black Count recalled a conversation he'd had with the duke, during the Feast of Saint Ignáce: "The Empire is a nation of lowborns, *led* by lowborns! Why should I fear them?"

The Black Count nervously rode down the path, trying not to look at the sea of bodies or the crucified men on display.

At Castle Moongold, the banners of the Grandvail-Bretagnes had been replaced with red-gold eagle banners of the Empire. Around the stone fortifications, the thirty thousand Imperial soldiers, which had defeated the much larger Zarube force, had pitched their tents and started campfires. The smell of cooking food mixed unpleasantly with the stench of rot.

Immediately a battalion of Imperial soldiers on white horses stormed forward, galloping down the road. They surrounded the Black Count, hemmed him in with spears. "I am a friend!" the Black Count said in his best, thickly-accented Imperial. "I am a servant of the great legate Marcus Sylla!"

The soldiers' eyes hardened with suspicion. "Come with us," one at last said.

The Black Count followed them to the castle doors at a gallop.

~

The bare corridors of Caste Moongold led to a drab Great Hall of sorts. Long wooden tables lay in the shadow of a dais and high seat where Marcus Sylla, grand legate, presided. He rose, smiling, and relief washed through the Black Count.

He is happy to see me. Immediately the Black Count dropped to one knee and bowed his head. "Your Honor. I salute you, Lord Sylla." He dared lift his head.

A confident air emanated from Sylla, and it was clear from the energy in the room that his top-ranking advisors and soldiers had never been more certain of victory. Sylla's blue eyes, cold as a serpent's but bright as sapphires, met the Black Count's. The scar running across a right eye, received in battle during the Imperial civil war, only intensified his estimating, examining gaze. In the manner of his fellow countrymen, he had shaved his face and was beardless as a boy. His once-thick brown hair had been trimmed to an inch in thickness all around. His black-gloved hands clutched an Imperial shortsword, out of its sheath, and on his body was a brocade tunic of red color, woven with gold thread.

Yet beneath this façade of a civilized commander of men

was one who ordered crucifixions, who butchered peasants and nobles alike, who—it was said—forced captives to dig their own graves and stabbed priestesses in the sanctuary of their churches. "My lord Sylla," the Black Count said, his deference and fawning tone more pronounced than ever. "I wish to reconsider our offer. I wish to cede the territory of Garrone to you, and become an Imperial citizen. I wish to leave Zarubain and never return."

A smile spread across Marcus Sylla's face, a smile that seemed wolfish. "My good Lord Jorjé, Count of Garrone, wishes to renege on our agreement." Sylla stood up on the dais. The Black Count's heart leapt in his chest. "He fears the consequences of what he has done... that his sovereign, the old, infirm and soon to die King Jourmande, will discover his treachery. Is this true?"

Lord Jorjé saw in those ice-cold blue eyes the fears and lost lives of Sylla's victim—even Dunstan, Duke of Ajernon, who had succumbed after infinite pain to black wilt and putrefaction. The bloodletting and soothing balms of ten physicians, the prayers and recitations of four fairy priestesses, had been unable to halt his descent into death, into hell. *How easily I could join him.*

"What use would giving you citizenship have for me, Signor Count?" Marcus Sylla said. "I could not have easily won Castle Holmgray without agreeing to Lord Grandvail-Bretagne's request, but you... you have nothing to offer me. Montée March is mine. The Count of Belidere has come here twice to negotiate terms, to pay me off with a hundred marks in gold and silver... he has been refused. Nothing is denied to me. Nothing is forbidden to me. I will have County Belidere before summer comes, and Silvan March and Rannier. I will have County Garrone, Lord Jorjé... and I will have your wife."

The Black Count gasped at the rude words. A few of Sylla's advisors laughed. The Black Count's heart burned with jealousy at the thought. His lady wife, Lysa, had been unfaithful before and he had forgiven her. But Lysa in the arms of an Imperial, even if by force—her fingers running through that dark hair, running the length of that scar—such a thing the Black Count could never forgive.

"Do you have children?" Marcus Sylla asked.

"Nine," the Black Count answered.

"I will have them all killed," Marcus Sylla said. "They will be hanging from the castle turrets, Lord Jorjé."

"You may have my wife, and my children," the Black Count said, "and all of County Garrone. But you must give me Imperial citizenship."

"Must I?" Marcus Sylla said. The wolfish smile returned. "The Imperials do not look well on traitors, my good Black Count. They do not look well on weasels and worms. A life in the Empire, for someone as debased as yourself, may be short."

"I want it anyway."

"You are old," Marcus Sylla went on. "You are old and tired. You could not bear to return to King Jourmande, could you? You could not bear to meet his gaze. How can you bear to meet your own, I ask. How can you behold your own reflection, and not hang yourself on a tree?"

The Black Count turned.

"*Shut the doors!*" Marcus Sylla thundered, and in an instant his command was obeyed. The great double doors reverberated as they slammed shut.

The Black Count turned back to face Marcus Sylla, innards turned to jelly. He felt like a child again, utterly at the mercy of a harsh father, unable to defend himself, unable to speak.

Marcus Sylla sprang from his high place on the podium, leaping from table to table like a deer, before landing inches from the now-cowering Black Count.

The Black Count could feel the cold edge of an Imperial blade on his neck. Tears were dripping down his face. He could not help but whimper and wail. He could not help but fall apart. "Please," he said. "Please… have mercy! Mercy!"

"Mercy," Marcus Sylla repeated, and pressed the blade edge closer to the Black Count's neck.

The Black Count leapt back and drew his sword. He struck and Marcus' sword went flying. He stabbed and Marcus leapt backward, taking a wound in the shoulder and falling back onto a table.

The Black Count kicked the doors open and fled out the corridor.

He was feet from the castle doors when gauntleted hands grabbed him by shoulder and yanked him to the ground. Seconds later, as more Imperials bound his hands and feet, Marcus Sylla appeared, still smarting from the wound, blood trickling down his arm. His cold blue eyes had never burned with such wrath.

Chapter Twenty-Three:
Avermere

Evart, Steward

"The town of Avermere is gone," the peasant said in Castle Moonsilver's Great Hall. "Every villager is gone… its homes are in ruins! The docks are broken! There is something in the water, Your Majesty! There is something in the water!"

"Something in the water," repeated Evart. His position as Steward of the Vale of Roy never ceased to attract strange visitors. Yet it was necessary; while His Royal Highness King Jourmande focused on the great problems that faced the nations, someone needed to tend the royal lands.

"Something in the water!" the peasant said. "Yes! I saw it with mine own eyes! Great feelers like worms coming out of the sea, bashing and breaking up the homes, and grabbing the townsfolk by the legs! You must do something about it, Master Evart!"

The knights in the Great Hall were glaring at the peasant.

"Is not Avermere in Duchy Lessant?" Evart said. "It would seem to me that this is a problem belonging to Ramone, Duke of Lessant."

"The Lord Ramone does not mind us, anymore!" the peasant said. "All he cares about are fortresses and soldiers and swords and shields! The war has consumed his mind! He will not listen to us! Four-hundred villagers are nothing to him… four-hundred villagers, snatched away and dragged to the briny deeps!"

Castle Moonsilver lay in the south of the Vale of Roy. It was late morning, and if he journeyed to Avermere he'd be back well before nightfall. "Very well," said Evart.

A great relief and sunny disposition overcame the peasant. He had expected to be ignored again.

"Master Steward," said Sir Garibold, a Knight of the Pillar, "we have great problems in Vale of Roy already. There are bandits in the woods, waylaying merchants and caravans. There is the threat of hunger and dissension among the peasantry."

"Quiet, Sir Garibold," Evart snapped. "I am going to Avermere, and you are coming with me… as are you, Sir Andival, and Sir Mattin and Sir Lyle."

There were many frustrated sighs in the Great Hall. Yet in the absence of the king, the steward's words were law.

~

They left south down the coastal road as it wound through the forests of hemlock, spruce, and great pines. The sky was blue and sunny but a wind was blowing westward and there were clouds in the horizon. Three times deer ran across the road. The air was cold, a reminder that winter was nearly upon them.

The forest fell away as soon as they crossed the bridge into Lessant. They turned down a new road. Here, miles from the coast, peasant villagers had already decorated their front doors with Yule wreaths, and parish priestesses had decked their stone churches with sprigs of holly. Yet a gloom began to take shape as they pressed westward to the coast, a gloom far beyond the quickly-cooling air, the roll of thunder, the sudden pattering of rain. The peasant led them to Avermere—or what was left of it. Where once a fishing village stood, only washed-up boards of timber and the sunken foundations of houses remained. The parish church of Avermere was a pile of rubble. The sandy shore had turned black as jet, stained by some strange ink. The villagers had died, and yet there were no bodies of humans or animals to be seen.

Evart's horse struggled as it slipped down the inky-black

ground. His eyes caught the stirrings of life—ten people in black cloaks, near the shore. One of them shouted. They took off and ran. "Arrest them!" Evart snapped.

Sir Garibold, Sir Andival, Sir Mattin and Sir Lyle galloped after them. Within seconds they had formed a ring around the black-hooded band. They had drawn daggers. Evart watched as one stabbed Sir Garibold's horse. The knights drew their swords and began to hack and slash, sending blood flying into the air.

Evart cursed. He had hoped to learn from them.

"I saw those black hooded folk, weeks ago!" the peasant said.

Evart rode up to the knights. "Curse you! I said arrest them!"

Sir Garibold dismounted and examined his steed's superficial wound.

The bloody, slashed up bodies were men and women both. Their daggers were of a design Evart did not recognize. He grabbed one and examined its simple, triangular shape, and its worn leather hilt. He discarded it, and ruffled through the black woolen cloaks. Inside each was a symbol in the shape of two snakes—one biting the other. He rolled up the woolen cloak and promised himself he would uncover the meaning of the symbol, and what—if any—connection these ruffians had to the destruction of Avermere.

"I saw them, weeks ago!" the peasant repeated. "They were making trouble at the inn."

Evart scanned the bodies for any more clues. He stooped down and grabbed the dagger again, examining it for a second time. Its simple triangular design seemed impractical. He decided to take it with him for further examination.

"Thank you, my good man," Evart told the peasant. "I will do my best to investigate. Come back in a few months to see what I have uncovered. May the Goddess bless you and light your path."

Evart prepared to mount the horse when his eyes ran across

the layer of inky blackness on the soil again. It was curious, indeed. He grabbed a leather pouch from his saddlebags and scraped some of the oily black soil inside. Only an alchemist would know truly what the substance was, and perhaps not even an alchemist. Still, it was worthy of a try.

Evart hopped back on his horse. "Come… Sir Andival, Sir Garibold, Sir Mattin, Sir Lyle… We must get back to Castle Moonsilver before dinnertime."

"Stay here!" the peasant cried. "A great and dark evil has landed on our shores! A terrible and most wicked thing!"

"Goodbye, my good man!" Evart answered his pleas. "May the Goddess be with you and protect you!"

Evart and his knights thundered away down the road, and the noise of the pounding hooves swallowed up the peasant's anguished pleas.

~

Darkness had settled in when the lights of Castle Moonsilver appeared. Men-at-arms and archers, fully suited in mail, were posted on the battlements. No small bit of alarm was raised when Evart and his knights appeared—there were a few shouts, a few arrows nocked to bowstrings, but as soon as Evart passed into the light the gates were opened, and the tenseness diminished.

In the castle yard, Evart's sergeant-at-arms met him. "The bandits are worse than we feared," he said. "There is an entire army of them… and all are elven slaves."

Peasants from the outlying farms north of Castle Moonsilver had packed the castle yard tight. Some had brought cots or sacks, but most slept on the cold, wet ground.

"An army of elves," Evart repeated. "It would seem, my good sergeant, that the nation has faced such a threat before, and prevailed."

"Indeed," the sergeant-at-arms answered, but his tone was less assured.

The flight of peasants would normally cause Evart concern, but there was no doubt this supposed elven "army" would be quickly destroyed.

Chapter Twenty-Four:
Surrender

Ramden

Ramden, sickened by the stench of rot and human waste inside his dingy prison, nonetheless screamed when the door opened again. Marcus Sylla was there, his hair cut to a new thinness, his piercing eyes just as cold and wolf-like as ever. And he had brought somebody into the torture-chamber as well—a quivering, crying man, blindfolded but with a pale, bloodless face that showed his fear.

Sylla slammed the door shut and it clicked into its locked position.

In his cold blue eyes was a new pleasure. Ramden had been reduced to this—crawling on all fours like an animal, his trousers stained, his fingernails scratched short by his efforts to escape. "Why?" Ramden found himself saying. "Why? Why do this to me? Why?"

Sylla tore the blindfold off his cowering captive. Ramden gasped as he beheld the face of Jorjé vis Garrone. His once salt and pepper hair had turned almost white. His brown eyes had a shallow look of terror. Like all the ducal families of the Seven Gems, Jorjé knew Ramden from his birth. Jorjé had been present at Ramden's naming, at his confirmation into the Fairy Faith. How many Yules had Jorjé spent with Ramden? At age ten, he had gone hunting with the Black Count, and brought home enough rabbits and wild fowl to feed all of Castle Garrone.

"You, too, Uncle Jorjé?" Ramden said. He did not want to believe what he was seeing.

In Sylla's right hand was a small morningstar with a dozen

iron spikes. Would he kill the Black Count in front of Ramden—Ramden, whom he had known all his life? Ramden, whom he loved as a nephew?

"I won't let you do it!" Ramden shouted. "I won't let you kill him." He strived furiously to stand up, but only slipped and fell. The binds that had bound his ankles—which he had been free of for more than a week—had broken them. He cried out and convulsed in pain.

"Did you know," said Sylla, and laid his fingerless left hand on the cowering Black Count's head, "that your friend here betrayed your kingdom?"

"Lies!" Ramden shouted. "My good uncle Jorjé is a good man, and brave! You can't change that with your lies, Sylla! Nothing you do can change that!"

"Tell him yourself," Sylla said to Jorjé, "and maybe I will free you."

"I let him have Castle Holmgray," the Black Count began to moan. "Me and the Bastard both."

"What?" Ramden cried. Though the Black Count was under threat of death, Ramden could almost believe him, though the things he was saying were too terrible to contemplate.

"Do you want your freedom?" Sylla said. "Do you want to go back to Duchy Lessant? Do you want to live the rest of your life crippled, but free?"

"More than anything!" Ramden shouted, and at the bright hope the Black Count's betrayal seemed secondary.

"Then perhaps the words from this man, who you call 'uncle,' will help you in your task. It is said, in my country, 'a king loves a treason but hates the traitor,'" Sylla said. "When we have used a traitor in all his capabilities, when we have extracted every bit of information from his lips, we refuse to give him shelter. It is also said in my country, 'a traitor is the lowest of criminals.' Even when they are to the Empire's advantage, they are despised and shamed."

"How can I be free?" Ramden wept. "Please, tell me."

"A life for a life," Sylla said. He tossed the morningstar to Ramden. "Kill the Black Count as I watch, and I will give you your freedom. Take his life, as he took the life of your country."

He was weak from poor rations, thirsty from little water, but Ramden grabbed the handle of the morningstar and threw it with all force across the room. The handle hit Sylla's leg and the head cracked against the floor.

"I would do anything for freedom," Ramden said, "but I will not betray my kin."

"Not even a traitor?" Sylla said. He grabbed the morningstar himself. "Will you make me do it, Ramden the Bold?"

"Please, no," Ramden shouted. "Please, do not hurt him. Do not hurt my good uncle! Do not hurt my friend Jorjé."

He could scarcely see through the tears. A watery silhouette lifted a weapon high, and brought it crashing down upon a head. Blood sprayed Ramden. He wiped his eyes and saw Jorjé lying still, his head split open. "My uncle, my uncle… my good uncle Jorjé."

"You disappoint me," said Sylla. "You also surprise me. I thought, for certain, you would strive for freedom above all. I thought you would see past your 'uncle' Jorjé's pleas for mercy, and see a treacherous snake."

"Do not speak ill of the dead!" Ramden snapped. But he, too, was dead, if not in body then in spirit.

Sylla laughed. "Oh, my good Ramden the Bold. You have squandered a great opportunity. You have shut the door that leads out. I fear you will be in my prison for all your life."

Ramden cried out. He tried to crawl out the door but the pain of his broken ankles forbade it. He shut his eyes and fell flat. A dark and troubled sleep overcame him.

~

Ramden dreamed he was in the Lady's Cathedral in Zarubad, having broken all his bones in battle. Before the altar he begged for forgiveness for all his sins, and pleaded to the Goddess to heal him and give him the gift of life. Yet when he turned his eyes skyward, all he saw were the ice cold, murderous blue eyes of Sylla, controlling his fate.

~

When he woke in the nighttime, the body of Jorjé and the ripe corpse of Crystelle had disappeared. The stench of the room remained. The thin, iron-barred window showed a dark night. Clouds hid the stars and a rain pattered constantly against the castle roof. There was a blue flash of lightning, and instantly thunder rolled across the countryside. What was Ramden to do now?

He crawled up to the door, ignoring the sharp, stinging pain of his broken ankles. He pounded on the door. There was no answer. He pushed the door—and it opened. Ramden gasped as he beheld the dingy stone corridor, lined with dozens of other cells. A dart of jealousy stung him. He crawled out, realizing this was likely a trap.

Ignoring the crushing pain of his feet, he crawled down the corridor. An open entryway led into a grand hallway. Portraits of the long-gone Grandvail-Bretagnes overlooked the red carpet. A crimson speck of blood stained the painted face of the Bastard Prince. A dozen specks discolored the gold hair of Leyna Grandvail. Once, and not long ago, a person's head had been bludgeoned in this hallway. These Imperials did not bother cleaning up.

Ramden crawled down the hallway. He heard voices speaking in the staccato Imperial language. He searched frantically for a place to hide, but saw no tables, no grand statues. Instead, he kept crawling. The hallway bent into another. Two Imperial soldiers stood chatting in the distance. Ramden went cold.

He turned around—and found himself facing an iron-toed

boot. "I thought you would find the temptation irresistible," said the voice of the devil himself. Ramden chanced a look up at the cold, baleful blue eyes, the very sum of all his fears. He was smiling. Ramden's torture was a game to him.

Sylla grabbed Ramden by the now-filthy shoulders of his tunic and hoisted him up. Burning, shattering pain roared through him. He screamed and his eyes instantly welled with tears. Such a pain he would never forget, never recover from. Sylla hauled him down the corridor, back to the place of torture. Ramden screamed again.

"You will learn, one day, that I am your master." Sylla bound Ramden's still-sore wrists in the cuffs that hung from the wall.

"No!" Ramden screamed as Sylla bound his broken ankles with binds, and pulled the chain as tight as ever.

Pain such as Ramden would never forget in all the days of his life brought tears streaming down his face, brought a scream from his lungs, brought a certain doom upon his mind.

Sylla left him there. Ramden hung his head and, at last, gave up.

Chapter Twenty-Five:
The Hall of Counsel

His Majesty King Jourmande vis Bretagne

A last attempt was necessary to repair the nation's grim situation. A last effort was needed to save the lords and ladies, and, indeed the peasantry, from certain death.

"The honorable Lord Dunstan, Duke of Ajernon, has passed away," said the messenger, in view of the Lion Throne. "He has succumbed to his arrow-wound. His son Vivien has assumed his place."

"Goddess guide him," said King Jourmande. Vivien was bold but brash, a young man strong of body but lacking in wisdom. Lady Jaine would have been a better replacement. Of all the duchesses, Lady Jaine was the wisest and most capable of rule. Goddess help them all if Roland were to fall and his lady wife Elsie were to take his place. Goddess help them all if Jourmande fell, and Alysant were Queen Regnant of Zarubain.

"The Imperial forces are massing in the north of Montée March," the messenger said. "It is feared that General Sylla will march on County Belidere."

Count Velyrrien was as strong a leader as any, but he would fall to the Imperials within weeks. He did not have the clout or the wealth of the Seven Gems. His men-at-arms and knights would break upon the Imperial legion and scatter. Only the Goddess could prevent the fall of Castle Veldair.

"We must act quickly," said King Jourmande. He would look past the Seven Gems, past the wealthiest and oldest region of Zarubain. He would call for a levy of all counties and viscounties within the reach of the capital. An army such as Zarubain had never seen would come pouring upon the Imperial legion, and its thus-far-lucky soldiers would be crushed before Jourmande's might.

A week had passed, and the levy just called, when the news arrived.

"Castle Veldaire has fallen!" the messenger cried, sparing no time as he ran into the throne room. "Its defenses are shattered! The villages are burning. The honorable Count Velyrrien is nailed to a cross in view of all!"

The Empire had drawn one step closer to the capital. The destroyer of nations lay within striking distance of the Seven Gems. The wicked foe had closed its iron claws in a death-grip around the neck of Zarubain.

"County Dracogne and County Garrone have both surrendered unconditionally!"

The news stole the breath from Jourmande's lungs.

"Emissaries have been sent from Silvan March and Cavon March to do the same!"

"Treason!" Jourmande cried. "They may not surrender without my will. The House Bretagne is a lion rampant; and a lion never surrenders!" He had half a mind to wrap his hands around the messenger's neck and squeeze until he heard something pop. Yet this messenger was only a bringer of news—even bad news.

"For all intents and purposes, the south is lost," the messenger said.

"Enough!" Jourmande said. "Tell me only the news, lowborn. Your mind is not sufficient to give me an interpretation." He heaved himself up from the throne, using the gold-forged lion armrests as leverage. "I call a meeting!" he shouted to the Royal Guard.

In the Hall of Counsel, King Jourmande vis Bretagne sat at

the head of a long table. A painting of Saint Melysant, founder of the nation, receiving her crown from the Lady of the Lake, faced him on the opposite end. How innocent did she look in that famed painting of Ranoul. A girl of just twelve years old had become Queen of Zarubain and laid the kingdom's foundations. How petty and small was Jourmande, compared to her.

Jourmande's advisors filtered in—some family, some friends, all highly born and highly qualified to give advice. "A crisis has been thrust upon us," he began. "A dark and dreadful chapter in our history. Montée March has fallen, and Castle Holmgray was seized after only a day's struggle. The demon Marcus Sylla—a lowborn if there ever were one—took County Belidere, and in an instant four other of my vassals declared for him! Count Julien of Dracogne... Countess Lysa of Garrone... Silvan March, and Cavon March too. This plague of cowardice will surely spread across the land if we do not act decisively."

"The Battle of Moonflower Field has severely diminished morale," said his advisor Sybold, a distant relation. "A great force of Zarubes, reduced to nothing by an Imperial army less than half its size? Some have begun to whisper that the Goddess has turned against us, that all of heaven's hosts are on the Empire's side."

"That is a lie," said Dame Alesandre, a retired Knight of the Pillar. "It can all be explained by luck, my king. A wondrous stroke of fortune has allowed these lowborn to prevail against a host much greater than themselves. We must try again, and we will surely prevail."

"And what of Count Julien and Countess Lysa, and the marquises? Shall we try them for treason?" said King Jourmande.

Sybold laughed. Lord Hierace, a baron and thrice-removed relation of Jourmande, no doubt spoke the mind of everyone at the table. "Why should we resurrect the treason charge? It has never been used against a highborn since..." For a moment, Lord Hierace appeared confused. "I cannot remember when."

"Since the time of Saint Ignáce, centuries ago," said Sybold.

For a moment, King Jourmande thought of the ill-fated peasant warrior, who had donned armor and borne sword and shield, championed the cause of the House of Hernaut and restored the true king to the throne, before the very one she helped turned against her. She had perished in the flame, cursing the king and the nation she had professed to love.

There was one remaining advisor who had not spoken, an advisor that few in the room respected. Dame Bernysse, a barely highborn Knight of Lorh from Tournay, nevertheless often gave indispensable advice.

"What of you?" King Jourmande said.

Even here, in the safe Hall of Counsel, Dame Bernysse wore a suit of mail and a sword. "To be bold, Your Majesty, I think we must go to our enemy, and seek terms of peace. I think you must go with only a hundred men in your retinue, and enter the land of the enemy. I think you must go before the emperor himself, and ask him for peace."

The room erupted with loud jeers and heckling. "Coward!" cried Sybold.

"A typical Knight of Lorh!" growled Lord Hierace.

"I have known you always to be bold, Dame Bernysse," said King Jourmande, and the room instantly quieted. "You fought to the last at the Battle of Delver's Dale. The Murghuls seized upon you and you did not falter. Even unhorsed, you took them head-on, and brought our nation to victory. My nephew Roland has said nothing but great things about you… and yet you are here, giving me craven counsel. Have you changed overnight?"

"The Imperials are not like the horse peoples," said Dame Bernysse. "They are well armed and well trained. If you don't act quickly on my advice, there may be no going back… and a storm of death and bloodshed will follow us until our destruction."

"Get out," said King Jourmande. His voice was firm, yet his

heart wavered and his mind questioned. "Get out, and never come back to Castle Royale. It is clear you do not want what is best for the kingdom."

"Your Majesty." Dame Bernysse stood up and bowed her head. Then she turned and left.

A week passed and the requested soldiers and knights from Duchy Valais to County Orr had begun to gather outside Zarubad. It was just days before Yule and a winter rainstorm had swept the city. News quickly reached Jourmande of a settlement between the two marches and the two treacherous counties; they were, in all but name, a part of the Empire, and the rulers had been left in place. The Empire knew how to conquer. Yet the demon Marcus Sylla would afford no such mercy and privileges to the King of Zarubain.

All ties to the Seven Gems were already under strain. In such a situation, perhaps even his beloved nephew Roland vis Valais would fail him, and surrender.

One morning, in the cloudy light, King Jourmande donned his skirt of mail and his gold-enameled breastplate, his great pauldrons and a light helm of steel. He was far too old for this, seventy-four years old, and should be preparing for a quiet and peaceable death in the halls of Castle Royale. His servants draped the surcoat of rich blue and gold over his armor, the lion rampant symbol of the House of Bretagne. To his belt they clipped the diamond-encrusted scabbard which hid *Fairbolt*, the royal blade of Zarubain which the Lady of the Lake blessed in ancient days.

If King Jourmande did not show courage, none of his vassals would. Even his dearest nephew Roland vis Valais would surrender to the Empire—and the high fastness of Castle Sunbow would fly its red-gold flag.

Within an hour, the forty-thousand strong army left. Thunder rolled across the fields and lightning flashed in the distance. Rain poured down from the steely clouds as they marched into a darkening storm.

Chapter Twenty-Six:
The Black Fox Reigns

Danitari

Once the walls of Castle Moonsilver were breached, the natural skill and precision of three thousand elven veterans quickly overcame the small host posted there. Danny had taken up a position on the battlements and hurled javelins into the fray, impaling a knight as he charged General Estilas. A slaughter had quickly ensued, and the Black Fox had taken charge of the castle. Yet not all was to his liking.

"We need banners," said the Black Fox. He had taken a seat where the Lord Steward had once reigned, and had never looked happier. "The black head of a fox on a red field. Black and red are the most fearsome colors, wouldn't you agree, Danny?"

"Danny" had become the apple of the Black Fox's eye, second only to General Estilas, who stood there with them. "Yes," he answered.

The Great Hall of Castle Moonsilver, where the steward had eaten his meals and conducted the day-to-day affairs of Vale of Roy, lay empty save for the three of them. Its wooden tables, seats, and bear rugs had taken on a grim look in the flickering torchlight.

"If I am a king," the Black Fox said, "then I must have a royal guard. There is none among my children that I trust more than you two."

The Black Fox called the elven slaves he had purchased his "children." It was his "children" he sent to war, to risk their lives and forfeit their souls as they embarked on killings and conquest. Only the Black Fox profited.

As the Black Fox retired to bed in what had been the steward's quarters, Danny poked through the room for the nominal reason of searching for assassins, but the true reason of curiosity. The wooden floors were covered partially in bearskins and lynx pelts. Inside the wardrobe were gowns of Mierese silk, painted in swirling patterns of blue, red, and green which fluoresced in the lamplight. On top of a wooden bookshelf was a length of elvencloth rope, dull yellow in color, and a looking glass. The shelves held dozens of books, some thin, some thick, in Zarube writing which Danny could not read.

"Perhaps an assassin is hiding in the bookshelf," said the Black Fox.

Danny had grown to loathe his voice. That man would be the bloody end of them all. The Zarube king did not tolerate lowborn bandits. "I am sorry," Danny said, then added reluctantly, "Your Majesty."

He turned to leave the room when he caught sight of something at the bed's end table: a pile of black cloaks, and a dagger lying on top.

"What is this, my lord?" Danny said, and walked up to the curious pile. The dagger was rigidly triangular and poorly suited for battle—a ritual weapon, no doubt. Its forging was high quality, and in the exact center of the blade was a blood-colored stone. Danny lifted it up and examined it in the light. The hilt was of black leather, and the pommel was forged into the face of a grotesque head. Its iron eyes bulged and its iron tongue protruded.

"I do not know," the Black Fox answered. "Perhaps our lord Evart had many secrets."

The ritual knife pointed to cultic activities. Could Lord Evart have worshipped a demon? Such a thing would not surprise him in

Zarubain, the Land of Darkness.

He dropped the evil weapon, shirking from the thought of it touching his hand. He grabbed one of the black cloaks—seeing that there were about ten—and beheld, on the back, the symbol of two serpents biting each other. A cultic significance was clear, and yet Danny had no idea what it could be. This "religion" was no faith of the gods or the Light. The steward Evart had found strength in the powers of darkness. No doubt he was part of some demonic cabal.

For once, Danny had no guilt. For once, he looked on the Black Fox with nothing more than respect. Danny was fighting on the right side. *"Illunaddori vadan,"* he told the Black Fox. "May your reign have no end."

Chapter Twenty-Seven:
Evergreen

The Reverend Alse-Lorie, High Priestess

"The leaves fall and the leaves grow again," said Alse-Lorie.

A crowd sat elbow-to-elbow in the pews. Few nobles attended every service, but to forgo Yule was inexcusable. Every healthy man and woman from the Inner City was in the Lady's Cathedral tonight.

"Yet the pines are ever green. The winter is upon us, yet the Lady who crowned Saint Melysant is still here. Her fey glory rides behind King Jourmande even now. As the pines are ever green, so she is ever present, even in these dark and challenging times."

Yule, which celebrated the victory of light over darkness and good over evil, had its origins in the Elven World—a fact widely known, but scarcely acknowledged. She eyed the people gathered in the Lady's Cathedral, wondering if they could tell she was a fraud. No duke or duchess of the Western Heartlands was here—all were fighting, save of course for Lord Roland—and no regular Yule revelers from the Eastern Heartlands or Further Zarubain had come, either. Everyone was consumed with the war, or making preparations for surrender.

"This Yule," said Alse-Lorie, "let us ask the Goddess for courage to those who fight in her name. Let us ask for bravery and fearlessness. Let us beg her that the ones who protect us will not surrender themselves into the power of the enemy. Let us ask that the King of Zarubain, Jourmande, will emerge victorious, that the wicked banner of the Empire will fall… that the battle-standards of the Eagle will be replaced with the blue and gold of the Lion."

There was a cheer from the crowd, a rude expression in the cathedral that Alse would expect out of a clueless peasant; but these were hard times. The people of Zarubain hungered for good news, yet only bad news arrived at the capital. All they had were Alse's idle promises. Her words, these worshipers would cling to, hoping they would bear fruit.

"On this, the darkest night of the year, remember the light is coming," Alse said. *Not for me.*

Seven junior priestesses holding candles—among them, Varysse—walked out from the shadows of the cathedral in a line. A gold candelabra with seven candlesticks lay unlit before the worshippers. One by one, the junior priestesses lit them, then blew out their own candles and dropped them to the floor.

"Give your Yule gifts gladly," Alse said. "Remember the light is coming."

"The light is coming," the worshipers said in unison.

"And now," Alse began. Her stomach twisted to knots at the thought of what she was about to do. She gazed down at the floor for a moment, then lifted her gaze up to the worshippers in the pews. "Today is a special day." She eyed Varysse's head of red hair; no doubt the snake was smiling. "I have great news for one of our junior priestesses. The Lady has smiled with fortune on one of them. Let me tell you a story…

"Our junior priestess Varysse was born in Ajernon in the House of Abrenard. She had not once thought of taking on the pink-and-green robes. It was not until her father Jon announced she was to marry a cripple, Lord Robyn in County Orr, that she announced her intentions to join the priesthood." If Varysse would blackmail Alse into this, there would be a healthy bit of pain involved. "The Lord Robyn is now dead. If only she had acquiesced, she'd be the ruling Countess of Orr. Instead, she has committed her life to the Goddess and the Fairy Faith. Of her virtue and virginity there is no doubt."

An awkward silence had overtaken the cathedral.

"Varysse has never done anything wrong in the eyes of the Goddess. She has not once betrayed her ideals. She has lived the perfect life according to anyone who knows her. Goddess help anyone who betrays her ideals in view of Varysse." Though Varysse faced the pews, Alse could tell she had gone a beet red. "With that said, I have no choice but to announce the promotion of Varysse to the full priesthood. She shall get a pink stole, and an assignment to a parish church in the wider kingdom. Goddess help any one of you if you sin before her eyes; for she is blameless."

There were a few claps, but the awkward silence reigned.

"Goodbye, worshipers!" said Alse-Lorie. "May you have a blessed Yule. Do not forget to ask the Goddess for victory, for courage, for stout-heartedness."

Behind Alse, the sounds of a dulcimer echoed through the hall. The worshipers gathered their belongings and began to exit. Yule music followed them as they left.

The seven junior priestesses—or, rather, six—glared at Alse as they left in a processional. None, however, glared as angrily as Varysse, the very one she had stooped so low to help.

~

Just minutes after Alse had retired to bed, her door flew open and the quivering form of Varysse appeared, angry and shaking like a wild beast.

"You pig!" Varysse howled. "You embarrassed me. I had relatives in the Yule service. You pig! You cow! You toad!"

Alse sat up on her bed. "I embarrassed you by raising you to the priesthood? It was far more than you deserved."

"Why did you have to bring up that sad bit about Robyn?" Varysse hissed. "Now the people of the Inner City will think I am some sniveling shrew! Robyn could not even *walk*, Alse. Sir Loy is gallant and full-bodied and strong—you have no room to criticize."

"You dare bring up the topic after I acquiesced to your demands?" All sleepiness had left Alse. She could feel her blood boiling. "I cave in and surrender to your outrageous request, at great risk to my reputation—"

Varysse backed down. For once this night she no longer looked like a cornered weasel. "I am sorry... Your Reverence." It was clear she did not mean her words.

"There is an opening in County Champiz. The count will be glad to have a reverend lady to lead his flock." Alse detected still-seething anger in Varysse's blue eyes. "Champiz has no small wealth. You will grow rich on the tithes. And I hear the Count of Champiz is handsome and gallant, and newly widowed."

"I do not intend to break my vows and debase the priesthood, like you," said Varysse. "And I will think on County Champiz. It is hundreds of miles away down the Royal Road. I may just want to stay here, in Zarubad."

Alse's gut twisted at the words. The parish of the Outer City had been open for a year now, and a junior priestess named Lysana ran it. The thought of Varysse being so close-by sickened her. But she could not deny a full priestess the parish she desired.

From such a close distance, Varysse would weave her web of entrapment and blackmail and bring the Lady's Church ever-closer in her grasp.

Goddess help me. She had only made a bad thing worse.

Chapter Twenty-Eight:
The Castle Dog

Ramden

An iron collar was bound to Ramden's neck and the accompanying chain was held by Marcus Sylla. He could only imagine what Master Marcus had in mind. But when he urged him forward and Ramden crawled ahead, splayed on his knees, through the hall, it dawned on him. Fighting through immense pain and burdensome shame, Ramden half-crawled, half-fell down two flights of stone stairs, further wounding his broken ankles. Sylla ordered him across the castle yard, through the cold, muddy ground. The sky was gray and cloudy. Ramden liked to stay indoors, where he felt safe. He did not know what Master Marcus intended, treating him like a pet dog, but he knew Master Marcus was very intelligent and wise, and he always had a purpose.

In the mess hall, the Imperial soldiers greeted them with a shout.

"Hail, legate!" said Salvatore.

"I have brought you a dog," said Master Marcus. "Caio, you said you missed your dog, so I have brought you one."

Caio, a centurion, laughed and stood up, raising his wineglass. All the wine-stores of Castle Holmgray had been brought to the mess hall, and most had already been drunk in this time of relative peace. "To our legate Sylla, and to our pet Ramden."

"*Ave!*" the legionaries cried, the Imperial word for "Hail!" Ramden had learned to speak much Imperial.

Through pain that brought tears to his eyes, Ramden crawled down along the benches and tables to more shouts of "*Ave!*" and

"Come, doggy!"

One soldier put a strawberry to Ramden's mouth and he gobbled it down like a dog, stem and all.

"Howl, doggy!" shouted Juno.

Ramden howled like a dog, like the hounds his father Ramir kept in the kennels of Castle Silvergold. He howled like they did when they caught the scent of a rabbit in the woods.

Another soldier dropped him some half-eaten bread and he gobbled it down, too. It was nasty and filthy, and lying on the floor, but Master Marcus wanted him to act like a dog, so why wouldn't he?

"Good doggy!" said the soldier.

A loud horn blew from outside, an Imperial horn. The jolly mood in the mess hall turned quiet. A minute had passed before a soldier entered, wearing full battle regalia of red and gold and a horsehair-crested helmet. "Grand legate. Tito Vitellius at your services." He dropped to one knee. "Our new holdings in County Garrone are threatened. A Zarube army has entered and the men in Castle Garrone are expecting a siege. The countess denies requesting help but I am not sure."

"The countess is likely as faithless as her husband. She cannot be trusted," said Master Marcus. His voice had lost its playful tone. "If the Zarubes want another massacre, they will get one. We will go to war... and destroy these pathetic northmen once and for all."

If the pain of crawling to the mess hall had been excruciating, the crawl back up to Ramden's holding cell was incomparable to anything he'd ever experienced or done. Eventually Master Marcus had to drag him by the chain up the stairs, and with each bump his ankles burned with pain. At last, eyes welling with tears, Ramden was deposited in the holding cell, and forgotten.

~

Master Marcus had neglected to give him water. Marcus often forgot to feed him, but he had never forgotten to give him water. By nightfall, Ramden was slurping the dirty water that had collected in pools in the room. In the morning, starving, he drank some more. This ordeal lasted another day, then another. On the fifth, starving and weak with hunger, he had drunk all the water in the room. A headache and chills assailed him, and Master Marcus had not given him a blanket. He had said that blankets were not fit for lions—which was what he called Zarubes—and said that lions deserved to suffer. Ramden tried to remember that as he slept in a corner of the room, shaking with cold and sickness.

On the sixth day, parched and hungry, Ramden feared he might die. He could scarcely sit there. A tremor had overtaken his body. Each movement was a bitter struggle. By evening, he had curled into a ball in a warm corner of the room. He dreamed of death, of his crossing over into the Otherworld where the Lady resided. Yet under Master Marcus' threat, he had forsaken the Lady and cursed Heaven. Under the threat of the knife, he called the Empire itself his god. He swore no higher loyalty, in Varda or Avenda, but to the red and gold eagle.

In the morning, noise stirred him from his light, uneasy sleep. Paralyzed with hunger, he remained in place. Master Marcus had returned. He had, no doubt, brought Ramden food… bits of hard bread, perhaps, maybe even some watered down wine.

There was a sharp pain in his stomach as he heard loud shouts and the whistling of arrows. The foul Zarubes must have attacked Castle Silvergold. The thought filled Ramden with fear, but he remained still, as motionless as a mannequin, unable to do anything for hunger and thirst.

It was late in the day when the door burst open. Light poured in from the hall.

"Goddess above!" said someone.

He spoke in Zarube.

"What is this?"

A knight entered, fully armored except for his bare head. A surcoat emblazoned with a black ram covered the breastplate. A greatsword, still dripping red, was in his iron-gauntleted hands. He had a beard of gold and bright blue eyes, and a silver headband damp with sweat.

"My good man…" The look of horror that overwhelmed the knight's face softened slightly at the sight of Ramden. He rushed over to him, and scooped the now-thin and slight scion of the House Rambée into his arms. "You have been in captivity for a long time, I see. I wonder why the Monster kept you alive, and not these others."

Ramden had become accustomed to the body-parts in the jars. Master Marcus had told Ramden about them, even their names. He had taken their lives during a time of peace. They had offended him and clearly deserved it.

"You look ill, my good man. You need good care."

In these six long days, Ramden had forgotten the feeling of the outside air. He had forgotten the soothing scent of wet pines. He had forgotten the feeling of the sun on his skin. The clouds had scattered and bright blue was visible. The castle yard was filled with Zarubes. The north gate had been shattered by a battering ram.

"That is Ramden! That is Ramir's son!" someone cried. Another knight came running up to them. Ramden recognized him from a prior life, before he became what he was now. It was Sir Bevin—long ago, a friend from Duchy Duranche. Yet now Ramden could scarcely remember the time and manner of their meeting.

A coldness was spreading through Ramden's body. The air was warm but his body had turned chill with dread. He was sure that somewhere, Master Marcus was watching. If he came back and saw that Ramden was out of the room, Master Marcus would tie him up again, and this time make good on his promise to flay his skin and rub salt on the tender flesh. Ramden struggled against the knight that held him. At last he fell to the floor and unable to walk, attempted to crawl. He slipped on the wet, muddy ground. *If I don't return soon, Master Marcus will find me out of place!*

"Goddess above, Ramden!" cried Sir Bevin. "What has the Monster done to you? Can you not walk? Relax, friend! Everything is okay! You are safe!"

Exhausted, Ramden paused his struggling in the cold, wet mud. Sir Bevin did not understand. Ramden was not safe. Master Marcus would come back at any moment. Master Marcus saw all. Master Marcus was present everywhere. He was present in the castle even now. He was present in the forest; he was present in the sky. Nothing could escape his eye.

He began crawling through the mud again, toward a castle door. A knight scooped him up again—this time, Sir Bevin.

"Relax!" Sir Bevin snapped, for once sounding angry. "You are safe! Good Goddess above, you are light as a feather! You are cold and haggard. We must send you home."

"No!" Ramden screamed. "He will find me."

"Castle Silvergold is safe," said Sir Bevin.

"What is the meaning of this?" A deep voice spoke, the voice of Eurelien, Duke of Duranche. A figure approached, girt in steel. His armor was gilded and polished, without a single mar or scratch. His helmet had so much gilding it appeared to consist of pure gold. Behind him two men-at-arms carried the banners of Duranche, a black ram on a silver field. Four knights bearing shields flanked him on either side.

"Your Lordship," said Sir Bevin.

A wild howl erupted from Eurelien's lips. "Ramden? Truly? Has the Monster no scruples? He has kept you captive… you, the son of Ramir? A son of House Rambée?"

In Ramden's prior life, he had seen Eurelien on occasion. Eurelien looked older, now, with more gray hairs poking through the helmet than black.

"Good Goddess, you need help!" said Eurelien. "You are starved, Ramden! You are thin as bone!"

Eurelien vis Námois could not protect Ramden from Master Marcus. Master Marcus saw all, controlled all. He struggled against Sir Bevin, but it was in vain; he was too weak. Sir Bevin's grip was like steel.

"I will cut down the one who did this to you!" Lord Eurelien cried, and drew his sword. The blue sapphires encrusted in the white blade gleamed in the sunlight. *Snowmourn* they called it, the ancestral blade of the House Námois, which in ancient days slew the rokahn king. "This sword will drink the blood of Sylla before all is done!"

Eurelien, Duke of Duranche, had such anger in his eyes that Ramden thought of Master Marcus, and whimpered. "I am afraid," he said. On the castle turrets, limber soldiers had climbed to the roof and thrown down the Imperial banners. The standards of the Zarubain—a brilliant gold lion on a bright blue field—were being fixed to the poles. Master Marcus would be enraged.

"I smell treachery," Eurelien said. He stuffed *Snowmourn* back into its sheath. "Castle Holmgray is strongly-built, yet it fell in the span of a night." He was speaking to Sir Bevin; he had already forgotten Ramden's distress. "And where is the Bastard Prince, and Leyna Grandvail? A man of Sylla's intelligence would surely know the profits of a ransom. The Grandvail-Bretagnes would be left alive. The king would have paid hundreds of *libres*."

"And yet," said Sir Bevin, "he bludgeoned the Black Count to death, and sent his body to His Majesty."

Ramden dared not speak of the Bastard Prince's betrayal. Master Marcus had not given him permission to do so.

~

In the mess hall, Ramden eyed the buttered bread before him. It had been so long since he ate anything other than dog scraps.

The Zarubes had even poured him a steep glass of wine.

Sir Bevin sat across from him in the mess hall. "Eat, Ramden," he said. "You need strength. You must put on more weight, if you are going to make the journey to Castle Silvergold."

Ramden shuddered at the thought. His brother Ramone could not protect him. His mother could not protect him. His sister could not protect him. When Master Marcus found out he had been freed, he would besiege Castle Silvergold and punish Ramden. He would take a sharp knife and remove the skin from his hands and arms, as he had promised. He would lay salt on the tender flesh.

Ramden grabbed the crisp bread and hesitated. He gazed into Sir Bevin's caring brown eyes. He had never seen such concern, such genuine worry. He ate the bread, amazed at the taste. His jaw flared from some forgotten injury. He remembered as he forced down the rich morsel—Master Marcus had punched him in the face with a steel gauntlet. Ramden had disobeyed his order to remain perfectly still. The binds that stretched his limbs had been so uncomfortable, so painful, that he had dared disobey. "I am afraid," admitted Ramden.

"I know," Sir Bevin answered. "But eat your bread. You have never been safer, not in your entire life. The Monster is far away, in County Garrone. He has been tricked. This castle will not fall—not in Lord Eurelien's capable hands."

"I do not think I will ever ride again," said Ramden.

Sir Bevin's grim demeanor darkened further. He knew Ramden's love for riding, his love for fighting. He knew of Ramden's daring escapades.

"I do not think I will ever walk again," said Ramden.

"I am sure your brother Ramone will give you the best life possible," said Sir Bevin.

"The best life possible." Ramden could not eat the bread without help. Tears of pain had formed in his eyes; his jaw flared with every chew. He tore off a bit of bread, dipped it in the wine, and swallowed it. "What is the best life possible, when I cannot walk, or ride?" He and his brother had never liked each other. A mutual animus and competition had haunted them their whole lives. "What maiden would ever desire a cripple?" Ramden continued. "Not even the peasant women in Lessant will spend a night with me. They will bar the doors to their hovels."

"Stop it," said Sir Bevin. "There are physicians. They may just heal your ankles. Then you will be Ramden the Bold again, gallant and brave."

"I will never be Ramden the Bold," he answered. "A miracle worker might heal my legs, but they can never heal my heart. I am afraid, Sir Bevin. I am so very afraid."

"Cavon March and Silvan March have broken their oath to Sylla and re-declared for King Jourmande," said Sir Bevin. "Sylla is trapped in Zarubain. He has already forgotten you. You are the last thing on his mind now."

Ramden hissed some curse. An anger rose up in him, a strange pang of hurt. "He has not forgotten me, Sir Bevin. He will never forget me." Of all the knights and warriors in Castle Holmgray, Ramden alone had been left alive. Master Marcus had seen something special in Ramden, something unique to torment. Master Marcus would not let his prey away so easily. He would never forget Ramden.

A puzzled expression had crossed Sir Bevin's face.

A trumpet sounded from outside, followed by three more. King Jourmande had arrived with reinforcements. Castle Holmgray had never in its history been so well defended. Yet Master Marcus would find a way in. He would snatch Ramden away, and spirit him off to some dark chamber. The torment would continue for all time.

Chapter Twenty-Nine:
The Faithless

His Majesty King Jourmande vis Bretagne

"Ramden!" King Jourmande could not believe his eyes. The strong, able-bodied young man he remembered—the one who had fought without fear or hesitation—had become a pale shadow of himself. Ramden had shed so much weight he looked like a skeleton as he sat there, nibbling on bread in the mess hall. Worst of all, the fire of courage had vanished from his eyes, replaced with fear. No longer was he a brave bear of the House Rambée, but a mouse. When he met Jourmande's eyes, he dropped the bread and spilled his wine on the table.

"Ramden," Jourmande said.

Yet he wondered if he could truly call this nervous boy Ramden. His long captivity with the Monster of Montée March had shattered him.

"Ramden," Jourmande said a third time, but the young knight remained silent. He had grown distant from Jourmande, distant from his surroundings, distant from his countrymen. "The Monster has done something terrible to you."

"Your Majesty!" bellowed a deep voice from behind.

Jourmande turned to see Eurelien, Duke of Duranche, kneeling before him, with *Snowmourn* sheathed. "Rise, friend," he said.

"A word," Lord Eurelien asked. "In private?"

Jourmande nodded, taking one last concerned look at the mousy Ramden, and followed Eurelien out of the mess hall, into a corridor, and at last into a bare stone room.

"My men have combed through the castle," said Eurelien. "We have uncovered many correspondences… with not just the defectors, but also with the Voraignes, and also with your nephew, Lord Roland."

"Goddess help us," Jourmande cursed.

"Lord Roland and the Voraignes may not be steadfast subjects… but there is something worse, Your Majesty," Eurelien said. "The King of Ardogne…"

"Roderigo."

"There is reason to believe is cooperating with Marcus Sylla… that he is actively supporting the Empire."

The blood drained from Jourmande's face. Ardogne, an island of warmth and plenty, had lived under the heavy influence of Zarubain for centuries. Jourmande had considered Roderigo a friend, even a close one. He had been more than an ally or a subject king; he had been dear to Jourmande. *Another great failure, added to my long list.*

"I will want a full report, with all the letters, when we next hold council," Jourmande said.

King Jourmande walked outside into the cool air. The skies had darkened. Thunder rolled across the marshes. A drizzle began, seeping into Jourmande's tunic. It struck him that he had never seen a sky so ominous. He had never seen a sky so filled with wrath. A wind jetted through Castle Holmgray's courtyard, scattering leaves. A storm was coming, a terrible storm.

Chapter Thirty:
Bubbles in the Sea

Danitari

As rain pelted Danny and winds howled through the glens and groves, the endless pines and firs vanished before the might of the sea. A sandy beach lay before him. The Golden Coast, he recalled, a region that spanned the western edge of Vale of Roy. Mignette had spoken of pirates harassing merchants as they tried to make their way south. Mignette had spoken of bandits that waylaid travelers, and worshipers of the death god who ate the flesh of men. So little of her words could be believed.

His Majesty the Black Fox had sent Danny and his friend Girion here to scout. Yet no one had expected a storm of this magnitude to arrive. The thunderheads were still rolling in, and the waves crashing in on the beach approached ten feet. The clouds themselves were dark purple like a bruise. In the comfort of a townhome or a castle, storms seemed benign, but here, in the open, Danny fought the urge to flee. Lightning flashed over the sea, and thunder immediately answered, crackling and booming as it echoed through the forest. The animals had already taken shelter and were wisely cowering; but what could Danny and Girion do?

"Hey!" Girion was pointing to something.

An islet lay some distance down the coast, and on it was a tower, extremely tall but without any features of fortifications—no arrow-slits or crenellations, but instead clear glass windows. The water that divided it from the land was untroubled and relatively still.

"Let's make a break for it!" said Danny.

Danny ran, and Girion followed. Another spear of lightning

crackled and boomed as the wind howled across the beach. The waves swelled to twelve feet and drove far into the beach. In their wake came white objects—no, dozens of bodies, and a giant pole— the wooden mast of a ship. The sight spurred Danny to run ever faster.

At the tower, Danny yanked on the door handle only to find it barred and locked. It had to be occupied. No doubt Zarubes were inside—cruel, elf-hating Zarubes. What was worse? Another look at the bruise-purple clouds, the corpses with still-terrified expressions on their lifeless faces, and the strange bubbling of the water far out to sea, and his mind was made up.

"Help!" Danny cried. "Help!"

Girion joined him, pounding on the door. "Help! *Help*!"

The wind howled across the sides of the tower, almost knocking Danny over. Girion fell onto the sand. Danny cursed himself for leaving the shelter of the forest. The crashing waves had grown so big that even hopping the thin strip of water to land was now a dangerous affair. Lightning sizzled again, followed by a crack of thunder. Danny pounded on the door harder than ever, but there was no answer.

The bubbling far out to sea gave the water the appearance of boiling, but the sea was ice cold. The doors flew open; there was a voice. A hand dragged Girion, and then Danny, inside.

"Good Goddess!" a woman shouted. "What have we here? Two elves?"

Danny cursed himself. Dying in a storm was better than slavery. In an instant, he recalled Mignette's harsh beatings, her curses, her belittling words. He remembered her husband's wrath, his hatred for elven-kind. Suddenly, the pouring rain, the crashing waves, and the cracks of thunder were no longer threatening. Sopping wet, Danny met the woman's eyes. She had on spectacles and a long, plain green dress. She reached out to touch him and Danny jerked away.

Her brown eyes were warm, but that, too, Danny knew was a trick. This woman would kill him, if given half the chance.

"Poor things," said the woman. "You look cold. Have you run from your masters?"

A man emerged from the tower stairwell, blond and blue-eyed. "Elves. Runaways. A great price could be fetched in the slave markets of Zarubad."

"We could," said the woman. "But not in this storm."

"We have a master!" Girion snapped. "He sent us to look after the beach."

"Hmmm," said the woman. "No lies are necessary. I am Cosette, and this is my assistant Lucien. We are with the Royal Observers Society, here on the Isle-of-Storms."

Thunder shook the walls of the tower, louder than any before it. Danny shuddered; Girion screamed.

"You are armed," Lucien observed. A look of disquiet overtook him. He fingered a dagger by his belt, still in its sheath.

"We mean no harm," said Danny.

"Indeed," Lucien said. "But it is illegal for elves to possess arms. Such is the law established by the king."

"Oh, do not bother them, Lucien," Cosette said. "Here, come with us!"

Cosette ran up the stairwell. Lucien followed half a second later. Danny met Lucien's gaze, hesitated a few moments, and then at last decided to follow. These two people were barely armed, practically harmless. And they seemed so very kind.

At the top of the tower, each wall was dominated by giant glass window. In the center of the room, a bronze-colored spyglass was aimed out to sea. The sky had darkened further; the waves had waxed to fifteen feet, and crashed well out to shore. Around the spyglass lay desks, filled with books stacked on top of each other, and papers scrawled with chicken-scratch.

"We at the Royal Observers Society have never seen such a

storm!" cried Cosette, with the enthusiasm of a religious fanatic. "These storms have been happening with increasing frequency. They are heralded by a great bubbling far out to sea! It is as if a giant is breathing underwater."

As Lucien took his place by the spyglass and adjusted the instrument as he peered inside, Cosette grabbed a book. "We have recorded sightings far out to sea… giant tentacles like forest vines… like the abominations of the sea that sometimes wash to shore, *octopi*. We do believe there is something in the water, that it approaches when the storm comes."

A sick feeling overcame Danny. *The idea of something in the water—a living, breathing thing…*

Cosette, excited beyond reason, opened the hefty tome and paged through it, coming at last to a poorly-drawn picture of a giant octopus. Sometimes, in Danarion, fishermen would accidentally net one of the abominations. Not even the most daring of gourmands would partake of one. "The men of Badelgard to the north call it the kraken. They believe it is the mother of all monsters. Here in Zarubain, there is a peasant tradition that the beast appears at times of great trouble—that it is a Beast of the End Days, a monstrous creature that will herald the destruction of Varda."

Danny had no time for such superstition. The end of the world would not come until the Tree of Life in elven lands began to wilt and die. Though ancient, the tree still lived, showing little sign of decay. All Danny had time for was to run.

"We are waiting until the beast pokes its head from the water," said Cosette. "I will draw, and make a most accurate depiction."

"We must go," said Danny. His insides had turned to jelly.

"Yes," Girion agreed. "Our master is waiting for us."

"The storm is deadly," said Cosette. "You had best wait until it passes.

Danny shook his head. "Come on, Girion," he said. His

voice trembled. He could only imagine a great beast rising out of the water, whether a kraken or a Beast of the End Days, stopping all their hearts with fright. He ran down the stairwell, with Girion only steps behind. He heaved off the wooden bar that held the door fast, and darted outside into the chilly dark day.

Soaked and trembling, the open gates of Castle Moonsilver seemed to Danny and Girion a doorway to paradise. They bolted into the courtyard where hundreds of elves loitered, and dashed into the warmth and safety of the inner castle. By the fire, they caught their breath. Moments later they realized the Black Fox was staring at them from the shadows, now wearing a poorly-forged crown of gold.

"Master," Danny acknowledged him.

"Your Majesty," the Black Fox corrected. "What does the Golden Coast look like? Are there king's men there?"

"No," said Danny.

"There was a tower," Girion added. "A tower of observation. Two people live there. They were quite kind."

The color drained from the Black Fox's face. "You left witnesses," he said. "Oh, sweet Goddess. We must go there... kill them... fortify the tower. It will be an outpost."

"No!" Danny cried. "We cannot kill them." Cosette and Lucien had been the first kind humans he had ever met, the first to treat Danny as an equal, as someone worthy of conversation. This Black Fox only treated them as tools to accomplish his dark ends.

"I am your king." The Black Fox narrowed his eyes. "You will do as I say."

Danny cursed as the Black Fox left. He kicked the wall and tore down a painting of Castle Silvermoon's former steward. Then he collapsed to the floor, and wept.

~

The day was sunny, blue, and unseasonably warm. A gentle

breeze blew across the forest as Danny, General Estilas, and a company of a hundred elves departed. The dirt path to the Golden Coast had dried, allowing for easy passage. The air smelled sweet, with a hint—dare Danny think it?—of spring. Yet at least a month of cold, rainy weather remained.

For hours, the company walked the path, and Danny could not enjoy the warm sunny day like the others. The chirping of birds could not quiet his anguish, his image of the task ahead—to stab a spear through the heart of two kind people, to answer their good graces with an act of unspeakable cruelty.

The pines and firs opened up into a sandy beach. Gulls circled overhead. The waves washed gently ashore. Not a single cloud marred the sky's blue expanse. All was quiet, all was still.

The tower was gone. Danny gasped. Where it once had proudly surveyed the sea, scattered stones lay strewn about. Only its base was standing; the rest of it had been pulled from the foundations. Queasy, Danny imagined the sea beast's tentacles yanking off the roof, grabbing hold of Cosette in the pouring rain, and dragging her into the depths.

"Ruins," said General Estilas. He turned, and growled some curse at Danny. "Is this some sort of joke?"

"Are you laughing?" Danny fumed. "I know what I saw. Yesterday night, this tower was standing."

General Estilas scowled. His grayish cheeks turned a shade of pink. "So someone besieged an observatory... knocked it down with a trebuchet? All while the storm was raging? Surely, the King of Zarubain has better things to do than that."

Danny growled a curse of his own. General Estilas—and all his men—looked so silly and unprepared in their mismatched leather jerkins, their odd assortment of stolen weapons. Danny hurled his spear into the sand. "I know what I saw."

"A waste of many hours," General Estilas said. "I am demoting you."

"Demoting me!" Danny laughed. "Oh, that's funny. Have you forgotten that we are all slaves? Have you forgotten that we call a bandit our king? That we are all doomed? That maybe tomorrow and maybe in a year, the King of Zarubain will burn us all at the stake?"

Estilas yanked the spear from the sand, rushed Danny and clubbed him across the face. Danny hit the sand hard. He grabbed his throbbing chin as tears of pain formed in his eyes.

"There is a monster in the sea," Danny wept. "A monster… a great tentacled monster. It tore the tower down."

"You are pathetic," said Estilas. "Come on, baggage boy. You are going to carry all our things. That is all you're good for."

Chapter Thirty-One:
Drastic Measures

His Majesty King Jourmande vis Bretagne

The warmth was exquisite, the sunny sky a blessing to Jourmande's soul. The gentle, warm winds blowing through the window had a scent of spring. In the keep of Castle Holmgray, in the highest room, Lord Eurelien vis Námois and his most senior knights had gathered at a makeshift Hall of Counsel. Advisor Sybold, traveled from Zarubain, and with him Dame Alesandre had gathered, there, too. Yet despite the grim situation of the nation, the Imperial army running wild and unchecked through the Western Heartlands, all Jourmande could do was watch the bright blue sky, feel the warm wind, and smell the sweetness of an early spring.

"Your Majesty," Dame Alesandre said.

Only she had the courage to rush him. Jourmande turned grudgingly. The beautiful day had vanished from his eyes; now only the grim innards of Castle Holmgray lay before him, and the dark-countenanced advisors huddled in the small room.

"We must decide on a course of action," Dame Alesandre began. "We have proven that the Imperials are not invincible. We have taken Castle Holmgray."

Jourmande laughed. Such a bold, confident comment was unsurprising from Dame Alesandre's lips. Disaster after disaster had befallen the Zarube army, yet the knight continued to have such confidence in Zarubain's prowess. Still she clung to the myth that Zarubain was strong. In her day it had been true; they had savagely laid waste to rebels in the east, and twice inflicted mass casualties upon the horse peoples. They had brought devastating destruction to the Elven World, inflicted humiliating terms of peace upon the Elven King and received his surrender. Yet against these Imperials, they were like lambs before wolves. Who could stand against the Empire? Who could make war against it?

"She speaks truth," said Advisor Sybold. "It is our first success. Surely more will follow."

Jourmande turned and again faced the window. The wind that blew now had a chill to it that was unbecoming. The day of spring had been so wonderful while it lasted. "My dear Alesandre," Jourmande said. "We overtook a castle manned by two-hundred soldiers, while using a force of ten thousand. It is true that the squalid swamps of Montée March are now under our control, but the counties of the Western Heartlands are falling like sheaves of wheat into Sylla's grasp. We cannot beat the Empire."

"What are you saying?" said Dame Alesandre. Jourmande heard her stand up. He could imagine her face quivering with indignation. "That we should surrender?"

"Surrender," Jourmande breathed. The sweetness of the air had begun to fade. "It is a funny word. It can mean so many things. Terms of peace. Peace is what we want, is it not?"

"Not without honor," said Dame Alesandre.

Jourmande laughed heartily. The mind of a soldier was a strange thing. "Honor. A funny word, too… You would see the hamlets and towns of the Heartlands burning, the castles besieged with catapults, and the River Zaros running red with blood—rather than a quaint concept like dishonor."

"I am a woman of war, Your Majesty," said Dame Alesandre. "I fought in your army. I brought the elves and the Murghuli to heel. You are strong, Your Majesty. We do not need to submit or surrender."

Jourmande let out a laugh, but this time it was sad, quiet. "You say you fought in *my* army. But it is King Gylles' army you fought in, and before that, Cyrien's." The statement was implied—

Gylles, at practically half Jourmande's age, had been twice the king. Yet he had disappeared one night from the Imperial Palace, and none had ever seen him since.

Jourmande risked turning around, no longer facing the bright blue sky but instead the dark grim council chamber.

"I heard there is a peasant legend," Jourmande began, "told in small villages and hamlets across the realm, in which King Gylles the Bold plays a part. The good king disappeared because he was plucked from Varda and stowed away in the Otherworld, and he will return at the Lady's behest, when Zarubain is in mortal danger. Even in myth, my young cousin is twice the king I am."

"Oh, come on," Dame Alesandre sneered. "Humility and despair is unbecoming of a king! Boldness and bravery is what the nation needs!"

Advisor Sybold shot up in his seat. "Oh, come off it, Alesandre. How dare you speak to His Majesty in such a tone?"

"Sit down, Sybold," said Jourmande. In all this time, Eurelien vis Námois, Duke of Duranche, had not spoken a word. His dark eyes were observing quietly. His knights and men of war followed him, saying not a word. Who knew what went on in that mind of his? All—even toadying Advisor Sybold—viewed Jourmande as a failure. *I could abdicate*, he thought, *but who would sit on the Lion Throne in my stead?*

"We must reconsider our strategy," said Dame Alesandre. "We must levy more peasant soldiers. All serfs in the Western and Eastern Heartlands must answer the kingdom's call."

Knights such as Alesandre had nothing but scorn for the lowborn soldiers that accompanied them on campaign, yet time and time again they had proven themselves essential. "And who will tend to the orchards, the cattle, and the grain?" Jourmande asked.

The thought had clearly not occurred to Dame Alesandre. She sneered. "We have grain stored away. Let the wellborn eat well. The serfs may eat acorns and twigs and grass, such as they deserve."

Jourmande sighed. "Every force we have thrown at Sylla has broken and scattered. Something drastic must be done. We… no, I… must make terms of peace."

"Coward!" snapped Dame Alesandre, such a breach of protocol that even Eurelien's hardened knights gasped.

Advisor Sybold was fuming. "This woman should be drawn and quartered."

"Quiet!" Jourmande snapped at Sybold for the second time.

Alesandre began to shout, and Advisor Sybold returned favor. Soon everyone at the council table was shouting at each other. The deafening cacophony shook the table.

At last, Eurelien slammed an iron-gauntleted hand on the table. A hush overtook the room. "His Majesty is right," said Eurelien. "Such a drastic move may be unprecedented. Shameful, even. But there are little other options. A maelstrom of blood and death, a ruined kingdom, a devastated peasantry… that would be the cost of doing otherwise. His Majesty must go to Sylla, and make terms. I will go with him."

Jourmande shook his head. "No, Eurelien. We are not going to Sylla."

Eurelien raised a brow.

"We will not beg for terms from a madman," Jourmande said. "We are going where the true power resides. Into the Empire… to Imperial City."

Chapter Thirty-Two:
Worlds Apart

The Reverend Alse-Lorie, High Priestess

With trepidation and deep regret, Alse-Lorie led Varysse down the dirty, chipped cobblestone of the Inner City. The harsh storms of this past winter had caved in several roofs.

"You will hate this place," said Alse.

"I know," Varysse said. "But it's worth it, if I get to be near my beloved mentor."

Alse ground her teeth together. She wondered if anyone would ask questions if she tossed Varysse into the River Zaros. She could say Varysse fell in of her own accord. Then this venomous snake would be gone from Alse's life forever.

As they passed by the rows of forward-leaning townhomes, there was a groaning sound. A shriveled old woman sat on the street corner, clothed in bare rags. Each rib was clearly defined on her emaciated body. Red sores, oozing yellow, pocked her skin. A dog, buzzing with fleas, lay with its head in her lap. She reached out a clay cup to Alse and Varysse. "A coin for a beggar," she croaked. "I haven't a single *aston*."

Alse reached into the folds of her robe, grabbed her coin purse, and opened it.

"Truly?" Varysse growled.

Alse dropped a whole silver *denier* into the beggar's cup.

"Oh! Bless you!" the beggar woman cried. "My dog and I shall eat like queens tonight!"

Varysse scowled at her as they walked on. "You've truly gone mad. Tossing money at every sick, diseased lowborn you see.

You should have let the poor wretch starve. Then the kingdom would be rid of her."

"You will do so well here as parish priestess," Alse said bitterly.

Soon the church appeared before them, a once-magnificent structure surrounded by caved-in townhomes and wooden shanties. The stained glass windows had been boarded up. Two statues guarded the giant double doors, both carved in the form of knights bearing swords and shields. The rain, wind, and long years had worn away all the detail. As Alse and Varysse drew near, the poor folk of the Outer City began to emerge from alleyways and shanty doors, taking a look at the newest full priestess.

"Goddess help me," Varysse murmured.

Alse opened the door. Varysse hurried inside.

"I will not see these wretches any more than I must," cried Varysse once Alse closed the door.

The junior priestess Lysana had been waiting for them. She was a waif of a girl, almost as thin as the starving wretches of her parish. Her hair was a golden brown, falling halfway down her back. Her eyes were fixed on Varysse, clear and blue. "You must see them a lot," said Lysana. "They are really not that terrible. They are quite endearing, really."

"Who is this girl?" Varysse howled. "Ah yes, this is the *junior* priestess Lysana."

Varysse had been one just weeks ago.

"This is the girl," Varysse began as she walked forward, "who will be attending to my every whim… who will be washing my robe and stole, and hanging it out to dry. This is the girl who will be my servant… no less than a lowborn deserves."

"I am noble," Lysana hissed. Alse had never seen such hatred in a person's eyes. "I am here because I have a heart."

"Noble," Varysse laughed. "And where is your domain? A diseased swamp? And your castle—a mud hovel?"

"Surrevere," said Lysana. "I am the viscount's own daughter."

"Ah, Surrevere," sneered Varysse. "Far from the capital, far from glory. When I visited Tournay, they had a name for you Surrevese—'those people on the wrong side of the bridge.' I am from Ajernon, of the House of Abrenard. You Surrevese are not worthy to lick the ground we walk on."

"Enough!" Alse-Lorie hissed. "Varysse, your insults end now. If you are one one-hundredth of the priestess Lysana is, the people of the Outer City would be lucky."

Varysse whipped around to glare at Alse. Her face had gone that familiar shade of bright pink. "You will regret your words."

Alse tried to put on a brave face, but eventually turned and left, feeling cold. Varysse's words had a ring of truth. Now the spoiled young woman was more powerful than ever.

~

The warmth of the day had evaporated; the clouds in heaven above had taken on a somber gray tone. A drizzle had begun. The stink of the Outer City lay all about her. These starved peasants and slaves had no compunctions about tossing their chamber pots out high windows with a cry of "Look out, water!" No official of the king's court had seriously considered attending to the Outer City's roads, which had been worn down and in places had been completely washed away, leaving bare dirt.

A group of bone-thin peasant children was staring at her from the shelter of a wooden shanty. They looked like they hadn't eaten in weeks. Alse might have thought the war had caused their hunger, but she—of all nobles—had been here, in the Outer City, the most. On these dirty, garbage-strewn streets, hunger was a way of life. No one thought about them; no one cared about them. The Inner City lay only yards from the Outer, yet in mind their distance was worlds apart.

Sadly Alse left the Outer City, knowing she had not seen the last of Varysse. The spider had only just begun to spin her web. The cucking stool awaited Alse. *The cucking stool, or something far worse.*

Castle Royale had taken on a somber tone since King Jourmande left. Who knew how the fool's errand had gone? Last Alse heard, he had taken Castle Holmgray, but had the invincible Sylla come back for the slaughter? She wound her way through the halls and narrow corridors. She no longer felt safe sleeping in her quarters at the Lady's Cathedral. Each corridor hid a spying eye, a listening ear. She and Sir Loy had taken great pains to be discreet, yet failed. In Castle Royale, the High Priestess's chambers were expansive. Moreover, the window panes were trimmed with gold; the bed sheets were made of silk; and the wardrobe was stuffed with Mierese gowns.

Her love for Sir Loy could no longer be quieted. The betrayal of her oaths had become unavoidable. She could no longer stop herself. The Goddess despised her now. The Goddess loathed the very one who sat on the High Chair and held the fairy rod. The Goddess would banish her from the Otherworld. Upon death, Alse would fall through fiery chasms into hell. But she had chosen her course; there was no forgiveness, no turning back.

As she made her way toward the upper stairwell, there were several shouting voices. A loud argument had ensued in the Great Hall. Alse hesitated, wondering whether chaos would suit her troubled mind. At last, curiosity got the best of her.

Queen Alysant and Lord Roland were shouting at each other

in the Great Hall. Following the departure of King Jourmande and the death of Lord Dunstan, it fell on Lord Roland to keep the nation in check. Few men were less suited to the task than the Young Duke.

"What is the meaning of this?" snapped Alse. "Why are you shouting at a pregnant woman, Lord Roland?"

The room grew quiet. A dark expression had overtaken the Lord Roland's handsome face, an expression Alse had seen before. "County Rannier has fallen to Sylla. The count is dead. The countess has been taken. Castle Rainbolt is occupied by the Imperials."

Queen Alysant, large with child and due any day now, was nonetheless standing on her feet, angry and roused. "Our dear friend Lord Roland will not agree to face him. He would rather the kingdom fall than live up to his lordly duties."

Alse frowned. She had little patience for Lord Roland, but she could see his point. All the force of Zarubain had been thrown at the madman, yet with a smaller army the Imperials had claimed devastating victory after devastating victory. "Lord Roland," she said, "there is an ancient order of things. The peasants sow, the priestesses pray, the nobles fight. You are a noble. You cannot stay hidden in Castle Sunbow with Elsie and Lord Mars."

"And where am I?" Roland growled.

"You are here," said Queen Alysant, "in body but not in mind."

"You are quarrelsome woman," said Lord Roland. "I pity my uncle."

"And I pity Elsie, your 'wife,'" sneered the queen.

"Enough!" Alse snapped. "Lord Roland, you are not behaving in a way that befits a noble. A nobleman treats women with utmost respect, never raising his voice nor cursing her. And Queen Alysant, Elsie *is* Lord Roland's wife. She is childless, but in some women the seed does not take root. It is to Lord Roland's credit that he has not put her away and disgraced her."

Queen Alysant glared at Alse cuttingly. "I am sorry that I

care about the safety of my child… I am sorry I care about the safety of our city… I am sorry I do not want Imperial men to abuse me."

She hurried out of the Great Hall as fast as a pregnant woman could. The sounds of weeping echoed from the corridor.

"It is strange what a baby does to a woman's head," said Lord Roland. "Their humors become imbalanced. They become hysterical. It is a good thing I am making the decisions."

Also had never cared much for Roland. It was his lack of chivalry that annoyed her. He did not open the door for a woman when she walked by. He did not listen to what a woman wanted; he believed he always knew better. Fleeing from battle was unchivalrous. Fighting in a church was unchivalrous. But belittling a woman was worse, second only to striking one. "To be honest, Lord Roland, I am sad you are in charge. King Jourmande—" She stopped short of finishing.

Lord Roland's expression darkened further. An angry glow had overtaken his eyes. "My uncle, King Jourmande, has failed in every endeavor he set his mind to. His armies have been massacred twice. The royal army cannot recover. Perhaps it is best I *am* in charge."

Also could see his point.

"So shut your pretty little mouth," Lord Roland continued with a newfound hatred in his eyes, "and leave the running of the kingdom to me."

Chapter Thirty-Three:
A Cold Reception

Ramden

The rain pattered constantly against the castle walls. After the warm, sunny day, it had rained for ten straight days. Ramden no longer wanted to sleep. Whenever he slept, a nightmare would overtake him… he was back in the torture chamber with Master Marcus. In some dreams, the dead body of the Montevillian whore would stir from its eternal rest, stand up on its two feet, and join Master Marcus' torments.

Even now, sitting in a secure room with Sir Bevin and three other knights, Ramden could see Master Marcus whenever he shut his eyes. Once, more than a week ago, Sir Bevin had left him alone. It had only taken Ramden a second to panic. Now, day or night, rain or shine, someone sat with him in this stone gray room. He could tell it had begun to wear on them. Even Sir Bevin, his friend, had shown signs of annoyance and bitterness.

"We need to get you back to Duchy Lessant." Sir Bevin had at last said what he'd been thinking this entire time. The boredom of sitting with Ramden had finally caught up to him. Sir Bevin had always gloried in battle. He had loved nothing more than war, and the excitement of the campaign. He would abandon Ramden now, leave him to his nightmares.

Thunder rolled across the castle. Ramden jumped at the sound. "My brother… he might sell me to Master Marcus."

"Ramone loves you," said Sir Bevin.

Sir Bevin knew their family well enough to know he spoke a lie. Ramone, Ramonette, and Mother would all sell him into slavery if it would earn them enough *libres*.

"Master Marcus… sorry, Lord Sylla… controls everything outside Castle Holmgray." Ramden could tell the matter was already settled by the look in Sir Bevin's eyes. Sir Bevin would rather risk his life needlessly than sit another day here in boredom.

Sir Bevin brought two horses into the castle yard. Then he helped Ramden out into the cold rain. Staggering and stumbling through the mud, Ramden could still not stand up. Sir Bevin heaved him into the saddle, and with a second Ramden fell, hitting the wet ground with a thud.

"We will ride two-a-saddle," said Sir Bevin.

"Sir Bevin… I do not think this is a good idea," Ramden half-spoke, half-wept.

"Nonsense," said Sir Bevin. Again he helped Ramden into the saddle, this time his own, and then leapt on behind. "With luck, you will be safe at home before tomorrow."

Sir Bevin galloped north out of the castle gates. The rain, pouring constantly, had flooded the River Zarube. The marshes around the road were flooded, too, and their reek had grown doubly. The filthy brown water sickened Ramden as he looked at it. He nodded in and out of sleep.

The sight of Monteville, perched on a hill, filled Ramden with hope at first. Then he saw a great breach in the wall, and as Sir Bevin galloped past it on the road, Ramden saw rotted bodies nailed to crosses, and the town buildings burn to blackened husks. The smell of the marshes mixed with the pungent smell of death. Ramden retched.

Hours later, they crossed the bridge into County Dracogne. Two tall Imperial standards, red and gold, flanked either side of it. It seemed all the world was under control of Master Marcus. Ramden wondered why he hadn't tried harder to escape. He could have fought, and clawed out Sir Bevin's eyes. He could have screamed for help. Instead, he allowed Sir Bevin to force him on this saddle and ride on a fool's errand, into certain death.

Blancheville, a castle town and the home of Count Julien, by all appearances looked normal as Ramden rode past. Yet instead of the blue-gold lion of Zarubain, a dozen Imperial flags circled the town walls. The thatch roofs of houses, shops and inns showed no sign of burning. No scent of mass death hung about it; only the septic smell of every town. Outside the town gate, a group of children kicked a leather ball around. They did not even look at Ramden and Sir Bevin as they rode by. The sound of their laughter fell away.

By dusk the clouds had scattered, and the sky had turned shades of red and gold. A deep quiet had settled over the vineyards of County Dracogne. The peasants had gone inside. The day's work had ended. A sickness overcame Ramden at the solitude of the night. As the shades of red and gold dimmed, the bridge to Duchy Voraigne appeared, a stone bridge that arched over the River Valles. A battalion of men-at-arms and knights stood guard. They startled at the appearance of Ramden and Sir Bevin.

"Halt!" cried a knight on a white horse. A greathelm obscured his face, revealing only two stern gray eyes.

Twin standards had been driven into the ground on the far side of the bridge, bearing the red hawk of the Voraignes.

"Where go you?"

"We are not Imperials," said Sir Bevin.

"I have gathered as much," said the knight. "And who is in your charge?"

"This is Master Ramden, of the House Rambée," explained Sir Bevin. "I intend to journey to Lessant."

"No one may cross the bridge," the knight continued. "It is

the express order of the honorable Lord Gouldair vis Voraigne. His unfriendly peace with the honorable Lord Sylla remains in place. Not may come; not may go."

"Give it up," groaned Ramden. "Master Marcus has won… he will kill us both… he will boil us in a pot… he will nail us to a cross…" That was the best scenario—to perish. He would kill Sir Bevin but keep Ramden alive as his pet.

"Our Master Ramden was once as bold as a lion," said Sir Bevin. "Now he is a pale glimmer of what he once was. Please… I beg of you…"

"Surrender," groaned Ramden. "Surrender and hope for mercy."

"Quiet," snapped Sir Bevin.

"I am sworn into the Lord Gouldair's service," the knight said. "I would betray my lord and Umbra his god if I disobeyed."

"Leave it alone," wept Ramden. "Master Marcus will skin us alive… he will rub salt on the tender flesh. Then he will boil us in a stew."

"Enough! Let them pass!" the knight said. The soldiers pulled back, and Sir Bevin galloped across the stone bridge, into the apple orchards and vineyards of Duchy Voraigne.

The next day was warm and sunny, a day that brought false hope of spring. The sun illuminated the firs and pines surrounding Castle Silvergold.

A woman ran out into the middle of the dirt road. Sir Bevin's horse stood up on its hind legs and whinnied. Ramden lurched out of the saddle, but Sir Bevin's steady hand caught him.

"Curse you, woman!" cried Sir Bevin. "A pox on you, and your family! You could have killed us."

"Killed you?" The woman's voice was familiar. Ramden recognized the filthy, matted gray hair, the cysts and boils, the golden lantern perched in her hands which swelled, then shrunk, and inside a glowing green will o' wisp. He had seen this woods witch before. She had not been burned at the stake, as was the custom; she had escaped justice. "I have seen this Ramden before. I have spoken to him once, when he was bold and brave as a lion. Now, look at him! I told you your boldness would ruin you! I told you! I told you!" The woods witch cackled.

Sir Bevin drew his sword. An invisible force tugged it from his hands. "Curse you, witch!" The sword hit the muddy road. The woods witch darted into the forest and disappeared.

Sir Bevin eventually recovered the sword from the ground, but he never recovered his confidence. In the feasting hall, where Ramden's brother gobbled down roast chicken and gulped down sweetwine, Sir Bevin's voice cracked as he spoke: "H-here is your brother, Lord Ramone."

"Why are you carrying him?" asked Ramone.

Ramonette and Mother entered from a side door.

"The Monster kept him captive," Sir Bevin explained. "The Monster tortured him and made him a slave. He will never walk nor ride again."

Mother's face darkened. "Never walk nor ride?"

"Indeed not, milady," said Sir Bevin. He set Ramden down at a table. Ramden shivered, suddenly feeling cold. He had never felt so unwelcome, nor so vulnerable. He knew Master Marcus' eyes and ears were all around Castle Silvergold, that it was only a matter of time before he fell back into his hands.

"I hope you will take care of him, Lord Ramone," said Sir Bevin.

Lord Ramone. Even broken and afraid, the title sent a surge of anger through his veins. He had deserved that title. Yet somehow, Father thought better of that fat fool than Ramden.

"I am sorry," said Sir Bevin. "I must depart. It will be dark soon. There is a war to win, and battles to fight. Be good to Master Ramden."

"Naturally," the fat fool said.

Mother had never seemed so disappointed. "Never walk nor ride again," she repeated.

"Never walk nor ride again," said Ramonette.

Chapter Thirty-Four:
The Naming

The Reverend Alse-Lorie, High Priestess

"A lightning offensive!" cried the messenger.

Lord Roland, standing in front of the Lion Throne, seemed perplexed. His indecision might cost the kingdom its life, Alse knew. His mind was inscrutable, his actions bewildering. He would not call another levy; he was insistent that Zarubain could not achieve a military victory. Lord Mars had come from Duchy Valais, and with him Roland's wife Elsie. Lord Mars had always been Roland's more violent, assertive half. He, too, was fed up. The King of Zarubain lay marooned, many miles away, in Castle Holmgray.

"They have swept through Duchy Voraigne!" the messenger continued. "They are in Duchy Duranche, now! It is only a matter of time before they reach the city!"

Lord Eurelien lay marooned with the king, holed up in Castle Holmgray and rebuilding the defenses. Alse-Lorie wondered how he felt now, knowing that the Monster rampaged through his lands, laying waste to the ancient orchards and vineyards of Duranche, setting fire to hamlets and villages across the duchy.

"We must call a levy," said Lady Esmette as she emerged from the shadows of the throne. The young Duchess of Arvogne had proven an important counterpoint to Roland's softness. "The Imperials are lowborn scum. They can be felled. With enough force, we can crush them."

"So said Lord Dunstan, and he is now dead," Lord Roland muttered. "A levy of peasant soldiers now would devastate our farms further. I will not call a levy. That is final."

"So you will grovel before the Empire," mumbled Lady Esmette. "Ask for humiliating terms of peace… grant them half the kingdom."

"Quiet, woman," Lord Roland said.

Alse-Lorie narrowed her eyes at the word. The unchivalrous Lord Roland seemed to use "woman" as an insult. If ever there were a less chivalrous warrior, Alse did not care to meet him. The Lady Goddess surely loathed this man—as much, perhaps, as she loathed Alse-Lorie.

"She is right, Roland," said Lord Mars.

He had gotten too comfortable in the court. The sun-bronzed peasant with his missing teeth had been ennobled by Lord Roland for some unknowable reason. He called Lord Roland by his first name only, a crime that called for public flogging. As a noble, now, there was no way to punish him. Lord Mars now served as the closest advisor of Roland vis Valais, his only assets a handsome, sun-darkened face and a furious temper. What Roland saw in him, Alse would never know.

"If I am not mistaken," said Lord Roland, "my uncle the king left me in charge. I am to serve in his stead. Many leaders make a poor nation. I beg of you, allow me to win this war."

"Allow you to lose it, you mean," hissed Lady Esmette.

"Be gone!" snapped Lord Roland.

The duchess, no more than a girl, stormed off. She had proven a better warrior than Lord Roland—"woman" or no.

Alse-Lorie sighed. With enough determination, the Imperial army could be at the gate of the Outer City by dusk. She smiled at the thought of Varysse, trapped in that chapel amidst the slaughter.

"What strategy is there?" said Alse-Lorie. "If the Royal City is to hold up against the Empire, then we must redouble our defenses… we must fill it with men-at-arms and knights."

"Leave the big decisions to me, *priestess*," said Lord Roland.

Alse muttered some curse. The sound of running feet

echoed through one of the throne room's many doorways. One flew open, revealing Princess Clarysse. Her blue eyes were wide and bright, her lip trembling. She looked as excited as she had when King Jourmande bought her a set of diamond earrings.

"The queen… it has begun… the birth!"

Alse-Lorie gathered her gown and ran after Princess Clarysse. The queen had begun to cry out in pain, lying in a room specially prepared with her and surrounded by midwives.

Hours later, when the morning light was trickling in through the window, she gave birth to a baby boy.

"What shall you name him, Your Majesty?" asked Alse-Lorie. With the royal brat, the line of Bretagne was perpetuated; provided he survived to adulthood, the kingdom had a proper heir.

The tiny thing cried out in his mother's arms, so vulnerable, so innocent. Would there be a kingdom to give, when all this war was over?

"Tyrol," said Queen Alysant.

"Truly?" said Alse-Lorie. "After Tyras, the god of war?"

"We will need a warrior, will we not?" said the queen. "A warrior he shall be… King Tyrol. Let the bells ring across the kingdom. He shall bear the lion banner, fierce and true."

"The Goddess…"

"Look at what the Goddess has done," said Queen Alysant, nuzzling the royal brat to her breast. "Look at what she has brought us to. Our prince will guide us to better days. Tyrol shall be his name, on his name-day. Tyras shall be his god."

"Goddess help us all," said Alse-Lorie. All this was a sign of her failure, of her failures upon failures.

"Tyras guide us to victory," Queen Clarysa answered her.

Chapter Thirty-Five:
The Ayri

Danitari

Danny had lives to answer for. The anger of General Estilas was the least of his concerns. He had fled from the observatory and left Cosette and Lucien to the sea monster. The two humans who had treated him well were dead. Somehow, Danny blamed himself for it.

The so-called King Bran looked displeased. In the makeshift throne of Castle Moonsilver where the steward had once conducted business, the Black Fox now sat. His dark eyes were examining Danny, evaluating the truth of his words.

"I do not lie," said Danny. "Everything I told you was true. The tower was standing tall when Girion and I left it. Just ask Girion."

"Girion has recanted the story," said King Bran. "Under pressure from General Estilas, he cracked—he said you coerced him into fabricating the story."

"He lies," Danny snapped.

King Bran's cheeks turned a shade of pink. "You bandy about that word freely, as only a liar can. I consider nothing more important than honesty, Danny. I have never told a lie, not in my entire life."

"Really? Never?" Danny knew King Bran just told one.

"General Estilas demoted you to 'pack mule.' I will go one further. I am demoting you to 'slave,' until you recant your lie," said King Bran. "Your lie is too fanciful to be true. You know this."

"I thought I was already a slave," said Danny.

"You are a slave among slaves, until you recant," said King Bran.

Danny felt two arms restrain him.

"Come with me," said Estilas.

General Estilas corralled Danny into the castle yard, then through an iron door into a dark stone room. The only light filtered through an iron-barred window. He took in the reek and the warm musk and realized he was not alone. A cursory look ahead revealed the truth—an elf, bare-chested and naked save a pair of worn, raggedy pants that might have once been yellow. He had a crazed look, this elf, and a head of bushy, dirt-filled hair. It was quite clear he had not bathed in months.

Estilas opened the door and left, then slammed it shut. A lock clicked into place.

"Hello," Danny said to his fellow prisoner.

"I am Ras! Ras is my name!" the elf howled. "Ras! Ras! They call me Ras!"

"A pleasure, Ras," Danny said.

"I am Ras! I am from Dongirion! Dongirion is where I am from!"

"You are from Dongirion," said Danny. "You are far from there." He did not know the place, but villages and towns filled the fruitful Great Elven Plain. In the shadow of the Dragonteeth, amid the tall green grass blowing in the wind, Danny had spent his childhood and young adult years. It is said the very soil was a gift from the Light. Plants grew easily from the dark rich earth, and there had not been famine in decades. Danny had worked the soil, planting beans in the gentle warmth of the sun. He had known everyone in the village of Donlamon, and everyone had known him. The filth and squalor of human cities had been blissfully unknown—all before the war began.

Danny wiped tears from his eyes.

"Don't be sad!" cried Ras. With his wild hair and long fingernails, he had the look of a beast. "There is a better place—"

"I am here," said Danitari, "because I refused to lie. Why are you here?"

"Ras did not lie, either. He knows there is a better place. A better place hidden from human eyes! In the woods, there is dancing, there is music, there is friendship."

Danitari sat up. It seemed Ras had invented an inner world. No doubt he was imprisoned for murder, or theft, or something worse. The tears welled up more furiously than before.

"In Dongirion I played the harp and I sang. I answered the King's call."

So had they all. They had left their fields in the wintertime, thinking they would return in time for the spring planting. Yet the armies rolling in across the Elven World had broken the King's strength, had laid waste to ancient citadels, had eradicated cities.

"I was captured," Ras said. "Yes, I was! And sold! To an arena, yes! Ras was to be pit fodder, but he killed the pit dog fair and square. And then he escaped. Yes, Ras escaped! He fled the stinking human city and ran into the woods… and he glimpsed the *ayri*."

"The *ayri*?" asked Danitari.

"A village in the woods where elves live… a village where they are free and hidden from sight! It had its own magister! It had its own town charter, its own laws! And all the elves were joining hands and dancing in a circle, and singing!"

Danitari shook his head. It couldn't be. It was too good to be true.

"I wanted to go the *ayri*, but they had a great starstone in the middle of the town, and everyone there was so full of Light. I felt so dirty, so vile, so filthy! I could have joined—oh, I could have joined—but I remembered what I had done. I had killed men in the pit… some very young. I had snuffed out young lives. Foolish young lives who thought they'd make a name for themselves in the Pit. I could not bear the *ayri* and its Light. I was not worthy to be among them."

Danitar wiped tears from his eyes.

"But King Bran won't believe me! He was so angry he threw me in here... he will never let me go, not until Judgment Day, he said." For the first time, tears came to Ras's eyes as well. "But I will not deny the *ayri*. I will not deny it. It is my last hope."

Chapter Thirty-Six:
Secrets

The Reverend Alse-Lorie, High Priestess

As expected, even in these dark times of war, the baby Prince Tyrol was the apple of the court's eye. Queen Alysant had a warmth in her eyes that only a mother's love could create.

Alse had brewed herself Grayman's beard tea each night. The life that might have taken root inside her was snuffed out. Grayman's beard was the domain of whores and women of ill repute; yet the very High Priestess consumed it by night.

Queen Alysant lay in the royal bed with Prince Tyrol, resting herself as he ate from her breast. Lady Elsie vis Valais was stooped over them, opposite Alse-Lorie. Her eyes had a sad, longing look as she watched the baby. No doubt Elsie felt badly that she had not borne Lord Roland a child; yet Lord Roland had displayed an uncharacteristic chivalry in remaining by her side. He had not petitioned Alse-Lorie once for divorce. Divorce, rarely granted by the Fairy Church, was not even afforded to the king or queen easily.

Despite Roland's devotion to her, Lady Elsie had never seemed happy. A gloom had worn away what joy she'd ever felt. Her hair was brown, yet in the light of the bedchamber it seemed some shade of gray. Lady Elsie had the tired look of a old maid. Alse wondered what troubled Elsie. She was highborn, the daughter of the Count of Belidere, true, but good birth did not always mean happiness. A devoted husband who stood by her side, despite her infertility, was a great gift.

"Forgive me for being rude," the queen said, "but would you leave Tyrol and I alone?"

"Of course," Alse said, and nodded to Elsie. "Mother needs her rest."

The corridor that led to the royal bedchamber was white and gilt with gold. Portraits of the King Lucien with his battalions and of Queen Melysant with her fey handmaids lined the walls. In some parts of the wood-carved wall, rubies and diamonds were inset. If Queen Alysant had half a mind to, a sale of one of these paintings or a single jewel could feed the Outer City for a week. *Why am I suddenly thinking of those lowborns? Perhaps I pity them, for dealing with Varysse.*

Halfway down the corridor, Lady Elsie stopped. Alse halted in kind. "I do not think he loves me," said Elsie.

"Who?"

"I know he does not love me," said Elsie.

Alse had an idea of who she meant—Lord Roland—but that did not match up with the facts, refusing to ask for a divorce when she did not bear his child.

Elsie turned to her. Tears had formed in her dainty face. The daughter of the Count of Belidere had never looked so sad. Her lips trembled. "He does not. Roland."

Alse, the supposed shepherd of the Zarube flock, embraced Elsie, then looked her in the eyes. "He loves you," said Alse. "He has stayed by your side. You are the envy of the Western Heartlands...you are a lucky woman, Lady Elsie."

"You do not understand," Elsie said. "He is unmanly."

"Unmanly?" Alse repeated. The word had a ring of truth; for weeks he had holed up in the Zarube capital, refusing to lead the army. "He is not unmanly. He merely thinks too much for his own good." A white lie never hurt anyone. "He has a strategy. He only *appears* weak. I'd hate to be under such pressure, wouldn't you?"

At Alse's encouraging words, tears began trickling down Elsie's cheeks. "You do not understand... you do not understand. He is *unmanly.*"

Alse frowned. What could she possibly mean? "I am sorry, Elsie. I do not understand."

"I have said too much," Elsie said and scurried off.

The matter was strange, but by the time she reached the throne room, it had vanished from her mind. Lord Roland stood in front of the Lion Throne, never daring to sit on it or rest his hands on the gold lion armrests. A knight knelt before him. A great smile had formed on Roland's face, brightening his dark features. He embraced Lord Mars. "Thank goodness!" he cried.

"What has happened?" asked Alse-Lorie.

But to Lord Roland, Alse was not even there. There was only him, and the knight, and Lord Mars.

"A minor setback," said Sir Loy.

Alse leapt at the voice.

"For the Empire," Sir Loy continued. He had crept up behind her.

"You scared me."

As a member of the castle guard, Sir Loy wore his steel gorget and breastplate, and over it a surcoat, white and black, a pillar: the Pillar Which Holds Up Creation. The Knights of the Pillar believed many strange things about the world. He wore no helmet, though, revealing his thick head of brownish-gold hair and his dark brown eyes. "They failed to capture Castle Hombard."

Castle Hombard, one of Duchy Duranche's strongest fortresses, had never fallen, but if anyone could break its fortifications, the Imperials could.

"They assaulted it for three days," said Sir Loy. "All their catapults and scorpions failed them."

Alse-Lorie smiled at the good news.

A young man—a castle page—walked through the double doors up to Alse-Lorie, holding a wax-sealed envelope in his hand. "A message, milady," he said. Alse took it and broke the seal as the page walked away.

"What is it?" said Sir Loy.

Also could scarcely breathe. She recognized the handwriting immediately. *Varysse.*

I loathe the Outer City as much as I feared. The people are horrid and the tithes are worse. What is one-seventh of ten astonnes, you wonder? Enough to buy me a hunk of stale bread. A townsman is lucky to make ten astonnes in a week, and not everyone tithes.

Also grinned. If she was asking for a transfer to County Champiz, Also might deny it. She liked the idea of Varysse suffering.

Just yesterday, I was asked to perform last rites for a poor lowborn with bleeding sores. I consented out of the goodness of my heart.

Also didn't believe it.

The hovel was filthy and stained with soot, as you could imagine. Nonetheless, Alse-Lorie, 'high priestess,' I require a payment of one-hundred sous every month from the treasury, or I will tell everyone our high priestess is a fraud.
Yours in the Lady's love,
V.

With one hundred *sous* a month, the spoiled brat could buy dresses of Mierese silk, a gaggle of servants and a chef. Also could feel her blood boiling.

"What is it, love?" said Sir Loy. "You've turned bright red."

"The shrew is blackmailing me," Alse growled. "She thinks she can get away with this. Well, I'll show her… I'll show her." She crumpled the letter and tossed it on the floor. She smothered it with her slippers.

"Do you want me to rough her up?" Sir Loy said. Alse slapped him in the face.

"Have some chivalry," Alse hissed.

Lord Roland, Lord Mars, and Lady Esmette—just returned from her pouting—were staring at her. Alse went from angry to afraid in an instant.

"Goodbye, everyone," Alse said. "I must return to the Lady's business."

She walked, then scurried out of the throne room, fearing everyone would suspect the truth.

Chapter Thirty-Seven:
Fading Glory

His Majesty King Jourmande vis Bretagne

This was the beginning of the end for the kingdom, Jourmande thought as he and his servants set foot on the ancient road. The broad road, which pierced southwards through the barbarian Mekara lands, was paved with carefully fitted stones—a rarity in the kingdom as a whole. It would be more than a fortnight before they reached the great wall which formed the border of the Empire.

On this shameful journey of acquiescence and surrender, he had not brought a full army, trusting in the Empire's legendary sense of honor and rule of law. Three hundred men-at-arms, fifty Knights of the Pillar, fifty Knights of the Sun, and a dozen of his Royal Guard joined him. His advisor Sybold joined him and even Dame Alesandre had come, albeit grudgingly. Lord Eurelien vis Námois remained behind in Castle Holmgray. On the day Jourmande departed, Eurelien, Duke of Duranche, had never looked so unsettled or afraid. And yet, *"the peasants sow, the priestesses pray, the noblemen fight."* It was his ancient duty, even if no great war had been fought in recent memory—even if the lords and ladies of the land had gotten used to peace. War in Zarubain had, of late, been a light, symbolic thing. Yet the Imperials viewed it in brutal, realistic terms. The diplomacy and pageantry with which Zarube nobles solved their disputes was alien to the violent, lowborn Imperial mind.

In Mekara, beyond the sight of the Westhorn Mountains, a light dusting of snow lay over the grass, but the sun was out and only a few clouds drifted through the sky. The air had warmed considerably since their arrival. Birds circled overhead. The snow was the last gasp of winter; spring was arriving, and soon.

Advisor Sybold rode with him at the front of the expedition. The presence of the fat, dim-witted relation of his—some great nephew thrice removed, not even a Bretagne but some lesser family from Further Zarubain—had begun to wear on him. His toadying words and flattery got him so far, but now Jourmande preferred the company of Dame Alesandre, who did not hesitate to rebuke him, castigate him, and give him unsparing, honest advice.

"The Wild Mekari haunt these hills," said Advisor Sybold. "Some say they collect the heads of their defeated war victims. But do not worry; they will not touch the head of the King of Zarubain, the Goddess's own hand on earth."

Perhaps we will all be lucky, and they will collect Advisor Sybold's head.

"It is said they worship a deer god," said Advisor Sybold. "A god with the antlers of a stag but the body of a man. They call him *Hernennos.*"

"Be quiet," King Jourmande answered him. "Else, I will give them your head as a gift."

Advisor Sybold gasped and fell back. He had spent all these weeks of flattery trying to scale the social ladder, but he had only succeeded in gaining Jourmande's—and Alesandre's—enmity. The fat fool from Further Zarubain had no more sage advice or insight than a common serf, and half one's charisma.

Eight days passed on the road, eight hard days that strained Jourmande's old bones. Some days he spent in the royal carriage, but that was no less uncomfortable, bouncing around on the pavestones. Throughout all those days merchants passed north or south—from the Empire, carrying reams of silk and jars of spices, casks of perfume and jars of olive oil; from the north, wool and *gerusivel,* beaver pelts and animal hides, sweet wines and dark ales. The shame of the situation nearly did King Jourmande in, but Dame Alesandre told a good story—that a diplomatic mission was a sign of strength, that it had been many years since a Zarube king visited the Empire. Those who had heard of the raging war, however, knew better.

The snow had completely melted, and a gentle spring warmth lay over the brown grass, when the ruins of Castle New appeared. The walls had been thrown down; the main keep had all but collapsed. The once numerous townhomes and shops had turned to piles of gray ash. The Church of the Forest Heart had not escaped Marcus Sylla's destruction—the stained glass windows, once in fairy pinks and greens, had all been smashed in. The roof had collapsed and now birds had nested within. Gold and red Imperial standards bordered the perimeter of the ruins. Not a soul lived there. The destruction had been absolute.

There, King Jourmande shed a tear, not for the Lord Viceroy Falerien, nor even the people of Castle New, but for the kingdom— and for himself. How far had they fallen? An inestimable distance, certainly—the King of Zarubain, the Goddess's own hand on earth, was traveling hundreds of miles to beg for mercy.

Six more days passed, six days of merchants' curious stares and Imperials' smug looks, six days of camping in the open air, six days of Alesandre's ashamed looks and Sybold's bitter glares. The warmth had intensified and the grass had turned a happier shade of green when the Wall appeared. The great wall towered above them, thirty feet high, stretching some nine hundred miles in an unbroken line. It was a great wonder of the world whose origins no one knew. Lying in ruins a thousand years ago, the Imperials had rebuilt it and manned it with two full legions. Advisor Sybold would know more— but since their confrontation a fortnight ago, he had grown bitter and reserved, and would not even look at Jourmande.

The shame of their situation became clear as the Imperial soldiers at the gate—staring scornfully at the visitors in their chain armor—asked, "What is the purpose of your visit, *signore?*"

No reverence, no "Your Majesty" or even "Your Honor." Just "signore."

Advisor Sybold answered in Imperial, though his expression was grudging, his resentment still clear. "His Majesty has come to speak to your king."

"Our emperor?" said the soldier. "His Undying Glory is exceedingly busy."

"We will speak to your *empereur* regardless of what you say, lowblood," snapped Sybold.

King Jourmande was a passive spectator to his nation's shame.

The soldier gazed at them. "An armed force is not allowed into the Empire," he said. "The citizens may bear arms but no foreigners may bring them. To enter you must disarm. We will return your weaponry when you leave."

"This is an outrage!" cried Sybold. "An outrage!"

"Quiet," said King Jourmande. Shame and embarrassment was a small price to pay for the life of a kingdom. All the armies of the Western Heartlands had broken upon a force of thirty thousand Imperials. What if the Empire sent in its full force? To resist would entail a maelstrom of destruction. "We will disarm."

Sybold quivered. "We will not."

"We will," Dame Alesandre answered. She offered her sword first, which the Imperial soldier took. One by one the knights and men-at-arms gave away their swords, their war axes, their halberds and their lances. Last of all King Jourmande handed *Fairbolt* to the soldier, a gilted sword studded with priceless sapphires, rubies, and emeralds. Never before had it been surrendered in such an indignified way.

The Imperial soldier shook his head. As his men stowed away the arms of the knights and men-at-arms, *Fairbolt* remained in King Jourmande's hand. "We will not disarm a king," the leader said.

"Besides, I could not promise this masterwork would remain here by the time you left."

Jourmande offered a weak, sad smile. Such indignity had never before been suffered on a diplomatic visit. *From failure to failure I have brought the kingdom.* The name of Zarubain had been tarnished. The glory of the old kings had vanished. The reverence and honor of the old kingdom had turned to shame and filth.

The stone-paved path continued beyond the Gate of Tidus. The road of sorrow and shame continued into the heart of enemy lands. King Jourmande had come into the Empire's northern frontiers, a land of mixed forest and plain, a brownish land of little development. A light drizzle began as they continued the path of sorrows. The weather and countryside were somber, yet the air was alive and palpable. A prosperous citizenry walked up and down these roads. Though Jourmande could scarcely understand their words, their happy gait, their bright smiles and cheerful conversation indicated a nation vibrant and alive. A renaissance was underway, and a mood of optimism contrasted starkly with the gloom and fear of Zarubad's Inner City. The travelers—merchant and pilgrim alike— were lowborns, yet their clothing was of fine wool, their appearance healthy and well fed. They looked at the Zarube highborns with contemptible nonchalance. Some even gazed at them with scorn. In Zarubain they would be put to forced labor. Yet they walked the Empire's roads with undeserved freedom and undeserved cheer. Although the Imperial authorities did not despise them or treat them as they deserved, King Jourmande and his party would.

Many towns of the Empire lacked proper walls, leaving them open to attack. In these giant settlements along the road, ten times the size of those in the Western Heartlands, the spring festival had overtaken the streets. Flower petals lined the paved streets, and bottles of sweet wine lay discarded in alleyways. Brooms lay across the door. The hills were green and bright after the winter's rain. Yet the weather was growing hotter, and drier.

It was three weeks through this vast and spacious land, through dry valleys and past brown mountains capped in snow, when the first signs of the capital appeared. Amid the dry heat and haze of the coming summer, grand villas appeared—white-pillared edifices perched on high, cypress-covered hilltops. The road had become intolerably crowded. The air was smoky and harsh to breathe, and the smell of human habitation was thick and fetid. For the first time since crossing through the gate, Jourmande wished he was back in Zarubain with its fresh air and lush greenery. He had never been on a road so densely packed, nor in a place so baking hot. He wished he was hunting stags and boars in Vale of Roy, or gallivanting through field and stream in the Westwood.

What was clear beyond all else was that King Jourmande had come to the center of enemy lands, that the glory of the old kings had passed away, that the nation of Zarubain had been brought to its knees, begging for mercy. In view of the white pillared villas, it grew increasingly clear that the kingdom's best days were in the past, and that the Empire was the future.

Interlude: Name-Day

The Reverend Alse-Lorie, High Priestess

Weeks Earlier…

It was a sign of her failure that the Reverend Alse-Lorie was a spectator to the royal baby's naming. Instead of a fairy priestess in pinks and greens, a black-hooded brother stood in the Lady's Cathedral. His only ornament was a gold belt that cinched his robe. He smelled of ale, and spoke like an easterner. He called himself Brother Archett, and served no less than thirty gods—Tyras, the god of war, included.

Queen Alysant offered him the royal baby. Brother Archett sprinkled the newborn's head with oil. "In the name of Tyras, the victory bringer, the mighty in battle… I bless this babe, the child of Alysant and Jourmande and heir to the Lion Throne." Brother Archett lifted the royal baby above his head, who began to cry. "Yea, in the name of Tyras I bless him, and call him Tyrol of the House Bretagne. May he honor his god in all ways, and may Tyras ride behind him in victory."

A tear fell from Alse's eye. She dried it with her pink stole. The rest of the nobles stood up in their pews and cheered. Alse followed them, moments late. Trumpets, shawms, and horns blared to the tune of *The Lion on the Ramparts*. Queen Alysant had abandoned the Goddess, and she had never looked happier with a decision in her life.

"Hail Tyrol! Hail Tyrol!" the nobles cried out amidst the deafening music. Brother Archett, holding young Tyrol high, walked down the aisle past the pews. Immediately bells began to ring in the Inner City and the Outer City. The bells would ring in parish churches across the kingdom, declaring the birth of the royal baby, the birth of a king.

The Eagle in Spring

OURS IS A NATION SET ABOVE, BUT IT IS NOT
WITHOUT TROUBLE.

—from *The Imperial Chronicles* by Primo Alleus

Chapter Thirty-Eight:
The City of the Gods

His Majesty King Jourmande vis Bretagne

King Jourmande had never imagined a city could grow so big. He had not believed Sybold when he said a million people lived in Imperial City—one thousand times one thousand—yet now he did. The folk of Imperial City lived in towering buildings of a strange material called cement. Beneath the streets, Sybold had told him, were sewers, which flushed the city's waste away into the Great Sea.

Yet greater wonders were yet to come. In giant open-air markets, in view of titanic temples, goods from everywhere in the world were sold. Jourmande even saw a brightly-painted Mierese silk, produced in Zarubain. Yet there was more, much more—bottles of wine, kegs of ale, pouches stuffed with pepper and nutmeg and saffron, sticks of cinnamon and bulbs of garlic, reams of fine silk cloth, even a dwarf elephant, in addition to hundreds of slaves.

In a gold lined cage were three tiny creatures similar to the dragonettes which fetched princely sums in the markets of Zarubad. Yet instead of the dragonettes' blue and green bodies, these had a fiery look. Their scales, a bright red, contrasted starkly with their coal black eyes. Their wings were bright orange on the outside and dark orange underneath. As they flitted about in the cage, one belched out smoke. A swarthy man in a white cotton turban stood by them. "A draco from the Far South... only one hundred *libra*, my signore!"

Beyond the market square, buildings towered overhead. Some were temples—giant pillared works of marble which made mankind ant-like in comparison. Others were titanic bronze statues of Imperial gods and goddesses whose legspans stretched from one end of the road to the other.

"Humans did not build this," muttered Jourmande.

Dame Alesandre, by his side, said nothing in reply. No doubt they, too, were wonderstruck by the monuments, the prosperity, and the vitality and energy which pulsed through these streets.

Yet greater things awaited them in the Imperial Square. One massive temple was under construction. Others were complete—and in size and grandeur, there was no equal in the Northern or the Elven Worlds. A basilica which dwarfed Castle Royale in Zarubain stretched to the sky, and above the doorway, etched in the Imperial language, were the words "The Imperial Treasury." On the opposite end and towering even higher, the Imperial Palace, overlooked the square. Its white columns and pillared domes indicated the fabulous wealth which the Empire enjoyed.

Yet another building was what stole Jourmande's breath. A tower stretched to the height of the Imperial Palace and was capped with a dome of white stone. In circumference it equaled the whole of Castle Royale.

"The Council House," said Sybold from behind him.

Ten soldiers in mixed plate armor guarded the gate to the Imperial Palace. Red capes and red horsehair-crested helmets stood out starkly against the dark metal they wore. Each had his own sword and shield.

"My good *seigneurs*," Jourmande began.

Their faces were unchanging and solemn.

"We wish to speak to your *empereur*."

Their faces grew angry, scornful. "Step away, signore. His Undying Glory has more pressing concerns than you."

Jourmande's heart sank. For a moment, the possibility that he might have come all this way for naught, that the Imperials might turn him back, crossed his mind. He panicked. "Please." The sovereign King of Zarubain fell to his knees, and the sable of his purple cape touched the bare ground for the first time. Dame Alesandre's cry of disgust echoed from behind. "Please!" Jourmande continued, heedless of the shame. Failure was unacceptable, an option too dark and terrifying to contemplate. The shame would be unbearable, and the nation done-for.

A loud voice cried out: "Hail! The northman king is in Imperial City!"

Jourmande turned.

A man in a white robe and purple sash was walking toward them. Jourmande stood up and brushed the dirt off his royal robe. "Greetings."

"Are you a man of import, *seigneur*?" said Jourmande. He noticed several soldiers flanking the man, carrying swords and shields.

The man answered in Zarube. "A man of the purple sash. An Imperial Councilor. Juliano Corvus, no less!"

"I wish to speak to the *empereur*," Jourmande said. "It is a matter of great import. We will resolve our nation's differences. It is best for both of us."

Corvus appeared confused. "Yes, yes, my good signore. But the emperor will not hear you. The Council will."

"I have not come all this way to speak to an advisory council!" Jourmande hissed. "This is madness!"

"The Imperial Council holds great power, my good signore," said Corvus, smirking. Jourmande's anger seemed to amuse him. "As much power as the emperor... and theoretically more!"

"Please," Jourmande said. "Let us meet at once."

"At once?" said Corvus. "I am afraid we are busy men. I will schedule a hearing before the full Council... in three weeks' time, at the latest."

"Three weeks," Jourmande groaned.

"You may stay in the guest villa. Signor Marco… show them to the Villa of Leto."

One of the gruff soldiers nodded. "Come with me, Signor King."

King Jourmande followed him. Jourmande's star had fallen far, and it was about to fall further.

As they passed through Imperial Square, the sounds of loud shouting erupted. A mob had gathered in front of a woman who was dancing and screaming. Her nude body dripped with wet pink paint. "Stop the war!" she cried.

Signor Marco stopped to watch, and Jourmande—by necessity—followed.

"Stop the war! Stop the war! The southrons have done us no harm!" She was writhing and leaping in a dance without music. "Stop the war! All soldiers are criminals! Stop the war! Death to the Empire! Stop the war! Stop the war!" A man came rushing in with an iron cudgel. Another darted in with a dagger.

The man with a cudgel struck her head before she could flee. The cracking of her skull echoed through Imperial Square. Bits of brain and blood flew everywhere. She slumped to the floor, and the man with the knife punched the blade repeatedly through her body.

"Good Goddess," Jourmande gasped. The lack of chivalry was unprecedented. The Empire may be mighty, and advanced, but they were barbaric.

The crowd was cheering. Signor Marco turned to Jourmande with a bright smile on his face. "A well deserved death," he said, positively glowing.

"Have you no chivalry?" Jourmande said.

"Chivalry or no, it was earned," said Signor Marco. "In years past, all speech was tolerated by law… but under our emperor Numa, no murder was committed… not with a person such as her."

"Good Goddess," Jourmande repeated.

In the Villa of Leto, Jourmande could scarce recover from the stresses of the day. The plants of the inner courtyard had all withered from disuse, and now hollowed out husks and shriveled vines were all that remained. Cockroaches skittered through the concrete floors, and the smell of mold and mildew was ever-present. The wall murals had faded, having lost all brilliance.

"This is what you think of the Zarube king," Jourmande stated.

"No," said Signor Marco. "This is what the Imperial Council thinks of you."

A spark of rage shot through Jourmande's veins, but the rage quickly vanished, changing to grief and mourning, for the death of his kingdom's honor.

Chapter Thirty-Nine:
Og

The Reverend Alse-Lorie, High Priestess

The spring had arrived, and warm weather had washed through the city. In the homes of the Inner City, chefs prepared spring pies and spring bread. Symbols of spring—rabbits, eggs, and birds—decorated doorsteps. The Feast of the Maiden was just days away. Yet no one felt like celebrating.

Alse-Lorie walked the streets of the Inner City, luxuriating in the warmth and the sunny sky but well aware that the sense of optimism when this war began had all evaporated. The Imperial Army lay just a mile from the city walls, having lain waste to the countryside, pillaging and robbing wherever it went. Those who had declared an oath of loyalty to the Empire remained unmolested and prosperous. Those who resisted were subject to Sylla's raids and atrocities. The news that Castle Hombard had, at last, fallen, sickened the nobles who remained. Alse had heard reports that in Duchy Voraigne, Lord Gouldair was considering striking a deal with Sylla, conceding to his land-thefts in exchange for peace. Whose loyalty could be bought when such a reward could be given—priceless life?

The galloping of hooves echoed like thunder across the Inner City. Alse-Lorie gasped as a hundred knights appeared, riding through the Inner City's cobblestone roads. At their head was a man Alse-Lorie recognized as Vivien vis Abrenard, Duke of Ajernon.

In a whirl Alse-Lorie followed the knights as they galloped toward the landing. Perhaps they intended to pay their respects to the royal baby Tyrol.

Alse had followed them into Castle Royale's throne room. The new Duke of Ajernon was half as old as his father, the late Lord Dunstan, and twice as imposing. His head of dark brown, almost black hair fell halfway to his shoulders, and his beard was thick and virile. He was half again the height of Lord Roland, who met him there.

Behind Lord Roland, king in all but name, stood Lord Mars and a pair of red wizards. "Lord Vivien," said Roland.

Vivien dropped to one knee. "Your Honor."

"Rise."

"Our war is not going well," said Lord Vivien. "Even the men of the Seven Gems are wavering. Our knights are the best in the world. We crushed the elves and the northmen alike. There is only one explanation. The Goddess is displeased."

"Yes," Lord Roland said. His dark eyes reflected a calculating mind.

Could Lord Vivien be speaking of the royal baby, Tyrol? Indeed, Queen Alysant had abandoned the holy name of the Goddess for a god of war and iron. Alse would not object to his re-naming.

"There is someone in the royal court who has betrayed our Goddess," said Lord Vivien. "Someone who has betrayed their duty… who has forsaken the Lady's trust."

"And how could we find out?" Lord Roland said, clearly unimpressed.

"By the old ways," said Lord Vivien. "Through trials of blood."

"The old ways will never be used again!" cried Alse-Lorie, at last roused to speak up. The old ways would expose her for the fraud she was.

"The Priests of Og," Lord Vivien continued. "And a sacrifice—a lowborn boy, a virgin."

"How will they tell if he is a virgin?" said Lord Roland.

"They have their ways," said Lord Vivien.

"Og'og will never be worshiped in the Royal City!" cried Alse-Lorie. "No demon will be honored in view of the Lady's Cathedral. No demon worshiper will set foot in Castle Royale!"

"Quiet, Alse," said Lord Roland with that sneering condescension of his. "We will get to the bottom of this. Our nation is in peril. Drastic measures must be taken, measures which a happier age would frown upon."

"The Goddess will be enraged!" cried Alse-Lorie. "To worship Og'og, a demon, to determine her displeasure…"

"It has been done before." Lord Vivien turned to snarl at her, with hatred burning in his eyes.

"Very well," said Lord Roland, then continued with a shout, "Summon the Priests of Og and a fitting sacrifice. We will learn the truth of what is necessary. We will save our nation."

"No! Please, no!" Alse cried. In dark times, when the kingdom's future seemed uncertain, drastic steps such as this had been taken. There was a reason why the cult of Og'og—a demon prince—was banned in public, but secretly kept alive.

The demon priests would expose her. They would shame her. She would be set on a cucking stool, shaved of hair, and dishonored for life.

It was less than an hour before thirteen dark shapes appeared, walking side by side with the high priest at the front. They all wore iron masks and covered their heads with black hoods. In the grip of the high priest, a little boy struggled. The priests in the back pounded a steady, doleful beat on drums. They and the others raised a chant in some dark tongue, half-singing, half-bellowing. The torches in the room flickered at their presence. Dread had consumed the room and a dark pall hung over all.

"Truly, Lord Roland?" cried Alse-Lorie. "This is what you

have brought us to? This is how low we have sunk?" Alse could run over and deliver punches to these vile demoniacs. Fey priestesses learned all sorts of fairy songs and fairy chants, but—forbidden to wield iron—they above all else learned how to deliver a strong punch. She clenched her fists—they were dripping in sweat.

Even beyond her selfish concerns, she was afraid of these Priests of Og. Another being walked with them, a being of terrible power, a being which spread fear wherever it traveled.

Lord Roland, in truth, did not look comfortable at all. Perhaps he regretted what he had done, seeing the innocent lowborn boy and feeling the terror which demoniacs naturally spread.

"*Oghog!*" they were chanting. "*Oghog meltoth!*"

A fourteenth demoniac ran in, tattered black cloak fluttering, with a giant wooden board in his hands. He cast it on the ground before the high priest and the struggling boy. It was covered in markings of Elvish characters and a six-pointed star. In the center was an iron spike, the spike which would take this little boy's life.

"No!"Alse screamed. "No! Unhand him!"

She ran to the high priest and punched hard. He fell to the ground, grunting, but his iron grip on the little boy remained fast. The other Priests of Og drew ritual knives.

"No!" Lord Roland shouted. "Do not harm the High Priestess."

One of Lord Vivien's knights ran to Alse, who was now weeping, and grabbed both hands. She kicked and screamed but she could not escape. The Priests of Og continued chanting. The High Priest of Og, having stood up, turned his iron-masked face to Alse-Lorie. "Do not take her away," he bellowed without emotion. "Let her watch."

He forced the boy toward the spike. Alse closed her eyes.

Chapter Forty:
Dreams of Home

Danitari

This dank cell had become his home; these chains, his only friends. Ras had died, succumbing to the cold and malnutrition. Danitari knew that he was next. The provisions of stale bread and water were more than Ras had ever gotten. The so-called King Bran wanted an apology for the so-called lie Danitari told. But he wouldn't get one. Danitari had spoken the truth.

Now, imprisoned and in the dark, Danitari quietly hummed elven songs. When he shut his eyes, he was running through the green grass of the Great Elven Plain. Colorful birds were flying overhead, and the vineyards were almost ready for harvest. When he shut his eyes, the peace that had existed for centuries had not been broken. When he shut his eyes, the elven people were unmindful of humanity, content and happy despite their lost prestige. "The Elven Age has come and gone," they would say, "but this is good too."

The promise of Yule had filled the air when the first of the raiders arrived. They stood taller than elves, the raiders did, when they first embarked on their mission of destruction. They raided the Shrines of the Light and came within miles of the World Tree before a devastating charge of the stag riders had massacred them in the midst of the Great Plain. Yet the trouble was just beginning—*indori mali vardoren*, the wicked king of the humans—would soon involve himself in the matter. He would prove worse than the raiders ever had. He had wanted more than gold or silver—he had wanted precious lives.

The air outside had grown warm, but the cell retained its

wintry chill. Spring had arrived and summer would come soon. The cold and rain had dissipated, but Danitari's state had only worsened. He had become bone thin and weak. A headache assailed him at all hours. He could scarcely think.

Yet when he shut his eyes, he was on the Great Elven Plain, and the wind was blowing through the green grass and the purple wildflowers, and he was alive and free.

Chapter Forty-One:
The Decree of Og

The Reverend Alse-Lorie, High Priestess

Alse-Lorie did not want to watch, but the foul knight forced her to. The poor lowborn boy was dead—Goddess rest his soul—and his shredded body had been cast aside. Now, blood and flesh stained the wooden board, smearing its once unblemished designs.

"Is the Goddess angry with us?" said Lord Vivien.

Roland had covered his eyes. He had not fully comprehended what he had agreed to.

"*Ké… ohé… gé…*" The High Priest was tracing the blood, which had formed a distinctive pattern over the letters. "Yes."

"Enough of this!" Alse-Lorie howled. "Kill these foul demoniacs."

"Quiet, woman," snarled Lord Vivien.

"This boy's blood is on your hands, Roland!" she cried.

Roland vomited on the throne room's floor.

"Why is she angry?" said Lord Vivien.

"Yes or no questions, fool," said Og's High Priest.

"Is she angry because we are not devout?" said Lord Vivien.

"*Mé… ohé… thé…* No."

"Is she angry," Alse-Lorie howled, "that we consult demons?"

"Quiet!" Lord Vivien screamed with an anger in his eyes she had never seen before. All tolerance for her was gone, replaced with a love for Og'og, demon prince of mysteries.

"*Ké… ohé… gé…* Yes."

"See?" Alse said.

"I will slice your head off, Alse-Lorie!" Lord Vivien howled. He put a hand on his sword hilt and glared at Alse with two burning, bright black eyes. "Is there something *you* aren't telling us about yourself?"

"*Ké... ohé... gé...* Yes."

The color drained from Alse's face. Yet Lord Vivien focused anew on the High Priest of Og. Roland, looking nauseous, bolted out of the room. Alse-Lorie struggled again to get out, but the knight's grip was iron strong.

"Is there any battle we can win?" said Lord Vivien.

"*Mé... ohé... thé...* No."

Lord Vivien looked desperate. His eyes had widened, and what little color there had been in his fair face had completely disappeared.

"Is the nation done for?"

"*Ké... ohé... gé...* Yes."

At the answer, a fresh burst of despair surged through Alse's bones. She let out a desperate wail, and in her sadness and darkness of heart a new strength filled her. She broke free of the knight's iron grasp and fled the throne room.

She fled all the way to the Lady's Cathedral and laid her hands upon the altar. *If you will not save me,* she prayed, *save our nation. If you curse me to shame and death, save our nation. For our nation's life is worth far more than mine...*

Chapter Forty-Two:
The Mouse

Ramden

Everyone in Castle Silvergold resented him—that much was beyond doubt. He could see how Mother looked at him when he was carried into the feasting hall. He could see the looks of scorn by Ramonette and the patronizing kindness of now Lord Ramone. He could see it in the castle servants when they brought him glasses of wine or plates of charcuterrie. To them he was Ramden the Cripple.

To himself, he was Ramden the Mouse. Once, he had been the bear rampant of House Rambée. Now every shadow could hide General Sylla's dark face, every unexplored space could hold a hand waiting to snatch him.

It was morning when the castle servants took him into the feasting hall. They set him on a bench with the rest of the ducal family. The morning meal was set on great trenchers—pan-fried eggs, crispy bacon, and great hunks of farmer's cheese. Bowls of raisins, dried fruits and nuts sat interspersed between them. Lord Ramone took his seat right after Ramden, followed by Ramonette, Ramondine, and Mother.

The knights and high-ranking castle officials had taken their place at the tables below. They had less charming fare.

"Your brother is getting married," said Mother.

Ramden didn't care. He took a bite of crispy bacon. Castle servants brought him a cup of tea, which he drank.

Mother was glaring at him. "To an Abrenard, no less. Aimee. You met her once, a few years ago—she was just a girl."

Ramden remembered what it was like to walk. He

remembered what it was like to run, leap, and ride. It was not long ago when he raced into Duchy Ajernon to steal a bottle of Ajernais gold. He and his fellow knights had drunk deeply that night. Everything had seemed so perfect. Now he was just a shadow of himself—or not even a shadow. Without his legs, without his feet, he was nothing. He could not bear it anymore. Perhaps it would be best if Sylla finished him off. That way, he wouldn't have to look at his fat brother basking in all the praise and glory of Castle Silvergold.

"Aimee vis Abrenard," said Mother. "Do you remember her?"

"I don't care," said Ramden.

"Excuse me?" Mother howled.

"I don't care." Ramden threw his trencher of food. It almost hit Ramondine, who ducked, before it skidded into the midst of the hall.

"Take him back into his room!" Mother snapped. The castle servants immediately laid hold of him. "Don't let him out until tomorrow."

Outside, through the window, the day was sunny and warm. The birds were chirping and the sweet smell of spring wafted through Castle Silvergold. Ramden looked at his shriveled legs, his swollen and disfigured ankles. He gazed at the scars on his hands and arms, were Sylla had slashed him with a knife. Sylla had taken more than his health—he had taken his will to live. But he did not hate Sylla. He was not angry at Sylla, only afraid. He was angry at Mother, and Ramondine, and Ramonette, and above all, at Ramone for taking what he deserved.

A wind blew through the window, hinting of pollen and spring. Ramden realized he had never been this defeated. He had never been so miserable—not even in the torture chamber of Marcus Sylla. Was it any wonder? Everything had been stolen from him in

Castle Silvergold—the dukedom, the respect of the knights and the love of the ladies. He needed to leave Castle Silvergold. He needed to go. Where, he did not know—but he needed to go, and quickly.

Chapter Forty-Three: Penance

The Reverend Alse-Lorie, High Priestess

Had it been a month since the Priests of Og defiled the throne room? Alse-Lorie had lost track. No doubt the shadow of demon fear still lingered there, the remnant of an unspeakable act of evil. In all the following days, she had not returned to Castle Royale. She had stayed within the confines of the Lady's Cathedral and left only briefly. She had forbidden Sir Loy from visiting her—it seemed the least of all things she could do, to stop breaking her vows for as long as she could. Sir Loy no doubt was hurt, as was Alse-Lorie, but the sight of the gallant knight and his handsome face would only compound the guilt.

She could have broken one more vow and brought a dagger to the throne room, then cut out the hearts of every last one of those foul demoniacs.

It was a warm day, more summer than spring, when a visitor entered through the open double doors of the Lady's Cathedral. A dozen knights waited just outside. Alse-Lorie, in her forest-green vestment and pink stole, ran to greet this person. In the sunny day, the stained glass windows' sylph yellows, puck blues, nixie greens and pixie pinks glowed like fire, illuminating the form of Lord Roland, Duke of Valais.

"Your Honor." Alse-Lorie bobbed her head.

"I have come to bring an offering of penance." Lord Roland clutched a bag of coins in his left hand. "One-hundred *sous*, Your Reverence. May the Goddess forgive Lord Vivien for his consultation of Og'og."

Alse-Lorie nodded.

Lord Roland raised his right hand, in which he clutched another bag. "For the Lady's victory and preservation, an offering of one mark in assorted coins. Gouldair vis Voraigne has strayed from faithful service. Our knights have intercepted a letter from Gouldair to the Monster, asking for mercy. Lord Vivien intends to set him straight."

Alse-Lorie gulped. *Lord Vivien, who consulted Og'og?* And was it not long ago that Lord Roland himself strayed, opening up communication with Sylla—the one Roland now called the Monster?

"Sylla will run out of food," said Lord Roland. "The *villeins* have fled into the castles. The grain stores are under close guard. We have severely damaged Sylla's siege machinery. When hunger sets in, Lord Vivien will set upon them… their soldiers will be scattered."

Alse-Lorie was perplexed by Lord Roland's newfound optimism. She took both heavy sacks of coins and set them on the altar. Such a grand sum of money would pay for many things. But she doubted it would buy the Lady's favor. It would buy Varysse's bribe. She could not let any junior priestesses know about this money. "What of the king?" said Alse-Lorie, turning back to Roland.

"He remains marooned at Castle Holmgray," Lord Roland said. "Goddess preserve him. He is in good company, though, with Lord Eurelien."

Alse-Lorie had no faith in Lord Roland's abilities, though she no longer questioned his will to claim the victory. She had less faith in King Jourmande's abilities and his will to succeed. She had faith only in King Jourmande's ability to lose, his ability to bring the kingdom low and then bring it lower.

Chapter Forty-Four:
Lies and More Lies

Eurelien vis Námois, Duke of Duranche

The gates of Castle Holmgray did not open for just anyone. Not even "a battalion of knights" as the eager servant said, "bearing the Red Hawk of the Voraignes."

Grudgingly Eurelien heaved his old bones out of the keep and up the wooden steps to the battlements. Indeed, a hundred knights waited below on the bridge, some bearing Voraignese standards—the Red Hawk on a rose field. The chief of them, Eurelien recognized as Gouldair's favorite, Sir Angres.

"Open the gates!" called out Sir Angres. "I demand to speak to the king."

Eurelien had kept up this game for many weeks now, and he'd be damned if he would back down now. "The king does not wait at your beck and call!" Eurelien shouted. "His Majesty is busy. He will not leave Castle Holmgray. Its defense is vital to our mission."

"I come with demands, directly from our lord Gouldair, Duke of Voraigne! It is about that pesky young boy, Roland, the king's own nephew!"

Rage was written all over Sir Angres' features. He had turned a shade of pink. "Lord Roland is the commander of the war effort!" Eurelien bellowed. "The king will not hear your futile petitions. The king is busy!"

"The king has not been seen in months!" Sir Angres shouted. There was a bloodthirsty look to his eyes. "Some have begun to say he is dead, and that you killed him, Eurelien!"

Eurelien sighed. Under the king's express orders, Eurelien had told no one about his visit to the Empire. It never struck Eurelien that he could suffer because of it.

"The king's pet Roland has been harassing the noble Lord Gouldair, even threatening violence against him!" Sir Angres snapped. "I have come far down country roads, through wild woods and burning fields! I demand to speak to King Jourmande *at once!* It is the least a duke of the Seven Gems deserves!"

"Roland is his deputy," said Eurelien. "Perhaps I can help."

"You cannot!" cried Sir Angres. "You have proven yourself useless as any! Under the Young Duke we have no hope of victory! Castle Hombard has fallen! *Castle Hombard!*"

Eurelien had heard of Castle Hombard's fall—the unassailable castle which had belonged to him, which had not once fallen in its almost thousand-year history.

"Tell your king Vale of Roy is overrun by bandits! Tell him bandits now live in Castle Moonsilver! Elven bandits. *Elves!*"

Eurelien had nothing to say.

"Perhaps that will wake him from his slumber!" hissed Sir Angres. "Or the death-blow you inflicted on him. Eurelien, you snake!" He turned and galloped north out of the village into the swamps of Montée March, along the upraised dirt path. The chirping of grasshoppers echoed through the otherwise quiet dusk. The sun was setting. Eurelien left the battlements, having never felt so alone.

Chapter Forty-Five:
Broken Faith

His Majesty King Jourmande vis Bretagne

In this city of the gods, Jourmande had never been so uncomfortable. His insulting living quarters, the Villa of Leto, crawled with cockroaches and scorpions. The chefs in Jourmande's retinue had no way to properly roast a pig or steam Swordfish Royeau, and thus Imperial meals would have to do. The Imperial cuisine was far too spicy to be healthy, and the wine was too harsh. Amid these towering buildings of marble—some of which could fit all of Castle Royeau snugly inside—vendors sold mass-cooked food in shops where Imperial lowborns actually sat down and ate. King Jourmande, even now, did not stoop to such a low.

One morning, in the dining room, as one of Jourmande's chefs was bringing back a dish to the villa proper, Dame Alesandre rushed in through the door. "Your Majesty," the gray-haired woman said, "I have something to show you."

Without hesitation, King Jourmande stood up from his seat at the table and followed her. Dame Alesandre led him to the common area where the court gathered at night, and pointed out a hole in the wall.

"I found it this morning," said Alesandre. "They have been watching us. Listening to us. I caught him this morning."

"Who?" cried Jourmande.

"A young man in a white tunic. He ran in the direction of the Imperial Palace. He disappeared into the crowd before I could catch him."

"Good Goddess," Jourmande said. 'Their disrespect for

me… it is unbelievable. And heartbreaking."

Dame Alesandre shook her head. "There are other spy holes, no doubt. I will find them and fill them in."

"We will not have to worry about it, anymore. Our meeting is today." At least there was that. Yet the event had its own share of stresses and sadness. He would have to convince the Imperial government, somehow, to stop this war, to agree to a peace—a peace which, by all accounts, would prove humiliating.

Around midday, long after Jourmande had eaten his fill of bread and olives, there was a knock on the door. He opened it, and there, found Councilor Corvus and a dozen Imperial soldiers in red capes. Over time, Jourmande had grown distrustful of the skeevy, slimy Councilor Corvus. There was something about his carefully-groomed black hair and manicured appearance that belied deceit. Surely Corvus was a weasel, as untrustworthy as he was important to Jourmande's cause.

"My Signor King," Corvus said, "I am very sorry. The Imperial Council must reschedule the hearing. Something important has come up… a matter of no small importance. I promise we will hear you out within two weeks, at the very most. The council looks forward to it."

Dame Alesandre rushed up to Jourmande's side, and even without seeing her face, Jourmande could sense her boiling anger.

"The Speaker of the Council, the August Gaius Vorenus, has expressed his regrets, and by a two-thirds vote the council agrees." Jourmande could not tell if Corvus was mocking them. Surely he was a slippery, skeevy man. "The councilors are all very busy people. We know the wait was hard for you and I wish I was bringing you better news."

"Enough of this!" howled Dame Alesandre. "We have waited for a long time. Too long! Longer than you or I deserve! This madness ends now."

Yet Dame Alesandre had been disarmed, like they all had been, besides Jourmande.

"If this is how you lowborn trash treat a king, then—*by the Goddess!*—I will… I will…"

Corvus stepped backward. "I am very sorry. When I scheduled you for today, I did not know the Maestro of Food and Wine would have a presentation for us. None of us knew before yesterday."

"The *Maistre* of Food and Wine—" howled Alesandre. "Words fail me. His Majesty has never been so disrespected! Our nation is being destroyed, and you postpone our meeting for two weeks! How dare you! How *dare* you! By the way, you sniveling snake, I know you've been spying on us. I know you've been listening in on us! I saw your spy this morning!"

"Enough, Alesandre!" shouted Jourmande. He glared at Corvus. There was still a smile on that skeevy weasel's face. "I cannot wait two weeks. I have waited long enough. I have traveled very far."

"That much is clear," said Corvus. "But the Imperial Council has many meetings. I am afraid we cannot reschedule. It must be two weeks… and I will do everything in my power to ensure you are not delayed any more—though, I am afraid, my Signor King, I cannot make any firm promises."

"*Seigneur King,* you call him!" howled Alesandre. "If I had my sword you'd be cut in two by now."

"Please, no threats of violence," said Corvus. "I know you have traveled far. The Imperial Council states its regret."

"Back off, Alesandre," Jourmande said, and she left in a huff. "Corvus, this is madness. We have already waited weeks. Our lodgings are poor. The food is inadequate. Surely there is something that can be done." No King of Zarubain had ever been so disrespected in history. He was treated like any other petitioner, like any lowborn off the streets which they called "citizens."

"If we may speak, man to man," said Corvus, "an hour after sundown, in front of the Imperial Treasury…"

"Of course," Jourmande said. What could this Corvus possibly have in mind?

"Come alone. Bring no guards, and I will not, either. Break protocol at all, and our deal is done."

~

Each minute that day seemed an hour, and each hour a life-age. Surely in the Otherworld the Goddess was weeping, and her fairy attendants lamented the fall of the Kingdom of Zarubain. Surely Saint Ignáce was full of scorn and hatred. Or perhaps the Goddess herself was a fiction, and the supposed fey were merely natural phenomena—such an idea had been posited before. It would not surprise Jourmande. What was life but a series of coincidences, destined to drag himself and his kingdom further into the ruin? The golden age of the Zarube kings was over—did he need any more evidence?

With only a dozen knights—Sir Pettigrew, Sir Didier and a few others—Jourmande left the squalor of the villa and entered the bustling streets of Imperial City. He needed to walk and clear his head. The titanic buildings which stretched to the sky, the young and vibrant population, the wealth and power which pulsed from this hive of humanity, might serve to pour further shame on King Jourmande, but he did not care. To stay another moment in that cockroach-filled villa was to lose his mind.

The air was dry and congested, a bit smoky. The sun—as always—beat down on them. No cloud could be seen in the sky. It had been bright blue every day since they had come. King Jourmande missed the clouds, the cool winds and rain. It was a true miracle that there was enough water for everyone.

In a market square, Jourmande was greeted by a fountain.

Floral patterns were etched along its circular rim. A woman's face had been carved in stone, and out of her puckered lips water spurted. The face had a glib, almost fey look to it. He wondered if it was a portrait of the fairy goddess herself.

Jourmande cupped some cool water in his hands and drank deep.

"Your Majesty!" cried Sir Pettigrew.

The water of the River Zaros was foul and deadly to drink, but Jourmande had never seen water so pure and clear. He did not fear as he drank the handful, and then another. He had lost all the respect of his knights and his lords and ladies; what did it matter that the King of Zarubain now stooped over a public fountain, shoveling water into his mouth like a beast of the field?

"It is good." Jourmande turned and eyed the dark-featured knight. "Like a mountain spring. Cool, and refreshing."

"I will not risk it," said Sir Pettigrew, "and neither should you."

The red-roofed buildings surrounding the market square had been defaced. In bold black paint, messages had been scrawled. "Vote Fioro," one said, and another—marred by a black slash—said "Vote Horatio." When the lords and ladies of Zarubain heard of this concept of "voting," they had been scornful and amused. But did Zarubain build temples that scratched the sky, or fountains that bubbled like mountain springs?

"You look like a rich man." A merchant had appeared in front of him. Jourmande stepped back and nearly fell. It was the foreigner from before, the dusky man in the white cotton turban. In his hand he held a golden cage, and inside a red-scaled dragonette, flitting about and breathing out burps of smoke. "She is my last one. A beautiful specimen. A great pet, certainly, and a wonder of the world. Such pets are bred in the Far South, my good man. Yes! The King of Kings himself has a menagerie. Take her home, and she will live for thirty years. She will be your steadfast and loyal companion!

She will never leave your side!"

"Back away from His Majesty!" thundered Sir Pettigrew.

But Jourmande poked his finger through the cage. The dragonette, no bigger than the finger itself, nibbled on it with tiny white teeth. Just as quickly Jourmande withdrew his finger. He wondered how this crazed merchant had followed him. In a city of incomparable size, how had he zeroed in on Jourmande? Jourmande supposed a bit of fear might be appropriate—after all, a city of this size was bound to have its share of madmen—but the merchant was not armed, and Jourmande still had *Fairbolt* at his side. "Have you been following me, *Seigneur* Merchant?"

"Why, no… not anymore than the others." The merchant smiled brightly. "The whole city is speaking of the strange appearance of the 'northman king.' I, Fharad, seller of all things weird and wonderful, am the only one bold enough to approach."

Jourmande sighed. "Leave me. I do not want your pathetic dragonette." He looked around and noticed, for the first time, Imperial lowborns staring at him, wondering at his presence. The whole city knew of his humiliation. Perhaps he should leave.

But in the dark of night, Jourmande left the Villa of Leto just the same. Music—lyres and lutes, singing voices and tambourines—echoed through the cool night air. In the windows of the towering buildings, lanterns were lit. Even after sunset, the streets bustled with people—yet an altogether different set. In Imperial Square, women in short skirts and skin-tight brassieres called after passersby. "Ten *denara*," one cooed at Jourmande, "for the night of your life."

The whorehouses of Zarubad did a roaring trade, and many even in the nobility took part in such excesses, but this scene was altogether different. All throughout Imperial Square, colored glass lanterns—bright reds, warm oranges, and brilliant blues—illuminated the colossal buildings and statues in a kaleidoscope of hues. The sounds of shouting and laughter were as thick as they had been in the afternoon, but the merchants had been replaced with revelers and ne'er-do-wells. The harsh scent of alcohol hung thick in the square. Journmande could use a thick class of Ajernais gold himself, right now—anything to soothe his nerves.

At the foot of the Imperial treasury were two towering bronze colossi. One, forged in the shape of a hooded woman, held a pair of scales in her hand—*Justice*. She was three times the height of of Journmande. Opposite her, another colossus towered—this, forged in the shape of a crowned woman, holding a cornucopia in one hand and a gold bar in the other. *Prosperity*. Just how much money could this immense building contain? Enough to buy up all the Seven Gems and the kingdom itself? Certainly, enough to fund the horrid war for a dozen years. He shuddered at his poor bargaining position—pleas of mercy, in exchange for peace.

A shadow stood beneath Justice—a dark shape in a hooded gray robe.

"Corvus," Journmande breathed. He drew near.

The shadow drew a knife from the folds of his robe. "Another step, northman, and I'll cut you ear to ear."

"Psst!" said another voice.

Journmande, faint with fear, turned. Corvus stood a short distance away behind him, wearing a light blue coat. Journmande walked up to him.

"Imperial Square is dangerous at night," said Corvus. "Didn't your mother ever teach you as much?"

"My mother," Journmande said, "taught me nothing about the Imperials at all. And my dealings with them taught me they are violent, destructive, and merciless."

"A pity," Corvus said. "I am sure your visit has changed your mind."

"It has added 'rude' to the list. After you kept me waiting many weeks, then asked me to wait more."

Corvus smiled. "The Imperial Council is confused about your visit. That is why they have refused to meet with you. They do not understand why you've come uninvited, and are understandably nervous."

"Understandably?" Jourmande laughed. "What threat could an ailing, seventy-five-year-old man possibly pose?"

Corvus laughed lightly. "My signore, we are naturally cautious. Our nations have not been on good terms since… since the war."

"Indeed." Jourmande remembered all too well the battle he had personally lost, the humiliating and costly victory which the Imperials had claimed. "Which is why, Corvus, as the only man I know in your Imperial Council, that I am begging you… as an old, harmless, seventy-five-year-old man, that you will hear me out. We must stop this war."

"The war." Corvus' eyebrows narrowed.

"The senseless violence must end."

"I can ensure a meeting tomorrow afternoon," Corvus said, "but you must come alone. You may not bring any of your knights or advisors. You must trust us completely."

"I do not trust you," Jourmande said, "but I will come."

Chapter Forty-Six:
The Lion on the Ramparts

Gouldair vis Voraigne, Duke of Voraigne

The trees of the forest seemed darker and gloomier, the gentle warmth of summer choking and oppressive. A great host had assembled outside the borders of Duchy Voraigne, threatening violence. The mood in Voraigne Manor had turned grim; the mood in the Ville, even worse. Gouldair could scarcely think. Out here, in the midst of the firs and pines, he at least felt at peace. The woodpeckers and kingfishers did not think about the troubles of the wider world, nor did they concern themselves with war. The stags which bounded through the mossy forest did not care who won—Imperials or Zarubes—and in truth, neither did Gouldair.

But if I surrender now, Roland will have me killed if he claims the victory. The road led past the lake just outside Voraigne Manor. The broad dirt path wound its way through the woods, eventually leading into the heart of the Ville of Jacquerre. Gouldair, not for the first time, considered mounting a horse and riding away, away from the problems of this world and the struggles of this life. Gouldair, a man of sixty-two, had seen little trouble before these dark events had come to pass. A relative peace had prevailed throughout the Seven Gems and the Eastern and Western Heartlands. The name vis Voraigne had been second only to vis Valais among the great ducal families. Yet in the wake of the Imperial onslaught, old friends and alliances had vanished. The future—for once in a millennium—had seemed uncertain. The peasantry in the Ville and the wider duchy were, for the first time in generations, being conscripted. Every knight in Gouldair's territory had been summoned, girt in steel, and asked to fight in the name of the Lion.

But Gouldair no longer cared about the Lion. He cared about the survival of the Red Hawk of the Voraignes, the preservation of its boundless wealth, the endurance of its prosperity and easy living. His wife Helysse felt the same way.

Yet here Gouldair was, in the woods of Duchy Voraigne, beside Silent Lake where the spring geese had returned. The ancient sword of the Voraigne was in his hand, outside its sheath, but wielded by an unwilling hand. The road stretched before him—and if he followed, where would it lead? Would it lead to the Royal City, where the king was conspicuously absent? Would it take him to far-off Badelgard, or the Elven World?

"Your Lordship!" a voice cried.

Gouldair turned and sheathed *Faircrys*. A messenger approached on a horse. There was a rolled-up letter in his hand.

"A message, Your Lordship!" the messenger continued.

A wax seal bound the letter. The red seal that bore the markings of an eagle. This was from none other than Sylla, the one they called the Monster. He broke it at once and let it unravel:

TO HIS EXCELLENCY GOULDAIR, THE
COMMANDER OF VORAIGNE:

I AM RUNNING OUT OF PATIENCE. I AM A MAN
OF GREAT RESOLVE AND INCREDIBLE SELF-
CONTROL, BUT I WILL NOT WAIT MUCH
LONGER. BEFORE SUNDOWN I EXPECT AN
ANSWER—WILL YOU DEFY ME AND MEET THE
SAME FATE AS JORJÉ? OR WILL YOU SUBMIT AND
RULE YOUR OWN LAND AS A CLIENT OF THE
GLORIOUS EMPIRE?

—SYLLA, GRAND LEGATE

Voraigne paled. The time had come to make a decision, a decision of impossible difficulty. He shuddered at the thought of the Black Count, beaten to a bloody pulp, discarded like trash. Gouldair dropped the letter and stamped it into the mud. "Summon all men-at-arms and knights into Voraigne Manor and the border posts. Tell the folk of the Ville to prepare for a siege. I have made my choice—to fight for the Lion."

That night, within the cold stone walls of Voraigne Manor, he had trumpets blare the tune of "The Lion on the Ramparts."

"The Lion," he sang along, "The Lion, The Lion on the Ramparts."

Time would tell if he acted wisely, or made a devastating mistake.

Chapter Forty-Seven:
A House of Cards

The Reverend Alse-Lorie, High Priestess

"Long term, Sylla's position is unsustainable."

Lord Roland's projections, spoken in the throne room, seemed overy optimistic to Alse-Lorie.

"He has destroyed the countryside. There will not be enough food to feed thirty thousand men."

"Or two hundred thousand city folk in Zarubad," quipped Sir Euliver, the knight grandmaster who had come to bring bad news. The hallowed throne room needed a good dose of pessimism. "The lowborn will riot."

"Shall we fear a mob of lowborns?" said Roland. "A poor, hungry mob of common men without proper weaponry or armor?"

Roland's sunny disposition did little to change what Sir Euliver, Knight Grandmaster of the Order of the Pillar, had told them. "The Vale of Roy is disintegrating," Sir Euliver repeated, a noble effort to instill sense into the Young Duke. "Bandit rule has replaced the rule of the steward. The southern marches have re-declared for the Empire. I do not think you know the gravity of the situation. It worries me that you are not concerned. Duchy Voraigne is on the verge of capitulating. Panic has set in throughout all the Seven Gems. And you refuse to take the lead."

"I am the leader. The king has appointed me."

"The king!" Sir Euliver cried, exasperated. "The king is gone. Most everyone considers him dead! He has not been seen in more than a month! Some say the Duke of Duranche killed him."

"He is right," Alse-Lorie said. "The king is gone. If he was alive he would have shown himself by now. We should force the Duke of Duranche to confess."

A familiar condescension appeared in Lord Roland's eyes as he glared at Alse-Lorie. His attention quickly turned back to Sir Euliver. "Whether he is gone or not, I am still the grand general of this war effort. I will not have a baby giving orders."

"If we declare the king dead," Alse sneered, "then Tyrol would inherit the throne by rights… and his mother the queen would assume command."

Lord Roland's cheeks turned a bright shade of pink. "The king is not dead. There has been no evidence of his death. He has appointed *me* head of the war effort… not Alysant, and certainly not *you*, priestess."

Alse-Lorie had grown to hate Roland over these past weeks. King Jourmande had been incompetent, a bumbling fool who had bungled the war and made poor choice after poor choice, but he had shown utmost chivalry. He had respected the opinions of his lady wife, and of Alse, in addition to all the princesses, maids, and ladies of the court. All the peasant girls and country maidens fawned over the Young Duke and spoke giddily of his handsome face and great gallantry—yet if they met him, all their love and worship would end. He was the least chivalrous duke in the nation. He treated his peasant-born advisor, Lord Mars, better than his own wife.

Lord Roland had focused once more on the only person in the conversation whom he respected—Sir Euliver. "We will wait Sylla out. He is running out of resources. His capacity to win sieges is diminishing. Much of the scorpions and catapults he brought have been destroyed. It takes skilled builders to fashion them. Sooner or later, he will be isolated and alone. Even his friends will abandon him. And every last one of the marquises will be marched to the gallows and hanged."

Such brutal justice had rarely been done to noblemen, and never in recent times, but on that point, at least, Alse could agree.

The faithless deserved death. *I am faithless, too,* she thought, *in my own way.* She considered running outside, leaping into the River Zaros, and having it carry her out to the sea.

Sir Euliver, obviously exasperated, turned and left.

"I do believe the Goddess is turning the tide," said Roland. To Alse's great surprise, his dark eyes were fixed on her.

She could not bear to meet his gaze. Her wrath would not end, not until Lord Roland had been put back in his place. Not until Roland was sent back to Duchy Valais where he belonged, with the ever-tearful Lady Elsie and the stupid Lord Mars.

~

That night, she lit a candle in her private quarters. High in the cathedral, she peered out a window. The thatch roofs of the townhouses and the towering steeples of the churches stretched far beyond the banks of the River Zaros. A hive of people lived there, poor and destitute. Here in the Inner City there was food and life. There was enough to weather the harshest siege. While the poor folk fed on vegetables and watered-down wine, the people of the Inner City feasted on roast boar or the king's dreaded high cuisine. Where the poor folk worried about fires, floods, and plague, here—in Zarube society's upper echelons—the concerns were petty jealousies over which duke was richer than whom, of which duchess wore the best Mierese gown, of which duke had the prettiest wife. The war had changed it somewhat. For the first time in their lives, the nobles had to honor their ancient commitment—to fight.

Alse wandered to her wardrobe. Tucked behind her silk nightclothes and wool slippers was a small jar. She opened it. Inside was powdered Grayman's beard, dried and pummeled in a mortar. A little bit would prevent pregnancy; a great swallow would terminate one. If anyone saw this, she would be forced out of the priesthood, stripped, shaved, and set on a cucking stool. In Lions Square in the

Outer City, she would sit in shame before the lowborn. A wooden sign would proclaim, "THE MOTHER OF WHORES."

She wetted her finger, dipped it in the Grayman's beard, and ate. She expected Sir Loy tonight. Their love could not and would not end. They had all but married. She said a prayer to any spirit or lesser god that would hear her—*stall the Goddess's justice, let this house of cards remain standing for another month, another year, another decade.*

Sir Loy was coming.

Chapter Forty-Eight:
Fever Dreams

Danitari

Thunder cracked and rolled across Castle Moonsilver, and the rain began immediately. Wind howled by the door of Danitari's prison, a dozen winds like angry ghosts. It seemed the foundations of the world were shaken and an apocalyptic beast was rising, a beast with iron teeth. The rain and wind might blow the castle away, Danitari thought. He couldn't do anything about it. He was hungry, tired, and weak. He was naked and weaponless, unable to survive outside these dark shadowy walls that had become his home.

Outside, his fellow slaves were screaming in panic. Another crack of thunder boomed across the castle, and the winds' ghostly choir shrieked at the birth of the beast. Danitari shut his eyes and tried to imagine the Great Elven Plain, but the storm had followed him there, and great purple thunderheads were rolling in. Flood and fire and destruction would surely follow him. The world's foundations would falter and sink under the sea. Though covered in sweat Danitari shivered. Though shivering in fear, he could not bring himself to pray.

Chapter Forty-Nine:
The End of the World

Ramden

Ramden had seen storms before, but never like this. He stared out the window, speechless. The sky had turned deep purple. A spear of lightning flashed and a deafening crack of thunder ripped across the woods. As rain pounded the roof of Castle Silvergold and fell in a flood off the stone walls, the wind howled and shrieked, almost forming words. Ramden did not know magic or dwemer-craft. He did not know what the winds were screaming.

Is the world ending? Ramden wondered. He did not want to die a cripple, lying in bed in his private room. But he did not want to live to age seventy like this either, unable to ride a horse.

The world was ending for someone, surely. Such a deluge would flood the rivers. Such a deluge would turn the seas into a boiling kettle. Waves would upturn ships and crack their hulls. Bodies would wash up days later. *At least I am not a mariner,* Ramden thought. But if he were a mariner, he would still have his feet. Mariners did not fight on land. Mariners were not captured by Syllas or crippled.

In the rain and thunder, Ramden slept easy. He dreamed—as he had every night—of Sylla. This time, he was riding a beast with iron teeth.

Chapter Fifty:
Hard Bargains

His Majesty King Jourmande vis Bretagne

Jourmande rose late. On the eighth hour after dawn, he gathered his courage and made his way to the door. Dame Alesandre nearly stopped him.

"You do not need to do this," she said. "We can always go back. We can always return. And you would return with your dignity."

"I want to return with more than my dignity," said Jourmande. "Perhaps, for you, that is enough."

He left into the baking hot streets of Imperial City, under a clear blue sky.

~

In the stifling heat, Jourmande made his way to the heavily guarded road which led to the Council House. The titanic building had a white pillared dome, and was connected to the vast complex of the Imperial Palace by a sky bridge.

A battalion of Imperial guards stood watch there. Red capes fell down their backs and red horsehair crests on their helmets contrasted with the dark steel of their armor. On their shields, golden eagles were painted against a red background. In their hands they gripped swords.

"Signores!" the tallest of them cried, then spoke some words in Imperial. Like ants they moved in unison, letting Jourmande by. The road would be lonely and Jourmande would have no protection.

I am at their mercy, he thought, *but they are my only hope.*

High walls guarded this elite pathway. The road—as all those in Imperial City—was of carefully-fitted stones. More ambitious kings than Jourmande had tried to pave Zarubad's narrow streets and winding thoroughfares, but their efforts had been neglected, left to be chipped and weathered. Imperial City's had been carefully maintained, and still gleamed white and fresh as the day they were first laid.

An eagle soared overhead. Jourmande had not yet seen a lion. He pressed on, gathering his thoughts, summoning all his courage. More soldiers appeared, guarding the narrow walkway. They paid him no heed. At last Jourmande entered the bright white edifice.

Inside, the walls were painted gold and red. The marble floor bore the sign of an eagle with a snake in its beak.

"Greetings!" said Councilor Corvus, who had been waiting for him. "We look forward to hearing your request."

The slimy councilor's words were empty, Jourmande knew. The shame of the situation weighed on Jourmande like a sack of stones. He cursed himself. He cursed the nation for falling this far.

Then he followed Councilor Corvus up the winding marble stairs.

~

The giant room at the top of the Council House made it clear who stood where, and who was more important. The thirty seats of the Councilors lay several feet above the marble floor. Two seats—one bright yellow and lined with gold, and another white and lined with silver—lay in the opposite direction, both elevated, but neither occupied.

The stern faces of the councilors examined Jourmande. Most were old, with white or salt-and-pepper hair. There were only a few young faces—and to his shock, a ratling stood there with black fur and whiskers, dressed in a purple-sashed white robe like the others. The Zarubes despised ratlings almost as much as elves. They were not even allowed in the Royal City. Yet here one stood in the attire of a councilor, a leader of the government. Jourmande withheld a gasp.

One of the councilors spoke, a middle-aged man with light brown hair: "Greetings, northman king. I am Gaius Vorenus."

Guards appeared at either doorway, bearing swords.

"What is your request?" Vorenus continued.

"My friends," said Jourmande, and immediately regretted it. *They are not my friends; they are my enemies. They are wolves, respecting only strength, hungering for the flesh of innocents.* "I wish to put an end to this war. We in Zarubain have canceled your debt. And yet you have attacked us. I wish for peace, as any good king does. I wish to end this war, and make amends. I wish—"

"I am confused," Vorenus said. "What war?"

Jourmande sighed. These Imperials wanted to play games. "Enough!" he cried. "I came to have a reasonable discussion, not to be mocked!" The deaths of all the innocents were a grave matter. He remembered Lord Falerien, burned at the stake. He remembered Lord Jorjé, the Black Count, bludgeoned and beaten beyond recognition. He remembered all the knights that had fallen, men and women from good families. He cursed the war, and he cursed this world.

"We are not mocking you," said Corvus. "We are earnestly confused."

"Your general Sylla has laid waste to the old Zarubain. He has burned the good men and women of our kingdom alive. He has torched cities and brought low ancient fortresses!" The emotion pouring from Jourmande was a tactical error, but he could not help himself. *Poor Falerien. Poor Jorjé.*

"Sylla," one councilor said, as if repeating a foreign word.

"Sylla," Corvus said in the same manner.

"Sylla!" snapped Vorenus. "Marcus Sylla! The Winter Wolf!"

A few gasps echoed through the dome-roofed council chamber.

"Northman King," said Vorenus, "are you saying Sylla has crossed into your territory?"

"With thirty thousand men," said Jourmande.

"Sylla is a war criminal," said Vorenus, "a wanted man in the Empire. Three legions were loyal to him. He called himself a grand legate but he was never appointed. In our civil war, he took advantage of the chaos. He rampaged across the province of Gad. He massacred entire towns. He raided the Temple of Sollust and cut off the head of the High Priest. He is a madman, a mass murderer…"

"And a brilliant general," added Corvus.

Jourmande gasped. *To think this war was never authorized. To think that the Empire is his enemy, too.*

"There is a rumor that in the winter of '01, his men resorted to cannibalism one snowy night," Vorenus said.

Jourmande gagged.

"There is no official war on the books, in short," said Vorenus. "We have no power to stop him."

All the relief that had washed through Jourmande's body dissipated. "You do," he insisted. "You can help us defeat his legions. You can send an army of your own."

Vorenus laughed openly. "And what would our Empire gain from such an action?"

"Our eternal friendship," said Jourmande. By the looks on their faces, the councilors were unimpressed.

Corvus wore that slimy smile on his face once more. "My Signor King, you will have to do better than that."

"The life of my nation is at stake!" Jourmande cried, but his words fell on deaf ears.

"Make it worth our while, Signor King," said Corvus.

"You can have all of Mekara," Jourmande said. "The entire region, from the River Zarube to your Wall. You can have what was

Castle New."

"Keep talking," said Corvus.

"You may post an official embassy in our Royal City, and trade missions in our great towns… and you can have a payment of ten marks."

"Make it a hundred," said Corvus.

"Very well," Jourmande said. The price was staggering, the terms unfair to the Zarube nation. But what more priceless than peace?

"We must deliberate," said Corvus, "and seek the approval of our emperor. You will hear back from us, soon."

~

Three days later, Corvus appeared at the door of the Villa of Leto. "Good news," he told Jourmande. "By a unanimous vote, and the approval of our emperor, we have agreed to your terms. Sylla will be destroyed."

Chapter Fifty-One:
Deepwood Hollow

Ramden

It was near summer and the tulips and roses were in full bloom when Ramden decided he had to flee. He had escaped the terror and dread of Sylla and had arrived into something far worse—despair. Mother, Ramondine, Ramonette and Ramone despised him above all else. They glared when the servants carried him in for dinner. They whispered about him when they thought he couldn't hear. Mother was going to remarry; a gentleman, a landless noble of the Poncée family, from Surrevere, had been staying with them. He was as plain, old, and boring as Mother. The thought of them together angered Ramden—it seemed an insult to his father, the honorable, courageous, and bold Lord Ramir.

Ramden, looking out his bedroom window, saw a wild and dangerous world. Beyond the red roses, the pink tulips and the fragrant lilacs lay a thick and dense wood where Ramden had once hunted. Beyond the forest, down the road, lay a kingdom at war, in peril of its life. Anything was better than the empty feeling that consumed him—anything, even death. He thought he still might be able to ride, even if he couldn't walk. His favorite horse Quicksilver was still alive. Of all the living things in Castle Silvergold, Quicksilver alone still respected him, still loved him.

His brother Ramone was getting married, too, to a young woman from Duchy Ajernon. Aimee was far too pretty for his fat, stupid brother. She had long golden hair and the brightest green eyes that Ramden had ever seen. She had a laugh that made Ramden think of a nymph or some fairy. Ramden had survived Sylla's hell and had received something worse. Ramone had sat on his rear for months and got what he didn't deserve—all of Duchy Lessant, and Aimee. Ramden hoped Sylla killed Ramone once and for all.

In the warm morning light a servant entered, bringing breakfast—stewed potatoes topped with crumbled bacon. Another servant had brought tea. "Master Ramden," one said—not "lord."

Ramden was not hungry. "My good men—take me to the stables. I have need of something."

"Yes, Master Ramden," a servant said.

It was a long and difficult journey for the servants before they reached the stables of Castle Silvergold. Ramden was no less uncomfortable. "There," he grunted, pointing to Quicksilver's stall. "Put on his saddle, and bind me to it."

"Master Ramden…" one of the servants objected.

"Now," Ramden ordered.

They set him down in the dirt and straw of the stable as they obeyed his command. They bound the saddle around Quicksilver's spotted white body, and then led the giant charger out of his stall.

"Are you sure?" said the servant.

"Now," Ramden grunted again. His legs and ankles burned with pain. For a second he doubted himself, wondering if he had made the right choice. Then he thought of Mother married to the old lout from Surrevere, and Ramone, Duke of Lessant, marrying beautiful Aimee. He cursed his family and himself, and no longer doubted his actions.

The servants heaved him into the saddle. They fit his feet into the stirrups. Ramden kicked the horse and clucked, then screamed at the pain. Quicksilver took off at a trot, leaving the stables of Castle Silvergold, and then the castle gate itself.

Pain spiked through Ramden's legs. Each step of Quicksilver

filled him with unbearable pain. Tears formed in his eyes. He could not scream or even think. Quicksilver was headed to the woods. Amid the fields of flowers and the tall grass, in the bright warmth of the sunny day, Ramden at last slipped and fell. He hit the ground hard, breaking something. He cried out in pain and began sobbing. Quicksilver wandered away.

Each breath Ramden caused spikes of pain to shudder through his torso. Each sob filled him with torment. How could he be so stupid? How could he be so foolish?

An hour of agony passed by. He drifted off to an uneasy sleep.

"Ramden! Ramden!" The angry howling of his mother woke him. It was late afternoon and the sun was low in the sky. "What in Varda have you done? Have you lost your mind?"

Ramden did not dare speak. His ribs were broken and even breathing was torture.

"I am ashamed of you!" she howled. "We have done so much to accommodate your injuries, and this is how you repay us! Well, I'll never!"

"Go away," Ramden moaned. Tears of pain trickled down his cheeks.

"Go away?" she howled again. "And leave you to the wolves?"

"Wolves are better than you," said Ramden.

"Very well!" Mother cried. "The wolves, then! Let me know if you change your mind!"

She turned and left.

At that moment, Ramden gave up. He asked the Goddess to kill him. He asked to never wake up again. Once more he drifted off into an uneasy sleep.

He dreamed of a world like Varda, but where the stars were bright and tinted pink and blue. He dreamed of a world where the grass, the tulips and the roses were as colorful and lively as a painting, and where the moon pulsed with greenish light. He dreamed of a world where there was no Castle Silvergold, just the wild woods and hills.

Then he woke up in the lesser world. It was the dark of night and the stars were shining. The moon was out, a pale white glow; and the grass, the tulips and roses were dim and dark. A shadow hovered above Ramden, a lithe shape that he recognized. *Who is it?* "Who are you?"

"Who am I?" said an old woman's voice. "I am Maude, nothing more, nothing less. Just Old Woman Maude."

It was the woods witch from before, the one Ramden had threatened to burn at the stake. Would she kill him now? Would she thrust a sharpened stone knife into his chest? "Are you going to kill me?"

"Kill you?" Maude exclaimed. "Oh, no, no, my sweet Ramden, of course not. Old Woman Maude is going to take you to her home. Old Woman Maude is going to help you. She is going to give you a good supper."

Maude, a wiry old woman, picked Ramden up as if he were a feather. She carried him into the dense dark woods, singing, "*Hey ho! Hey ho! To Deepwood Hollow we go!*"

Unable to resist, Ramden peered around the dark woods. It seemed he had returned to the old world of his dream, with bright blue and pink stars and the rich colors of a painting. The giant pines and firs seemed larger than before. The moss growing on the forest floor had taken on a fey green hue.

The dark woods opened up into a hollow. In the middle lay a house, low to the ground, of wattle and daub and with a roof of thatch. A menagerie of animals was waiting for Maude—squirrels, a black bear, two foxes and a number of weasels.

"Hello, friends!" Maude called out. "Do not be afraid of this Ramden. He will not hurt you—I'll make sure of it."

Inside Maude had prepared a bed for him. Gently she laid him down, light as a pebble, and wrapped him in warm linen sheets.

"Hush, hush," cooed Maude. "Hush, hush… now sleep."

Within seconds Ramden had drifted off, dreaming of that bright colorful world, a world where there were no towns or cities… a world where there was no Castle Silvergold, no war, no pain—a world as the gods had intended, a world of unspoiled nature and eternal plenty.

Chapter Fifty-Two:
Diminished Capacity

Gouldair vis Voraigne, Duke of Voraigne

Gouldair had set up bowls of water all throughout Voraigne Manor. They did not tremor. There were no sappers digging under the manor's stone walls. Three hundred men-at-arms and a dozen knights had not seen anyone stirring through the ducal wood. It was—as his wife Helysse said—completely tranquil.

He left the safety of the keep in the morning. A light fog had rolled in, as it often did. The air was cool, more spring than summer. He climbed the walls up to the battlements. A dozen men-at-arms had been posted there with crossbows.

"Nothing?" Gouldair murmured.

"Nothing at all, milord," said one of them.

It had been the better part of a week. Sylla had an army that could crush all the kingdoms of this world, and yet he had not shown his face once. Reports from the Ville said something similar—all peaceful, all tranquil, no sign of Sylla or the dreaded Imperials. There was not even a hint of war. He had heard no calls of distress from the castles and Villes of the outer parts of the duchy.

"Could he truly have retreated?" said Gouldair, mostly to himself.

These past days had been unnerving. His wife Helysse said she had never seen him this afraid. Gouldair said he had never so firmly stood up in the name of the Lion, so he deserved to be a little afraid. The southern marches had declared for the Empire, quietly accepting submission for the sake of peace. Gouldair had been foolhardy enough to risk his life, and that of sweet Helysse, for the sake of honor or duty or some other vague, ill-defined notion that he—as nobleman—was supposed to follow. He had been relatively sure it would end in death. But if Roland eventually claimed the victory, he would be no less cruel. In ancient days, the punishment for treason had been the most severe of all. One would be burned at the stake, or boiled alive. True, it was not ancient days anymore, and Roland might prove merciful…

Do not second guess yourself now, Gouldair, he chided himself.

An hour later he was back on top of the battlements, summoned on behalf of a messenger. The messenger was clearly a knight. He rode on a white charger and wore a full suit of armor. His shield was painted with the swordfish of Ajernon, white on red. "Your Lordship!" cried the knight. "The honorable Lord Vivien seeks your help desperately in his hour of need! The armies of the Monster rampage through Ajernon! They are slaughtering peasants, setting fire to vineyards… smashing the stained glass of churches. We need reinforcements. We need soldiers and men-at-arms—fighting men!"

Gouldair stood silently, pondering this news. The knight's tone was desperate, yet a smile had formed on Gouldair's face against his own will. The "monster" Sylla had indeed retreated from Duchy Voraigne. He lacked the capacity to take Voraigne Manor or even the lackluster walls of the Ville.

"He is outside Stormhold!" cried the knight. "I beg of you, Your Lordship—"

"No," said Gouldair.

Chapter Fifty-Three:
A Word In Secret

The Reverend Alse-Lorie, High Priestess

It was the first day of summer and Duchy Ajernon was up in flames. The year had been dark and it promised to grow darker.

Alse-Lorie stood before the Lion Throne out of duty. She no more stood beside Lord Roland, Duke of Valais, than she stood by Varysse. The Young Duke had a strategy of doing nothing, and he seemed to think it was working. The hacked and burned vineyards of Ajernon did not bother him. The demolished churches did not seem to bother him. The army's proximity to Vale of Roy and the Royal City did not bother him. He was today, as always, cold, distant, and uncaring. In mind, he was a thousand miles away from everyone in the court. Even Queen Alysant despised him. His own wife Elsie shot him frequent glares. The so-called "Lord" Mars was his only support.

Honey Crumbles had taken the stage once more and was juggling knives. Alse imagined him slipping and making a mistake, cutting open a giant wound, and bleeding to death. She laughed. The thought was the only entertainment this jester had provided in all these months of performances.

"You bore me, jester," said Lord Roland.

Honey Crumbles began to sing in a harsh, howling voice. "The Ol' Cow Bess… The Ol' Cow Bess… Farmer Piers did milk her…"

"Good Goddess," cursed Alse under her breath. She looked to the throne room's open double doors wistfully, thinking she might flee.

Varysse was there. Alse gasped.

"Your Reverence!" Varysse called out with a knowing, irreverent smile.

The blood drained from Alse. She wiped sweat from her neck with her stole. She ran to Varysse.

"My dear!" Alse said. "What is wrong?"

"A word, Your Reverence," Varysse said.

"I am terribly busy."

"Then I will tell your secret to everyone in Castle Royale," Varysse snapped in a voice loud enough for the Royal Guards at the door to hear.

"Come on!" Alse hissed, and made her way up Castle Royale's winding corridors and towering steps.

Eventually, Alse-Lorie made it to her castle quarters and slammed the door shut. Then she screamed at the top of her voice, "What is wrong with you?"

A wry smile crossed Varysse's strawberry lips. "I am unsatisfied."

"Really," Alse murmured. Varysse deserved worse—she deserved to be miserable.

"The people of the Outer City are not like you and me," said Varysse. "I cannot relate to them. They wear rags and dirty clothes. They don't know Ranoul from Aglond. They don't eat the high cuisine or listen to high music. They are *villeins,* my sweet. They are loathsome, dirty creatures."

"You are unworthy of them," said Alse.

Varysse laughed lightly. "Oh, and you are a saint." She smiled darkly. "What would King Jourmande think if he knew the High Priestess was a whore?"

Alse wanted to strike her. No, she wanted to club her. To death. "I have given you more than you deserve... an ordination you do not deserve. A payment you do not deserve." She drew close to Varysse, within biting distance. "Do you know what you deserve, my sweet? Six feet of dirt, and a mouth full of gravel."

Varysse pushed her away, so hard Alse almost fell onto the carpet. The derisive smile had vanished, replaced with glaring eyes. "People do not get what they deserve. The Goddess is a lie. I curse her, as I curse you. She is a figment of peasants' imaginations, the last desperate hope of *villeins* toiling in the fields."

"And so the truth comes out." Alse realized she was crying. "You should never set foot in a church again."

"Indeed," said Varysse. "But the Lady is a profitable lie. Thousands of dim-witted fools tithe each month. I want that money, Alse. That is why I serve."

Alse wiped her eyes. "Why did you come? You are not welcome here."

"I want the High Priesthood," said Varysse. "I want your title. And I want you to serve the Outer City parish instead of me."

Alse laughed. Varysse's cruelty had at last reached a zenith, a level beyond belief. "Be gone, snake. I refuse your offer. And you will not get a penny more from the cathedral's treasury. No one will believe your tales." Alse thought they might believe, but how could they prove it besides an ordeal by fire?

"Very well," Varysse said. "You have chosen your path. So have I."

Varysse left and Alse fell, weeping, to the floor.

Chapter Fifty-Four:
Fairy Brew

Ramden

Visions swirled by Ramden as he slept—visions of ancient stars, seen from a primordial forest. In the unspoiled wilderness there were no houses. There were bushes filled with berries and trees bursting with fruit. There were ice cold lakes in view of mountains capped with snow. There were marshes dank and cold in the shadow of the trees.

Ramden was not alone in these visions. Pixies with bright blue wings and nixies with bright green skin sang in the primordial forest. Sprites flew by like shooting stars, white and gold and yellow. Fairies with the legs of grasshoppers chirped in the night, and pucks played songs on pipes made from reeds. Yet they did not see Ramden nor acknowledge his presence. Ramden did not feel entirely there—he was only an observer to this forest that time forgot. He wandered amongst the trees in the light of the green will o' wisps, hoping he would never return to the harsh cruel world he had left behind. Ramone and Ramonette, Ramondine and Mother were the last things on his mind. He had not been this happy since before his injury.

He startled awake. The wizened face of Maude, the woods witch, sent a shudder through him. The morning light was filtering in through her cottage in Deepwood Hollow. The black bear from before sat against the wall, and in its lap a fox slept.

I am never going back to that happy forest. It was all a dream.

"Oh, my sweet little boy," said the witch. "You are still sick and injured. But Old Woman Maude has made you some stew. Turnips and onions and carrots. Oh, my, you will love it."

"No meat?" Ramden asked.

"No meat," Maude answered. "I would not want to insult our guests. These bears and foxes and squirrels are my friends. They shan't be eaten."

"I meant venison or beef..." A deer had wandered into Maude's cottage, a white-tailed doe.

"Venison," Maude uttered as if it were a curse. "We witches do not eat meat at all—not beef and certainly not venison." She walked up to the hearth, where a pot was simmering in the fire. She grabbed a bowl from the hearthside table and ladeled in the vegetable stew.

"Maude... I'm not sure." Ramden did not want to eat vegetables. He cursed himself for leaving Castle Silvergold, where bacon, beef and venison had never been in short supply.

"You will love it!" said Maude. She grabbed a spoon from the table and made her way over to Ramden.

"Vegetables are what peasants eat," insisted Ramden. He realized he had never been this comfortable, lying on this silken-soft bed with not a care in the world.

"Peasants?" said Maude. "There is no peasant or nobleman to Old Woman Maude. There is only an injured young man who needs help. Here! Open up! Eat!"

The vegetable stew looked terrible in the bowl, but the onions were juicy, the carrots tender, the turnips soft and flavorful. The meatless mash formed a perfect complement. There was no trace of salt, pepper, or cormorant, just vegetables and wild forest herbs.

"See?" said Maude. "I told you that you'd like it."

Ramden ate the stew willingly from then on, savoring each tender carrot and each bit of the oniony broth.

"The Lady loves the forest animals," said Maude. "She does not like it when the lords hunt. Foxes and rabbits and bears—she is *their* lady too!"

Even in this warm room, in these comfortable sheets, and with a full stomach, the slightest movement shocked Ramden with pain. A rib had broken when he fell from the horse, and his feet were as aching and pain-filled as ever. "Your faith impresses me," said Ramden, "but you are not a priestess. You are a wild woods witch, a heathen. The Goddess hates you."

Maude laughed. She was so shriveled, so ugly. "On the contrary, my dumpling. The priestesses are heathens in her sight. They are no closer to the Fair Folk than you. They spite her by building churches of stone and glass and metal. They do not meet in forest hollows like they used to. They are wrapped up in politics and court intrigue. They are an abomination."

A whiff of this kind of speech and his brother Ramone would burn her at the stake. But Ramden didn't want to burn her at the stake. He no longer viewed this woods witch as an enemy.

"I am half in this world, half in the Other," said Maude. "I can see the fey. Why, Ramden, there are two pucks on your shoulder, one blue and one brown. They are playing a sylvan melody on miniature fiddles."

Maude turned and grabbed something from her bed—a gold hob lantern. "What do you see?"

There was a glowing orb of green light within the gold and brass of the lantern. Such objects were banned by the Fairy Church.

"A hob lantern."

"And inside?" Maude pressed.

"A glowing light."

"A will o' wisp," Maude said, "trapped in this world by the hob lantern and faer power. The will o' wisps are the most spiteful and vicious of fey. They love nothing more than leading folk into quagmires and quicksand. Death is a practical joke to them! The Fair

Folk of the Otherworld are happy to have a will o' wisp removed from their presence. And I am happy to have a light that illuminates my path. I call this will o' wisp Good Man Jack. He doesn't want to be trapped in this hob lantern but he has no choice." She eyed the glowing orb. "Do you, Good Man Jack?"

"It seems cruel," said Ramden.

"Do you know what's cruel?" said Maude. "The one who did this to you." She set down the hob lantern and walked over to Ramden. She ran her pruned old fingers over his swollen red feet.

"Careful," Ramden cautioned.

Maude hummed a tune softly. She shook her head. "Who could do this to a young man in his prime of life?"

"Marcus Sylla." The name still sent shivers through Ramden's body.

"Sylla," Maude repeated. "A queer name."

"He is from the southlands… the Empire," Ramden muttered. "No one can beat him. No one can stand up to him. I think the kingdom is doomed."

"Doomed?" Maude said, clearly unmoved. "It takes a great deal to doom a nation." A cross expression seized her face. "Hey, you two. Don't laugh. That isn't nice."

She was talking to the invisible pucks on her shoulder. Ramden wasn't completely convinced of their existence—Old Woman Maude might just be barking mad.

"The nation's doom will require something extraordinary, something cataclysmic," said Maude.

"Sylla is extraordinary," Ramden explained. "He is unbeatable. Everyone is afraid of him. I don't think there's any way our kingdom will survive."

"You have great respect for this Sylla, don't you, hmmm?" said Maude.

Ramden bristled at the comment. Respect was not the right word. Fear, maybe. Awe, perhaps.

"To be honest, I don't care if the kingdom survives after how I've been treated."

Maude wagged her finger. "No, no, now. Don't be a sour apple. You're just like Good Sir Black Bear over there... whenever he doesn't get his honey, he throws a big tantrum. I know you've been mistreated. But that's no excuse to give up hope!"

"My father gave my fat brother the duchy," Ramden muttered. "I'm the castle outcast now. No one respects me anymore. I can't ride. I can't walk. I can't even fight."

"Would it mean the world to you if I healed your feet?"

"Truly?" Ramden gasped. "Can you really do that? Can you heal me?" His heart leapt in his chest. The thought was too wonderful to contemplate seriously. No physician had been able to help. Was it beyond the realm of possibility for this Maude to do it instead?

"I can heal you," said Maude. "With the help of my friends, you will be able to walk again. But you have to make me a promise."

"Anything!" Ramden cried. "Anything in this world that I can give you, you can have!"

"Don't go back to Marcus Sylla," said Maude.

Ramden laughed in disbelief. The thought was mad. He would never even consider it. Putting on the best act he could, he muttered demurely, "All right."

Maude smiled. "Very well. I'll get to work."

The old woman turned and left the room, disappearing behind a door. She returned with a bundle of herbs in her hands— green sprigs, dried stems, and thorny tendrils. She smiled at Ramden, then poured water into a pot from her laver and dropped the herbs inside. She set it in the fire.

Stirring, she muttered to herself: "Rosemary and fairywort, witches broom and Grayman's beard."

Ramden had shut his eyes and was on the verge of sleep

when Maude poked him. His bowl of vegetable stew had been reused—this time, with an inky back fluid.

"The process of healing shall be incredibly painful," Maude said. "I shall spare you it. Here, drink my fairy brew."

Ramden swallowed Maude's fairy brew and gagged at the bitter, poison taste. He tried to spit it up, but Maude gently forced it down. He drank every last drop, and seconds later was unconscious.

When Ramden awoke he lay on the edge of the woods in view of Castle Silvergold's grim stone walls and towering donjon keep. He wondered if it had all been a dream, if he had only imagined the entire ordeal. Then he shifted his feet and felt no pain. He took an uncertain step forward. He stood up. Joy filled him. He took another cautious step and fell. He had forgotten how to walk.

Within moments he stood up again. He walked carefully up the hill toward the castle, amidst the purple and pink wildflowers and the tall grass. He basked in the warmth of the air and the new day. He walked further ahead, and then he ran. "Thank you, Maude," he muttered. "Thank you…" He ran up the hill and into the castle yard, shouting with joy.

Chapter Fifty-Five:
A Knife in the Dark

Roland vis Valais, Duke of Valais

The enemy was starving. Their siege engines had been damaged and destroyed in all the fruitless battles. Alse-Lorie and Queen Alysant despised Roland, thinking him unmanly, but his strategy was clearly working. Soon the Imperial Army would be hungry and desperate. They would grow weak and demoralized. Then, and only then—at their breaking point—would Roland gather what strength the Seven Gems possessed, and crush the Imperials in a final battle.

He stood only inches from the Lion Throne. Each day he dared stand just a little closer. One day, perhaps, he would venture to sit in it. He would never be king, however. The Bretagne dynasty had ruled for hundreds of years. His uncle was—perhaps—the least of all the Vis Bretagne kings, but his wife and infant son were by law the rightful rulers.

He would eagerly look forward to doling out justice. The marquises of the south who had defected to the Empire would be punished according to the ancient law books. A traitor was to be burned at the stake or boiled alive. Such a punishment had never been used against a nobleman in recent times. Only peasants received such a cruel end—for heresy, or insurrection, or witchcraft. It would all change when Roland finally acted, delivering a crushing blow to the Imperial Army and sending their soldiers scattered to the four corners of Varda.

A knight walked past the Royal Guard and into the throne room. The High Priestess, Alse-Lorie, was staring daggers at him.

Her hatred, he did not understand. He understood the hatred of his wife Elsie, and to an extent that of the queen, but Alse's he did not comprehend. He had not done anything to Her Reverence. In the royal court only Lord Mars took his side, and then only grudgingly. Roland wondered if Lord Mars hated him too, if the peasant thought his ennoblement had come at a terrible price.

On the knight's shield was the swordfish of Ajernon, white on red.

"Has Lord Vivien fallen?" asked Roland. *Perhaps I am too direct.*

"Goddess, no," said the knight. "The Lord Vivien is as well as he has ever been. Castle Rose has stood firm. The Imperial Army has left Ajernon."

Roland smiled, his suspicions confirmed. The Imperials had grown desperate. With each passing day their capabilities were reduced. Soon they would have no defenses, no energy, no will to fight.

"It is something else, Your Lordship," the knight said. "Something altogether different... something worse."

"Worse?" Roland said. "Worse than your liege falling."

"Portents in the sea," said the knight. "Troubled waters... storms..."

Roland was not impressed. "Truly? This is what you've come to tell me?"

"There is a monster in the water, Your Lordship."

"A monster," Roland repeated, "in the water."

"Lord Vivien saw it. I saw it, too." The knight's face paled. "Its head was the size of a city... it had a hundred arms. The Lord Vivien fears the portent. He fears what it might mean. He fears what he has done with the Priests of Og."

The throne room had grown colder.

"He said the priests of Og torment him in his dreams," said the knight. "And the peasants say they know of this beast. They say it is a beast of the apocalypse… the beast which heralds the end of the world."

"Does he want me to attack it with ships?" Roland scoffed. "Shall I build a fishing pole the size of a city and drag it onto the shore?"

"He asks for priestly guidance," said the knight. "He asks for Alse-Lorie."

The priestess looked shock. "I… I have things to take care of. I…"

Perhaps this was an opportunity for Roland to clear the castle of his opponents. Perhaps they would all be better off with Alse gone—even her. "It is your duty to care for the Zarube flock," Roland insisted. "I demand you go."

The familiar hateful glare returned. "I can make my own decisions, 'Lord' Roland."

"You say the word 'lord' with bitterness," Roland sneered, "but it is the truth." He did not understand this woman. "I am the lord of this castle—Castle Royale—and my edicts are final. I demand you go, and you *will* go." Part of him hoped she would fall to bandits on the way there.

Alse-Lorie's hateful glare softened slightly. "Your Lordship."

"Off you go to Ajernon. I hear it is lovely this time of year."

"Indeed." Alse-Lorie stalked off coldly, and the knight followed a step behind.

By dusk, Roland had retired to his quarters. His wife was gone, probably sulking somewhere, thinking hateful thoughts about him. Roland pitied young Elsie. The thought of marrying the handsome Young Duke was the wild dream of every peasant maiden and lady in waiting, but the reality had proved different.

Lord Mars stood there, dressed in light linens. He was staying in the guest quarters adjacent. There was a long hunting knife in his hand, and he was stroking it. "When I served Your Lordship as a man of the fields, I ended the lives of pigs and sows. It is surprisingly hard to kill them. I hated it at first, but I became accustomed to it. It became easy to end lives."

The light of dusk, filtering through the window, illuminated Lord Mars' bronzed skin.

"Jourmande stands in your way," said Lord Mars.

Roland couldn't help but glare. "King Jourmande is dead. I do not want to admit it. He would have shown himself by now if he was not. He fell in battle, or Lord Eurelien killed him. Maybe there is plague in Montée March. It may surprise you that the thought makes me sad. I do not want Jourmande to die. He is my uncle, and I like him."

"Do you?" said Lord Mars. He continued stroking the hunting knife.

"More than Jourmande stands in my way," Roland said. "The laws of succession... the hatred of the court... the fact that I am a Valais and not a Bretagne. You'd have to kill all the nobles in the Seven Gems to make me king."

"The offer remains," Lord Mars said, and stooped down to one knee. "I would lie for you... I would kill for you..."

"Would you die for me?" said Roland.

Lord Mars looked hesitant.

"That is good," said Roland. "I would not want you to die for me. I would not die for you."

Lord Mars smiled. Half his teeth were missing, and those that were not were brown and decayed. "I would not want you to die for me either, my lord. Life is precious. Mine is, I mean. And yours."

"When this war is over," Roland said, "you can put that knife to its proper use. We will go hunting in the woods, in the height of summer." His words felt empty. *This war will never end... the nation will fall, and we will all be slaughtered. I will be nailed to a cross and left to suffer and die. The Royal City will burn...*

"Indeed, my lord," he answered.

Chapter Fifty-Six:
A Cruel World

The Reverend Alse-Lorie, High Priestess

In the morning, filled with dread, Alse set out for Ajernon. A dozen knights flanked her as she rode, but it was not bandits or Imperials she feared. As she left the Lion Gate on horseback and found herself on the wide dirt road, the thing that terrified her, the thing that filled her with panic was the fact that Varysse had free reign. Would she find the powdered Grayman's beard and prove, once and for all, that Alse was a fraud?

Her words last night with Sir Loy had been curt. She had glared at him like she had never glared before. She had accused him of causing all her troubles. She had blamed him for everything she had done.

It was those things she thought of as she rode south down the road.

~

The sky was bright blue and the sun beat warmly on the tall grass and the fields of wildflowers. Amid the woods and streams, smoke billowed from tiny hamlets and country villages.

An hour had not passed before all turned grim. By the side of the road, the fire-gutted ruins of an inn lay. A bit of burned, blackened wall formed the outline of the building. Shriveled blackened bodies lay amid the ash and ruin, and the stench of death hung hot in the summer day.

In the woods beyond the inn, bodies dangled from trees—

ripe, bloated, and some sickly shade of green.

"Bandits," said one of the knights. "The king has been distracted so long they think they can terrorize the countryside with impunity. They are as bad as I have ever seen them… they are elves."

"Elves?" asked Alse. "Elven bandits?" She had not heard of such a thing.

"Elven slaves, indeed," the knight explained.

The bodies in the woods were male and female, young and old. Alse could not believe anyone could be so cruel. She could not imagine elven slaves doing such a thing. The Empire, certainly, but not elves.

"Once that inn was a lovely place," the knight said. "I stayed there last summer. The Spring Goose, it was called. Goddess rest those poor folk."

"Goddess rest them," said Alse, "and Goddess rest us all."

From that point on, the last thing on her mind was Varysse. A shaved head and a cucking stool was nothing compared to the threat to her life. Bandits that could burn down an inn and hang people from trees would certainly not show mercy to a priestess.

"Why can't we take a different route?" asked Alse at one point late in the morning.

"Because, Your Reverence," said the knight whose name she had learned was Sir Leonel, "everywhere else is under threat of the Imperials—and they, if you can believe it, are far worse."

Alse could not believe it, but she chose to just the same.

The hamlets and villages of Vale of Roy were mostly unwalled. The air was thick with the smell of burning and smoke. Vineyards had been hacked down and bodies lay discarded like garbage off the side of the road. The corpses, ripe and bloated, emitted a sickening stench. Maggots feasted on the exposed flesh and none of these dead were given a proper burial. Without the last rites, the Fairy Church taught that the slain could not pass over into the Otherworld—but Alse-Lorie thought that perhaps, just perhaps, the Goddess was merciful.

Halfway through Vale of Roy, as the sun had dipped low in the sky, Alse cried out, "How could the king let this happen?" The situation had clearly spiraled out of control, and in the king's backyard. "The robbers control the whole Vale!"

"Some say the king is dead," answered a knight named Sir Neville. "Our lord Vivien says that ol' Duke Eurelien has killed him!"

Alse-Lorie had her doubts about that. She had seen Eurelien many times throughout her young life and had never thought of him as anything more than an unexceptional, boring old man. He did not harbor any great love for Jourmande, but neither did he harbor any hate.

Yet did he kill him? Alse-Lorie could say nothing anymore for certain in this dark, topsy-turvey world – this world where Varysse had Alse by the throat, where the king disappeared out of thin air and robbers overran the sacred Vale.

Above her, dangling from a high tree branch, were the hanged bodies of three more victims—two women and a man— bloated and dripping their fetid juices onto the roadway. Alse cursed this topsy-turvey world and everything in it.

~

Late in the night they crossed the stone bridge into Duchy Lessant. By evening tomorrow, they would find themselves in Ajernon.

Chapter Fifty-Seven:
Dreams

Danitari

Hungry, weak and cold, Danitari dreamed in vivid color—for in this prison, the dream was all he had.

~

The beast visions did not cease. They only worsened and gathered strength. He dreamed that the beast with iron teeth and iron claws wore a crown of gold on its black-furred head. He dreamed the beast devoured kingdoms and remade them in the vision of itself. He dreamed of men and women wearing cloaks of black, making the sign of the serpent and falling down before the beast.

He dreamed that the foundations of the earth were shaken, and the pillars which held up the sky began to crack. He dreamed of ice and snow, of dryness and burning heat, of the earth itself groaning in pain.

He dreamed without cease. Hungry, weak, cold and imprisoned, the dream was all Danitari had.

Chapter Fifty-Eight:
Broken Ties

Ramden

When Ramden walked into the Hall of Feasting, there was a loud cry.

"My Ramden!" cried Mother. "What has happened to you?"

"Disappointed, Mother?" asked Ramden. He glared at the one who birthed him, the one he had come to despise. Ramone sat his fat self up from his plate of bacon and hash. His beautiful bride-to-be stood there beside him, Aimee. Her hair was a golden blonde, her eyes a bright emerald green. She carried herself like a graceful nymph, even when Ramden stormed in so rudely.

"Has the Goddess herself favored you?" asked Mother.

The gall. After all the ill treatment, Ramden would not easily forget. Ramonette and little Ramondine came running in.

"My brother!" cried Ramonette. "A miracle!"

"A miracle of the Goddess herself!" cried Mother. "Unless I am dreaming, or seeing an apparition!"

"I am no apparition." Ramden's clothes were torn and muddied from the elements. His hair was wild and knotted. If he were an apparition, he would be a harbinger of death. He drew his sword.

Mother flinched.

"I was healed by fairy craft," said Ramden. "By Good Woman Maude in Deepwood Hollow."

"A woods witch?" Ramone howled, incredulous.

"I owe her my life," said Ramden.

Mother's face had flashed red. "They who consort with

witches are equally culpable. Stay your tongue, my son, before you incriminate yourself further!"

Clueless Aimee took a step back, utterly bewildered.

"Good Woman Maude saved my life," Ramden snapped. "I will not hear her name dishonored."

"Be careful what you say!" screamed Mother. "Men higher born than you have been burned at the stake for less!"

In his room, Ramden shut his eyes and stewed. The red tulips and purple wildflowers outside the window glowed like fire in the sun. He cursed Castle Silvergold and cursed the kingdom. His family had become his enemies. Besides Good Woman Maude, what friend did he have?

An eagle soared overhead.

Chapter Fifty-Nine:
Filth

The Reverend Alse-Lorie, High Priestess

The concerns of the Royal City had returned to the forefront of her mind. The quaint beauty of Ajernon did not soothe her troubled spirit. The red brick walls which marked the boundaries of farmers' vineyards lent a summery feeling to countryside. The warmth and the sun, peeking through the clouds, might—in any other circumstance—fill Alse's heart with gladness. In market squares in the hamlets and villages, fishmongers sold tuna and swordfish and lobster by the bucketful, but the Reverend Alse-Lorie was not entirely there. Part of her remained in the Royal City, where even now Varysse spread her snaring web. Alse laughed at the thought of Varysse the spider with eight legs and a spinneret. Then she shuddered and felt cold.

Castle Rose appeared, towering above the horizon. Its towers, curtain walls, and donjon keep were the same color as the red brick of the vineyards. In its shadow lay the large town of Abreville, a place of squalor where the lowborn eked out meager subsistence. Alse-Lorie had never been to Castle Rose, nor visited Lord Vivien. After Vivien summoned the priests of Og, she had not cared to visit. The Imperial attack seemed an act of divine justice, and one she did not disagree with. *Though who am I to judge? I have forsaken the Goddess's oath.*

Amongst the peasant village of brick hovels, the lowborns hawked their wares—fresh fish of the day—tuna, swordfish and whitefish as before—but also bottles of last year's wine, no doubt watered down for maximum profits. Others sold roots and tubers with dirt still clinging to it. All meat—rabbit, venison, and beef alike—was forbidden to the lowborns and given to His Lordship Vivien. The lowborns ate poorly and were treated as less than slaves, yet theirs was a life of busy commerce in a world all their own.

As Alse and the knights passed down the way, the lowborns scurried off. A man selling chewets pushed away his whole cart, dropping the little pies onto the road. Girls and boys—taught by their parents to respect the highborns—ran away at the sight. No doubt Lord Vivien had made an example of those who got in his way. He did not take kindly to lowborns standing obstinately in the road.

The portcullis opened at the sight of the knights, revealing the castle yard. Within was a garden of shrubberies and bright flowers, smelling sweet in the warm summer air. The yard was flanked by pointed arches, and Alse felt she had entered the southlands. The walls stretched high above, and the donjon keep in the center seemed to scrape the clouds. All along its staggering extent, marble statues depicting the great rulers of the House Abrenard peered down from alcoves. The wealth of the House Abrenard radiated from its glorious home, Alse mused.

In the castle yard itself, there was hardly room for Alse's party. A scullery maid, her face white with flour, raced past the knights with a bundle of vegetables in her arms. A dozen gardeners trimmed the bushes of the castle yard and examined the flowers carefully. Knights and men-at-arms stood guard at every door.

The Castle Rose was a city unto itself, all designed to serve the whims of the House Abrenard—all to serve the whims of Lord Vivien. Was it any wonder that the lords of Further Zarubain looked upon the west with envy?

Alse dismounted and the knights followed. Immediately, servants came running out to grab the horses' bridles and lead them into the lord's stable. She and the knights walked toward the grand doors of the donjon keep. A servant girl ran across the castle yard and nearly tripped, almost spilling a bucket of water on a knight. "I am sorry, milord! Show mercy on me!"

These servants acted in unison like the many parts of a body served a human being, all—in concert—benefiting the Lord Vivien and his lady wife, whom Alse had not yet met.

If the outside of Castle Rose stunned Alse-Lorie, the inside awed her. Mosaic floors depicting flowers and potted plants covered the entire hallway. Statues of bronze and silver dotted the corridors. Some statues were dancing girls, others women riding tigers. "What is this?" Alse said. She had heard of something like this before. "Are we in Carribor?"

"The castle in City Carribor portrays the Near South, milady," said Sir Leonel, the captain of their party. "An Imperial would be home there. But this—this castle portrays the Far South, more exotic than anything you will find in Zarubain. Our lieges the Abrenards gutted the place and made it in the image of the Far South not long ago. They hired a native… his name was Maubrouk of Sheva."

Alse-Lorie thought of Varysse. The spoiled now-full priestess was an Abrenard. These glorious halls would have been intimatey familiar to her. "And these statues…" she said to distract herself.

"They are all sacred to the goddess Isdar, it is said."

Alse grimaced. The goddess Isdar was treated as a juicy morsel of gossip among the northerners. To think of those dark-skinned, mysterious southerners worshipping the goddess of pleasure, holding drunken debauches in dim-lit brothels. To think of women sworn to serve her—sacred whores that debased themselves on behalf of their divine patron. "I should hope that the Abrenards do not worship her," Alse said simply.

"I assure you, milady, they are devout worshippers of the Goddess and the Goddess alone," said Sir Leonel.

It was more than they could say for the Voraignes, worshipping the lord of shadows, or even Queen Alysant, who had found a new reverence for Tyras lord of war. Alse hoped the Goddess would curse Brother Archett, who had led Alysant astray—and spare Alse. Alse had not yet gotten the punishment due to her—stripped naked and sat on a cucking stool, shamed and barred from ever entering a church again. Penniless she would starve, the pariah of the Goddess's kingdom. She asked the Goddess silently for another day, another week, another year.

Alse-Lorie followed Sir Leonel through hall after hall, through corridor after corridor of pointed arches. The mosaic tiles continued: bowls of fruit, perhaps representing fertility; dark-skinned dancers holding tambourines; black rocks; silver idols; and palm trees. She sincerely hoped that Sir Leonel spoke the truth—that the folk of Castle Rose did not worship the Fertile Goddess or hold candlelit debauches by night.

~

On an immense black throne fit for the most megalomanic southern tyrant was the Duke of Ajernon, Lord Vivien. The throne's armrests were carved in the shape of tiger heads and layered with gold. Steps of white marble led up to it. On either side were statues of the Goddess—but this was not the noble Goddess in white samite, but the Goddess dressed in the brassiere and skirt like Isdar.

A lady stood beside Lord Vivien.

"My lady wife," Vivien explained, apparently noticing Alse's gaze. "She is from Miere."

Oh, was she ever from Miere. Her long, raven black hair contrasted starkly with her pallid white skin. Her silken gown was colored in ivy patterns and gold—Mierese paintwork if there ever was any. Her hands glistened with gold rings and ornaments. A dragonette was perched on her finger—a tiny creature no bigger than her fist with green scales and a pink and purple ridge running down its neck. It breathed, and a puff of yellow gas emerged, wafting up then disappearing into the air.

"A pleasure," said Alse-Lorie. She glared at Vivien. Perhaps it was unfair to still hate him. But how could she forgive him? In this—the darkest hour—he had surrendered himself to demons and asked Og the Lord of Secrets for help. The Fairy Church had always despised the existence of Og's antipriests, but what could they do? No king from Joules to Jourmande ever had the moral character or the courage to destroy the demoniacs.

"I have seen a most troublesome thing, my priestess," Vivien said.

"So have I," said Alse. "A young boy sacrificed. A demon, summoned for help. A nation brought low by your hand."

"Enough!" snapped Vivien. "Such words would get anyone here killed—lowborn or high—but I need your counsel."

"Do you," huffed Alse. She couldn't help herself. What was that boy's name? What were his wants, his desires? Did he have dreams of a better life? Did he have grand plans? Her blood boiled at the thought of it—the life of a peasant boy taken by Vivien's hand.

"I was near the seashore on a bright and cloudless day," Vivien said. "I was looking at the seashells, searching for a sand dollar."

Also could scarcely bear to listen.

"My lady wife was not there, Goddess be thanked." Vivien's face had turned pale. His eyes grew shallow and afraid. "A cold wind blew. The skies darkened until they blotted out the sun—if clouds rolled in I did not see them coming. The air grew still but the waves began to stir. I had never felt so vulnerable. There was lightning and a crack of thunder. The clouds had a shade of red fire. It seemed the foundations of the earth had trembled. Then the sea began bubbling…"

"Bubbling," Alse repeated.

Vivien was reliving the episode. Even from a distance Alse could see his hands grow clammy, wet with cold sweat. "Out of the depths it arose… a creature with a head the size of a city, and a dozen arms the thickness of towers. I could hear the sounds of the restless dead wailing. The wind began to blow. I ran for Castle Rose. The knights beside me had begun to scream. The wind knocked me down three times but I made it inside. The knights did not."

A pity on both accounts.

"They were dragged out to sea," said Vivien.

Alse sighed. She hated herself for feeling the same dread Vivien did. She did not want to pity him. She did not want to care for him. She had heard of this beast before. She had seen an Elvish book before with brightly colored illustratons. The text had been lengthy. Priests across the Northern World considered its words true. She remembered its name, too. *"Lormon Narssanad."*

"Pardon?" said Vivien.

"She speaks Elvish," said Vivien's wife. "Curse her. Isn't that right, Regulus?" The dragonette burped its yellow gas in approval, then flitted up and nested in her black hair.

"Lormon Narsannad," Alse repeated, unfazed. "That is what it's called. It is in a book in the Lady's Cathedral. It was part of my education but glossed-over. I thought the picture was absurd. That is probably the fault of the artist. You say it had legs like tree trunks— were they sinuous, like vines?"

Vivien nodded. He was still pale and shaken.

"Tentacles… like the filthy creatures of the sea—octopi." Alse had not expected anything from this journey. "May I see your library?"

"Of course," said Vivien.

In the library of Castle Rose, books of medicine, science and geography predominated. Alse recognized some histories from the Southern World, translated into Zarube—"A People's History of the Empire" by Priscilla Marianus and "The Seánine War" by Aquilla. The religious texts were fewer. There were psalteries and prayer books, having collected dust from disuse. There was the Book of the Winter Fairies, one of the primary texts of the Fairy Church; and "Seven Fairy Songs" by Saint Hilgrid. Her heart leapt when she saw what she was looking for—an immense canonical tome of all the northern churches' sacred writings, called "The Holy Book" or simply the Book.

Alse-Lorie grabbed the giant tome and nearly fell over at its weight. She opened it to the front, finding a table of contents. She skipped over the table's pages of writing, skimming, then focusing on the most ancient of all writings. Her blood pulsed with excitement when she recognized the entry—"The Seven Visions of Sinderion."

She paged through the visions one by one—a beast, a tree, and others. The last was the sea beast, the *lormon narsannad.*

The page had been cut out. By whom? Who would abuse the Holy Book so?

Alse cursed. Yet this raised more questions. Who would have an interest in this? Could someone possibly be responsible for this beast's apparition? Moreover, could someone have also entered the library of the Lady's Cathedral and cut the page from the Holy Book there?

Alse cursed again. She shoved the tome back on its place in the shelf. She could spare no time, not another moment. She had to get back to Zarubad at once.

When she told Vivien as much, the Duke of Ajernon frowned.

"She is of no use," said his lady wife, and her green

dragonette burped yellow smoke in agreement.

"She is of use," said the duke. "I am most concerned about the book… hidden safe in our library. An entire page cut from the Holy Book. Who would have such a mind to do it?"

Someone who could summon demoniacs and ask Og'og for help. Her skin crawled at the thought. But how could anyone wander the grand halls of Castle Rose with impunity? Surely someone had seen something.

"I will make sure you are safely guarded."

"No," said Alse. "I cannot be slowed down. I will make the journey in a day."

"That is a difficult task for a fine lady such as yourself," said Vivien.

Had the woman-hatred of Roland seeped into the Duke of Ajernon? She cursed the family banners—white swordfishes on red backgrounds. *He is only concerned for my safety.* She forgave him. "I am not afraid," Alse said, and as soon as she spoke realized it was a lie. She had a feeling, a feeling she couldn't shake, that whoever had cut the page from the Holy Book intended to do so in the Cathedral Library too.

The same day she had arrived she departed. The red brick walls and green vineyards of Ajernon passed her by. The dry summer had begun to turn the grass a shade of yellow. The warmth was exquisite. But the image of the sea monster, the *lormon narsannad*, stuck in her mind. It meant something terrible, something baleful for the whole world.

Lormon was a word for beast, but it carried a deeper meaning. It had the implication of filth, of abomination, of primeval slime. Even in Zarubain, where elves were despised more than the lowborn, priestesses knew Elvish, the language of religion.

Lormon narsannad. She did not know what the second word

meant. But the implications of the beast's arrival could only be grim.

Chapter Sixty:
Heresy

Ramden the Bold

Ramden's tongue had gotten him in trouble again. His praise of the woods witch had damned him in the eyes of Castle Silvergold—in the eyes of Mother and Ramone, Ramonette and Ramondine—but also the knights he had considered friends, and even the scullions, servants and chefs. One morning when he saw the parish priestess of Duchy Lessant, the Reverend Tetienne, standing in the feasting hall, he knew his luck was up.

Mother, that unvanquishable scold, glared at Ramden from the table. Ramone's hatred was more subtle—a sullen, even sad look in his eyes—and his sisters appeared more afraid than anything.

"Hello, Ramden," said Tetienne. The young woman wore a green robe and the pink stole of the priesthood. Her hair was bound up in a conical hat—a hennin—and a length of transparent cloth fell from the tip down to her shoulders. "It appears that you are the only one in Castle Silvergold that does not take heresy seriously."

Ramden glared at Tetienne. Castle Silvergold saw very little of her—only on Yule and feast-days—and he had always considered that a good thing.

"The priesthood is the only body which is equipped to serve the Lady," said Tetienne. "All others who purport to serve the Lady are heretics. All witches must be burned. You know this. The witch knows it, too. Their seeming powers are devilry. *The Lady despiseth the witches.*"

"Devilry," Ramden repeated and laughed. "The devilry healed my legs. The devilry fed me… and gave me strength."

"False strength!" howled Tetienne shrilly. "It shall backfire, surely. The Lady does not grant her power. Do you disagree?"

"Yes," Ramden said.

Mother cursed.

"You are a heretic, then, too!" snapped Tetienne. "You will be examined by the High Priestess in Zarubad. The punishment for heresy is burning—lowborn or high."

That was a lie. No noble had been burned at the stake in recent history. The church court would find him not guilty. Only peasants could be heretics.

"I will grant you mercy if you help us find this woods witch," said Tetienne. "If you lead me to her hole, I will not accuse you before the high priestess."

"She does not live in a hole," Ramden answered. "She has a house, and quite a nice one."

"Quiet," hissed Tetienne. "You will lead me to her with a company of knights, and she will get her justice. She will be burned before the peasants of Lessant, to serve as a lesson. The woods witch knew what she did when she embarked upon that dark path; now, she must die."

Ramden glared at Tetienne. Though young, she had a shrill voice and the presence of a crone.

"Furthermore," said Tetienne, "her dark powers must be reversed. The devilry she inflicted upon you must be dispelled."

Ramden laughed. "Will you wash me in a fairy spring and expect it to go away?"

"No," Tetienne said. A hint of a smile crossed her plain face. "Your ankles will be broken, such as they were before. The Goddess decided that you would be a cripple, and *you*, Ramden the Bold, reversed her decision with dark powers."

Ramden laughed incredulously. "Are you hearing this, Mother? Truly?" Mother looked away. She did not have the stomach to stop this. Nor did Ramone, Ramonette, or little Ramondine.

Ramden's father would have stopped it. Ramden's father had been as brave and bold as him. Yet the broken House Rambée now let Tetienne walk all over him.

"It is the Goddess's command," said Tetienne. "It is the ancient custom."

"You think you can worship the Goddess in houses of stone," Ramden said. "You think you can worship in cathedrals cut with *iron*. You are wrong."

"You repeat the woods witches' foul propaganda," Tetienne said darkly. "Now I will not lift the charge of heresy—not even if you help."

"Then I will not help," said Ramden.

Tetienne's cheeks flashed pink. She glared. It was clear she had little experience with disobedience and dissent—the lowborn feared her, and the nobles did too. Even Mother had a sheepish look.

Ever since his healing, Ramden wore his sword openly. He drew it from the sheath.

"You draw swords before a lady?" howled Tetienne.

"You are no lady." Ramden raised the blade, ready to strike if need be.

Tetienne's mouth hung agape. The disrespect, now, had become incomprehensible. Even Mother was glaring at the lack of chivalry, and Ramonette, and Ramondine. Pity was written on brother Ramone's face. "I sentence you hear and now, by the authority of Her Fey Glory, to death by burning. Since you will not oblige, a death by sword will do. Kill him!"

Knights—men Ramden had known since childhood—betrayed their friendship in the blink of an eye. Sir Percival came running at him, heaving his sword. Ramden blocked with his own and the fresh clang of steel rang through the feasting hall.

Sir Martin came next, leaping onto a table and then crashing down, sword in hand. Ramden ducked out of the way.

Sir Guliver betrayed their friendship last, charging Ramden

headlong and sending servants and scullions fleeing. Ramden blocked his blow easily, but these three all wore chainmail. There was no way he could defeat them, not when they acted in concert. Ramden let his sword drop. He fell to his knees. "I accept my punishment," Ramden said, "even death."

"And death you will receive," Tetienne boomed. "Bind him and take him to a cell."

They stripped him to his breeches and bound his fists with cloth. Sir Martin, Sir Guliver, Sir Percival—all of them—set him in the cold, dank stone room. They shut the door and locked it, having abandoned their ancient friendship. They had gone on daring raids together, learned to wield the sword together—but all of that had been cast aside. They cared more about their social standing than they did about Ramden. And a friend of the woods witches was worse than anything, even a friend of elves. The woods witches and the marsh witches did something far worse than not worshipping the Goddess—they worshipped her incorrectly.

Ramden cried. He sat down on his stone bed with no cloth to cover him. He curled up and tried to warm himself with just his arms. The wind howled against the stone walls. *You've really done it now, Ramden.* A pyre awaited him—all because he couldn't keep his mouth shut.

Face streaked with tears, he shut his eyes and an hour later, drifted to sleep.

He awoke with a jump in the dead of night. He did not remember what he had dreamed, but the dream he had just experienced warmed his body and soul. All the terror and misery of the prior day had been washed away.

And the lock on the door clicked. The door creaked as it

opened. A female figure stood in the dim light of the torches. A gray cowl hid her face, but Ramden recognized her just the same—even before she spoke.

"Ramden, my sweet Ramden," the woods witch purred. "I care so very much about you. I do not want to see you burn."

"Thank the Goddess," said Ramden. "I do not want to see you burn either. I would rather I burn than you. You are the only good person in this world… the only one I can call 'friend.'"

"Do not worry about Good Woman Maude," she said. "I have put everyone in Castle Silvergold to sleep—your family, the jailer, even the dogs."

"How did you know?" asked Ramden, terrified despite her reassurances. "How did you find me?"

"Hush," Good Woman Maude said. "Do not ask questions. My spell will not last forever. You must leave Lessant, my sweet. You must go elsewhere."

"Where will I go?" said Ramden.

"You will find safe haven somewhere," said Good Woman Maude. "Your life is precious. Do not throw it away."

"I… of course not." Ramden gulped. More than anything, he wanted to live.

"You have your horse and your sword," said Good Woman Maude. "Make me a promise, sweet Ramden." She lowered her gray cowl, revealing that wrinkled, boil-covered face of hers. "Do not run from death into death. Stay away from Marcus Sylla, though you call him master."

"I will," promised Ramden.

"Hurry," Good Woman Maude embraced him. "Run from here. Do not return. Not even Deepwood Hollow is safe for you. Flee the wicked knights and the false priesthood. The Goddess favors you and does not wish you harm."

"Of course," Ramden said. He hurried away. Good Woman Maude vanished behind him.

It was dark but the moon and stars were radiant. In the cool air Ramden rode his horse out of Castle Silvergold's stables. It seemed, as he galloped out of the castle yard and onto the wide dirt road, that he had returned to that forest that time forgot. The stars shone so bright in the sky, the flowers and lilacs smelled so fragrant in the air, that Ramden expected fairies to greet him on his way. But no pucks or goblins, pixies or sprites could be seen on either side of the dirt road. Ramden remembered Zarubain was still a troubled kingdom—a kingdom in the grips of war.

Chapter Sixty-One:
Homeward

His Majesty King Jourmande vis Bretagne

Too late and too openly, Jourmande left Imperial City. Dame Alesandre would not even look at him. Sybold's flattery had lessened. The knights wore their hatred openly, glaring in Jourmande's presence and whispering quietly. Yet they were all fools. What was the worth of peace? It was invaluable. Peace, certainly, was more valuable than Mekara. The Imperials would take possession of it, but they would also do something better—they would defeat the renegade war criminal Sylla, and bring lasting peace. For that, there was no price too high—honor be damned. Jourmande would have made this agreement again in a heartbeat.

Behind him marched thirty thousand Imperial soldiers, three legions in total, led by their "grand legate," or supreme general. The white pavestones of the great road gleamed in the sun. The giant buildings, white colonnades and bronze statues disappeared behind them. An urban sprawl of tall ugly buildings called apartment blocks and an amalgamation of dirty streets, market squares, and low-lying hovels greeted them instead. It was late in the day before the squalor disappeared, and Jourmande had returned to nature.

Cypress-covered hills greeted them, and tall yellow grass. White villas appeared in the distance, surrounded by vineyards. The air was hot and dry, smoky and poor in quality. It was just as well— Jourmande, King of Zarubain, was headed home. *Home.* But would there be a home to greet him when he returned?

Chapter Sixty-Two:
The Fox's Kingdom

Danitari

Hungry, cold and weak, Danitari was at death's door. He could feel his body deteriorating. He had forgotten what the sunlight felt like. He had forgotten the smell of wildflowers in the meadows. He had forgotten the look of white apple blossoms and the taste of sweet red cherries. *No, I have not forgotten. I just yearn for them.*

Meanwhile the visions continued apace. Danitari felt like the great seer Sinderion, assailed with god-sent dreams, locked in the Tower of Everwinter amid the swirling white snow. Yet his dreams were meaningless. He was Sinderion only if Sinderion was barking mad. Just last night, he had dreamed he was collecting seashells by the beach. The observatory still stood. Lucien and Cossette were outside, too, collecting seashells. Bran, the Black Fox, had appeared behind him, startling Danny and causing him to drop the seashells.

"See?" the Black Fox had said. "There is no monster that pulled the tower down. I was right to imprison you. You are a liar."

"A liar?" Danny had answered. "I know what I saw."

"Come with me," the Black Fox had said.

Then a lion came springing from the nearby woods, a lion with a golden mane and two glowing blue eyes. The lion clawed the Black Fox to death until the sand had turned red. Danny had run away. He saw Lucienne and Cosette being dragged into the sea by two monstrous tentacles. Then the lion savaged Danny—yet the clawing only lasted a second. A great bird with brown feathers—the size of an ox—carried the lion away into the sky. Danny had been bleeding. He had collapsed, resigning himself to death. Then he had awoken in the cold, dark prison—hungry, tired, and shivering. He had yearned for that lion to come and end his misery.

The door opened. Bran the Black Fox stood there with a clay cup of watered-down wine and a bowl of cold pottage. "Breakfast," said Bran. "Are you ready to recant? Honesty is all I require."

"I have given you honesty," Danny said.

The Black Fox handed him the cup, and Danny gulped it down. The Black Fox handed him the bowl and Danny cautiously began to eat with his fingers. As expected it was tasteless. "We are winning the war," said the Black Fox. "The folk of the Vale are terrified. The king dares not question my power. You could be one of us, Danny—a royal prince, a kingdom official. The right hand of His Majesty King Brand."

"I could," said Danny, "but then I'd have to be a liar."

"Another month. Is that what it will take to stop your lying tongue?"

"It will take more," Danny said, "before I stop telling the truth."

Bran's black-bearded face darkened. A hint of a glare touched his coal-dark eyes. "Goodbye, Danny."

The door slammed shut and then locked.

~

That day Danny saw more visions. He dreamed of home— of great green plains bursting with wildflowers, washed with rain. He dreamed of the bean fields, the vineyards, the apple orchards and cherry orchards. He dreamed of Yuletide and the storms that would roll across the village of Donlamon. He dreamed of the old stories his grandfather would tell. He dreamed of his mother, gray with years, baking cherry pies and making fruit bowls. He dreamed of the trouble that had assailed the Elven World. Who knew when the human raiders from Sorelda had come, that the peace and serenity they had known was ending?

"Yours is the world and everything in it." So had said the gods to the first elf, Lumas, and to his wife Luvé. Yet the elves' time had passed away with the wind. Their ancient glory and power was forever gone. The silver Age of the Elves had been tarnished, then thrown into the fire. Now was the time of iron, the time of violence and suffering, the time of plague and fire and endless war. Who knew the destruction and ravages of the wider world could come to the elves' happy shore? Who knew the rich, happy life of Danitari could end in slavery and chains?

A darkness was coming, greater than before. This new evil had become normal. He dreamed of the apocalypse. *War and bloodshed, plague and famine, destruction and entropy… from now, until the end.*

Chapter Sixty-Three:
The Order of Things

The Reverend Alse-Lorie, High Priestess

Thunder rolled across the Vale of Roy and a rain began. The woods along the road were dark and impenetrable but Alse did not fear bandits; they were the last thing on her mind. Though signs of their ravaging lay everywhere around her—bodies dangling from trees, burned-down houses and ruined villages—the thing Reverend Alse-Lorie feared above all was the *lormon narsannad*, the beast which had emerged from the sea's briny depths. Imperials she did not fear, though their cruelty had no bounds. The end of the kingdom she did not fear. There were things worse than death.

Blue lightning flashed. The leaves of the elms and lindens rustled; the pines groaned under the wind. The Golden Coast, which ran the edge of Vale of Roy down the shoreline to Ajernon, had claimed many lives. Pirates and ne'er-do-wells were the least concern; flashes of lightning killed just as often, and with impunity. An inn appeared off-road on a hill. The thatch roof would offer protection. She hurried there as another spear of lightning cracked and sizzled. A boom of thunder immediately followed, rattling her entire world. A sign stood in the front, depicting a sprig of green holly. A misspelled lowborn scrawl gave its name: The Green Man's In."

In the yard, no one hurried outside to stable Alse's horse. She hopped off her steed as sheets of rain fell all about her. The wind tossed her gown this way and that. She pounded on the wooden door. "My good man!" she cried. *Or is it a woman.* "Let me inside!" There was no answer. She tried the door—and it opened. It was unlocked.

Could the bandits have murdered the innkeeper? Would a scene of carnage greet her?

The couches and chairs had been thrown all over. Flour and spilt wine marred the floor. A crack of thunder echoed—and then whimpering. She could hear it through a door.

"Please," the voice was mumbling, "please…"

"Who is it?" said Alse.

"Who do you think?" the voice answered. "The innkeeper."

Alse opened the door. Hands pushed her against the wall. A knife flashed.

Stunned, Alse staggered backward. "A message from the Black Fox, our savior." This was no elf. It was a peasant man, tall and strongly built, wearing brown russet clothing. "I have caught us a big one! A priestess, yes, a devotee of the Goddess! The Goddess is dead!"

Alse gathered herself. She had thought elves were responsible for all this destruction—but the bandit lord had won over the peasantry. Now, the lowly *villeins* were given over to their basest impulses. The domestic pigs had become wild boars—fearsome, wild, and rude. *Goddess help me.* "You should be in the vineyards," said Alse, "trimming the vine. You should be milking the cows. Instead you wreak violence. You lie in wait for travelers. Repent and ask for the Goddess's mercy."

The peasant laughed darkly. It was not a knife he held but a sword. Peasants were forbidden to bear arms. No doubt he had pocketed it from a fallen knight or man-at-arms.

"Lay down your arms, my friend," said Alse. In her years of training as a priest, she had been forbidden to wield iron. The Goddess hated iron. Iron killed fairies with a simple touch. Iron was poison to the fey. Therefore, priestesses had to compensate.

"Soon, we will throw off our shackles!" the peasant cried. "We will stop the suffering we've endured for thousands of years!

The lord will have to work. The lady will have to spin. The king will be a jester. The peasants will rule."

Such a thing would never happen. It was the order of things. One could not rebel against nature or rewrite things that had been in place since the beginning—the peasants sow, the priestesses pray, the nobles fight. It had always been and it always would be. No cog in society's grand machine was lesser than the other, though it seemed that way. Each was imperative for a healthy and functional society. The peasants did not deserve pity and the nobles did not deserve scorn.

"How much money do you have, my sweet?" said the peasant.

Alse did not know what to say. She had more money than this peasant had ever seen, though it was a pittance compared to her total wealth. Ten *sous*, enough to travel comfortably. The peasant would be happy with one.

"Ah, it does not matter! I will search your body when I am done with you!"

The peasant charged. Alse dodged just as the sword would have taken her in the head. She stepped forward and punched hard. The peasant howled in pain and fell over. Two brown teeth had fallen from his bleeding jaw.

The priesthood taught many things—lessons of theology and of the geography of the Otherworld, yes, but among the most important lessons was a good, solid punch.

She fled outside.

~

The horse was gone. The lightning had terrified it. It would run through Vale of Roy, panicked, and fall into the hands of the bandits. Alse cursed her luck. The Goddess despised her but this seemed overly cruel. It was still a long journey to Zarubain. She would have to make it on foot.

The peasant came dashing out. His face was red and contorted, wild with rage. Blood trickled from his mouth as he charged again. And again Alse dodged him just at the last moment, but this time did not strike. Her foot caught his and he went flying to the ground. The sword skidded from his grasp, just out of reach. Alse walked over calmly in the midst of the sheeting rain. She grabbed him by the shoulders and locked his neck in her arms, then heaved him onto his feet. "I do not kill unless it is necessary," she said. "Is it necessary?"

"No," the peasant mumbled through a mouth of blood.

"Know I hold your life in my hands. A twist of the arm and you would be dead." Alse tightened her grasp on his neck. "I have mercy on you. Now have mercy on me. Run and tell your bandit 'king' to leave the Reverend Alse alone."

"Yes, milady," the peasant grunted.

She released him and the peasant went sprinting down the road, leaving his sword behind. Alse-Lorie cursed her luck again. She wondered if her mercy had been folly. It was too late to question herself now. She walked over, grabbed the sword and headed to the wood's edge. She pitched back her arm, and hurled the wicked iron into the brush. Then she turned and walked inside.

Chapter Sixty-Four:
Squalor

Ramden the Bold

Healthy and strong, riding without a problem on his horse and with a sword buckled to his side, Ramden should have been as happy as ever. Yet clouds of uncertainty hung above him as the morning light dawned. The peasants of Lessant tended the vineyards, the fields of beans and the dairy farms. Once they had called Ramden lord. Now Ramden was even less than them—a heretic, a man of great dishonor. He had shamed his family line, and from that there was no returning. He would never bear his father's standard again. No proud bear rampant for Ramden—just the life of an outlaw from hereon.

He reminded himself of Old Woman Maude's words. *Do not return to Deepwood Hollow.* Most of all—*do not return to Sylla.* The thought, still, was laughable. The worst weeks of his life, a traumatic hell of Sylla's own making, were something he still dreaded. The nightmares would surely continue. The wounds, the devices of torture, the sadistic smile of Sylla—those would haunt him to the grave.

Ramden was a man of the sword. Fighting had long been his only profession. He could not till the fields or milk the cows, nor did he want to. Ramden was the most energetic, the most himself, at the vanguard of an army, fully girt in armor with a lance in hand, charging his hapless prey. Ramden could not cook or clean. Moreover, he would not. But now, a renegade, he had to find some way of supporting himself. There was only one way—to sell his sword to the highest bidder, to become a mercenary.

Mercenary companies operated with impunity. They did not ask questions. Murderers, thieves, heretics and disgraced noblemen alike lined their coffers. The only thing required was skill. No moral judgments were permissible. Therefore, Ramden would head east along the Royal Road which bisected the kingdom. He would go to the lands of the petty noblemen, the much-scorned Eastern Heartlands. There, in the great town of Tournay, he would pledge himself to a mercenary company and rebuild the ruins of his life.

~

In late morning, Ramden the Bold found himself on the Royal Road. The wide dirt thoroughfare bisected the kingdom. Travel long enough, and you would find yourself in the Eastern Region, where no westerner wanted to be. Eventually it would take you out of Zarubain, to unknown lands which geographers had not charted.

Yet here, the environs were decidedly familiar. Vineyards—some, unfortunately, in disarray—lay in view of whitewashed castles. Peasant and lord alike had grown weary of the war, but the common *villeins* still toiled here, in the ancient lands of Duchy Valais. Along the road, every mile, was a country inn.

On and on Ramden traveled. The Royal Road would take him far from home—far from the life he had always known.

~

It was near the end of the journey, having traveled three days through unfamiliar counties and through regions that he did not know the name of, that Ramden questioned his decision. He did not want to admit his mistake. He did not want to admit that, at long last, his mouth had gotten him in more trouble than he could handle. He wondered if he should have stayed home, begged Tetienne for mercy—mercy she would have almost certainly granted—and lived the rest of his life as a cripple. What, in the end, was the value of a witch's life? Surely Good Woman Maude would have a way to escape the burning, some spell or sleight-of-hand that she would use to escape.

Late in the third day the towering stone walls of Tournay appeared. Above them peaked the steeples of cathedrals and churches and tall bell towers. The stench of human habitation—the waste and the garbage—mixed with the fetid scent of the tanneries. Ramden had always loathed the sickening smell of towns. The Royal City could not escape it. There was a reason lords and ladies stayed put in their castles and did not leave the countryside without dire necessity. The lowborn *villeins* had a saying—"town air makes free"— but there was nothing more unnatural, more unhealthy, more plague-ridden and congested than a Zarube town.

The gates were wide open despite the Imperial War that now raged. Men-at-arms had been posted on the walls with bows. Others stood by the gate, wielding halberds.

"My good man," one of them began.

Not milord. And he had a detestable lowborn accent. The townsmen acted so arrogantly despite their low birth. It was an offense against nature that these peasants were able to walk about in this self-enclosed world, considering each other equals.

"Are you bringing anything to trade?" said the man-at-arms. "If so, I must check your baggage."

"I am not," Ramden sneered. "Only my sword."

The man-at-arms began to speak again but Ramden galloped off before he could hear.

The roads of Tournay were paved and well kept, but garbage was strewn about. The cobblestones were soiled with human waste where the townsmen had pitched their chamberpots, and no amount of street-cleaning could fully erase it.

The homes of Tournay were tall and crammed together and leaned so far into the road that Ramden felt he was traversing a tunnel. And Ramden, with his horse, could barely fit among the street traffic. From one edge to another, the lowborn *villeins* walked side-by-side, struggling to pass through the street.

The church bells rang. The street opened into a market square and the sound of merchants hawking their wares drowned the bells out. Bottles of wine, spices from the south, elvish swords and elvish jewelry were all on display. It seemed there was a contest going on—whoever screamed the loudest won.

"A fine red wine!" one merchant howled. "One hundred years old this day!"

"A fine book!" another cried. "A romance of the ancient trouveres! Ten *sous* and not an *aston* more!"

"Dragonettes!" shouted a woman. "Five reds and a rainbow! Fifty crowns for the discerning nobleman!"

The swarming mass of people and the cacophony of voices overwhelmed Ramden.

"Look at him, mother!" A little boy was pointing at him. "He has a horse—he must be rich!"

"Hush," the boy's mother hissed and jerked him away. "We must find our supper."

Ramden had forgotten how out of reach horses were to the common people. A good destrier could cost as much as twenty *libres*, and a common riding horse not much less.

Not soon enough, Ramden left the swarming, shouting mass of the market square and entered once again the tunnel-like streets of Tournay.

"Look out, water!" cried a woman from a high window and

emptied her chamber pot onto the street. A fetid stench greeted Ramden as he walked by. *I am too good for this*, he thought. *Any noble is too good for this.*

Amid the twisting, winding streets Ramden rode, through crammed alleys and broad, waste-filled thoroughfares. It was clear these lowborns had begun preparing for the Feast of the Lady—an insignificant festival back home but apparently of great significance here, in this backwater, lowborn dump. A summer wreath hung on every door, and bouquets of flowers lay on doorsteps. It was clear these lowborn *villeins* were of serious faith and of a happy disposition, but that did not forgive the circumstances of their birth. It did not matter if they had received a charter of self-rule from the king—they were lowborns, of *villein* stock, and that would never change, no matter how prosperous they became.

Past the Road of the Bakers, the Road of the Tanners, the Road of the Fullers and Dyers, the Road Saint-Jermaine and the Road Saint-Croix, Ramden—at last—found what he was looking for late in the day. The Road of the Swords stretched along the wall, paved and cleaner than the residential areas. Ramden passed the famed Knights of Lorh Commandery where the Knight Grandmaster of the order resided. The most hated order of knights, they were well overdue for a purge. Popular opinion and noble opinion had alike turned against them—elf-lovers they were called, traitors to the realm and haters of the king. A great iron gate prevented easy access to the commandery. The whitewashed stone of the building seemed strangely radiant despite the shadow of the townhomes behind it. The windows were iron-grilled—and with good reason.

In the shadow of the wall, Ramden continued. More commanderies passed by, of knightly orders he had never heard of. He came to the end of the road, ready to abandon hope, when a wooden sign caught his eye. Words were written on it: "The Gold Drake Company."

Ramden dismounted. He trusted his warhorse never to flee

or disobey.

In the commandery, a man sat behind a desk, clearly not a warrior. He was thin and gaunt and had the look of a scholar or a wizard, not a knight. His hair was gray and his eyes a shade of blue. He peered intently at Ramden, curious yet dismissive.

"Can I help you, my good man?" He did not bother disguising his disdain.

"Good man" was what peasants were called. Ramden's face flushed hot. He wanted to strike this cur for speaking rudely. *But I am not a Rambée anymore.* "I wish to join your company. I am good with the sword, and fleet of foot."

"'Good with the sword and fleet of foot.' I have heard such talk from street urchins and haggard old men before." The man's glare intensified. "The Gold Drakes take great pride in their work."

Ramden drew his sword. "I have a sword and a warhorse. I can fight with the best of them. I am a nobleman—of House Rambée." Desperation strained Ramden's voice. He had only a few *deniers* left, not even enough for a night at Tournay's most ramshackle inn.

"My good man," the man continued, his condescension only growing, "The Gold Drakes have no need of swords or horsemen. We also find nobles to be overly proud and self-centered. They rarely make good matches."

Ramden scoffed. *The nerve of this man.*

"We are seeking red wizards to join. Do you practice magic? I do not think so."

Ramden seethed.

"If you could practice magic and belonged to the Red Robes, then we could talk. Unfortunately, I must ask you to leave. *Now.*"

"I will not be treated so poorly," Ramden shouted. "I am a noble. You will treat me with respect, lowborn scum. Your life is worth a small sum—and I will pay the fee to see your throat cut. There will be no gallows for me."

Ramden charged but a blinding light stunned him and sent him staggering backwards against the wall. The lowborn's outer clothes had slipped off him, revealing a crimson robe. A staff was in his hand. The room had gone cold. "Leave," the red wizard said, "before I do something drastic."

Ramden charged again. In an instant his sword turned scalding hot. He dropped it to the floor, where it turned red and began to melt. Another blinding flash burst before him and Ramden half-fell, half-staggered, toward the now-open door.

"Go," boomed the red wizard. "Go and never come back, Master Rambée."

Swordless and penniless, Ramden mounted his warhorse once more. He wept. He could sell the beast for a large sum, but was that truly the best course of action? He'd be stuck among these lowborns forever, and *aston* by *aston* his wealth would dwindle until he truly had nothing. He could only imagine the shame. One day, perhaps, his brother Ramone and Ramone's wife would visit Tournay and see him, dirty and clothed in rags.

The crowded streets and thick stench of Tournay sickened Ramden and he gagged. He did not want to leave, yet he did not want to stay. What else was there to do? He grabbed his coinpurse and counted the money—there were eight *sous* left, only eight, and a handful of copper *astonnes* that could buy him, at best, one paltry loaf of bread. He had spent all the money at roadside inns, and now he truly had nothing.

The words of Good Woman Maude echoed through his mind: *Promise me—don't go back to Sylla.* Ramden laughed at the thought. Even now, he could not do it. As he laughed peasant woman in patched-up flannel scowled at him. He rode by her, leaving her in her filth.

He kept laughing at the thought. How could Ramden ever be that desperate? Even at the threshold of death and starvation, could he possibly consider the idea? He had been tortured and abused for weeks. His skin had been ripped from his flesh, and salt rubbed into the wounds. He had been terrified for his life, fearful of Master's anger or—even worse—his sadistic smile. How could he possibly go back?

The winding alleyways, garbage-choked avenues and waste-blackened cobblestone of Tournay confused him. Still he rode on. He passed by a great church with a bright rose window and statues of pixies flanking the double doors—a rare thing of order and culture in this tunnel-darkened, lowborn squalor. The day had grown late before he at last found himself in the market square. Quickly he made his way to the gate.

Rejected by the mercenaries, his last hope extinguished, Ramden left Tournay, heading west. But there was nowhere to go.

Chapter Sixty-Five:
Iron Teeth

Danitari

What day was it? What month was it? Were there truly gods in heaven?

Those three questions bounced through his mind. His visions and his reality had become blurred. He had begun to forget what the outside world looked like. He could not envision the color of the sky on a clear day, or the shade of the green pines of Zarubain.

Yet he could remember vividly the color of the grass in the Great Elven Plain, the wildflowers wafting in the wind, the purple and yellow blossoms which drifted this way and that. He remembered the warmth of summer, the young boys playing war with wooden swords and wooden helmets. He remembered the village priest telling tales of the world's beginning—of Lumas and Luvé in the light of the first dawn. He remembered the elder women teaching young girls how to weave and spin. He remembered when he had first learned to plow and tend the fields.

Yet freedom was now out of reach. Not long ago, a prisoner named Ras had lived here. He had woven a grand tale about an *ayri*, a community of elves in the woods out of the sight and mind of human civilization. Danitari laughed at the thought—the last desperate hope of an oppressed creature, a vivid dream, a wild yearning for what could never be. The humans knew all, saw all. They could sense an elf smiling from miles away—and would travel all that distance just to cut him down.

Here in this dank, cold prison, weakened by a diet of bread and water, Danitari had begun to enter the world of dreams. It was a better world than the one he had lived in before. In the real world, he was hated and despised, cursed to live a life of despair. In the dream world, he was back home, in the village with Mother and Father. He was about to propose marriage to Badré. He was stuck in the happy days, right before his world had come crashing down, before the king had summoned every able-bodied man in the Elven World to fight.

Danitari slipped against the wet walls of the prison. His hands were shaking and his legs began to quiver. A warmth settled over him. He could see the beast from his visions, devouring a lion in its iron jaws.

Chapter Sixty-Six:
Freedom

The Reverend Alse-Lorie, High Priestess

Alse had spent the night in the abandoned inn, and no one had come to harass her. When she returned to the capital, she would have to tell Lord Roland the news. Not only had bandits overrun the Vale of Roy, but the lowborn peasants—those who had once tilled the fields for the steward Evart—had joined in. They had formed a perverse lowborn government, a government based on robbery and violence. It was to be expected from lowborns. You could not expect beasts to behave like men. You could not teach a castle dog to think like a man. The peasants needed to be controlled—for the lords and ladies, yes, but also for themselves. Alse pitied them as much as she scorned them. Lord Roland, however, would not be so forgiving.

The sun was just rising when she left through the open doors. Her horse now gone, she set out, walking down the road. The pines and hemlocks flanked either side. It was only when the inn had left her vision that she became worried, painfully aware of her dangerous predicament.

The dark woods continued. Every time Alse heard a rustle she jumped. She had a strong arm and a good sense of balance, but against a group of outlaws she was severely outmatched. Add enough swords and spears and no amount of agility and strength could overcome them.

I have to get back to the city. I have to find the Holy Book before the page is destroyed. Even here in the lonely woods, she remembered keenly the *lormon narsannad,* the great beast which had appeared in the water. There was great meaning there, something of incredible import. Something that might determine the fate of the nation.

A twig cracked in the woods. *I will not be stopped by outlaws.*

Still she stopped. The boughs of the firs and pines dripped with last night's rain. The woods were bright with moss and lichen. A tuft of Grayman's beard dangled from one of the branches—an unwelcome reminder of what awaited her. *A cucking stool, a shaved head, poverty, starvation, exile.* It was nothing less than what she deserved. Yet the worst thing was the Goddess's scorn, the knowledge that Alse was despised by the Lady herself.

In the darkness she could not see any movement. The deer here were fat and well fed. A stag could easily have broken the branches. There were black bears, too, and deer. Any number of forest creatures could have caused the noise. Still, she trembled, and her heart was seized with dread. Cold, and with clammy hands, she continued on apace.

~

The cold creeks, babbling brooks and lush glades of the Silver Woods disappeared behind her. The firs and pines were replaced with vineyards. The rows of green were abandoned. In the distance, on high hills, the blackened remains of a village emitted smoke into the blue sky. The peasants had exchanged their honest work for robbery and destruction. They had joined with the elves. The lowborn—left to their own devices—had predictably become wild beasts. It was not their fault—they were naturally base and savage. Without lords and ladies to restrain their worse impulse, this was the natural result.

Once this walk had been merry. The journey from Zarubad southward along the coast had filled Alse-Lorie's heart with joy. The sight of the peasants harvesting grapes in the vineyards, gathering apples and pears in the orchards, and stamping their feet in the winepresses had given the illusion of prosperity and eternal peace.

That had all changed with the war.

On the sides of the road, blackened bodies appeared. The corpses were shriveled and burned beyond recognition. No doubt the elven bandits had done this—could a human being be so cruel? She remembered the savagery of the Imperials, and thought to herself, "Yes, they could."

Just a dozen yards beyond, hanged bodies dangled from an ash tree like ornaments. They had bloated and turned green and brown, and the stench of death hung all around the road—thick, foul, and sickening. Alse retched. She could not tell just by looking at the bodies what their class was, but the tattered remnants of blue fustian cloth clung to their flesh like a layer of skin. *Merchants, perhaps—or even highly born.* When the peasants' murders extended even to their betters, Alse-Lorie knew all semblance of the rule of law had disappeared.

On this, the Great South Road, she had seen not a single merchant. Only she, a priestess armed with her fists, was foolish enough to travel. The thought sickened her.

A horse came galloping by. Alse-Lorie leapt back and tripped, falling squarely onto her back, soiling her green robe. Dazed, Alse stood up. When she came to, the rider loomed above her, a young man with thick brown hair and dark eyes. "Milady," he said. "Are you going to Zarubad?" He spoke like a lowborn.

Alse-Lorie bit her lip, wondering if she should lie.

"I can take you there quickly, if you need a quick hand."

"What is a lowborn doing riding on a horse?" Alse said. A fine brown horse like that would cost ten *libres* at the least, well out of the range of any commonblood.

"A lowborn," the peasant repeated, and a scowl formed on his face. "An insult is what I get for the offer of help. Oh, yes, I see. Thank you, milady."

He galloped off, and Alse-Lorie cursed herself for the mistake. *If he was one of the bandits, he would not have left me here.*

A mile further down the road, she came to a short extent of woods. A dozen elves stepped out of the darkness of the pines and firs, some carrying bows, some wielding daggers, and others heaving greatswords. Behind them were twice their number in peasants, wearing tattered homespun clothes and wielding sticks and kitchen knives.

"My lady," said the foremost of them, dressed in scale armor, in that horrid elvish accent. "You must pay a toll to travel this road. Give us ten *sous* and we will leave you alone."

"You aren't getting one *aston*, bandit," hissed Alse-Lorie. The rebellion of a peasant was one thing, but to see an elf—the lowest of all the lowly born—speak so rudely to a priestess was something utterly uncalled for. She could scarcely believe his arrogance.

"If you will not comply," said the elf, "we will take you to King Bran for trial."

"There is only one king, and there is only one kingdom," said Alse-Lorie. "The king is Jourmande vis Bretagne. There is no King Bran."

"Take her," said the elf. His light brown eyes were hesitant, unwilling. Alse-Lorie had no doubts he was being compelled. This so-called King Bran, a bandit leader, had perhaps purchased these elves wholesale and enlisted them in an army. It would not end well for "King Bran"—and it certainly would not end well for the elves. Their daring exploit would end in a torturous death. It would be another failure in the long history of insurrections and peasant rebellions. The Bretagnes could not be beaten. Not even great dukes had successfully broken away from their control. This foolish bandit king would be burned at the stake or boiled alive. So, too, would the elves foolish enough to surrender.

The elven slaves bound her hands with cord. She did not struggle. The peasants were smiling, positively glowing at this injustice. *It will not end well for them either.*

They marched Alse-Lorie back down the road until again they had entered the Silver Woods. By then it was midday. Zarubad was a distant memory. Alse was quivering. She was saying prayers under her breath to the Lady, prayers of hope and protection. Yet the Lady In White would not hear her; her ears were deaf to Alse, the harlot who betrayed her vows. *Yet Sir Loy is worth it,* she thought. She remembered his dark brown eyes, his gallant demeanor, his mastery of the sword, his surefootedness. He had won tourneys and jousts without fail. The ladies of the kingdom would surely envy her—but not now.

Late in the day they came to a castle of grim gray stone. Four towers, connected by high walls, protected an immense inner keep. She knew in an instant where she was—Castle Moonsilver, once the home of the steward Evart. The trees had been cleared for a hundred yards around, and in their place grew tall grass and weeds. A moat surrounded it. The portcullis was lifted, and a mixture of elves and peasants in tattered homespun clothes lingered outside, bearing swords, spears, and scythes.

It is forbidden for elves to bear arms—and peasants, also.

In the castle yard, they patted her down, at last finding her coinpurse. The chief elf counted the coins—twenty gold *libres*, several dozen silver *sous*, and a handful of *deniers* and copper *astonnes*. "She lied," said the chief elf. "She carried much money."

"Shall we let her go?" said another elf.

"Only King Bran can decide," he answered.

She eyed Castle Moonsilver's dark donjon keep. Only then, seeing the lack of blue-and-gold lion flags, did the reality dawn on her. These bandits and elves had successfully stormed a castle. Castle Moonsilver was the backbone of Vale of Roy, the seat of administration for the king's fief. It had become, in effect, a rogue bandit state. The world had truly gone mad.

They led her inside the donjon keep. Torches on sconces lit the walls of dark grim stone. Portraits of the Lord Steward, Evart, were nowhere to be seen. Nor did this King Bran have any portraits on display; who could trust a crude peasant's hand to paint the highly born?

She had her doubts that this King Bran was highly born.

~

In the steward's Great Hall, the bandit king sat, eating a meal of braised vegetables and drinking a glass of wine. It had not occurred to Alse-Lorie that elves might know how to cook—yet there were people in Zarubain without a sense of propriety who would eat what elves had touched.

King Bran looked up. He was in his early middle age. He had a thick black beard, immaculately trimmed and cleaned, and a handsome, dark face. His eyes were the color of coals. "A captive, Eldion?" said King Bran.

"Yes, Your Majesty," answered the chief elf.

"And what is your name, good woman?" said the false king. He spoke without a peasant accent, nor a false, social-climbing merchant affectation. This man was highborn—or once had been.

He had called her "good woman"—a term used for wet nurses and chamber maids, fishwives and peasant women. "Good woman," Alse scoffed. "You will call me 'my lady' or 'your ladyship.'" Out of the corner of her eye Alse saw her once-pristine priestly robes, muddied and dampened. The pink of her stole was scarcely recognizable.

"I should have known," said Bran. "Your robe is dirtied as to be expected. You are a priestess of the Goddess."

"And you," said Alse-Lorie. "I hear the way you talk. You are a king only of bandits, and yet your speech is refined. You are a nobleman, Bran… albeit one who threw his life away."

At her words, Bran glared. "Yes, good woman."

Alse bristled at the knowing insult.

"I am one of the highly born," he said. "Once I lorded over peasants in the vineyards of County Orr. They called me Master Brandon. I was the firstborn of the House of Cardigne."

Alse did not want to encourage him by asking more. She could already sense his disrespect.

"I grew unduly close to the peasants," said Bran. "I drank in their alehouses and played dice with the common farmers. I despised the strict rules of noble life which had been forced upon me. Countless times I was warned—by my parents, by my priestess, by the visiting noblemen… but I did not listen. When my father died I realized they had cut me out of the will—they had given the county to my crippled brother Robyn. I was so angry I fought in the castle's Great Hall—I killed two knights. I was exiled and forbidden to ever return."

She had heard the name Robyn before, the cripple who once ruled County Orr. "Robyn is dead."

"I have heard," said Bran. "They have found someone else—I am dead to them."

Alse-Lorie still had no sympathy for this man. He had, after all, overrun this once-tranquil vale, laid hold of its treasures and butchered thousands of innocents. He had joined hands with elves and wrought destruction everywhere. He was not to be pitied—he was to be condemned.

"I stole money from the county treasury. I swore I would become an enemy of the king and the high-blooded. I purchased a hundred elves… I began robbing. And with each new bit of treasure I bought more. I liberated Vale of Roy and made the peasants—all of them—free men."

"Quiet!" snapped Alse-Lorie. Such talk of "freedom" and "liberation" would get his tongue cut off in any more civilized place.

"Do not speak to me so," said Bran. His expression turned stormy; his coal-black eyes were filled with a dark hate.

Suddenly Alse-Lorie had little care for the *lormon narsannad,* or the imminent threat of exile and shame. She had only concern for the preservation of her life, and for the dark-hearted bandit king who wanted to end it.

"There is no fiercer warrior than one who has tasted freedom," Bran said. "These peasants will find unto their deaths to preserve it. They have come to hate the highly born, as I have."

"Are you going to kill me?" said Alse-Lorie. Tears welled in her eyes. She did not want her life to end like this, amid the angry peasant mob and the elf-polluted air. "Give me a quick death. It is no less than the High Priestess deserves. No torture, no burning, no boiling."

The hate in his eyes diminished but did not disappear. "The High Priestess does deserve more. A ransom. The king would pay a handsome sum for her life. You will be kept prisoner until he writes back. You may move around the castle under careful guard."

Relief washed through Alse-Lorie. Her tense muscles loosened; the cold dread in her heart melted. The concerns of the prior day—much less pressing than the threat of imminent death—began to return. She remembered the filth of the sea, the *lormon narsannad*, and her curiosity returned. "Do you have a library, Your Majesty?" said Alse.

Bran nodded.

"Thank the Goddess," Alse breathed. The elves led her away to her cell. Thunder rolled across the castle. Rain began to pour against the roof, and a wind picked up.

~

That night in the castle library, amid the flashing lightning and the deafening thunder, she laid hands on Castle Moonsilver's copy of the Holy Book. She paged through it, finding "The Seven Visions of Sinderion." Again the *lormon narsannad* had been excised from the page. Alse-Lorie wept, exhausted and utterly defeated. The dark forces which sought to prevent this knowledge had succeeded. Had they truly cut the page from each book? It seemed impossible that this band of thieves had stretched their arms into every county castle in Zarubain, into every library, and succeeded in their dark goals.

Chapter Sixty-Seven:
Good News and Bad

Roland vis Valais, Duke of Valais

"Sylla was driven from Duchy Arvogne," the knight said to Lord Roland before the Lion Throne. He had been sent by his patrons, the House of Alerie, and on his shield their symbol was painted—a gold beaver against a green background. "He failed to take Castle Neves."

Roland smiled. His plan, at last, had come together. The Imperial soldiers had begun to lose their capabilities. Their siege weapons had been destroyed utterly and their strength and morale had begun to fail. There was little food for them. *They may well turn back and flee for the Empire—but not if I kill them first.*

"Lord Alerie chased them out of Arvogne. They crossed the river. They've taken safe haven in County Garrone."

"Good news," said Roland, perhaps the understatement of the year. *If only Queen Alysant were here, to swallow her words.* Lord Mars would be so proud of him and so delighted. The baby King Tyrol would have a large and prosperous realm to inherit, and he would owe Lord Roland all of it. The first defeat of the Imperial Army would shatter their morale and send shock waves rippling through the kingdom. There was only one last cog in the grand machine, only one last piece to the grand puzzle. "Tell your liege to prepare for battle," said Roland. "Prepare to gather up all his remaining strength. At my word, all the armies of the Seven Gems will gather. We will drive the Empire out of Zarubain and destroy them utterly."

The massive operation would be only weeks away, at most. Roland did not know what would be better—a crushing victory over a once-invincible foe, or seeing Queen Alysant and Princess Clarysse, his wife Elsie and the Reverend Alse-Lorie swallow their words. He could not quite decide, just yet.

"I shall tell them," the knight said. He bowed slightly and then turned to leave.

Esmette vis Alerie and her husband Lord Alivere had been to the capital before and had harshly disagreed with the way Roland conducted the war. But now they saw for themselves Roland's strategy. The crushing victory would cement in their minds Roland's wisdom and overarching strategy. When the death blow for the Empire came, Roland's patience and seeming softness would be shown in its true light—a strategic patience that was a coherent and effective course of action all along.

That very hour, Roland sent messages to each duke of the Seven Gems to prepare for war.

~

Late that day, in the company of Lord Mars, another messenger arrived. He had in his hands a letter written on lambskin. "Your Lordship." He dropped to one knee.

"Rise," said Roland.

"I have a message from the Vale of Roy."

The vale was overrun with bandits. Some said that Castle Moonsilver itself had been taken, and that the lord steward had been killed publicly. One thing was certain—all semblance of order had been demolished, and anarchy reigned.

He opened the rolled up lambskin. "To the King of Zarubain. Here it says, 'word from King Bran.'"

"Another king. Quaint." Roland laughed lightly.

"I have in my possession the High Priestess of Zarubain. For her safe return, I demand five marks paid in gold. You have until the Feast of the Crone. On that day I shall kill her."

Roland scoffed. The bandits had grown overbold. Surely it was a lie. Who would dare capture Alse-Lorie? Who would dare call himself "king?"

"The bandit has done us a great service, getting rid of that shrew," said Lord Mars.

"Shut your mouth," Roland snarled. Such words were beneath his station. Yes, Lord Mars was—at heart—a peasant, but it was beneath his dignity. Roland was Lord Regent. He could not associate himself with such talk.

Lord Mars was glaring at him. *So be it. Let him be angry.*

"The Lady Alse-Lorie," Roland murmured. "A pious woman, the proclaimer of the Faith—as I am its defender. There is a rule with a long history in our kingdom. We do not hold talks with bandits, nor do we pay ransoms except to a nation's sovereign. Yet what else could we do? The bandits will kill her…"

"Five marks," Lord Mars repeated, apparently a new expert at finances and coinage. "To a bandit lord and an insurrectionist."

"As Lord Regent I do not know what can be done," said Roland. "I will think on it. I would not dare to disregard our ancient rule—but it may be necessary."

~

Another visitor arrived before the Lion Throne late in the day. Lord Roland vaguely recognized her red hair and freckles. She wore the green gown and the pink stole of a priestess.

Great, Roland thought, *another one.*

"My lord Roland," she said. "I am Varysse, parish priestess of the Outer City."

Perhaps she had brought back fleas from the stinking, squalid streets. Roland found himself inching away.

"I bring to you an accusation of incredible importance," she said. "Namely, that your own High Priestess, who pretends to rule the faithful, is a liar and a harlot, a breaker of her vows. She has lain with a man."

Roland felt his hackles rise. Lord Mars stiffened uncomfortably. The members of the Royal Guard eyed this Varysse and tightened their grip on their swords. "I do not have time for this," said Roland.

"Do not think me a madwoman." Varysse's face had flushed a shade of bright red. Her blue eyes burned with wrath. "I have proof—incontrovertible proof. On my honor. If I do not show it beyond all doubt, then I will accept death. You may burn me at the stake if it is necessary."

"Again," sneered Roland. "There is no time." Such a thing would cause an outcry across the whole kingdom—but what did it matter? There were graver concerns. There were far more pressing issues than broken vows and minor sins. The greatest sin of all hovered over Roland—failure—and he would not let it consume him. Failure to defend the kingdom would be the greatest sin of all.

Varysse was apoplectic. "You do not care about the integrity of the priesthood! Why, I should expect nothing better from you, 'Lord' Roland. Or should I call you 'Lady?'"

"Drag her out!" bellowed Roland. "Throw her into the streets, and make it hurt."

The Royal Guard consented. Whatever concern Roland had for the integrity of the priesthood vanished. A woman who spoke so rudely to the Lord Regent did not deserve his attention.

Chapter Sixty-Eight:
The Trap Is Set

The Reverend Varysse, Priestess

The beginning of the end for Alse-Lorie had not gone as Varysse had hoped. But Varysse's victory was assured. She had crept into Alse's bedchamber—against all the rules of the priesthood—and found the Grayman's beard she had been consuming. There was only one reason for it to be there, and that was enough proof for any sensible person. One only consumed Grayman's beard to prevent pregnancy, or to end one. Varysse needed only to find someone in the royal court with a sense of honor—honor Varysse could exploit, and use to bring about Alse-Lorie's catastrophic end.

Chapter Sixty-Nine:
Westward

Ramden the Bold

Ramden traveled west down the road. Where else was there to go? What else was there to do? If he had crossed the Tournay Bridge into Surrevere he would find himself in Further Zarubain and eventually the Eastern Region. Such a place was alien to everything Ramden had known. The further from the heartlands, the greater the chaos and instability, the lesser the rule of law. The grand dukes of the Eastern Region ruled as autonomous monarchs. They would have no use for a westerner.

Therefore, all Ramden could do was go home and beg for leniency and mercy. He would apologize with weeping eyes, and soften the harsh glares of the Reverend Tetienne. He would lead his brother's knights to Deepwood Hollow. He would let them burn Old Woman Maude at the stake, the same one who had healed him. And he would let Ramone's men break his ankles once more. What was the life of a cripple in exchange for comfort and wealth?

Days later he crossed into Duchy Duranche. Home was only a short journey away. In the warm sunlight he remembered the respect his family once had for him. He had been the greatest warrior in the family, ten times the strength of Ramone. The peasant girls had fawned over him. The knights had esteemed them above everyone, even his father, Lord Ramir.

Then he thought of the life he'd soon return to—a cripple, with his ankles broken. Day by day, month by month, year by year, he would waste away. His muscles would loosen from disuse. He would grow fat and useless like Ramone. The peasant girls of Duchy

Lessant would look on him with barely-disguised disgust every time he was carried outside. *And that is what I'm going back to.*

Castle Hombard appeared. No longer did the Imperial flags fly; now the Ram of the House of Námois fluttered on the turrets. *They have driven Sylla out.* Ramden wondered why the news disappointed him. It struck him like a blow, twisted his insides. Perhaps he had found a sick comfort in seeing these bad people, these noblemen who treated Ramden poorly and knew nothing of suffering, struggle in vain against the Empire.

Rules set in stone were shown to be porous: *The Empire is not invincible. The Empire does not always win.*

In a thick wood on the edge of Duranche, Ramden—exhausted—found his way to an inn. "The Horn of Plenty" it was called, a large building of two stories with a thatch roof. Its boards were painted in rich creamy hues and its stable and yard commanded a wide space. Such a place was beneath the dignity of a nobleman, who stayed—as a rule—with highborn friends. Yet Ramden had only two *sous* left, and no honor to speak of. No self-respecting highborn would associate with the rogue Master Ramden, who befriended woods witches and defended their honor.

A pair of elven slaves ran out—a boy and a girl. "We will take your horse," they said. Ramden dismounted and they led the beast away, into the stable.

~

In the inn's common room, a fire blazed despite the relative warmth outside. The floors were of dirt but padded with straw. The sound of the lute and dulcimer echoed throughout the open space. Around the dozen tables a thick crowd had gathered, each with a full glass of wine. There were merchants in fine purple cloaks and pilgrims in grim gray clothes perhaps heading to the Church of Saint Ignáce in Naines or Saint Delphine-upon-the-Zandie. All were travelers, and their faces were merry as they feasted on breads and thick stews. The musicians, standing on a stage, had begun to play *Ol' Cow Bess.*

"Ol' Cow Bess," the lowborns started singing, "Ol' Cow Bess… Farmer Piers did milk her…"

Far off in a corner, a group of knights played dice. Dice and gambling were considered a lowborn's hobby, but more knights and even highborn played than would admit it. A pool of silver *sous* and *deniers* sat in the middle of their table. They had not joined the patrons in song.

"Hello, my good man!" The innkeeper stood before him, a plump man with a buttoned-up coat. His hands were stained white with flour. "A stay at The Horn of Plenty will ruin all other inns for you. I shall make it so."

"I'd like a room," said Ramden. "A room with a bed. And a glass of wine… that's all I need."

"Two sous for the room, and one *denier* for a glass of wine…"

"Just the room, then." Ramden felt like weeping. He was hungry and thirsty, deeply ravished and weak. What he wouldn't give for a glass of wine, a mouthful of bread. He would give up the use of his legs—no, he would not give up anything for that.

He handed the innkeeper the two *deniers,* the last bit of wealth he had. Now he was penniless—penniless and hungry.

"You know, my friend, if you do some work, I can serve you a good glass of wine. The best wine you'll ever taste."

"That's all right," said Ramden. There was no wine glass worth working under a lowborn's employ.

He sat at a table by himself. He eyed his ankles, perfectly healed. He remembered they would be broken tomorrow, when he returned to Castle Silvergold. The humiliation would be severe, even worse than seeing Deepwood Hollow put to the torch, the woods witch Maude burned at the stake, and the woodland creatures butchered and roasted for dinner.

He wept into his hands. The knights snickered at his unmanliness. It did not matter. Nothing mattered, anymore. He had consigned himself to a life of torment, a living death as cruel as hell. The scorn he faced in The Horn of Plenty meant exactly nothing.

"The Imperials have gone south," one of the knights said. "They're holed up in Silvan March, by the sea."

"I think their time is up," said another. "If the Aleries can break them, they'll all be dead soon."

~

Ramden awoke early in the morning and set out in the nascent light of dawn. The rosy rays of the sun glanced through the pine bows and the air smelled thickly of wildflowers. He had not ridden an hour before he came to the Duranche Bridge. He stopped at its edge. A little further and he would once again be home—but not altogether home. His family's scorn had turned to hatred. The priestess Tetienne wanted blood. He would be a cripple again, as useless as before. Old Woman Maude would be burned alive in view of the peasantry, and Deepwood Hollow would be demolished and scorched to ash. No longer would he ride his horse. No longer would he run or wield the sword. No longer would he fight—the thing he had relished more than all else.

Ramden wheeled his horse and galloped the other way. He would ride east and then south, south into the marches, south into Silvan March, south into the Empire's hands.

Chapter Seventy:
Back to Master

Ramden the Bold

The journey should, by any reasonable thought, have taken him three days, but Ramden rode swiftly. He did not stop to eat or drink. Hungry and thirsty, he ignored his body's needs.

He crossed the tranquil woods of Duchy Voraigne, leaving its Ville and Voraigne Manor itself behind. He skimmed the edge of Ajernon in the light of the sunny day, seeing its productive vineyards but thinking little of them. He passed beside the vineyards and bean fields of Duchy Arvogne and reached County Rannier by dusk. It was dark before he galloped through the covered bridge into Silvan March.

A battalion of Imperial soldiers stood on the edge of the covered bridge, bearing swords of steel and shields of red and gold. "Signore!" they cried. "State your business!"

But Ramden rode past them, ignoring their shouts. His mind was utterly focused at the task at hand—to rejoin Sylla, to pledge his life to Sylla, to live or die by Sylla's command. Of everyone only Sylla had treated him with respect. Sylla had tortured him, yes. He had crippled him. But he had never betrayed him like his family did. Was there anything more painful and destructive than a family turning its back on a son in need? For that there was no ailment. Not even Good Woman Maude could cure that.

The stars and moon soon appeared. Exhausted, Ramden dismounted and led his horse off road. He tied him to the trunk of a fir, wrapped himself in a cloak, and slept in the open air.

He awoke at dawn. The pine forest was all around him, bright with moss and well watered. Birds were chirping and the sky was rosy. An owl with great big eyes had perched nearby, hooting loudly. In an instant it flew away. Ramden breathed in the fresh morning air. The salt scent of the coast filled it. He remembered he was in Silvan March. He stood up and unfastened his horse. Red and gold glinted before him.

Imperial standards lined the road—a gold eagle on a red field, fluttering in the wind. Ramden hopped on his horse and ascended to the road—and was stopped by spears.

"What is your business, *signore*?" an Imperial soldier said in his staccato accent.

"None of yours," said Ramden.

There were five of them on the road. The one who spoke slashed him across the chin with his spear.

Ramden grabbed his cheek, now covered in hot blood. His eyes welled with tears of pain. It would be days before the deep cut healed. "I come to speak to your general, Lord Sylla."

"Lord Sylla," the soldier repeated and laughed. "Commander Sylla does not speak to the likes of you."

"I think you are mistaken," Ramden said. "Where is he?"

"In Camp Victory," he answered. "Of course. Where else would he be? Guarded by thousands of soldiers... you would be dead before you broached the outskirts, barbarian."

"Sylla knows me," Ramden said. "He and I have a special bond."

The soldier recoiled. A grimace touched his face. "Signore... you are mad."

"Where is Camp Victory?"

The soldier smiled. "Down this road, just outside Celine Castle. You will die if you try to enter, my signore."

Castle Celine, overseeing the scant farmland of Silvan March, was rumored to stretch to the clouds. Ramden touched his cheek once more. The blood continued to trickle, wet and hot. He cursed the Imperials who had done this to him. *They are not all alike. Sylla would not do this to me.*

For miles and miles the road wound south-westward through the thick pine forest. Bright green moss grew on the forest floor and green hanging moss draped from the pine boughs. The ever-present rain of the Western Heartlands ensured that there was no plant un-watered. The deer here were large and strong and all the beasts of the forest were well fed. *The Lady looks after her woodland creatures.*

Eventually, the woods fell away, and the road descended into a great vale. To the south, the River Zarube flowed, wide and gushing. North of its banks lay a ridge of high hills on which Castle Celine perched—a towering gray edifice that overlooked the surrounding farmland. Wheat fields and vineyards stretched far into the distance. To the west lay a range of low mountains, and just beyond them, the sea. The breadbasket of Silvan March had escaped the travails of war—all by allying with the enemy.

As Ramden rode past Castle Celine proper, he could not help but glare. The marquis, sworn to protect the border, had thrown his lot in with the enemy. *So have I.* At the thought, Ramden's hatred crumbled. *I am just like him. No, I am worse. I refuse to take my punishment. Instead I join hands with the Empire.*

Camp Victory, as the soldiers said, lay just a short ride from Castle Celine. The wooden palisades had been constructed hastily. Imperial flags flew at the tips. Above it a superstructure hovered, all built of wood.

Here I am, at the threshold of the enemy. I can still turn back. I can still return to Castle Silvergold... accept my punishment... live my life as a cripple, but an honorable cripple.

He kept riding until he reached the gate.

The soldiers there glared at him. Ramden envied their artful armor—the thick breastplates of steel, and, on their heads, helmets with bright red horsehair crests.

"What do you want, Zarube worm?" one barked.

"I wish to speak with Sylla," said Ramden.

"So do all," another answered, his tone dripping with scorn. "The grand legate is a busy man… too busy for the likes of you."

"Tell him Ramden wishes to see him."

"Get out, worm!" snapped the soldier. "Sylla has better things to do than speak with barbarians."

Ramden rode closer.

"Another step and we'll have you crucified!" the soldier shouted. "Flee, Zarube worm! This is your last warning! You aren't worthy to breathe the same air as us."

Ramden could think of only two things—how far and how difficult the journey he had taken, and the terrible end that awaited him if he went back to Lessant.

Ramden galloped full-speed ahead. The soldiers threw themselves out of the way. Ramden's horse leapt over a wooden barrier but then stumbled. Ramden went flying. He hit the dirt hard. An alarm was raised. A horn blew. Shouting overwhelmed him. Thousands of soldiers crowded him and they were all gathering their weapons. *This is the end,* Ramden thought. *This is the end.*

The wind had been sucked from his lungs. He stood up and drew his sword, then flung it to the ground. He fell to his knees in surrender. His mind was whirling. In an instant a dozen Imperial soldiers had hemmed him in with swords and spears.

"Shall we kill him?" one said.

Ramden tried to catch his breath. There was a soldier among them with dark iron armor and a purple horsehair crest on his helmet. "Go ahead, Caelio," he said.

"Wait!" Ramden shouted. His mind was still spinning. The loss of his life, he did not fear. What he feared most was living in his brother's shadow, a cripple, despised by all in Castle Silvergold. "Wait!"

"Let him speak," said the soldier in dark armor. "He has one chance to preserve his life."

"Marcus Sylla," Ramden breathed. "Tell him Ramden has come."

But Marcus Sylla would not come for him. Perhaps that was best. He would die on his feet, able bodied, strong and self-sufficient.

"Go, Caelio," the soldier in dark armor continued. "Tell him, since you were so eager to spill blood."

Ramden was still dizzy and it hurt to breathe. He took in his surroundings. Thousands of soldiers lived here, too many to count. The wooden palisades were high, but the central keep was higher— and also built of wood. It would not last a day in a siege, but no sane Zarube general would attack the Imperial Army.

One of the soldiers left. The rest lowered their spears and swords, but poured scorn on Ramden with their glaring eyes. The day was clear and sunny yet Ramden was cold. The warnings of Good Woman Maude returned to him. A thought dawned on him with terrible certainty that he had made the worst mistake of his life. His recklessness had gotten him in trouble once more. He thought of the beatings, the manacles, the torture he had endured. *But it is better than living life as a cripple.*

Ramden again surveyed his environs. The countless multitude sat around fire pits. There were smiths sharpening weapons, too, and tailors mending clothes. There were leatherworkers and cobblers, working in the warmth of the day. There were hundreds of slaves and there were Zarube girls, too—no doubt harlots from the countryside or professional whores from the Storm Coast, making a quick *sou* off these lonely soldiers far from home.

Camp Victory, he realized, was a self-sustaining town. *And victory they will get, if they hold on a bit longer.* One by one the duchies would fall. King Jourmande would be hanged, and his head set on a pike for all to see. Lessant would become an Imperial dependency. Ramondine and Ramonette would be married to Imperial dukes, and Mother would work in an Imperial peasant's vineyard. The worst punishment would be saved for Ramone—a crucifixion and then a burning. He would not even receive a burial.

Ramden smiled. All his joy vanished when Caelio returned, and worst of all, when he spoke—"Signor Sylla will see you."

~

With hands bound in rope, Ramden approached the wooden fort in the center of Camp Victory. Imperials cursed at him in their own tongue. *"Zarubo!"* they called him—"Zarube," which had become the gravest of insults. Others he did not recognize. He had been held prisoner, starved and tortured by Sylla for weeks, and yet he had learned no word. The trauma had blotted out all memory, only the dreadful fear—fear that was beginning to return.

~

The soldiers opened the door to Sylla's chamber and hurled Ramden inside.

Ramden stumbled and fell onto the hard wooden floor. Two feet stepped near him—feet he recognized. Ramden was shaking. He could not help himself. *Sylla is a wild beast—if he senses weakness he will take advantage.*

"Have you gone mad?" said Sylla.

Ramden struggled to his feet. He met those ice blue eyes and fell backward against the door. The room was warm, yet gooseflesh had spread across all of his skin.

"All Zarubes are mad," said Sylla. "You are highborn in your land… a land of little development or sophistication."

There was a dagger in Sylla's hand—the hand that had fingers. He was tossing it and catching it.

"Why did you come back?" said Sylla. "Did you miss the skinning knife and the garrote?"

A desk sat in the middle of the room, filled with papers. A map of Zarubain hung against the wall, marked up with black ink. On a high shelf there were jars filled with yellow fluid, and in them were organs. Sylla's sick anatomical obsession had not ended.

"I have another theory," said Sylla. "You have acknowledged that I am your master... and you cannot live without him."

The words were not true. Ramden was not entirely sure why he had come. His shaking had lessened; he could breathe again. Sylla was walking closer. "Why do you have no fingers on your left hand?" he said.

"Once, in the heat of battle, a lawgiver sliced them off."

"What is a lawgiver?" said Ramden. He could only imagine—a man made of iron, bringing order and law to the world at threat of death.

"A lawgiver is the worst type of man," said Sylla. "Far worse than you silly Zarubes." He lifted up his fingerless left hand. "I overcame him eventually. I bashed his head against the rock until his skull cracked. I cut off his head. I tore up his black robe and stuffed it in his mouth. He gave me these wounds—but I took his life."

"A poor trade?" Ramden asked.

"No," Sylla answered, looking at the fingerless hand with a pensive expression. His right hand tightened on the dagger. "You still have not answered my question. Why did you come?"

"How did you really lose your fingers?"

Sylla pursed his lips. He was so unlike the Sylla Ramden had remembered—the tormentor who had delighted in pain. He seemed reasonable, maybe even compassionate. *No, not quite compassionate.*

"You are a monster, you know," said Ramden. "Did one of your prey bite your fingers off?"

"Monster," Sylla repeated without emotion. Thought filled his cold blue eyes. He turned and walked to the desk, set down his dagger, and opened a shelf. Out of it he drew a sword of steel, its gold pommel forged into an eagle's head. "There were some in my country who called soldiers monsters. They called warriors demons in human form. They said there was no difference between a mass murderer and a legionary."

"So," Ramden said, "were they killed?"

"No," Sylla answered. "We tolerated them for too long. We allowed them too much space. Some still remain."

Ramden peered into the cold blue eyes, wondering what thought went on behind them.

"Those limbs in jars, those folk I killed—they scorned soldiers and men of war. They deserved what they got."

"And Crystelle?" It beggared belief that Ramden could remember the Montée March whore.

Surprise touched Sylla's eyes. It appeared he hadn't considered it. Sylla then glared. "Do you consider soldiers killers, monsters, mass murderers?"

"Of course not," said Ramden. "I am one of them, after all. Only a simpleton would think so. But I *do* think you are a monster."

"A monster you respect," Sylla said. "A monster you love."

"Perhaps, I do respect you," Ramden said. "I am not sure why I came here."

"To join the Imperial legion," Sylla offered.

"Yes." It was an easy out, the simplest of all explanations. He had lost respect for Zarubain and its countrymen, its dukes and duchesses, its lords and ladies, all stuck in their old ways.

"Then you will join," Sylla said. "It is simple enough... you must make an oath."

"How did you really lose your fingers?"

Sylla smiled faintly. "A victim bit them off—she had cursed soldiers as they walked the street. I found her later that night, surprised her…"

"You lie," Ramden said. What could possibly be more evil than the story he told? But there was something else, something darker. He had barely scratched the surface of Sylla's depravity. Again he asked, "How did you really lose your fingers?"

"There is an old law in the Empire. A baby who is deformed must be killed—exposed, left to die in the elements. It is not taken seriously in the Empire except by followers of the old ways."

"You were born with it," Ramden said.

Sylla lifted up his left hand, which only had a thumb. "Indeed. A worse tale than any I could possibly tell. My father was not a follower of the old ways."

"Clearly," said Ramden.

"I am, though," Sylla said. "I should be dead."

"I can help you."

Sylla laughed. "Honor has been instilled in me since birth. But I cannot bring myself to correct my father's wrong—nor let anyone else help."

"I am ready to join the legion," Ramden said.

~

An Imperial slave took a razor and shaved every bit of hair from Ramden's face. Then he cut the thick hair from Ramden's head until it was short and square, identical to the rest of the Imperials.

That dusk, he received his Imperial armor, a suit of chainmail and steel leg guards. He received his sword and shield. Then, before Sylla, he repeated the Imperial oath—"I pledge my life to the Empire."

He was an Imperial, now.

Chapter Seventy-One:
The Final Battle

Roland vis Valais, Duke of Valais.

Two weeks later, and summer had arrived in its full strength. The Feast of the Lady had passed them by. Now Roland stood a mile south of Zarubain. An army awaited his beck and call. Knights from the Western Heartlands to Further Zarubain had massed just off the road. Twenty thousand peasant soldiers had joined them, and ten thousand men-at-arms. The Imperial Army was starved and weak. They would crumble before him. They would be driven from the kingdom, and no one would call them invincible anymore.

Chapter Seventy-Two:
Beast Visions

Danitari

The beast towered above the earth, chest puffed out, smoke escaping from its nostrils. The lion was perched in its hand, light as a plaything.

~

Lumas and Luvé stood in the primordial forest in the light of the first dawn. Their hands were interlocked, their fingers knit together. Evil had already entered into the world, but they were ignorant—and in their ignorance they were happy. The end of the world was eons away. The forest hummed with life, and the stars glowed with brilliant light. Danitari could see his face reflected in their eyes, yet they could not see him. *The world is coming undone. The end is now.*

~

Starved and shivering, ribs showing clearly through his skin, Danitari lay in a waking dream, lost in his visions, lost in another world.

Chapter Seventy-Three:
Haste

King Jourmande vis Bretagne

King Jourmande breathed a sigh of relief when the endless hills and woods of Mekara had vanished behind him and the River Zarube appeared. The river that he loved, that he had known since childhood, in which he had left offerings of gold and silver, filled him with warmth and relief. *I am home.* Castle Holmgray lay before him, forming a bridge across the waters. Archers had been posted at the walls.

A horn blew—a horn of alarm—followed by a dozen others. The gate was already firmly shut. Panic seized the archer's faces. Even from this far away, Jourmande could see them turn white. *They think the Empire wants to annex the kingdom.* He laughed at their foolishness. Nothing could be further from the truth.

King Jourmande left the safety of his royal carriage. He hopped on a horse and rode to the gate. "My good men!" he cried. "My good subjects, do not fear!"

"Your Majesty?" hollered one of the archers. He turned back and shouted, "His Majesty is kidnapped!"

"I am not!" shouted Jourmande. "The Empire is our ally. They are intent on hunting down the war criminal Sylla! I am proud to say we have made a deal! Open the gates—Lord Eurelien would understand."

"That's madness!" the archer cried, perhaps forgetting who he was speaking to.

Jourmande drew *Fairbolt*, feeling his hackles rise. The archer was lucky Jourmande stood so far away—he would not have hesitated to kill him for such impudence. A swift, clean stroke would lob his head off.

Dame Alesandre rode forward on her horse. "He speaks the truth! You are speaking to folk well above your station, Goodman Archer! Fetch Eurelien at once—he understands!"

Dame Alesandre had been less happy about this deal than anyone. *A deal with the devil,* she had said, *was no deal at all.* She had forgotten her place as a knight—a place far beneath His Sovereign Majesty. Jourmande was the supreme ruler of the kingdom, the vicar of god on earth.

Soon enough the gate opened, and the Imperial Army began to pour in.

In the castle yard, Eurelien vis Námois, Duke of Duranche, met Jourmande. His face was pale and colorless; his eyes were filled with doubt. "Your Majesty," he said, "are you sure—?"

Jourmande, however, was positively giddy. "I have never been more certain of a thing in my life, Eurelien."

Eurelien's doubt did not diminish. He too, was far beneath Jourmande. Eurelien was only a Námois, only a duke of the Seven Gems. The gold lion of the House of Bretagne flew far higher than the black ram of Námois.

Eurelien's fear did not dispel Jourmande's daydreaming—of a realm without war, where peasants tilled happily in the fields, where granaries were filled to overflowing, where elves did what was expected of them, where lords and ladies from across the kingdom came to the Royal City on St. Ignáce Day to dance and drink away the hours. This awful business of war would soon be behind them.

"Your Majesty," he said, "Sylla is cornered in Silvan March. His days are numbered. Lord Roland—"

"Lord Roland is regent," Jourmande hissed. "I am king. I will not be questioned by anyone, let alone you." He would not let all this turn to humiliation once again. Lord Roland was no hero.

"The counts and countesses who switched sides are imprisoned," said Sylla. "They await punishment on Prison Isle."

"Prison Isle!" Jourmand could hardly believe it. "I am king, not Roland. No man or woman of high blood will be treated so. They did what they thought was best for *themselves*; no one can question that. I demand their release."

"They betrayed the country."

Jourmande kicked Eurelien to the ground. He had spoken out of turn. He had dishonored the kingdom by insulting the king. If anyone deserved to rot on Prison Isle, it was Eurelien.

Jourmande found Councilor Corvus near the vanguard of the Imperial Army.

"We must make haste," Jourmande said. "To Silvan March."

"Indeed," the councilor answered. He was surveying Castle Holmgray with a more slimy, skeevy look than usual. He was estimating the cost of everything and everybody. It did not matter— he would be gone soon.

Chapter Seventy-Four: Departure

Eurelien vis Namois, Duke of Duranche

Lord Eurelien watched the last of the Imperial Army leave Castle Holmgray, barely able to contain his rage. The tyrant King Jourmande had burst into the kingdom at the worst possible moment. Again he had bungled the effort. There would be no justice. The king's words were law. The craven counts and countesses on Prison Isle would be released. Eurelien had supported Roland's intentions, to make an example out of them for lords and ladies whose hearts were faint. For these past weeks and months—more than once—he had hoped Jourmande was dead. But the Goddess had sent no bandits on the Imperial roads. She had sent no Mekari war party at the exact right time. If the Goddess truly cared for the kingdom, she would have slain Jourmande some way or the other.

But the Lady is a superstition. She is powerless because she is false. The world is in disorder because there is no order. There are no gods. Of that Eurelien had become convinced. The view was shared widely among the dukes and duchesses of the Western Heartlands, but never spoken publicly. It was natural for a peasant, worked to exhaustion in the fields, to believe—not so much for a man of wealth who could see clearly. There was no hell to fear, nor an Otherworld to look forward to. On that, Eurelien had staked his life.

Either way, his task here was done. His castle awaited him. The kingdom would endure, of that he was certain—but in a humiliated state, with the Empire close at hand. Eurelien absolved himself of all guilt. It was not his decision. It was not his doing. All blame rested squarely on Jourmande, and his incredible ability to wrest defeat from sure victory.

Chapter Seventy-Five:
The Battle of Vale Merysse

Roland vis Valais, Duke of Valais

Vale Merysse stretched before him. The Imperial camp, the one they called ironically Camp Victory, lay a short distance from Castle Celine, where the craven marquis Ivain ruled. On the far end lay high hills and the Storm Coast; all around lay peasants' fields and cattle ranches. Roland did not know what excited him more—a final crushing victory over the Imperial Army, or the delivery of Ivain to Prison Isle.

Queen Alysant had regained respect for him. Elsie did not glare at him quite so much. The whole kingdom, once saved by Roland, would see the strategy in his patience and failure to act. The crushing victory would prove him the warrior he had always been. Roland as Lord Regent was a defender of the kingdom, more so than Jourmande had ever been.

Lord Roland rode at the vanguard like his uncle never had. On a white horse he rode, on a gold saddle, sword in hand. Behind him were thousands upon thousands, all ready to deal the final death blow. For once the Empire would be humiliated. For once, the Zarubes would reign supreme. "Today will be a day of glory! Today will be a day of victory! Today will be the day we bring an end to the Empire! Sound the horns! Ride with me, brothers!"

Horns pealed from one end to the army to the other. Lord Roland charged ahead toward "Camp Victory," and his knights followed, pouring like water down the hill. The vale was theirs. Castle Celine would fall. Victory was at hand.

Chapter Seventy-Six:
Standstill

Roland vis Valais, Duke of Valais

The battle had raged all day. Hundreds of Imperials had died, but many more Zarubes. Exhausted, Roland had fallen back. At night, the fighting stopped. The fortifications of Camp Victory were demolished, but the Imperials held fast. Roland had overestimated their weakness. But now, resting in the general's tent and drinking water, his resolve had not failed. He had never been more certain of his victory. It was only a matter of time before the Imperial ranks faltered, the knights of the realm charged in, and their dreadful power was forever broken. *Victory is at hand.* Roland gulped down the life-giving water, and smiled.

Chapter Seventy-Seven: Marching

Roland vis Valais, Duke of Valais.

Ramden had begun to learn why the Empire had not found its match. Fighting at the front of the legion, his shield had formed a living wall. When he fought in the heat of the day, he had lost his individuality. He had become a body part, a limb, in a greater life form. Marching in lockstep with the Imperial soldiers, he became something greater than one man or one sword. The charging knights had broken upon them; the ranks of the legion were too deep, their combined strength too much, their morale too great. In the darkness the Zarubes had fallen back. In the morning there would be more fighting. The legion stayed ever alert. No wine was consumed, only water and meager rations. The time of celebration was not now.

Ramden thought of Mother, of Ramone, of Ramonette and Ramondine, of the comfortable and privileged life he had left behind. He wondered, not for the first time and certainly not for the last, whether he had made a mistake.

Chapter Seventy-Eight: Death At Dawn

Roland vis Valais, Duke of Valais

At dawn there were horns, but not horns Roland recognized. In the pink-and-gold sunlight, Roland beheld a sight that drained all heat from his body. He could scarcely breathe. Another Imperial army had arrived, twice as large as Marcus Sylla's. All the confidence he had vanished at that moment. *Zarubain has no chance. We must surrender.* There was no chance of beating them.

The knights behind him stirred uncomfortably. There were a few screams. *Their hearts are melting. Panic is setting in.* Roland would hold firm. "Hold firm!" he said.

The peasants sow, the priestesses pray, the nobles fight. Roland would fight. He was not the craven coward everyone believed.

"Stand fast!" Roland cried.

To his bewilderment, King Jourmande rode at the head of the Imperial Army. Beside him was Dame Alesandre and the fat advisor Sybold. Roland cursed under his breath. He could not make sense of it. Had King Jourmande been captured and allowed to ride freely?

Or had he made a deal with the Imperial devils? *Goddess, no.* That would be the worst of all possible worlds.

The three armies met in the shadow of Castle Celine, amid the burnt and broken wreckage of Camp Victory. The new Imperial Army was far larger than the first. King Jourmande had a smug, self-pleased look on his face. *He has made a deal.* Roland wished he could cut that face off, and the head too.

A carriage rode up to the front. Its axels were lined with gold, its wheels painted a bright yellow and rimmed with gemstones—ruby, emerald, and lapis lazuli. The wooden carriage car was painted red with yellow trim. One of the doors opened and a man stepped out. He had graying black hair, cut short in that contemptible Imperial style. His face was hairless as a newborn—no moustache or beard to speak of. His eyes were dark, his mouth perked with contemptful humor. Around his white tunic was a purple sash. He was clearly a man of great importance, or—at least—someone who considered himself to be.

Roland removed his helmet.

"My nephew," Jourmande explained.

I do not consider him uncle, anymore.

"Signor Roland, a pleasure," said the man with the purple sash. "Juliano Corvus."

The staccato Imperial accent ruined all the beauty and subtle contours of the Zarube language.

Out of the ranks of Sylla's army a man emerged too—the commander himself, Marcus. He wore no helmet, only a breastplate with that horrid eagle emblazoned upon it. The Monster who had tormented the kingdom for all these months did not bear the horns and red skin Roland envisioned. He looked normal, even handsome, despite the widespread atrocities he had inflicted. He had brought suffering and death to the kingdom, yet here Roland was, looking down at him. He could do nothing—the rules of war denied it. He would get an equal say in whatever went on.

"Marcus Sylla," Corvus said, "we meet after long last. I do not wish to shed blood. I demand you come home, to the Empire, for trial."

"Trial!" Sylla looked at him in shock.

"For the Boracum massacre."

"The Boracum Massacre!" Sylla laughed. "You mean the Battle of Boracum, which I won for the Empire's cause?"

"A word in private," said Corvus.

"Indeed." Sylla led Corvus away.

"What is the meaning of this, uncle?" cried Roland.

His uncle was no longer the reticent, uncertain man he remembered. He looked sure of his course of action—and angry that his nephew would question it. "A deal," he snarled. "The best deal I could make, with the devil himself."

"The devil indeed." Roland couldn't fathom it. He believed in the Lady and the Fairy Faith, but had been uncertain of devils. The Imperials had made him believe. "A nation who nails highborns to crosses... who treats highborns like the lowest of elven slaves."

"Enough with it!" snapped Jourmande, his face a shade of pink.

Dame Alesandre and Sybold walked up to flank him. "Back off," Alesandre said and rested her hand on her sword. It seemed she had forgotten how old she was. With long white hair and wrinkles on her hands, she still saw herself as threatening—still, the lioness who fought with the best of Jourmande's knights. She did not scare Roland in the slightest.

"I had won this war," Roland said. No one would dare speak to the king so—not even him, until now.

"Another word," said Dame Alesandre, "and I will cut off your head."

"You are less fearsome than you think, old woman."

In a single movement Alesandre drew her sword and slashed. Roland, a second late, drew his sword too, but lost balance and fell back onto his rump. *She is fearsome.* "Your Majesty," he said. He could not bear to see his victory ruined. He whistled and his stallion came to him. He rode away from Vale Merysse. Would he return to Castle Royale, to Elsie and Lord Mars? Or would he lock himself in Castle Sunbow and never leave? Only the road would tell him.

He ignored the army he had amassed, riding past them, cursing his luck, cursing his king and cursing the kingdom.

Chapter Seventy-Nine:
As It Has Been

His Majesty King Jourmande vis Bretagne

Roland would overcome his pouting. A few days and he would be the jolly Young Duke again. Jourmande had no doubts he had done the right thing. The region of Mekara had been a drain on the kingdom's resources. The land had proved difficult to till, and the natives had raided the cattle farms constantly. Now the Empire would deal with it. And the Kingdom of Zarubain would know peace.

Marcus Sylla and Councilor Corvus emerged from the ranks of the former's army. "My good Signor King," said Corvus, "I have come to announce a deal. Marcus Sylla will return with us to the Empire. He will stand trial for his crimes. A hefty fine or an execution is probable. And you will hand over the province of Mekara."

Jourmande had hoped for a bloody battle. "You will execute him here," he told Corvus, "in Lions Square, in the Royal City."

Corvus shook his head. "I am sorry, Signor King. An Imperial citizen will face Imperial justice."

Jourmande had little leverage. "A committer of heinous deeds will face justice where he committed them."

"Would you risk conflict, my signore?" Corvus asked. A patronizing smile appeared on his face. "With all these legions at your door?"

"Goodbye" was Jourmande's answer. Like ants marching in step the legions moved south down the road. Jourmande watched as they left. His problems were leaving. War and conflict was leaving.

He had achieved peace. The peasants in the fields would work the land. The priestesses would pray and study. The nobles would enjoy the feast days and grand parties of the Inner City. *Everything will be as it has been.*

Chapter Eighty:
Old And New

Ramden, Legionary

The King's Highway—or the Path of Tidus as the Imperials called it—wound south-eastward toward Mekara. At last, at Further Zarubain, it crossed over the Garavel Bridge in Further Zarubain. There the legions camped. Tomorrow, Ramden would venture into territory he had never seen. He had risked his life, and still did not feel safe. The language was difficult. He was an outsider to the extreme. And he was always within grasp of Sylla. The tortures and beatings could begin. Sylla could make good on his promise and skin him alive. As night fell, Ramden struggled to sleep. The full moon arose in a sea of stars. It was glowing and luminous, almost a shade of green. The air smelled of flowers and pollen. A foot kicked him. He looked up. A hooded figure towered over him. *Maude.*

She lowered the hood, revealing the warts and boils of her face. "Will you truly leave the Lady's land?" she said.

"I have no choice," said Ramden.

"But you do." No one was paying attention to either him or Maude. For all intents and purposes they were invisible and inaudible.

"I will face death by burning," Ramden said. "They will force me to lead them to Deepwood Hollow. You will be burned too."

"A good witch always escapes," said Maude. "And if not we have our ways. My cries of agony may be staged. Do not worry for me, Ramden."

"I want to leave," Ramden said. "I hate the kingdom. I hate the land."

Maude smiled. "A pity. The Lady has watched you with great interest. The kingdom is *her* land, you know."

"But I hate it nonetheless."

"The southerners are a folk of iron and smoke and wheels. No fairies dare live there save in the highest mountain recesses. The air is very hot in summer, too." Maude's smile had not disappeared. "And you will not be waited on, hand and foot. The strong survive and the weak perish. High birth is not respected, nor is it a guarantor of life."

"You are only convincing me further, Good Woman Maude."

"Very well," Maude said. "I had thought beyond all doubts that you would perish. I thought Lord Roland would succeed and his army break the legion at last. But unforeseen events transpired."

The king Jourmande had proven the Empire's greatest ally. The Battle of Vale Merysse could easily have been disastrous for Ramden. He could have been pierced straight through by a knight's lance, or hacked to bits by a man-at-arm's broadsword. The Empire was strong but not invincible. Another day of battle and Roland might have worn them down.

"I remember Ramden the Bold," Maude persisted. "The wild bear of the House Rambée, tearing across the battlefield. He loved the Lady and served king and country. But that Ramden is dead."

"The old is gone," Ramden said. "The new is here. There is no more Ramden the Bold. No longer a wild bear, but a soldier marching in lockstep among his brothers-in-arms."

"The Lady and the fey give you their blessing," Maude said, "as long as you do not bring the land of iron and smoke and wheels into the north."

"I can promise nothing," Ramden said. "But I give you my blessing, Good Woman Maude. May the animals of Deepwood Hollow protect you. May the forest burst with raspberries and mushrooms. May you forever elude capture."

"Goodbye," said Maude.

She left, and Ramden startled awake, amazed to see the sun rising with a new day. A new day had arrived, banishing the night. *The old is gone. The new has come.* The Empire awaited him.

Chapter Eighty-One:
The Lion Throne

His Majesty King Jourmande vis Bretagne

The air had turned cool and Castle Royale shone with a fresh new coat of whitewash. Here, in the Inner City, King Jourmande was insulated from the problems abroad. The full-fledged revolt in Vale of Roy seemed distinctly less threatening than the Empire. How could legions rampaging across the Western Heartlands possibly compare to brigands and bandits? It was for this reason that they were able to elude capture. Having been driven out of Castle Moonsilver, the elven bandits and renegade peasant "warriors" had hidden away in the Silver Woods. It was a matter of time before they were starved out. The peasants who had surrendered were put to forced labor, more severe and taxing than anything they'd ever known.

And Alse-Lorie was due back any day now. The High Priestess had been extracted at a high cost. The royal treasury had paid a sum of ten marks to the bandit "king" Bran for her safe return. Now Jourmande would quickly seize the king *and* his money. Lowborn bandits were insufferably stupid.

The ash and linden trees which grew along the river banks had turned shades of dull brown and gold. The Feast of Saint Ignáce would be upon them soon. Only a year ago, the great war had begun. It seemed so long ago. It had been the longest year of his life. Now, at a venerable seventy-five years old, death stalked the corners. He questioned himself as he walked. Had he been the worst king to ever sit on the Lion Throne? *No, I have brought peace, a great and lasting peace.*

But the Empire had seized Mekara, and on the ruins of

Castle New a town was being built. Mekara Territory they called it. They had promised to keep their distance. *But how easy would it be for them to break their word?*

At the docks a royal boat had been prepared for him. A gaggle of servants helped him in. The boat coasted down the water, then docked at Castle Royale.

King Jourmande took his seat on the Lion Throne, wondering just how much time he had left. He feared no threats to his rule, though hatred and scorn was not lacking among the dukes of the Western Heartlands. His nephew Roland, holed up with Lord Mars in Castle Sunbow, refused to speak to him and said he would never come to Castle Royale again. The struggles of the present age would continue after Jourmande's death, but life would soon pass him by. He had a son now, Prince Tyrol, who would carry on his legacy. His wife Alysant was taking very good care of him.

A figure appeared in a pink robe and a green stole. Jourmande stood up, breathless, at the thought of Alse-Lorie returning. The High Priestess had always been a welcome presence in Castle Royale.

But alas it was not her. This woman had bright red hair, freckles and the brightest blue eyes Jourmande had ever seen. A few yards from the throne, she fell to her knees. "Your Majesty."

King Jourmande was a busy man. He did not have time for this. "Rise," he said, pitying her.

"I have something to tell you," she said. "Alse-Lorie, the High Priestess—"

"What is your name, priestess?" Jourmande snapped.

"Varysse, Your Majesty," she said. "Alse-Lorie, the High Priestess, is a fraud."

"A fraud," Jourmande repeated. The insubordinate words did not endear Varysse to him.

"She has been bedding Sir Loy."

Jourmande scoffed at the accusation. The Knight of the Pillar was a great swordsman and a great man. Alse-Lorie had always taken the Fairy Faith seriously. Her record had been nothing but exemplary.

"I can prove it," said Varysse. Her eyes were uncertain, as if she hadn't expected such a cold reception. "There is Grayman's beard in her closet."

Jourmande grumbled some curse. "What were you doing in her private chambers?"

"I am not the *villein* here," Varysse said. "I saw them abed. I was looking for proof."

"Looking where no one should have been," Jourmande said.

The Royal Guard stood silently at the door.

"Go!" he shouted. "Find the Grayman's beard. If you can't find it, it's off with Varysse's head.

~

An hour passed and Jourmande had completely forgotten the matter. His memory was reawakened when he saw the Royal Guard return, clutching a cask full of grayish powder. He recognized it in an instant. Varysse seemed positively radiant. *She loves the idea of sending Alse to a cucking stool. What in Varda did she do to her?*

As poorly as Alse had behaved, Jourmande loathed this Varysse woman even more. There was no excuse for breaking vows, but this priestess was giddy at the prospect of Alse's punishment.

"My lord," Varysse said, "you are a wise and just king. I beg of you, Your Majesty, deal with her as the law demands."

Only then did Jourmande realize she had returned with a hefty book. He recognized the markings—it was a hefty tome of law. Few nobles or even judges read it with care.

Varysse pulled it open and pointed to an entry.

"Punishments for breaking vows. A full priestess must be shaven and set on display in a cucking stool. But a high priestess breaking the vows is to be taken to Avelogne, to be led up the mountain to the Life Well, and drowned within. Her lover must die with her."

Her words deepened Jourmande's anger. "I am a man of laws. The king's word is law. Leave me. I will see what is to be done."

Varysse furrowed her brow in disappointment. "But, Your Majesty… a firm commitment first…"

"Leave me!" Jourmande boomed, louder than before.

Varysse bit her lip. Then she curtsied and scurried away.

~

Late in the autumn morning, Alse-Lorie returned. She was thin and pale. The effort of walking to the Lion Throne seemed to have taxed her to her limits. All joy had left her. She seemed grim and deathly. "You know," she said.

"Did someone tell you?" Jourmande asked.

Alse shook her head, another monumental effort. "I just know the secret is out. Many weeks have passed. Will you set me on a cucking stool?"

"Your fellow sister Varysse advocates a worse punishment," Jourmande said. "She says a high priestess must be drowned in the Life Well, and her lover with her."

"I expect nothing less from sweet Varysse," said Alse. "Which shall you foist upon me? I do not know which is worse."

Jourmande sighed. He observed Alse's light brown hair, her tender green eyes. He looked at the pitiful creature before him, starved and haggard, in the light of the flickering torches. He could not hate her. "You have a choice, my sweet," he said. "I have seen much death and bloodshed in this past year. I have seen faithlessness and treason, of immeasurable suffering. Enough suffering has been dealt. I will not punish you."

Alse cried and relief washed through her. She fell down on her knees. Her pink gown was caked with mud and dirt.

"But you have a choice," Jourmande continued. "I honor the ancient law when it is necessary. You may continue as high priestess, or you may abdicate and be with Sir Loy."

"The high priesthood is all I want."

"Then I will send Sir Loy to the Eastern Region," Jourmande said, "and I will speak of your deed no longer."

Alse wept, whether from joy or sadness he did not know.

Chapter Eighty-Two:
Light

Danitari

It was late in the day when the horns blew. The knights and men-at-arms were far away. King Bran, several dozen elves and a hundred poorly armed peasants stood in the way of total obliteration. Danitari was weak from hunger, ill, and shivering cold. He could not decide whether he wanted to live or die. He would not have a choice. They lay in the midst of the Silver Woods, among the towering firs and pines. The sea was so close the rush of the waves was clearly audible. King Bran had thought he could take his ill gotten money and hire a pirate fleet to take him south. Instead the pirates had assaulted him and taken the ten marks in gold *libres*. Now they were stranded. The loyalties had frayed over the past months. After spending so long in the prison, Danitari had no love for King Bran. Hatred alone had consumed his soul, had poisoned his outlook. Bran's thin veneer of kindliness and goodwill had vanished in this dark hour, replaced with open scorn for elves and peasants.

I will die, Danitari decided. A short pain would end this life, and he would rest eternally in the ground.

The horn blew louder, just a hundred yards away at most. Panic seized Danitari. He did not want to die. He could not face death with calm. He ran. King Bran started screaming, "I'll kill you!"

But Danitari ignored it. The doomed party vanished from his sight and Danitari was alone and running.

~

The Silver Woods had no end it seemed. Danitari constantly slipped and fell over tree roots. There were mushrooms and he ate them without discernment. They tasted like the richest of feasts after months of slop and mash. He drank from the forest pools and licked the water from the boughs of pines, and it tasted like the finest of wine.

The day ended and a rain began. A bit of strength had returned to Danitari's body. He took shelter under a pine and fell asleep. As he drifted off he remembered he could not flee death. He was an escaped slave and he would be burned alive or something worse. He should have let the knights kill him. He lay in the cold damp, shivering and improperly clothed. The rain dripped through the pines and his rags did not protect him.

He awoke cold and hungry. He kept running.

The woods were brilliant green. Moss—hanging and creeping—filled the forest with brilliant color. Birds chirped and squirrels scurried. There were black bears in the Silver Woods. The thought scared him, but it was humans he should fear the most—humans, the cruelest and most evil of all animals that walked the earth, the elves' wicked cousins, the shame of the Light's creation. Not one of them was good, not a single one.

Danitari tripped over a tree root. His ankle caught on something and a cracking pain surged through his body. He screamed. Tears filled his eyes but there was no one to hear. There was no one to help in this dark world. He was completely and utterly alone. *Light help me.* The Light would not help him. No one would help him. He was all alone in a world that despised him. The Light had forsaken him—or else there was no Light.

He crawled through the mud and pine needles of the forest, tearing up patches of moss. He had never felt this hopeless. At last he gave up. Even crawling filled his ankles with pain. He wept. If only he had a knife, to finish the deed and slash his wrists. If only…

At dusk, he awoke to loud, angry roaring. A black bear approached. He would be shredded to pieces.

His sleep had not cured his despair. In the past, sleep had banished the bad thoughts and the sad thoughts, but no longer. He welcomed the beast as it roared. Its black fur was so beautiful, its muzzle and fangs so awe-inspiring.

Again panic filled him. *I do not want to die,* he realized. Why in Varda did he not want to die? Intellectually he knew there was nothing in this life for him. But he could not withstand the panic. He tried to climb a tree but fell, hitting the dirt hard.

The bear clawed at him. Danitari flipped over to face the black bear. It clawed him again, shredding the tattered tunic and lacerating tender flesh. Danitari screamed. He would be eaten. He cursed the Light and cursed heaven. Panic was coursing through his veins. The black bear was hungry enough to eat an elf, and its dark eyes sensed fear. Danitari was wounded prey.

Blood was flowing from the claw wound. As Danitari backed away his body grew slippery. The black bear charged again and mauled him, harder than ever before.

This life was passing him by. Death was knocking at the door, welcoming him to the kingdom of shades. He wept.

Blood was pouring from his body. He slipped across the forest floor as he backed away. The hot blood drenched his rags. *This is not the end I wanted.* He should have stayed by King Bran's side. He should have bedded Mignette. There were so many things he should have done.

The black bear perked up, standing on its two front legs. Its wet muzzle sniffed.

An arrow pierced its chest.

Danitari could not celebrate. He could not think at all. His life was fading. His vision was dimming. His will to live had finally begun to wither.

Another arrow struck the bear and it staggered backward.

"Lunitari!" someone shouted, and then, in Elvish—the language he loved—"Hurry."

Spritely, an elf darted at the stunned bear. A curved saber was in his hands. Relentlessly he slashed the bear but the bear fought back, angrier than ever.

Soon it had collapsed.

These elves had come to save him, but Danitari was already gone. *The irony*. At least he would pass on among his people.

A woman appeared above him—an elf maiden with hair of reddish gold, the color of autumn leaves. She crouched above him and a sweet, warm wind blew, scattering the pine nettles. In her eyes, there was Light. She was humming an Elvish tune. Her eyes were bright and blue. Her lips were pale and colorless. She laid a soft hand against his cheek. "He is almost gone," she said. She clutched a staff of yew in her left hand.

She lifted her right hand above Danitari. A nimbus of golden light surrounded it. The air grew cold and Danitari's skin was seized with gooseflesh. He eyed his torn, lacerated body. His body jerked with pain as the wounds began to close.

"What is your name?" Danitari said. This was a Healer, in the Zarube woods no less.

"Hush," the Healer said as she continued to work her magic.

The most pain came when his ankle was healed, as the fractured bone connected and then sealed back together. Then Danitari was all new—but incredibly weak. "My lady," Danitari said in Elvish.

"Lunitari? Albi? Help him."

Two strong arms helped Danitari to his feet. "Where are we going?" he said.

"Hush," the Healer said a third time. "Do not worry. Relax.

Breathe slowly."

"Where are we going?" Danitari said, unfazed.

"To *Benidori Ayri*," the Healer answered. "To your new home, a safe place."

Danitari could not believe it. Relief washed through him. Darkness and despair built up through many long years fell away, melting like snow in summer. He wept for joy. The myth was true—there were elves in deep woods, living lives far from the ears of human persecutors. Danitari could not believe his luck. "What if the humans find us?"

"Quiet," said the Healer. "In *Benidori Ayri* there is no worry nor fear."

A short walk through Silver Woods and the Ayri appeared, a village in a forest clearing well hidden—perhaps by magic—in the brush. There, crude houses were built in the human style. No less than a hundred elves lived within, some men, some women, some maidens, some children. Music filled the air. There were harps and lyres and singing voices. Everyone was smiling. Danitari had never seen a people so happy, not even back home, in the Elven World.

These slaves had escaped from the Silver Woods and formed a community far from human eyes. Ayris dotted the entire kingdom, self-sustaining communities with high-minded ideals and tenants of equality and the common good. Here Danitari would spend the rest of his days, singing and praising the Light, which had not abandoned him.

That evening, he ate berries and drank wine. He sang and danced well into the night. He had never lived so well. Surely providence and prosperity woud follow him until the end of his days. Surely he would never weep again. Surely he would live forever in this paradise on earth, far from slavery and all trouble.

Chapter Eighty-Three:
A Chance Meeting

The Reverend Alse-Lorie, High Priestess

On the bridge between Emerald Isle and Convent Isle, in the shadow of the Lady's Cathedral, Alse-Lorie took Sir Loy's hands in hers and said, "Goodbye."

Sir Loy had never looked so sad. A gloom had overtaken him—not because of his journey to the Eastern Region, but because he would lose Alse-Lorie forever. "My love," he said.

"It is for the best," said Alse-Lorie. "For both of us."

The sun bathed them in cold autumn light. Soon the rains of winter would pour and the frosts and winds would return. Where Sir Loy would venture, snow would fall. He would long for the mild weather of the Western Heartlands. The Eastern Region, far from the king's power, was not for the weak. But he had accepted his duty without complaint.

She dared not kiss him, not now. Their love was at an end. The Goddess might never forgive her. Everyone in the Royal City would soon know. "Goodbye, my love," she said.

"Goodbye," he said, and gasped. A spear head stuck out through his chest. Alse screamed.

Varysse stood there, behind him. She pulled out the bloodied spear and Jourmande stumbled back.

"How could you!" Alse cried.

Jourmande fell off the bridge, into the water. Varysse thrust the spear forward and stabbed Alse in the chest.

"Justice," Varysse said.

Warm blood ran like a river down her skin. Alse stumbled

back, in disbelief.

City guards were running at her with swords. Alse staggered back and fell headlong off the bridge. She hit the cold water with a splash. The flow carried her out of the city, out to sea.

~

In the roiling waves of the ocean, it was not death she feared. The hatred of the Lady was what she feared. She had forsaken the Goddess… the fires of perdition awaited her.

In the cold darkness of the sea, as her last bits of breath ran out, she cried out for mercy. She swallowed water and lost all consciousness.

She could feel Sir Loy's hand in hers, and before her was a lady in shining white samite. A crown of stars was on her fiery red hair, and her face shone like the sun.

Her radiance was forgiveness. Her brilliance was compassion. Her light was life.

Alse-Lorie cried out for joy, for relief, for deep sadness.

Here, in the summer land, she would walk until the end of time. Here, in the Otherworld, she had been accepted; here, in the land of the Lady, she would find her rest.

Chapter Eighty-Four:
An Offer

His Majesty King Jourmande vis Bretagne

Roland, Duke of Valais, sat on his bed in Castle Sunbow.Weeks had passed since Jourmande's humiliation and Roland still fumed. Victory had been within reach until the bumbling fool threw it all away.

Lord Mars, standing before him, sensed this as he seemed to sense all Roland's thoughts. He drew from his sheath his dagger. "I would kill for you, you know." He stroked the steel.

"So I have gathered," Roland said, "but he will die soon. Queen Alysant will reign. She is twice the man Jourmande is."

"Indeed," Lord Mars said, disappointed. He did not stop stroking the blade.

Chapter Eighty-Five:
The Beast of the Apocalypse

The Knight of Lorh

The ice-gray waves crashed far and forcefully on the Golden Coast, spreading their foam almost to the road. The few lindens and ashes had shed their leaves and only the great firs and pines remained green. The gales of winter blew harsh and cold across the sea, piercing Sir Darius' cloak and burning him with cold. His horse neighed. The air was as ice; the sun had not been seen for days.

Sir Darius had escaped the traitors—the Bastard Prince, who thought he'd been tortured to death. But the Knights of Lorh had their ways of survival. They had to. Their long persecution had not ended, and would not end until the end of days.

Far out to shore, the water was bubbling. Sir Darius had half expected it but his blood still turned to ice. His horse bucked up and whinnied.

A form rose from the depths—a beaked head the size of a city with purple fleshy skin and a flat and primitive head. An army of tentacles surrounded it, grabbing and wriggling. The *lormon narssanad* was before him. Gods help the king's subjects if they ever found out what it meant. A dark end awaited all. Waves the height of castles surged at its presence.

Sir Darius paid it no mind. His horse galloped down the road. There were things to do.

Epilogue

Marcus Sylla, Grand Legate

"That was easy," said Sylla to Councilor Juliano Corvus.

"Almost too easy," Corvus answered.

They were building a fortress around the ruins of the castle. The air was cold but the sky was sunny here in the Mekara plains. Slaves were digging a giant foundation. The construction would take perhaps years, but when completed, the Empire's power over the north would be complete. Zarubain was in their sights. The kingdom had proven itself divided and weak.

Sylla felt safe on Imperial ground, in new Mekara Territory. He eyed his left hand and the fingers he had cut off in service to Og'og. The power of the lord of mysteries and deep secrets lay about him. He would make a bloody return to the Kingdom of Zarubain. Its petty counties and duchies would fall. Its people would die in a maelstrom of destruction and blood. Its forests would become a smoking ruin.

The Empire's armies would remake the world and the Empire's name would be exalted above the gods. The Empire would rule the whole world—an iron beast with its head stretched to the heavens.

THE END

Glossary

Currency

Aston: A copper coin. Also called a penny.

Denier: A silver coin worth twenty *astonnes*, the most basic unit of currency.

Sou: A large silver coin, worth twelve *deniers*.

Libre: A gold coin, worth also called a "crown," worth twenty *sous*.

Mark: A unit of measurement equal to one thousand *deniers*.

Dates

Zarubain uses the dating system Waking Year (W.Y.), about 126 years ahead of the Imperial system, Year of the Empire (Y.E.)

Terms

Aglond: A famed sculptor.

Ajernon: A duchy in the Western Heartlands, one of the Seven Gems, ruled by the Abrenard noble family. For three years, Duchy Ajernon was engaged in a petty war with Duchy Lessant over a small portion of grape-growing territory in which Ajernon lost. Its symbol is a white swordfish on a red field.

All-Seeing Eye: (1) An All-Seeing Orb or (2) a term for the Wizards Council.

Alzdorf: A large town in the far east of Zarubain in the Grand Duchy of Almania.

Avermere: A seaside village, population 300, on the northern edge of Lessant.

Avenda: See the Otherworld.

Avelogne: A large island west of Zarubad, the training ground and ancient center of the fairy priesthood. Sometimes called the Green Isle or the Emerald Isle.

Ardogne: An island far south of Zarubain. Its climate, unusually warm for its northerly location, allows for the growth of palmettos. Ardogne's main exports are saffron and iron ore.

Arvogne: A duchy in the Western Heartlands, one of the Seven Gems, lead by the Alerie noble family. Its symbol is a gold beaver on a green field. The Aleries claim to be the richest family in Zarubain besides the Bretagnes.

Badelgard: A kingdom just north of Zarubain on a high mountain plateau. Its people are considered violent raiders and robbers.

Battle of Delver's Dale: Fought between Murghul raiders and Roland, Duke of Valais, in autumn 1222 W.Y., ending in a costly Zarube victory.

Bretagne, House of: The royal family. Their symbol is a gold lion rampant on a blue field.

Carribor: A city in central Zarubain, reputed for its lawlessness and immorality.

Castle Holmgray: A bridge castle over the River Zarube in Montée March.

Castle Hombard: A castle in Duranche.

Castle Celine: A castle in Silvan March.

Castle New: A recently-founded fortress and town in the region of Mekara.

Castle Neves: A castle, the county seat of Arvogne. The town of Neville surrounds it.

Castle Moonsilver: A castle in Vale of Roy.

Castle Silvergold: A castle in Lessant, the seat of the House Rambée.

Castle Sunbow: A castle in Duchy Valais, perched on high ground overlooking Delver's Dale.

Castle Rose: A large castle in Duchy Ajernon, home to the duke, named for its light red color.

Castle Royale: A castle in the Inner City of Zarubad, the royal family's residence.

Castle Veldair: The central fortress of County Belidere, surrounded by the county seat, Veldois, population three thousand.

Carribor: A large city in a region known as the Robber Baronies. It is legendary as a haven for vice and corruption.

Civil War: A war taking place just prior to the events of this novel, fought in the Empire between governmental elements and the now-emperor, Numa.

Commandery: The headquarters of a knightly order.

Dongirion: An elven village in the region of Lamdar.

Dragonettes: Sometimes called toy drakes, these tiny reptilian creatures are kept as pets in Zarubain. Instead of true drakes' corrosive breath, they emit colorful burps of gas. They are most often silver in color, but sometimes red, gold, brown, or, rarely, rainbow. They can fly but are tempting food for eagles and birds of prey.

Duranche: An ancient duchy of the Western Heartlands, one of the Seven Gems. The House of Námois rules it. Its symbol is a black ram on a silver field.

Dwemer-craft: A term for ancient or unreachable knowledge.

Eastern Heartlands, the: An inland region considered to stretch from the edge of the Western Heartlands to the edge of County Orr.

Eastern Region, the: The far east of Zarubain. Its counts and dukes are practically self governing, being so far removed from the king. Winters in the Eastern Region are extremely harsh.

Elven World, the: A term for all of elven civilization.

Empire, the: A vast nation south of Zarubain and Mekara. Its ruler is Emperor Numa Adamantus.

Fairbolt: The ancient sword of Zarube kings.

Fairy Priestess: A priestess dedicated to the goddess Feanara. Men are not allowed into her priesthood. They are sworn to remain virgins until the age of thirty-three, when they may marry a man of the noble class.

Fair Folk, the: A term for the fey.

Fairy Faith, the: The religion of the Lady Goddess, Feanara, who is the patron deity of Zarubain.

Feanara: The patron deity of Zarubain. A goddess who rules over woodland creatures and the fey. She resides in the Otherworld, the realm of the fairies.

Feast of the Maiden, the: A celebration of spring held on the equinox which celebrates Feanara as a young maiden, as opposed to the Feast of the Lady in summer and the less-celebrated Feast of the Crone in spring.

Further Zarubain: A region beyond the Eastern Heartlands, considered a backwater between the great duchies of the west and the wealthy counties of the Three Sisters—Lys, Miere, and Renseur.

Garrone: One of the oldest counties in Zarubain, ruled by a family of the same name. Its symbol is a white stag on a black field.

Goddess, the: See Feanara.

Golden Coast, the: A region running roughly from Zarubad down to Ajernon, named after its great wealth.

Grayman's beard: A silver-colored hanging moss that grows in Zarube forests, which—when consumed—stops pregnancy.

Great Elven Plain: A vast coastal plain with rich soil, dotted with cities and villages. It is considered the heart of elven civilization.

House of Hernaut: The original dynasty of Zarubain, now extinct, which was superseded by the House Bretagne.

High Chair, the: A tall chair lined with silver and gold in the Lady's Cathedral where the High Priestess sits. Used figuratively, the High Priesthood, or, rarely, the Fairy Faith itself.

High cuisine: The royal cuisine of Zarubain, often using strange ingredients that are distasteful to the inexperienced.

Isdar: The goddess of fertility and erotic love.

Joules vis Bretagne: The first king of the Bretagne dynasty.

Knights of Lorh: A faction of knights who practice a form of mysticism. They revere the god Orbuus and only allow initiates with magical talent to join. They have a contentious relationship with the Wizards Council and the wider kingdom.

Knights of Marabelle: A faction of knights dedicated to the goddess Marabelle, Queen of Horses.

Knights of the Sun: An order of knights dedicated to Alabaster, the so-called king of the gods. Its symbol is the sun, the "light-bearer."

Knights of the Pillar: A secretive order of knights. Their symbol is "the pillar which holds up creation." They hold nothing in higher esteem than order, obedience, and law. Their commandery is located in Port Bratteau in the Vale of Roy.

Lady, the: See Feanara.

Lamdar: A region of the Elven World, north of Zarubain and Badelgard, considered the heart of elven civilization.

Lamen: See Lamdar.

Lessant: A duchy of the Western Heartlands, one of the Seven Gems. Its current ruler is Ramir vis Rambée. Its symbol is a blue bear against a white field.

Lady, the: A colloquial term for the goddess Feanara.

Lady In White, the: A term for the goddess Feanara in her aspect as the Lady of the Lake, dressed in white samite.

Lady of the Lake, the: A term for the goddess Feanara who appeared to the first queen of Zarubain out of the deep waters of a lake.

Life Well, the: A holy spring in the isle of Avelogne, said to be the place where the Lady of the Lake appeared to Melysant, the first queen of Zarubain.

Lys: A county in the middle of Zarubain, held in high regard by the nobles of the realm, one of the Three Sisters along with

Miere and Renseur.

Melysant Hernaut: The founder of the Kingdom of Zarubain and its first queen.

Miere: A large county in the middle of Zarubain, one of the Three Sisters along with Lys and Renseur. Much of it lies in an ancient fairy-haunted forest called the Eldenwood.

Mierese silk: Silk clothing, painted by the women of the lake town region of County Miere. Their methods of painting are a closely guarded secret, and the end products sell for hundreds of *sous* each.

Montée March: A border region, home to Castle Holmgray and its adjacent bridge. The ruling family was traditionally the Grandvails, but this has changed following the marriage of the Bastard Prince to Leyna Grandvail. Now the family is known by the name Grandvail-Bretagne.

Moon Dust: A crushed and powdered form of mooncrystal which the Knights of Lorh employ. It can hold magic energy.

Murghuls: A people north of Zarubain, considered barbaric nomads.

Name-day: Among Zarube nobility, a ceremonial day thirteen days after birth when the child receives his or her name, and is considered a full member of the family.

Nuns: Fairy priestesses who are sworn to lifelong celibacy and live in convents. Most belong to peaceful orders dedicated to the study of the fey, but others are trained in hand-to-hand combat.

Nurnen: A race of elves, sometimes called the Gray Elves due to the faint silver tint of their skin.

Og: Also called Og'og. Considered by his followers to be a god, but by the mainstream priesthood as a savage demon prince. His cult has been banned for hundreds of years, but a small sect has existed in the Royal City, under the strict supervision of the king. No churches are built to him, however.

Orr: A county of lush vineyards, considered the gateway to Further Zarubain. Ruled by the Cardigne noble family, its largest town is Tournay.

Orbuus: The god of mysteries, hidden knowledge, and magic.

Otherworld, the: The world of the fey.

Port Bratteau: A small town by the Western Sea, Vale of Roy's only port outside of Zarubad.

Pretender, the: Also called the Black Knight, Mortimer Thorne rebelled against the rightful king and banned the worship of the Lady. He was killed by Saint Ignáce, a peasant girl and warrior from Naines.

Primogeniture: Among the Zarube nobility, the long-established right of the firstborn son to inherit his father's estate.

Pit, the: An informal term for the arena. Pit fighters kill each other for the entertainment of the crowds. Pit fighting is illegal in Zarubain, but done in secret.

Prison Isle: An isle off the coast of Zarubain which holds accused criminals awaiting trial.

Ranoul diu Jakov: A famous painter, born a peasant in County Champiz.

Rambée, House of: A noble family that rules over Duchy Lessant. Their standard is a blue bear rampant against a white field. Its current head is Ramir vis Rambée, and its heir-apparent is Ramir's son, Ramden the Bold.

Red Wizards: Wizards of the Red Robes. The Red Robes are the only order of wizards which allows members to serve as mercenaries.

Renseur: A county in the middle of Zarubain, wealthy and highly regarded, one of the Three Sisters along with Lys and Miere.

Rokahn: Warlike humanoids that live in the Dragonteeth Mountains north of Zarubain. Once numerous and fearsome, their population has declined so much that the Rokahn Wars of ancient days are but a distant memory.

Royal Road, the: A road beginning in the royal capital of Zarubad and ending in the faraway city of Galiope.

Samite: A white cloth made from silk. The fabric is extremely expensive and beyond the means of any except the most wealthy.

Saint Delphine-upon-the-Zandie: A large shrine in Tournay, holding the bones of the Zarube saint Delphine. Delphine, a martyr for the Goddess, was killed during the time of the Pretender.

Saint Ignáce: Also called the Maid of Naines, Ignáce was a peasant girl who became a great warrior and defeated the Pretender (see above) allowing the true king to return to the Lion Throne. Some nobles, resentful of her peasant origin, accused her of witchcraft and had her burned at the stake. She was later declared a saint and revered across the kingdom.

Seven Gems, the: The "seven gems in the king's crown" are seven regions in the Western Heartlands, the oldest and wealthiest territories in Zarubain. They are Vale of Roy, which includes Zarubad and the king's own holdings, and the six duchies of Valais, Lessant, Ajernon, Voraigne, Arvogne, and Duranche. Though small in size compared to other duchies, they lie upon fertile ground and have benefited disproportionately from Zarubain's wars, leading to fabulous wealth and resources, and disproportionate power in politics.

Silver Woods: A large forest which covers much of Vale of Roy.

Sinderion: An elven seer, born thousands of years ago. He saw his visions while locked in a mountain tower.

***Snowmourn*:** A white-colored sword, the ancient weapon of the Duke of Duranche. Its crafters embedded seven sapphires into the blade, representing the Seven Gems.

Surrevere: A viscounty in Further Zarubain. The House of Poncée rules it from the seat, Castle Goldmane.

Storm Coast, the: A region along the western coast of Zarubain, running roughly from the northern tip of Ajernon to the mouth of the River Zarube. It is legendary as a haunt of pirates.

Stormhold: A large walled town on the Storm Coast in southern Duchy Ajernon.

The Lion on the Ramparts: Zarubain's national anthem.

Tournay: A large town in County Orr. It has received a royal charter of self-rule.

Trouvere: A royal court musician, especially in the west. Those in the east, especially in the Three Sisters, are called troubadours.

Tyras: The god of war.

Vale of Roy: Also called Vale Royeau, a region in the Western Heartlands which the king rules directly.

Valais: A duchy just east of Vale of Roy, one of the Seven Gems, ruled by a family of the same name. Its current leader is Roland vis Valais, the youngest duke in Zarubain at age 29. Its symbol is a white wolf on a gold field.

Voraigne: A duchy, one of the Seven Gems, ruled by a family of the same name. Its seat is Voraigne Manor. Its current leader is Gouldair vis Voraigne. Its symbol is a red hawk on a rose field. Unique among the Seven Gems, the Voraignes revere Umbra, the god of shadows, rather than the Goddess.

Wall, the: A wall, thirty feet tall along its whole extent, which marks the border of the Empire.

Westwood, the: A lush forest north of Zarubad and favored hunting ground of the nobility.

Witch: In Zarubain, a term for a non-ordained devotee of the Goddess. They often have closer relations to the fey and, sometimes, magic-like powers. If caught, witches are burned at the stake.

Wizards: Powerful magic weavers of the north, wizards are present throughout Zarubain but are not considered under the king's control or beholden to his laws. They are governed by a grand council and an Archwizard.

Zarubain: A kingdom of the Northern World. Its flag is a yellow lion against a blue field.

About the Author

Cursed at birth with a wild imagination, Andrew Cooper spent his youth dreaming of worlds more exciting than Earth.

He is a graduate of the Odyssey Writing Workshop. His stories have appeared in Morpheus Tales, Fear and Trembling, Residential Aliens and Mindflights, among others.

Contact the Author

Visit **www.aj-cooper.com** to sign up for the newsletter and stay up-to-date on new releases.

Find him on Facebook at:

www.facebook.com/AJCooperauthor